Her Father's Daughter

by

Gene Stratton-Porter

List of Characters

LINDA STRONG, Her Father's Daughter
DR. ALEXANDER STRONG, a Great Nerve Specialist
MRS. STRONG, His Wife
EILEEN STRONG, Having
Social Aspirations
MR. AND MRS. THORNE, Neighbors of the Strongs
MARIAN THORNE, a Dreamer of Houses
JOHN GILMAN, a Man of Law
PETER MORRISON, an Author
HENRY ANDERSON, an Architect
DONALD WHITING, a High School Senior
MARY LOUISE WHITING, His Sister
JUDGE AND MRS. WHITING, a Man of Law and a Woman of Culture
KATHERINE O' DONOVAN, the Strong Cook
OKA SAYYE, a High School Senior
JAMES HEITMAN, Accidentally Rich
MRS. CAROLINE HEITMAN, His Wife

CHAPTER I. "What Kind of Shoes Are the Shoes You Wear?"

"What makes you wear such funny shoes?"

Linda Strong thrust forward a foot and critically examined the narrow vamp, the projecting sole, the broad, low heel of her well-worn brown calfskin shoe. Then her glance lifted to the face of Donald Whiting, one of the most brilliant and popular seniors of the high school. Her eyes narrowed in a manner habitual to her when thinking intently.

"Never you mind my shoes," she said deliberately. "Kindly fix your attention on my head piece. When you see me allowing any Jap in my class to make higher grades than I do, then I give you leave to say anything you please concerning my head."

An angry red rushed to the boy's face. It was an irritating fact that in the senior class of that particular Los Angeles high school a Japanese boy stood at the head. This was embarrassing to every senior.

"I say," said Donald Whiting, "I call that a mean thrust."

"I have a particular reason," said Linda.

"And I have 'a particular reason'," said Donald, "for being interested in your shoes."

Linda laughed suddenly. When Linda laughed, which was very seldom, those within hearing turned to look at her. Hers was not a laugh that can be achieved. There were a few high places on the peak of Linda's soul, and on one of them homed a small flock of notes of rapture; notes as sweet as the voice of the white-banded mockingbird of Argentina.

"How surprising!" exclaimed Linda. "We have been attending the same school for three years; now, you stop me suddenly to tell me that you are interested in the shape of my shoes."

"I have been watching them all the time," said Donald. "Can't understand why any girl wants to be so different. Why don't you dress your hair the same as the other girls and wear the same kind of clothes and shoes?"

"Now look here," interposed Linda "You are flying the track.I am willing to justify my shoes, if I can, but here you go including my dress and a big psychological problem, as well; but I think perhaps the why of the shoes will explain the remainder. Does the name 'Alexander Strong' mean anything to you?"

"The great nerve specialist?" asked Donald.

"Yes," said Linda. "The man who was the author of half-dozen books that have been translated into many foreign tongue' and are used as authorities all over the world. He happened to be my father There are two children in our family. I have a sister four years older than I am who is exactly like Mother, and she and Mother were inseparable. I am exactly like Father; because we understood each other, and because both of us always new, although we never mentioned it; that Mother preferred my sister Eileen to me, Father tried to make it up to me, so from the time I can remember I was at his heels. It never bothered him to have me playing around in the library while he was writing

1

his most complicated treatise. I have waited in his car half a day at a time, playing or reading, while he watched a patient or delivered a lecture at some medical college. His mental relaxation was to hike or to motor to the sea, to the mountains, to the canyons or the desert, and he very seldom went without me even on long trips when he was fishing or hunting with other men. There was not much to know concerning a woman's frame or he psychology that Father did not know, so there were two reason why he selected my footwear as he did. One was because he believed high heels and pointed toes an outrage against the nervous province, and the other was that I could not possibly have kept pace with him except in shoes like these. No doubt, they are the same kind I shall wear all my life, for walking. You probably don't know it, but my home lies near the middle of Lilac Valley and I walk over a mile each morning and evening to and from the cars. Does this sufficiently explain my shoes?"

"I should think you'd feel queer," said Donald.

"I suspect I would if I had time to brood over it," Linda replied, "but I haven't. I must hustle to get to school on time in the morning. It's nearly or quite dark before I reach home in the evening. My father believed in having a good time. He had superb health, so he spent most of what he made as it came to him. He counted on a long life. It never occurred to him that a little piece of machinery going wrong would plunge him into Eternity in a second."

"Oh, I remember!" cried the boy.

Linda's face paled slightly.

"Yes," she said, "it happened four years ago and I haven't gotten away from the horror of it yet, enough ever to step inside of a motor car; but I am going to get over that one of these days. Brakes are not all defective, and one must take one's risks."

"You just bet I would," said Donald. "Motoring is one of the greatest pleasures of modern life. I'll wager it makes some of the gay old boys, like Marcus Aurelius for example, want to turn over in their graves when they see us flying along the roads of California the way we do."

"What I was getting at," said Linda, "was a word of reply to the remainder of your indictment against me. Dad's income stopped with him, and household expenses went on, and war came, so there isn't enough money to dress two of us as most of the high school girls are dressed. Eileen is so much older that it's her turn first, and I must say she is not at all backward about exercising her rights. I think that will have to suffice for the question of dress but you may be sure that I am capable of wearing the loveliest dress imaginable, that would be for a school girl, if I had it to wear."

"Ah, there's the little 'fly in your ointment'—'dress that would be suitable.' I bet in your heart you think the dresses that half the girls in high school are wearing are NOT SUITABLE!"

"Commendable perspicacity, O learned senior," said Linda, "and amazingly true. In the few short years I had with Daddy I acquired a fixed idea as to what kind of dress is suitable and sufficiently durable to wear while walking my daily two miles. I can't seem to become reconciled to the custom of dressing the same for school as for a party. You get my idea?"

"I get it all right enough," said Donald, "but I must think awhile before I decide whether I agree with you. Why should you be right, and hundreds of other girls be wrong?"

"I'll wager your mother would agree with me," suggested Linda.

"Did yours?" asked Donald.

"Halfway," answered Linda. "She agreed with me for me, but not for Eileen."

"And not for my sister," said Donald. "She wears the very foxiest clothes that Father can afford to pay for, and when she was going to school she wore them without the least regard as to whether she was going to school or to a tea party or a matinee. For that matter she frequently went to all three the same day.

"And that brings us straight to the point concerning you," said Linda.

"Sure enough!" said Donald. "There is me to be considered! What is it you have against me?"

Linda looked at him meditatively.

"You SEEM exceptionally strong," she said. "No doubt are good in athletics. Your head looks all right; it indicates brains. What I want to know is why in the world you don't us them."

"What are you getting at, anyway?" asked Donald, with more than a hint of asperity in his voice.

"I am getting at the fact," said Linda, "that a boy as big as you and as strong as you and with as good brain and your opportunity has allowed a little brown Jap to cross the Pacific Ocean and a totally strange country to learn a language foreign to him, and, and, with the same books and the same chances, to beat you at your own game. You and every other boy in your classes ought to thoroughly ashamed of yourselves. Before I would let a Jap, either boy or girl, lead in my class, I would give up going to school and go out and see if I could beat him growing lettuce and spinach."

"It's all very well to talk," said Donald hotly.

"And it's better to make good what you say," broke in Linda, with equal heat. "There are half a dozen Japs in my classes but no one of them is leading, you will notice, if I do wear peculiar shoes."

"Well, you would be going some if you beat the leading Jap in the senior class," said Donald.

2

"Then I would go some," said Linda. "I'd beat him, or I'd go straight up trying. You could do it if you'd make up your mind to. The trouble with you is that you're wasting your brain on speeding an automobile, on dances, and all sorts of foolishness that is not doing you any good in any particular way. Bet you are developing nerves smoking cigarettes. You are not concentrating. Oka Sayye is not thinking of a thing except the triumph of proving to California that he is head man in one of the Los Angeles high schools. That's what I have got against you, and every other white boy in your class, and in the long run it stacks up bigger than your arraignment of my shoes."

"Oh, darn your shoes!" cried Donald hotly. "Forget 'em! I've got to move on or I'll be late for trigonometry, but I don't know when I've had such a tidy little fight with a girl, and I don't enjoy feeling that I have been worsted. I propose another session. May I come out to Lilac Valley Saturday afternoon and flay you alive to pay up for my present humiliation?"

"Why, if your mother happened to be motoring that way and would care to call, I think that would be fine," said Linda.

"Well, for the Lord's sake!" exclaimed the irate senior. "Can't a fellow come and fight with you without being refereed by his mother? Shall I bring Father too?"

"I only thought," said Linda quietly, "that you would like your mother to see the home and environment of any girl whose acquaintance you made, but the fight we have coming will in all probability be such a pitched battle that when I go over the top, you won't ever care to follow me and start another issue on the other side. You're dying right now to ask why I wear my hair in braids down my back instead of in cootie coops over my ears."

"I don't give a hang," said Donald ungallantly, "as to how you; wear your hair, but I am coming Saturday to fight, and I don't think Mother will take any greater interest in the matter than to know that I am going to do battle with a daughter of Doctor I Strong."

"That is a very nice compliment to my daddy, thank you, said Linda, turning away and proceeding in the direction of her own classrooms. There was a brilliant sparkle in her eyes and she sang in a muffled voice, yet distinctly enough to be heard:

"The shoes I wear are common-sense shoes, And you may wear them if you choose."

"By gracious! She's no fool," he said to himself. In three minutes' unpremeditated talk the "Junior Freak," as he mentally denominated her, had managed to irritate him, to puncture his pride, to entertain and amuse him.

"I wonder—" he said as he went his way; and all day he kept on wondering, when he was not studying harder than ever before in all his life.

That night Linda walked slowly along the road toward home. She was not seeing the broad stretch of Lilac Valley, on every hand green with spring, odorous with citrus and wild bloom, blue walled with lacy lilacs veiling the mountain face on either side; and she was not thinking of her plain, well-worn dress or her common-sense shoes. What she was thinking was of every flaying, scathing, solidly based argument she could produce the following Saturday to spur Donald Whiting in some way to surpass Oka Sayye. His chance remark that morning, as they stood near each other waiting a few minutes in the hall, had ended in his asking to come to see her, and she decided as she walked homeward that his first visit in all probability would be his last, since she had not time to spare for boys, when she had so many different interests involved; but she did decide very finely in her own mind that she would make that visit a memorable one for him.

In arriving at this decision her mind traveled a number of devious roads. The thought that she had been criticized did not annoy her as to the kind of criticism, but she did resent the quality of truth about it. She was right in following the rules her father had laid down for her health and physical well-being, but was it right that she should wear shoes scuffed, resoled, and even patched, when there was money enough for Eileen to have many pairs of expensive laced boots, walking shoes, and fancy slippers? She was sure she was right in wearing dresses suitable for school, but was it right that she must wear them until they were sunfaded, stained, and disreputable? Was it right that Eileen should occupy their father and mother's suite, redecorated and daintily furnished according to her own taste, to keep the parts of the house that she cared to use decorated with flowers and beautifully appointed, while Linda must lock herself in a small stuffy bedroom room, dingy and none too comfortable, when in deference to her pride she wished to work in secret until she learned whether she could succeed.

Then she began thinking, and decided that the only available place in the house for her use was the billiard room. She made up her mind that she would demand the sole right to this big attic room. She would sell the table and use the money to buy herself a suitable worktable and a rug. She would demand that Eileen produce enough money for better clothing for her, and then she remembered what she had said to Donald Whiting about conquering her horror for a motor car. Linda turned in at the walk leading to her home, but she passed the front entrance and followed around to the side. As she went she could hear voices in the living room and she knew that Eileen was entertaining some of her many friends; for Eileen was that peculiar creature known as a social butterfly. Each day of her life friends came; or Eileen went—mostly the latter, for Eileen had a knack of management and she so managed her friends that, without their realizing it, they entertained her many times while she entertained them once. Linda went to the kitchen, Laid her books and package of mail on the table, and, walking over to the stove, she proceeded deliberately and heartily to kiss the cook.

"Katy, me darlin'," she said, "look upon your only child. Do you notice a 'lean and hungry look' on her classic features?"

Katy turned adoring eyes to the young girl.

"It's growing so fast ye are, childie," she said. "It's only a little while to dinner, and there's company tonight, so hadn't ye better wait and not spoil your appetite with piecing?"

"Is there going to be anything 'jarvis'?" inquired Linda.

"'I'd say there is," said Katy. "John Gilman is here and two friends of Eileen's. It's a near banquet, lassie."

"Then I'll wait," said Linda. "I want the keys to the garage."

Katy handed them to her and Linda went down the back walk beneath an arch of tropical foliage, between blazing walls of brilliant flower faces, unlocked the garage, and stood looking at her father's runabout.

In the revolution that had taken place in their home after the passing of their father and mother, Eileen had dominated the situation and done as she pleased, with the exception of two instances. Linda had shown both temper and determination at the proposal to dismantle the library and dispose of the cars. She had told Eileen that she might take the touring car and do as she pleased with it. For her share she wanted her father's roadster, and she meant to have it. She took the same firm stand concerning the Library. With the rest of the house Eileen might do as she would. The library was to remain absolutely untouched and what it contained was Linda's. To this Eileen had agreed, but so far Linda had been content merely to possess her property.

Lately, driven by the feeling that she must find a way in which she could earn money, she had been secretly working on some plans that she hoped might soon yield her small returns. As for the roadster, she as well as Eileen had been horror-stricken when the car containing their father and mother and their adjoining neighbors, Mr. and Mrs. Thorne, driven by Marian Thorne, the playmate and companion from childhood of the Strong girls, had become uncontrollable and plunged down the mountain in a disaster that had left only Marian, protected by the steering gear, alive. They had simply by mutual agreement begun using the street cars when they wanted to reach the city.

Linda stood looking at the roadster, jacked up and tucked under a heavy canvas tent that she and her father had used on their hunting and fishing trips. After a long time she laid strong hands on the canvas and dragged it to one side. She looked the car over carefully and then, her face very white and her hands trembling, she climbed into it and slowly and mechanically went through the motions of starting it. For another intent period she sat with her hands on the steering gear, staring straight ahead, and then she said slowly: "Something has got to be done. It's not going to be very agreeable, but I am going to do it. Eileen: has had things all her own way long enough. I am getting such a big girl I ought to have a few things in my life as I want them. Something must be done."

Then Linda proceeded to do something. What she did was to lean forward, rest her head upon the steering wheel and fight to keep down deep, pitiful sobbing until her whole slender body twisted in the effort.

She was yielding to a breaking up after four years of endurance, for the greater part in silence. As the months of the past year had rolled their deliberate way, Linda had begun to realize that the course her elder sister had taken was wholly unfair to her, and slowly a tumult of revolt was growing in her soul. Without a doubt the culmination had resulted from her few minutes' talk with Donald Whiting in the hall that morning. It had started Linda to thinking deeply, and the more deeply she thought the clearly she saw the situation. Linda was a loyal soul and her heart was honest. She was quite willing that Eileen should: exercise her rights as head of the family, that she should take the precedence to which she was entitled by her four years' seniority, that she should spend the money which accrued monthly from their father's estate as she saw fit, up to a certain point. That point was where things ceased to be fair or to be just. If there had been money to do no more for Eileen than had been done for Linda, it would not have been in Linda's heart to utter a complaint. She could have worn scuffed shoes and old dresses, and gone her way with her proud young head held very high and a jest on her lips; but when her mind really fastened on the problem and she began to reason, she could not feel that Eileen was just to her or that she was fair in her administration of the money which should have been divided more nearly equally between them, after the household expenses had been paid. Once rebellion burned in her heart the flames leaped rapidly, and Linda began to remember a thousand small things that she had scarcely noted at the time of their occurrence.

She was leaning on the steering wheel, tired with nerve strain, when she heard Katy calling her, and realized that she was needed in the kitchen. As a matter of economy Eileen, after her parents' passing, had dismissed the housemaid, and when there were guests before whom she wished to make a nice appearance Linda had been impressed either to wait on the table or to help in the kitchen in order that Katy might attend the dining room, so Linda understood what was wanted when Katy called her. She ran her fingers over the steering wheel, worn bright by the touch of her father's and her own hands, and with the buoyancy of youth, found comfort. Once more she mechanically went through the motions of starting the car, then she stepped down, closed the door, and stood an instant thinking.

"You're four years behind the times," she said slowly. "No doubt there's a newer and a better model; I suspect the tires are rotten, but the last day I drove you for Daddy you purred like a kitten, and ran like a clock, and if you were cleaned and oiled and put in proper shape, there's no reason in the world why I should not drive you again, as I have driven you hundreds of miles when Daddy was tired or when he wanted to teach me the rules of good motoring, and the laws of the road. I can do it all right. I have got to do it, but it will be some time before I'll care to tackle the mountains."

Leaving the cover on the floor, she locked the door and returned to the kitchen.

"All right, Katy, what is the programme?" she inquired as lightly as she could.

Katy had been cook in the Strong family ever since they had moved to Lilac Valley. She had obeyed Mrs. Strong and Eileen. She had worshiped the Doctor and Linda It always had been patent to her eyes that Mrs. Strong was extremely partial to Eileen, so Katy had joined forces with the Doctor in surreptitiously doing everything her warm Irish heart prompted to prevent Linda from feeling neglected. Her quick eyes saw the traces of tears on Linda's face, and she instantly knew that the trip the girl had made to the garage was in some way connected with some belongings of her father's, so she said: "I am serving tonight but I want you to keep things smoking hot and to have them dished up ready for me so that everything will go smoothly."

"What would happen," inquired Linda, "if everything did NOT go smoothly? Katy, do you think the roof would blow straight up if I had MY way about something, just for a change?"

"No, I think the roof would stay right where it belongs," said Katy with a chuckle, "but I do think its staying there would not be because Miss Eileen wanted it to."

"Well," said Linda deliberately, "we won't waste any time on thinking We are going to have some positive knowledge on the subject pretty immediately. I don't feel equal to starting any domestic santana today, but the forces are gathering and the blow is coming soon. To that I have firmly made up my mind."

"It's not the least mite I'm blaming you, honey," said Katy.

"Ye've got to be such a big girl that it's only fair things in this house should go a good deal different."

"Is Marian to be here?" asked Linda as she stood beside the stove peering into pans and kettles.

"Miss Eileen didn't say," replied Katy.

Linda's eyes reddened suddenly. She slammed down a lid with vicious emphasis.

"That is another deal Eileen's engineered," she said, "that is just about as wrong as anything possibly can be. What makes me the maddest about it is that John Gilman will let Eileen take him by the nose and lead him around like a ringed calf. Where is his common sense? Where is his perception? Where is his honor?"

"Now wait, dearie," said Katy soothingly, "wait. John Gilman is a mighty fine man. Ye know how your father loved him and trusted him and gave him charge of all his business affairs. Ye mustn't go so far as to be insinuating that he is lacking in honor."

"No," said Linda, "that was not fair. I don't in the least know that he ever ASKED Marian to marry him; but I do know that as long as he was a struggling, threadbare young lawyer Marian was welcome to him, and they had grand times together. The minute he won the big Bailey suit and came into public notice and his practice increased until he was independent, that minute Eileen began to take notice, and it looks to me now as if she very nearly had him."

"And so far as I can see," said Katy, "Miss Marian is taking it without a struggle. She is not lifting a finger or making a move to win him back."

"Of course she isn't!" said Linda indignantly. "If she thought he preferred some other girl to her, she would merely say: 'If John has discovered that he likes Eileen the better, why, that is all right; but there wouldn't be anything to prevent seeing Eileen take John from hurting like the deuce. Did you ever lose a man you loved, Katy?"

"That I did not!" said Katy emphatically. "We didn't do any four or five years' philanderin' to see if a man 'could make good' when I was a youngster. When a girl and her laddie stood up to each other and looked each other straight in the eye and had the great understanding, there weren't no question of whether he could do for her what her father and mither had been doing, nor of how much he had to earn before they would be able to begin life together. They just caught hands and hot-footed it to the praste and told him to read the banns the next Sunday, and when the law allowed they was man and wife and taking what life had for them the way it came, and together. All this philanderin' that young folks do nowadays is just pure nonsense, and waste of time."

"Sure!" laughed Linda. "When my brave comes along with his blanket I'll just step under, and then if anybody tries to take my man I'll have the right to go on the warpath and have a scalping party that would be some satisfaction to the soul."

Then they served the dinner, and when the guests had left the dining room, Katy closed the doors, and brought on the delicacies she had hidden for Linda and patted and cajoled her while she ate like any healthy, hungry young creature.

CHAPTER II. Cotyledon of Multiflores Canyon

"'Ave, atque vale!' Cotyledon!"

Linda slid down the side of the canyon with the deftness of the expert. At the first available crevice she thrust in her Alpine stick, and bracing herself, gained a footing. Then she turned and by use of her fingers and toes worked her way back to the plan, she had passed. She was familiar with many members of she family, but such a fine specimen she seldom had found and she could not recall having seen it in all of her botanies. Opposite the plant she worked out a footing, drove her stick deep at the base of a rock to brace herself, and from the knapsack on her back took a sketchbook and pencil and began rapidly copying the thick fleshy leaves of the flattened rosette, sitting securely at the edge of a rock. She worked swiftly and with breathless interest. When she had finished the flower she began sketching in the moss-covered face of the boulder against which it grew, and other bits of vegetation near.

"I think, Coty," she said, "it is very probable that I can come a few simoleons with you. You are becoming better looking ever minute."

For a touch of color she margined one side of her drawing with a little spray of Pentstemon whose bright tubular flower the canyon knew as "hummingbird's dinner horn." That gave, her the idea of introducing a touch of living interest, so bearing down upon the flowers from the upper right-hand corner of her drawing she deftly sketched in a ruby-throated hummingbird, and across the bottom of the sheet the lace of a few leaves of fern. Then she returned the drawing and pencil to her knapsack, and making sure of her footing, worked her way forward. With her long slender fingers she began teasing the plant loose from the rock and the surrounding soil. The roots penetrated deeper than she had supposed and in her interest she forgot her precarious footing and pulled hard. The plant gave way unexpectedly, and losing her balance, Linda plunged down the side of the canyon catching wildly at shrubs and bushes and bruising herself severely on stones, finally landing in a sitting posture on the road that traversed the canyon.

She was not seriously hurt, but she did not present a picturesque figure as she sprawled in the road, her booted feet thrust straight before her, one of her long black braids caught on a bush at her back, her blouse pulled above her breeches, the contents of her knapsack decorating the canyon side and the road around her; but high in one hand, without break or blemish, she triumphantly held aloft the rare Cotyledon. She shrugged her shoulders, wiggled her toes, and moved her arms to assure herself that no bones were broken; then she glanced at her drawings and the fruits of her day's collecting scattered on the roadside around her. She was in the act of rising when a motor car containing two young men shot around a curve of the canyon, swerved to avoid running over her, and stopped as abruptly as possible.

"It's a girl!" cried the driver, and both men sprang to the road and hurried to Linda's assistance. Her dark cheeks were red with mortification, but she managed to recover her feet and tuck in her blouse before they reached her.

"We heard you coming down," said the elder of the young men, "and we thought you might be a bear. Are you sure you're not hurt?"

Linda stood before them, a lithe slender figure, vivid with youth and vitality.

"I am able to stand," she said, "so of course I haven't broken any bones. I think I am fairly well battered, but you will please to observe that there isn't a scratch on Cotyledon, and I brought her down—at least I think it's she—from the edge of that boulder away up there. Isn't she a beauty? Only notice the delicate frosty 'bloom' on her leaves!"

"I should prefer," said the younger of the men, "to know whether you have any broken bones."

"I'm sure I am all right," answered Linda. "I have falling down mountains reduced to an exact science. I'll bet you couldn't slide that far and bring down Coty without a scratch."

"Well, which is the more precious," said the young man. "Yourself or the specimen?"

"Why, the specimen!" answered Linda in impatience. "California is full of girls; but this is the finest Cotyledon of this family I have ever seen. Don't mistake this for any common stonecrop. It looks to me like an Echeveria. I know what I mean to do with the picture I have made of her, and I know exactly where she is going to grow from this day on."

"Is there any way we can help you?" inquired the elder of the two men.

For the first time Linda glanced at him, and her impression was that he was decidedly attractive.

"No, thank you!" she answered briskly. "I am going to climb back up to the boulder and collect the belongings I spilled on the way down. Then I am going to carry Coty to the car line in a kind of triumphal march, because she is the rarest find that I have ever made. I hope you have no dark designs on Coty, because this is 'what the owner had to do to redeem her.'"

Linda indicated her trail down the canyon side, brushed soil and twigs from her trousers, turned her straight young back, carefully set down her specimen, and by the aid of her recovered stick began expertly making her way up the canyon side. "Here, let me do that," offered the younger man. "You rest until I collect your belongings." Linda glanced back over her shoulder. "Thanks," she said. "I have a mental inventory of all the pencils and knives and trowels I must find. You might overlook the most important part of my paraphernalia; and really I am not damaged. I'm merely hurt. Good-bye!"

Linda started back up the side of the canyon, leaving the young men to enter their car and drive away. For a minute both of them stood watching her.

"What will girls be wearing and doing next?" asked the elder of the two as he started his car.

"What would you have a girl wear when she is occupied with coasting down canyons?" said his friend. "And as for what she is doing, it's probable that every high-school girl in Los Angeles has a botanical collection to make before she graduates."

"I see!" said the man driving. "She is only a high-school kid, but did you notice that she is going to make an extremely attractive young woman?"

"Yes, I noticed just that; I noticed it very particularly," answered the younger man. "And I noticed also that she either doesn't know it, or doesn't give a flip."

Linda collected her belongings, straightened her hair and clothing, and, with her knapsack in place, and leaning rather on heavily on her walking stick, made her way down the road to the abutment of a small rustic bridge where she stopped to rest. The stream at her feet was noisy and icy cold. It rushed through narrow defiles in the rock, beat itself to foam against the faces a of the big stones, fell over jutting cliffs, spread in whispering pools, wound back and forth across the road at its will, singing every foot of its downward way and watering beds of crisp, cool miners' lettuce, great ferns, and heliotrope, climbing clematis, soil and blue-eyed grass. All along its length grew willows, and in a few places white-bodied sycamores. Everywhere over the walls red above it that vegetation could find a footing grew mosses, vines, flowers, and shrubs. On the shadiest side homed most of the ferns and the Cotyledon. In the sun, larkspur, lupin, and monkey flower; everywhere wild rose, holly, mahogany, gooseberry, and bayoneted yucca all intermingling in a curtain of variegated greens, brocaded with flower arabesques of vivid red, white, yellow, and blue. Canyon wrens and vireos sang as they nested. The air was clear, cool, and salty from the near-by sea. Myriad leaf shadows danced on the black roadbed, level as a barn floor, and across it trailed the wavering image of hawk and vulture, gull and white sea swallow. Linda studied the canyon with intent eyes, but bruised flesh pleaded, so reluctantly she arose, shouldered her belongings, and slowly followed the road out to the car line that passed through Lilac Valley, still carefully bearing in triumph the precious Cotyledon. An hour later she entered the driveway of her home. She stopped to set her plant carefully in the wild garden she and her father had worked all her life at collecting, then followed the back porch and kitchen route.

"Whatever have ye been doing to yourself, honey?" cried Katy.

"I came a cropper down Multiflores Canyon where it is so steep that it leans the other way. I pretty well pulverized myself for a pulverulent, Katy, which is a poor joke."

"Now ain't that just my luck!" wailed Katy, snatching a cake cutter and beginning hurriedly to stamp out little cakes from the dough before her.

"Well, I don't understand in exactly what way," said Linda, absently rubbing her elbows and her knees. "Seems to me it's my promontories that have been knocked off, not yours, Katy."

"Yes, and ain't it just like ye," said Katy, "to be coming in late, and all banged up when Miss Eileen has got sudden notice that there is going to be company again and I have an especial dinner to serve, and never in the world can I manage if ye don't help me!"

"Why, who is coming now?" asked Linda, seating herself on the nearest chair and beginning to unfasten her boots slowly.

"Well, first of all, there is Mr. Gilman, of course."

"'Of course,'" conceded Linda. "If he tried to get past our house, Eileen is perfectly capable of setting it on fire to stop him. She's got him 'vamped' properly."

"Oh I don't know that ye should say just that," said Katy "Eileen is a mighty pretty girl, and she is SOME manager."

"You can stake your hilarious life she is," said Linda, viciously kicking a boot to the center of the kitchen. "She can manage to go downtown for lunch and be invited out to dinner thirteen times a week, and leave us at home to eat bread and milk, bread heavily stressed. She can manage to get every cent of the income from the property in her fingers, and a great big girl like me has to go to high school looking so tacky that even the boys are beginning to comment on it. Manage, I'll say she can manage, not to mention managing to snake John Gilman right out of Marian's fingers. I doubt if Marian fully realizes yet that she's lost her man; and I happen to know that she just plain loved John!"

The second boot landed beside the first, then Linda picked them both up and started toward the back hall.

"Honey, are ye too bad hurt to help me any?" asked Katy, as she passed her.

"Of course not," said Linda. "Give me a few minutes to take a bath and step into my clothes and then I'll be on the job."

With a black scowl on her face, Linda climbed the dingy back stairway in her stocking-feet. At the head of the stairs she paused one minute, glanced at the gloom of her end of the house, then she turned and walked to the front of the hall where there were potted ferns, dainty white curtains, and bright rugs. The door of the guest room stood open and she could see that it was filled with fresh flowers and ready for occupancy. The door of her sister's room was slightly ajar and she pushed it open and stood looking inside. In her state of disarray she made a shocking contrast to the flowerlike figure busy before a dressing table. Linda was dark, narrow, rawboned, overgrown in height, and forthright of disposition. Eileen was a tiny woman, delicately moulded, exquisitely colored, and one of the most perfectly successful tendrils from the original clinging vine in her intercourse with men, and with such women as would tolerate the clinging-vine idea in the present forthright days. With a strand of softly curled hair in one hand and a fancy pin in the other, Eileen turned a disapproving look upon her sister.

"What's the great idea?" demanded Linda shortly.

"Oh, it's perfectly splendid," answered Eileen. "John Gilman's best friend is motoring around here looking for a location to build a home. He is an author and young and good looking and not married, and he thinks he would like to settle somewhere near Los Angeles. Of course John would love to have him in Lilac Valley because he hopes to build a home here some day for himself. His name is Peter Morrison and John says that his articles and stories have horse sense, logic, and humor, and he is making a lot of money."

"Then God help John Gilman, if he thinks now that he is in love with you," said Linda dryly.

Eileen arched her eyebrows, thinned to a hair line, and her lips drew together in disapproval.

"What I can't understand," she said, "is how you can be so unspeakably vulgar, Linda."

Linda laughed sharply.

"And this Peter Morrison and John are our guests for dinner?"

"Yes," said Eileen. "I am going to show them this valley inside and out. I'm so glad it's spring. We're at our very best. It would be perfectly wonderful to have an author for a neighbor, and he must be going to build a real house, because he has his architect with him; and John says that while he is young, he has done several awfully good houses. He has seen a couple of them in in San Francisco."

Linda shrugged her shoulders.

"Up the flue goes Marian's chance of drawing the plans for John Gilman's house," she said. "I have heard her say a dozen times he would not build a house unless Marian made the plans."

Eileen deftly placed the strand of hair and set the jewelled pin with precision.

"Just possibly things have changed slightly," she suggested.

"Yes," said Linda, "I observe that they have. Marian has sold the home she adored. She is leaving friends she loved and trusted, and who were particularly bound to her by a common grief without realizing exactly how it is happening. She certainly must know that you have taken her lover, and I have not a doubt but that is the reason she has discovered she can no longer work at home, that she must sell her property and spend the money cooped up in a city, to study her profession further."

"Linda," said Eileen, her face pale with anger, "you are positively insufferable. Will you leave my room and close the door after you?"

"Well, Katy has just informed me," said Linda, "that this dinner party doesn't come off without my valued assistance, and before I agree to assist, I'll know ONE thing. Are you proposing to entertain these three men yourself, or have you asked Marian?"

Eileen indicated an open note lying on her dressing table.

"I did not know they were coming until an hour ago," she said. "I barely had time to fill the vases and dust, and then I ran up to dress so that there would be someone presentable when they arrive."

"All right then, we'll agree that this is a surprise party, but if John Gilman has told you so much about them, you must have been expecting them, and in a measure prepared for them at any time. Haven't you talked it over with Marian, and told her that you would want her when they came?"

Eileen was extremely busy with another wave of hair. She turned her back and her voice was not quite steady as she answered. "Ever since Marian got this 'going to the city to study' idea in her head I have scarcely seen her. She had an awful job to empty the house, and pack such things as she wants to keep, and she is working overtime on a very special plan that she thinks maybe she'll submit in a prize competition offered by a big firm of San Francisco architects, so I have scarcely seen her for six weeks."

"And you never once went over to help her with her work, or to encourage her or to comfort her? You can't think Marian can leave this valley and not be almost heartbroken," said Linda. "You just make me almost wonder at you. When you think of the kind of friends that Marian Thorne's father and mother, and our father and mother were, and how we children were reared together, and the good times we have had in these two houses—and then the awful day when the car went over the cliff, and how Marian clung to us and tried to comfort us, when her own health was broken—and Marian's the same Marian she has always been, only nicer every day—how you can sit there and say you have scarcely seen her in six of the hardest weeks of her life, certainly surprises me. I'll tell you this: I told Katy I would help her, but I won't do it if you don't go over and make Marian come tonight."

Eileen turned to her sister and looked at her keenly. Linda's brow was sullen, and her jaw set.

"A bed would look mighty good to me and I will go and get into mine this minute if you don't say you will go and ask her, in such a way that she comes," she threatened.

Eileen hesitated a second and then said: "All right, since you make such a point of it I will ask her."

"Very well," said Linda. "Then I'll help Katy the very best I can."

CHAPTER III. The House of Dreams

In less than an hour, Linda was in the kitchen, dressed in an old green skirt and an orange blouse. Katy pinned one of her aprons on the girl and told her that her first job was to set the table.

"And Miss Eileen has given most particular orders that I use the very best of everything. Lay the table for four, and you are to be extremely careful in serving not to spill the soup."

Linda stood very quietly for a second, her heavy black brows drawn together in deep thought.

"When did Eileen issue these instructions?" she inquired.

"Not five minutes ago," said Katy. "She just left me kitchen and I'll say I never saw her lookin' such a perfect picture. That new dress of hers is the most becoming one she has ever had."

Almost unconsciously, Linda's hand reached to the front of her well-worn blouse, and she glanced downward at her skirt and shoes.

"Um-hm," she said meditatively, "another new dress for Eileen, which means that I will get nothing until next month's allowance comes in, if I do then. The table set for four, which, interpreted, signifies that she has asked Marian in such a way that Marian won't come. And the caution as to care with the soup means that I am to serve my father's table like a paid waitress. Katy, I have run for over three years on Eileen's schedule, but this past year I am beginning to use my brains and I am reaching the place of self-assertion. That programme won't do, Katy. It's got to be completely revised. You just watch me and see how I follow those instructions."

Then Linda marched out of the kitchen door and started across the lawn in the direction of a big brown house dimly outlined through widely spreading branches of ancient live oaks, palm, and bamboo thickets. She entered the house without knocking and in the hall uttered a low penetrating whistle. It was instantly answered from upstairs. Linda began climbing, and met Marian at the top.

"Why, Marian," she cried, "I had no idea you were so far along. The house is actually empty."

"Practically everything went yesterday," answered Marian. "Those things of Father's and Mother's and my own that I wish to keep I have put in storage, and the remainder went to James's Auction Rooms. The house is sold, and I am leaving in the morning."

"Then that explains," questioned Linda, "why you refused Eileen's invitation to dinner tonight?"

"On the contrary," answered Marian, "an invitation to dinner tonight would be particularly and peculiarly acceptable to me, since the kitchen is barren as the remainder of the house, and I was intending to slip over when your room was lighted to ask if I might spend the night with you."

Linda suddenly gathered her friend in her arms and held her tight.

"Well, thank heaven that you felt sufficiently sure of me to come to me when you needed me. Of course you shall spend the night with me; and I must have been mistaken in thinking Eileen had been here. She probably will come any minute. There are guests for the night. John is bringing that writer friend of his. Of course you know about him. It's Peter Morrison."

Marian nodded her head. "Of course! John has always talked of him. He had some extremely clever articles in The Post lately."

"Well, he is one," said Linda, "and an architect who is touring with him is two; they are looking for a location to build a house for the writer. You can see that it would be a particularly attractive feather in our cap if he would endorse our valley sufficiently to home in it. So Eileen has invited them to sample our brand of entertainment, and in the morning no doubt she will be delighted to accompany them and show them all the beautiful spots not yet preempted."

"Oh, heavens," cried Marian, "I'm glad I never showed her my spot!"

"Well, if you are particular about wanting a certain place I sincerely hope you did not," said Linda.

"I am sure I never did," answered Marian. "I so love one spot that I have been most secretive about it. I am certain I never went further than to say there was a place on which I would love to build for myself the house of my dreams. I have just about finished getting that home on paper, and I truly have high hopes that I may stand at least a fair chance of winning with it the prize Nicholson and Snow are offering. That is one of the reasons why I am hurrying on my way to San Francisco much sooner than I had expected to go. I haven't a suitable dinner dress because my trunks have gone, but among such old friends it won't matter. I have one fussy blouse in my bag, and I'll be over as soon as I can see to closing up the house and dressing."

Linda hurried home, and going to the dining room, she laid the table for six in a deft and artistic manner. She filled a basket with beautiful flowers of her own growing for a centerpiece, and carefully followed Eileen's instruction to use the best of everything. When she had finished she went to the kitchen.

"Katy," she said, "take a look at my handiwork."

"It's just lovely," said Katy heartily.

"I quite agree with you," answered Linda, "and now in pursuance of a recently arrived at decision, I have resigned, vamoosed, quit, dead stopped being waitress for Eileen. I was seventeen my last birthday. Hereafter when there are guests I sit at my father's table, and you will have to do the best you can with serving, Katy."

"And it's just exactly right ye are," said Katy. "I'll do my best, and if that's not good enough, Miss Eileen knows what she can do."

"Now listen to you," laughed Linda. "Katy, you couldn't be driven to leave me, by anything on this earth that Eileen could do; you know you couldn't."

Katy chuckled quietly. "Sure, I wouldn't be leaving ye, lambie," she said. "We'll get everything ready, and I can serve I six as nicely as anyone. But you're not forgetting that Miss Eileen said most explicit to lay the table for FOUR?"

"I am not forgetting," said Linda. "For Eileen's sake I am I sorry to say that her ship is on the shoals. She is not going to have clear sailing with little sister Linda any longer. This is the year of woman's rights, you know, Katy, and I am beginning to realize that my rights have been badly infringed upon for lo these many years. If Eileen chooses to make a scene before guests, that is strictly up to Eileen. Now what is it you want me to do?"

Katy directed and Linda worked swiftly. Soon they heard a motor stop, and laughing voices told them that the guests had arrived.

"Now I wonder," said Linda, "whether Marian is here yet."

At that minute Marian appeared at the kitchen door.

"Linda," she said breathlessly, "I am feeling queer about this. Eileen hasn't been over."

"Oh, that's all right," said Linda casually. "The folks have come, and she was only waiting to make them a bit at home before she ran after you."

Marian hesitated.

"She was not allowing me much time to dress."

"That's 'cause she knew you did not need it," retorted Linda. "The more you fuss up, the less handsome you are, and you never owned anything in your life so becoming as that old red blouse. So farewell, Katy, we're due to burst into high society tonight. We're going to help Eileen vamp a lawyer, and an author, and an architect, one apiece. Which do you prefer, Marian?"

"I'll take the architect," said Marian. "We should have something in common since I am going to be a great architect myself one of these days."

"Why, that is too bad," said Linda. "I'll have to rearrange the table if you insist, because I took him, and left you the author, and it was for love of you I did it. I truly wanted him myself, all the time."

They stopped in the dining room and Marian praised Linda's work in laying the table; and then, together they entered the living room.

At the moment of their entrance, Eileen was talking animatedly about the beauties of the valley as a location for a happy home. When she saw the two girls she paused, the color swiftly faded from her face, and Linda, who was watching to see what would happen, noticed the effort she made at self-control, but she was very sure that their guests did not.

It never occurred to Linda that anyone would consider good looks in connection with her overgrown, rawboned frame and lean face, but she was accustomed to seeing people admire Marian, for Marian was a perfectly modeled woman with peach bloom cheeks, deep, dark eyes, her face framed in a waving mass of hair whose whiteness dated from the day that the brakes of her car failed and she plunged down the mountain with her father beside her, and her mother and Doctor and Mrs. Strong in the back seat. Ten days afterward Marian's head of beautiful dark hair was muslin white. Now it framed a face of youth and beauty with peculiar pathos. "Striking" was perhaps the one adjective which would best describe her.

John Gilman came hastily to greet them. Linda, after a swift glance at Eileen, turned astonished eyes on their guests. For one second she looked at the elder of them, then at the younger. There was no recognition in her eyes, and there was a decided negative in a swift movement of her head. Both men understood that she did not wish them to mention that they ever had seen her previously. For an instant there was a strained situation. Eileen was white with anger. John Gilman was looking straight at Marian, and in his soul he must have wondered if he had been wise in neglecting her for Eileen. Peter Morrison and his architect, Henry Anderson, had two things to think about. One was the stunning beauty of Marian Thorne as she paused in the doorway, the light misting her white hair and deepening the tints of her red waist The other was why the young girl facing them had forbidden them to reveal that two hours before they had seen her in the canyon. Katy, the efficient life-saver of the Strong family, announced dinner, and Linda drew back the curtains and led the way to the dining room, saying when they had arrived: "I didn't have time in my hour's notice to make elaborate place cards as I should have liked to do, so these little pen sketches will have to serve."

To cover his embarrassment and to satisfy his legal mind, John Gilman turned to Linda, asking: "Why 'an hour'? I told Eileen a week ago I was expecting the boys today."

"But that does not prove that Eileen mentioned it to me," answered Linda quietly; "so you must find your places from the cards I could prepare in a hurry."

This same preparation of cards at the round table placed Eileen between the architect and the author, Marian between the author and John Gilman, and Linda between Gilman and the architect, which added one more tiny gale to the storm of fury that was raging in the breast of white-faced Eileen. The situation was so strained that without fully understanding it, Marian, who was several years older than either of the Strong sisters, knew that although she was tired to the point of exhaustion she should muster what reserve force she could to the end of making the dinner party particularly attractive, because she was deeply interested in drawing to the valley every suitable home seeker it was possible to locate there. It was the unwritten law of the valley that whenever a home seeker passed through, every soul who belonged exerted the strongest influence to prove that the stars hung lower and shone bigger and in bluer heavens than anywhere else on earth; that nowhere could be found air to equal the energizing salt breezes from the sea, snow chilled, perfumed with almond and orange; that the sun shone brighter more days in the year, and the soil produced a greater variety of vegetables and fruits than any other spot of the same size on God's wonderful footstool. This could be done with unanimity and enthusiasm by every resident of Lilac Valley for the very simple reason that it was the truth. The valley stood with its steep sides raying blue from myriad wild lilacs; olives and oranges sloped down to the flat floor, where cultivated ranches and gardens were so screened by eucalyptus and pepper trees, palm and live oak, myriads of roses of every color and variety, and gaudy plants gathered there from the entire girth of the tropical world, that to the traveler on the highway trees and flowers predominated. The greatest treasure of the valley was the enthusiastic stream of icy mountain water that wandered through the near-by canyon and followed the length of the valley on its singing, chuckling way to the ocean. All the residents of Lilac Valley had to do to entrance strangers with the location was to show any one of a dozen vantage points, and let visitors test for themselves the quality of the sunshine and air, and study the picture made by the broad stretch of intensively cultivated valley, walled on either side by mountains whose highest peaks were often cloud-draped and for ever shifting their delicate pastel shades from gray to blue, from lavender to purple, from tawny yellow to sepia, under the play of the sun and clouds.

They had not been seated three minutes before Linda realized from her knowledge of Eileen that the shock had been too great, if such a thing might be said of so resourceful a creature as Eileen. Evidently she was going to sulk in the hope that this would prove that any party was a failure at which she did not exert herself to be gracious. It had not been in Linda's heart to do more than sit quietly in the place belonging by right to her, but when she realized what was going to happen, she sent Marian one swift appealing glance, and then desperately plunged into conversation to cover Eileen's defection.

"I have been told," she said, addressing the author, "that you are looking for a home in California. Is this true, or is it merely that every good Californian hopes this will happen when any distinguished Easterner comes our way?"

"I can scarcely answer you," said Peter Morrison, "because my ideas on the subject are still slightly nebulous, but I am only too willing to see them become concrete."

"You have struck exactly the right place," said Linda. "We have concrete by the wagon load in this valley and we are perfectly willing to donate the amount required to materialize your ideas. Do you dream of a whole ranch or only a nest?"

"Well, the fact is," answered Peter Morrison with a most attractive drawl in his slow speech, "the fact is the dimensions of my dream must fit my purse. Ever since I finished college I have been in newspaper work and I have lived in an apartment in New York except while I was abroad. When I came back my paper sent me to San Francisco and from there I motored down to see for myself if the wonderful things that are written about Los Angeles County are true."

"That is not much of a compliment to us," said Linda slowly. "How do you think we would dare write them if they were not true?"

This caused such a laugh that everyone felt much easier. Marian turned her dark eyes toward Peter Morrison.

"Linda and I are busy people," she said. "We waste little time in indirections, so I hope it's not out of the way for me to ask straightforwardly if you are truly in earnest, about wanting a home in Lilac Valley?"

"Then I'll have to answer you," said Peter, "that I have an attractive part of the 'makin's' and I am in deadly earnest about wanting a home somewhere. I am sick in my soul of narrow apartments and wheels and the rush and roar of the city. There was a time when I ate and drank it. It was the very breath of life to me. I charged on Broadway like a caterpillar tank charging in battle; but it is very remarkable how quickly one changes in this world. I have had some success in my work, and the higher I go, the better work I feel I can do in a quiet place and among less enervating surroundings. John and I were in college together, roommates, and no doubt he has told you that we graduated with the same class. He has found his location here and I would particularly enjoy having a home near him. They tell me there are well-trained servants to look after a house and care for a bachelor, so I truly feel that if I can find a location I would like, and if Henry can plan me a house, and I can stretch my purse to cover the investment, that there is a very large possibility that somewhere within twenty miles of Los Angeles I may find the home of my dreams."

"One would almost expect," said Marian, "that a writer would say something more original. This valley is filled with people who came here saying precisely what you have said; and the lure of the land won them and here they are, shameless boosters of California."

"Why shameless?" inquired Henry Anderson.

"Because California so verifies the wildest statement that can be made concerning her that one may go the limit of imagination without shame," laughed Marian. "I try in all my dealings to stick to the straight and narrow path."

"Oh, kid, don't stick to the straight and narrow," broke in Linda, "there's no scenery."

Eileen laid down her fork and stared in white-lipped amazement at the two girls, but she was utterly incapable of forgetting herself and her neatly arranged plans to have the three cultivated and attractive young men all to herself for the evening. She realized too, from the satisfaction betrayed in the glances these men were exchanging among each other, the ease with which they sat, and the gusto with which they ate the food Katy was deftly serving them, that something was happening which never had happened at the Strong table since she had presided as its head, her sole endeavor having been to flatter her guests or to extract flattery for herself from them.

"That is what makes this valley so adorable," said Marian when at last she could make herself heard. "It is neither straight nor narrow. The wing of a white sea swallow never swept a lovelier curve on the breast of the ocean than the line of this valley. My mother was the dearest little woman, and she used to say that this valley was outlined by a gracious gesture from the hand of God in the dawn of Creation."

Peter Morrison deliberately turned in his chair, his eyes intent on Marian's earnest face.

"You almost make me want to say, in the language of an old hymn I used to hear my mother sing, 'Here will I set up my rest.' With such a name as Lilac Valley and with such a thought in the heart concerning it, I scarcely feel that there is any use in looking further. How about it, Henry? Doesn't it sound conclusive to you?"

"It certainly does," answered Henry Anderson, "and from what I could see as we drove in, it looks as well as it sounds."

Peter Morrison turned to his friend.

"Gilman," he said, "you're a lawyer; you should know the things I'd like to. Are there desirable homesites still to be found in the valley, and does the inflation of land at the present minute put it out of my reach?"

"Well, that is on a par with the average question asked a lawyer," answered Gilman, "but part of it I can answer definitely and at once. I think every acre of land suitable for garden or field cultivation is taken. I doubt if there is much of the orchard land higher up remaining and what there is would command a rather stiff price; but if you would be content with some small plateau at the base of a mountain where you could set any sort of a house and have—say two or three acres, mostly of sage and boulders and greasewood and yucca around it."

"Why in this world are you talking about stones and sage and greasewood?" cried Linda. "Next thing they'll be asking about mountain lions and rattlesnakes."

"I beg your pardon," said Gilman, "I fear none of us has remembered to present Miss Linda as a coming naturalist. She got her start from her father, who was one of the greatest nerve specialists the world ever has known. She knows every inch of the mountains, the canyons and the desert. She always says that she cut her teeth on a chunk of adobe, while her father hunted the nests of trap-door spiders out in Sunland. What should I have said when describing a suitable homesite for Peter, Linda?"

"You should have assumed that immediately, Peter,"—Linda lifted her eyes to Morrison's face with a sparkle of gay challenge, and by way of apology interjected—"I am only a kid, you know, so I may call John's friend Peter—you should have assumed that sage and greasewood would simply have vanished from any home location chosen by Peter, leaving it all lacy blue with lilac, and misty white with lemonade bush, and lovely gold with monkey flower, and purple with lupin, and painted blood red with broad strokes of Indian paint brush, and beautifully lighted with feathery flames from Our Lord's Candles, and perfumy as altar incense with wild almond."

"Oh, my soul," said Peter Morrison. "Good people, I have located. I have come to stay. I would like three acres but I could exist with two; an acre would seem an estate to me, and my ideas of a house, Henry, are shriveling. I did have a dream of something that must have been precious near a home. There might have been an evanescent hint of flitting draperies and inexperienced feet in it, but for the sake of living and working in such a location as Miss Linda describes, I would gladly cut my residence to a workroom and a sleeping room and kitchen."

"Won't do," said Linda. "A house is not a house in California without a furnace and a bathroom. We are cold as blue blazes here when the sun goes down and the salty fog creeps up from the sea, and the icy mist rolls down from the mountains to chill our bones; and when it has not rained for six months at a stretch, your own private swimming pool is a comfort. This to add verisimilitude to what everyone else in Lilac Valley is going to tell you."

"I hadn't thought I would need a fire," said Peter, "and I was depending on the ocean for my bathtub. I am particularly fond of a salt rub."

So far, Eileen had not deigned to enter the conversation. It was all so human, so far from her ideas of entertaining that the disapproval on her lips was not sufficiently veiled to be invisible, and John Gilman, glancing in her direction, realized that he was having the best time he had ever had in the Strong household since the passing of his friends, Doctor and Mrs. Strong, vaguely wondered why. And it occurred to him that Linda and Marian were dominating the party. He said the most irritating thing possible in the circumstances: "I am afraid you are not feeling well this evening, Eileen."

Eileen laughed shortly.

"The one perfect thing about me," she said with closely cut precision, "is my health. I haven't the faintest notion what it means to be ill. I am merely waiting for the conversation to take a I turn where I can join in it intelligently."

"Why, bless the child!" exclaimed Linda. "Can't you talk intelligently about a suitable location for a home? On what subject is a woman supposed to be intelligent if she is not at her best on the theme of home. If you really are not interested you had better begin to polish up, because it appeals to me that the world goes just so far in one direction, and then it whirls to the right-about and goes equally as far in the opposite direction. If Daddy were living I think he would say we have reached the limit with apartment house homes minus fireplaces, with restaurant dining minus a blessing, with jazz music minus melody, with jazz dancing minus grace, with national progress minus cradles."

"Linda!" cried Eileen indignantly.

"Good gracious!" cried Linda. "Do I get the shillalah for that? Weren't all of us rocked in cradles? I think that the pendulum has swung far and it is time to swing back to where one man and one woman choose any little spot on God's footstool, build a nest and plan their lives in accord with personal desire and inclination instead of aping their neighbors."

"Bravo!" cried Henry Anderson. "Miss Linda, if you see any suitable spot, and you think I would serve for a bug-catcher, won't you please stake the location?"

"Well, I don't know about that," said Linda. "Would it be the old case of 'I furnish the bread and you furnish the water'?"

"No," said Peter Morrison, "it would not. Henry is doing mighty well. I guarantee that he would furnish a cow that would produce real cream."

13

"How joyous!" said Linda. "I feel quite competent to manage the bread question. We'll call that settled then. When I next cast an appraising eye over my beloved valley, I shan't select the choicest spot in it for Peter Morrison to write a book in; and I want to warn you people when you go hunting to keep a mile away from Marian's plot. She has had her location staked from childhood and has worked on her dream house until she has it all ready to put the ice in the chest and scratch the match for the living room fire-logs. The one thing she won't ever tell is where her location is, but wherever it is, Peter Morrison, don't you dare take it."

"I wouldn't for the world," said Peter Morrison gravely. "If Miss Thorne will tell me even on which side of the valley her location lies, I will agree to stay on the other side."

"Well there is one thing you can depend upon," said the irrepressible Linda before Marian had time to speak. "It is sure to be on the sunny side. Every living soul in California is looking for a place in the sun."

"Then I will make a note of it," said Peter Morrison. "But isn't there enough sun in all this lovely valley that I may have a place in it too?"

"You go straight ahead and select any location you like," said Marian. "I give you the freedom of the valley. There's not one chance in ten thousand that you would find or see anything attractive about the one secluded spot I have always hoped I might some day own."

"This is not fooling, then?" asked Peter Morrison. "You truly have a place selected where you would like to live?"

"She truly has the spot selected and she truly has the house on paper and it truly is a house of dreams," said Linda. "I dream about it myself. When she builds it and lives in it awhile and finds out all the things that are wrong with it, then I am going to build one like it, only I shall eliminate all the mistakes she has made."

"I have often wondered," said Henry Anderson, "if such a thing ever happened as that people built a house and lived in it, say ten years, and did not find one single thing about it that they would change if they had it to build over again. I never have heard of such a case. Have any of you?"

"I am sure no one has," said John Gilman meditatively, "and it's a queer thing. I can't see why people don't plan a house the way they want it before they build."

Marian turned to him—the same Marian he had fallen in love with when they were children.

"Mightn't it be," she asked, "that it is due to changing conditions caused by the rapid development of science and invention? If one had built the most perfect house possible five years ago and learned today that infinitely superior lighting and heating and living facilities could be installed at much less expense and far greater convenience, don't you think that one would want to change? Isn't life a series of changes? Mustn't one be changing constantly to keep abreast of one's day and age?"

"Why, surely," answered Gilman, "and no doubt therein lies at least part of the answer to Anderson's question."

"And then," added Marian, "things happen in families. Sometimes more babies than they expect come to newly married people and they require more room."

"My goodness, yes!" broke in Linda. "Just look at Sylvia Townsend—twins to begin with."

"Linda!" breathed Eileen, aghast.

"So glad you like my name, dear," murmured Linda sweetly.

"And then," continued Marian, "changes come to other people as they have to me. I can't say that I had any fault to find with either the comforts or the conveniences of Hawthorne House until Daddy and Mother were swept from it at one cruel sweep; and after that it was nothing to me but a haunted house, and I don't feel that it can be blamed for wanting to leave it. I will be glad to know that there are people living in it who won't see a big strong figure meditatively smoking before the fireplace and a gray dove of a woman sitting on the arm of his chair. I will be glad, if Fate is kind to me and people like my houses, to come back to the valley when I can afford to and build myself a home that has no past—a place, in fact, where I can furnish my own ghost, and if I meet myself on the stairs then I won't be shocked by me."

"I don't think there is a soul in the valley who blames you for selling your home and going, Marian," said Linda soberly. "I think it would be foolish if you did not."

The return to the living room brought no change. Eileen pouted while Linda and Marian thoroughly enjoyed themselves and gave the guests a most entertaining evening. So disgruntled was Eileen, when the young men had gone, that she immediately went to her room, leaving Linda and Marian to close the house and make their own arrangements for the night. Whereupon Linda deliberately led Marian to the carefully dusted and flower-garnished guest room and installed her with every comfort and convenience that the house afforded. Then bringing her brushes from her own room, she and Marian made themselves comfortable, visiting far into the night.

"I wonder," said Linda, "if Peter Morrison will go to a real estate man in the morning and look over the locations remaining in Lilac Valley."

"Yes, I think he will," said Marian conclusively.

"It seems to me," said Linda, "that we did a whole lot of talking about homes tonight; which reminds me, Marian, in packing have you put in your plans? Have you got your last draft with you?"

"No," answered Marian, "it's in one of the cases. I haven't anything but two or three pencil sketches from which I drew the final plans as I now think I'll submit them for the contest. Wouldn't it be a tall feather in my cap, Linda, if by any chance I I should win that prize?"

"It would be more than a feather," said Linda. "It would be a whole cap, and a coat to wear with it, and a dress to match the coat, and slippers to match the dress, and so forth just like 'The House That Jack Built.' Have you those sketches, Marian?"

Opening her case, Marian slid from underneath the garments folded in it, several sheets on which were roughly penciled sketches of the exterior of a house—on the reverse, the upstairs and downstairs floor plans; and sitting down, she explained these to Linda. Then she left them lying on a table, waiting to be returned to her case before she replaced her clothes in the morning. Both girls were fast asleep when a mischievous wind slipped down the valley, and lightly lifting the top sheet, carried it through the window, across the garden, and dropped it at the foot of a honey-dripping loquat.

Because they had talked until late in the night of Marian's plans and prospects in the city, of Peter Morrison's proposed residence in the valley, of how lonely Linda would be without Marian, of everything concerning their lives except the change in Eileen and John Gilman, the two girls slept until late in the morning, so that there were but a few minutes remaining in which Marian might dress, have a hasty breakfast and make her train. In helping her, it fell to Linda to pack Marian's case. She put the drawings she found on the table in the bottom, the clothing and brushes on top of them, and closing the case, carried it herself until she delivered it into the porter's hands as Marian boarded her train.

CHAPTER IV. Linda Starts a Revolution

The last glimpse Marian Thorne had of Linda was as she stood alone, waving her hand, her cheeks flushed, her eyes shining, her final word cheery and encouraging. Marian smiled and waved in return until the train bore her away. Then she sat down wearily and stared unseeingly from a window. Life did such very dreadful things to people. Her girlhood had been so happy. Then came the day of the Black Shadow, but in her blackest hour she had not felt alone. She had supposed she was leaning on John Gilman as securely as she had leaned on her father. She had learned, with the loss of her father, that one cannot be sure of anything in this world least of all of human life. Yet in her darkest days she had depended on John Gilman. She had every reason to believe that it was for her that he struggled daily to gain a footing in his chosen profession. When success came, when there was no reason that Marian could see why they might not have begun life together, there had come a subtle change in John, and that change had developed so rapidly that in a few weeks' time, she was forced to admit that the companionship and loving attentions that once had been all hers were now all Eileen's.

She sat in the train, steadily carrying her mile after mile farther from her home, and tried to think what had happened and how and why it had happened. She could not feel that she had been wrong in her estimate of John Gilman. Her valuation of him had been taught her by her father and mother and by Doctor and Mrs. Strong and by John Gilman himself. Dating from the time that Doctor Strong had purchased the property and built a home in Lilac Valley beside Hawthorne House, Marian had admired Eileen and had loved her. She was several years older than the beautiful girl she had grown up beside. Age had not mattered; Eileen's beauty had not mattered. Marian was good looking herself.

She always had known that Eileen had imposed upon her and was selfish with her, but Eileen's impositions were so skillfully maneuvered, her selfishness was so adorably taken for granted that Marian in retrospection felt that perhaps she was responsible for at least a small part of it. She never had been able to see the inner workings of Eileen's heart. She was not capable of understanding that when John Gilman was poor and struggling Eileen had ignored him. It had not occurred to Marian that when the success for which he struggled began to come generously, Eileen would begin to covet the man she had previously disdained. She had always striven to find friends among people of wealth and distinction. How was Marian to know that when John began to achieve wealth and distinction, Eileen would covet him also?

Marian could not know that Eileen had studied her harder than she ever studied any book, that she had deliberately set herself to make the most of every defect or idiosyncrasy in Marian, at the same time offering herself as a charming substitute. Marian was prepared to be the mental, the spiritual, and the physical mate of a man.

Eileen was not prepared to be in truth and honor any of these. She was prepared to make any emergency of life subservient to her own selfish desires. She was prepared to use any man with whom she came in contact for the furtherance of any whim that at the hour possessed her. What she wanted was unbridled personal liberty, unlimited financial resources.

Marian, almost numbed with physical fatigue and weeks of mental strain, came repeatedly against the dead wall of ignorance when she tried to fathom the change that had taken place between herself and John Gilman and between herself and Eileen. Daniel Thorne was an older man than Doctor Strong. He had accumulated more property. Marian had sufficient means at her command to make it unnecessary for her to acquire a profession or work for her living, but she had always been interested in and loved to plan houses and help her friends with buildings they were erecting. When the silence and the loneliness of her empty home enveloped her, she had begun, at first as a distraction, to work on the drawings for a home that an architect had made for one of her neighbors. She had been able to suggest so many comforts and conveniences, and so to revise these plans that, at first in a desultory way, later in real earnest, she had begun to draw plans for houses. Then, being of methodical habit and mathematical mind, she began scaling up the plans and figuring on the cost of building, and so she had worked until she felt that she was evolving homes that could be built for the same amount of money and lived in with more comfort and convenience than the homes that many of her friends were having planned for them by architects of the city.

To one spot in the valley she had gone from childhood as a secret place in which to dream and study. She had loved that retreat until it had become a living passion with her. The more John Gilman neglected her, the more she concentrated upon her plans, and when the hour came in which she realized what she had lost and what Eileen had won, she reached the decision to sell her home, go to the city, and study until she knew whether she really could succeed at her chosen profession.

Then she would come back to the valley, buy the spot she coveted, build the house of which she dreamed, and in it she would spend the remainder of her life making homes for the women who knew how to hold the love of men. When she reached the city she had decided that if one could not have the best in life, one must be content with the next best, and for her the next best would be homes for other people, since she might not materialize the home she had dreamed for John Gilman and herself. She had not wanted to leave the valley. She had not wanted to lose John Gilman. She had not wanted to part with the home she had been reared in. Yet all of these things seemed to have been forced upon her. All Marian knew to do was to square her shoulders, take a deep breath, put regrets behind her, and move steadily toward the best future she could devise for herself.

She carried letters of introduction to the San Francisco architects, Nicholson and Snow, who had offered a prize for the best house that could be built in a reasonable time for fifteen thousand dollars. She meant to offer her plans in this competition. Through friends she had secured a comfortable place in which to live and work. She need undergo no hardships in searching for a home, in clothing herself, in paying for instruction in the course in architecture she meant to pursue.

Concerning Linda she could not resist a feeling of exultation. Linda was one of the friends in Lilac Valley about whom Marian could think wholeheartedly and lovingly. Sometimes she had been on the point of making a suggestion to Linda, and then she had contented herself with waiting in the thought that very soon there must come to the girl a proper sense of her position and her rights. The experience of the previous night taught Marian that Linda had arrived. She would no longer be the compliant little sister who would run Eileen's errands, wait upon her guests and wear disreputable clothing. When Linda reached a point where she was capable of the performance of the previous night, Marian knew that she would proceed to live up to her blue china in every ramification of life. She did not know exactly how Linda would follow up the assertion of her rights that she had made, but she did know that in some way she would follow it up, because Linda was a very close reproduction of her father.

She had been almost constantly with him during his life, very much alone since his death. She was a busy young person. From Marian's windows she had watched the business of carrying on the wild-flower garden that Linda and her father had begun. What the occupation was that kept the light burning in Linda's room far into the night Marian did not know. For a long time she had supposed that her studies were difficult for her, and when she had asked Linda if it were not possible for her to prepare her lessons without so many hours of midnight study she had caught the stare of frank amazement with which the girl regarded her and in that surprised, almost grieved look she had realized that very probably a daughter of Alexander Strong, who resembled him as Linda resembled him, would not be compelled to overwork to master the prescribed course of any city high school. What Linda was doing during those midnight hours Marian did not know, but she did know that she was not wrestling with mathematics and languages—at least not all of the time. So Marian knowing Linda's gift with a pencil, had come to the conclusion that she was drawing pictures; but circumstantial evidence was all she had as a basis for her conviction. Linda went her way silently and alone. She was acquainted with everyone living in Lilac Valley, frank and friendly with all of them;

aside from Marian she had no intimate friend. Not another girl in the valley cared to follow Linda's pursuits or to cultivate the acquaintance of the breeched, booted girl, constantly devoting herself to outdoor study with her father during his lifetime, afterward alone.

For an instant after Marian had boarded her train Linda stood looking at it, her heart so heavy that it pained acutely. She had not said one word to make Marian feel that she did not want her to go. Not once had she put forward the argument that Marian's going would leave her to depend entirely for human sympathy upon the cook, and her guardian, also administrator of the Strong estate, John Gilman. So long as he was Marian's friend Linda had admired John Gilman. She had gone to him for some measure of the companionship she had missed in losing her father. Since Gilman had allowed himself to be captivated by Eileen, Linda had harbored a feeling concerning him almost of contempt. Linda was so familiar with every move that Eileen made, so thoroughly understood that there was a motive back of her every action, that she could not see why John Gilman, having known her from childhood, should not understand her also.

She had decided that the time had come when she would force Eileen to give her an allowance, however small, for her own personal expenses, that she must in some way manage to be clothed so that she was not a matter of comment even among the boys of her school, and she could see no reason why the absolute personal liberty she always had enjoyed so long as she disappeared when Eileen did not want her and appeared when she did, should not extend to her own convenience as well as Eileen's.

Life was a busy affair for Linda. She had not time to watch Marian's train from sight. She must hurry to the nearest street car and make all possible haste or she would be late for her classes. Throughout the day she worked with the deepest concentration, but she could not keep down the knowledge that Eileen would have things to say, possibly things to do, when they met that evening, for Eileen was capable of disconcerting hysteria. Previously Linda had remained stubbornly silent during any tirade in which Eileen chose to indulge. She had allowed herself to be nagged into doing many things that she despised, because she would not assert herself against apparent injustice. But since she had come fully to realize the results of Eileen's course of action for Marian and for herself, she was deliberately arriving at the conclusion that hereafter she would speak when she had a defense, and she would make it her business to let the sun shine on any dark spot that she discovered in Eileen.

Linda knew that if John Gilman were well acquainted with Eileen, he could not come any nearer to loving her than she did. Such an idea as loving Eileen never had entered Linda's thoughts. To Linda, Eileen was not lovable. That she should be expected to love her because they had the same parents and lived in the same home seemed absurd. She was slightly disappointed, on reaching home, to find that Eileen was not there.

"Will the lady of the house dine with us this evening? she asked as she stood eating an apple in the kitchen.

"She didn't say," answered Katy. "Have ye had it out about last night yet?"

"No," answered Linda. "That is why I was asking about her. I want to clear the atmosphere before I make my new start in life."

"Now, don't ye be going too far, lambie," cautioned Katy "Ye young things make such an awful serious business of life these days. In your scramble to wring artificial joy out of it you miss all the natural joy the good God provided ye."

"It seems to me, Katy," said Linda slowly, "that you should put that statement the other way round. It seems that life makes a mighty serious business for us young things, and it seems to me that if we don't get the right start and have a proper foundation life Is going to be spoiled for us. One life is all I've got to live in this world, and I would like it to be the interesting and the beautiful kind of life that Father lived."

Linda dropped to a chair.

"Katy," she said, leaning forward and looking intently into the earnest face of the woman before her, "Katy, I have been thinking an awful lot lately. There is a question you could answer for me if you wanted to."

"Well, I don't see any raison," said Katy, "why I shouldn't answer ye any question ye'd be asking me."

Linda's eyes narrowed as they did habitually in deep thought She was looking past Katy down the sunlit spaces of the wild garden that was her dearest possession, and then her eyes strayed higher to where the blue walls that shut in Lilac Valley ranged their peaks against the sky. "Katy," she said, scarcely above her breath, "was Mother like Eileen?"

Katy stiffened. Her red face paled slightly. She turned her back and slowly slid into the oven the pie she was carrying. She closed the door with more force than was necessary and then turned and deliberately studied Linda from the top of her shining black head to the tip of her shoe.

"Some," she said tersely.

"Yes, I know 'some'," said Linda, "but you know I was too young to pay much attention, and Daddy managed always to make me so happy that I never realized until he was gone that he not only had been my father but my mother as well. You know what I mean, Katy."

"Yes," said Katy deliberately, "I know what ye mean, lambie, and I'll tell ye the truth as far as I know it. She managed your father, she pampered him, but she deceived him every day, just about little things. She always made the household accounts bigger than they were, and used the extra money for Miss Eileen and herself—things like that. I'm thinkin' he never knew it. I'm thinking he loved her deeply and trusted her complete. I know what ye're getting at. She was not enough like Eileen to make him unhappy with her. He might have been if he had known all there was to know, but for his own sake I was not the one to give her away, though she constantly made him think that I was extravagant and wasteful in me work." Linda's eyes came back from the mountains and met Katy's straightly.

"Katy," she said, "did you ever see sisters as different as Eileen and I are?"

"No, I don't think I ever did," said Katy.

"It puzzles me," said Linda slowly. "The more I think about it, the less I can understand why, if we are sisters, we would not accidentally resemble each other a tiny bit in some way, and I must say I can't see that we do physically or mentally."

"No," said Katy, "ye were just as different as ye are now when I came to this house new and ye were both little things."

"And we are going to be as different and to keep on growing more different every day of our lives, because red war breaks out the minute Eileen comes home. I haven't a notion what she will say to me for what I did last night and what I am going to do in the future, but I have a definite idea as to what I am going to say to her."

"Now, easy; ye go easy, lambie," cautioned Katy.

"I wouldn't regret it," said Linda, "if I took Eileen by the shoulders and shook her till I shook the rouge off her cheek, and the brilliantine off her hair, and a million mean little subterfuges out of her soul. You know Eileen is lovely when she is natural, and if she would be straight-off-the-bat square, I would be proud to be her sister. As it is, I have my doubts, even about this sister business."

"Why, Linda, child, ye are just plain crazy," said Katy. "What kind of notions are you getting into your head?"

"I hear the front door," said Linda, "and I am going to march straight to battle. She's going up the front stairs. I did mean to short-cut up the back, but, come to think of it, I have served my apprenticeship on the back stairs. I believe I'll ascend the front myself. Good-bye, darlin', wish me luck."

Linda swung Katy around, hugged her tight, and dropped a kiss on the top of her faithful head.

"Ye just stick right up for your rights," Katy advised her. "Ye're a great big girl. 'Tain't going to be long till ye're eighteen. But mind your old Katy about going too far. If ye lose your temper and cat-spit, it won't get ye anywhere. The fellow that keeps the coolest can always do the best headwork."

"I get you," said Linda, "and that is good advice for which I thank you."

CHAPTER V. The Smoke of Battle

Then Linda walked down the hall, climbed the front stairs, and presented herself at Eileen's door, there to receive one of the severest shocks of her young life. Eileen had tossed her hat and fur upon a couch, seated herself at her dressing table, and was studying her hair in the effort to decide whether she could fluff it up sufficiently to serve for the evening or whether she must take it down and redress it. At Linda's step in the doorway she turned a smiling face upon her and cried: "Hello, little sister, come in and tell me the news."

Linda stopped as if dazed. The wonderment in which she looked at Eileen was stamped all over her. A surprised braid of hair hung over one of her shoulders. Her hands were surprised, and the skirt of her dress, and her shoes flatly set on the floor.

"Well, I'll be darned!" she ejaculated, and then walked to where she could face Eileen, and seated herself without making any attempt to conceal her amazement.

"Linda," said Eileen sweetly, "you would stand far better chance of being popular and making a host of friends if you would not be so coarse. I am quite sure you never heard Mama or me use such an expression."

For one long instant Linda was too amazed to speak. Then she recovered herself.

"Look here, Eileen, you needn't try any 'perfect lady' business on me," she said shortly. "Do you think I have forgotten the extent of your vocabulary when the curling iron gets too hot or you fail to receive an invitation to the Bachelors' Ball?"

Linda never had been capable of understanding Eileen. At that minute she could not know that Eileen had been facing facts through the long hours of the night and all through the day, and that she had reached the decision that for the future her only hope of working Linda to her will was to conciliate her, to ignore the previous night, to try to put their relationship upon the old basis by pretending that there never had been a break. She laughed softly.

"On rare occasions, I grant it. Of course a little swear slips out sometimes. What I am trying to point out is that you do too much of it."

"How did you ever get the idea," said Linda, "that I wanted to be popular and have hosts of friends? What would I do with them if I had them?"

"Why, use them, my child, use them," answered Eileen promptly.

"Let's cut this," said Linda tersely. "I am not your child. I'm getting to the place where I have serious doubt as to whether I am your sister or not. If I am, it's not my fault, and the same clay never made two objects quite so different. I came up here to fight, and I'm going to see it through. I'm on the warpath, so you may take your club and proceed to battle."

"What have we to fight about?" inquired Eileen.

"Every single thing that you have done that was unfair to me all my life," said Linda. "Since all of it has been deliberate you probably know more about the details than I do, so I'll just content myself with telling you that for the future, last night marked a change in the relations between us. I am going to be eighteen before so very long, and I have ceased to be your maid or your waitress or your dupe. You are not going to work me one single time when I have got brains to see through your schemes after this. Hereafter I take my place in my father's house and at my father's table on an equality with you."

Eileen looked at Linda steadily, trying to see to the depths of her soul. She saw enough to convince her that the young creature in front of her was in earnest.

"Hm," she said, "have I been so busy that I have failed to notice what a great girl you are getting?"

"Busy!" scoffed Linda. "Tell that to Katy. It's a kumquat!"

"Perhaps you are too big," continued Eileen, "to be asked to wait on the table any more."

"I certainly am," retorted Linda, "and I am also too big to wear such shoes or such a dress as I have on at the present min. ute. I know all about the war and the inflation of prices and the reduction in income, but I know also that if there is enough to run the house, and dress you, and furnish you such a suite of rooms as you're enjoying right now, there is enough to furnish me suitable clothes, a comfortable bedroom and a place where I can leave my work without putting away everything I am doing each time I step from the room. I told you four years ago that you might take the touring car and do what you pleased with it. I have never asked what you did or what you got out of it, so I'll thank you to observe equal silence about anything I choose to do now with the runabout, which I reserved for myself. I told you to take this suite, and this is the first time that I have ever mentioned to you what you spent on it."

Linda waved an inclusive hand toward the fully equipped, dainty dressing table, over rugs of pale blue, and beautifully decorated walls, including the sleeping room and bath adjoining.

"So now I'll ask you to keep off while I do what I please about the library and the billiard room. I'll try to get along without much money in doing what I desire there, but I must have some new clothes. I want money to buy me a pair of new shoes for school. I want a pair of pumps suitable for evenings when there are guests to dinner. I want a couple of attractive school dresses. This old serge is getting too hot and too worn for common decency. And I also want a couple of dresses something like you are wearing, for afternoons and evenings."

Eileen stared aghast at Linda.

"Where," she inquired politely, "is the money for all this to come from?"

"Eileen," said Linda in a low tense voice, "I have reached the place where even the BOYS of the high school are twitting me about how I am dressed, and that is the limit. I have stood it for three years from the girls. I am an adept in pretending that I don't see, and I don't hear. I have got to the point where I am perfectly capable of walking into your wardrobe and taking out enough of the clothes there and selling them at a second-hand store to buy me what I require to dress me just plainly and decently. So take warning. I don't know where you are going to get the money, but you are going to get it. If you would welcome a suggestion from me, come home only half the times you dine yourself and your girl friends at tearooms and cafes in the city, and you will save my share that way. I am going to give you a chance to total your budget, and then I demand one half of the income from Father's estate above household expenses; and if I don't get it, on the day I am eighteen I shall go to John Gilman and say to him what I have said to you, and I shall go to the bank and demand that a division be made there, and that a separate bank book be started for me."

Linda's amazement on entering the room had been worthy of note. Eileen's at the present minute was beyond description. Dumbfounded was a colorless word to describe her state of mind.

"You don't mean that," she gasped in a quivering voice when at last she could speak.

"I can see, Eileen, that you are taken unawares," said Linda. "I have had four long years to work up to this hour. Hasn't it even dawned on you that this worm was ever going to turn? You know

19

exquisite moths and butterflies evolve in the canyons from very unprepossessing and lowly living worms. You are spending your life on the butterfly stunt. Have I been such a weak worm that it hasn't ever occurred to you that I might want to try a plain, everyday pair of wings sometime myself?"

Eileen's face was an ugly red, her hands were shaking, her voice was unnatural, but she controlled her temper.

"Of course," she said, "I have always known that the time would come, after you finished school and were of a proper age, when you would want to enter society."

"No, you never knew anything of the kind," said Linda bluntly, "because I have not the slightest ambition to enter society either now or then. All I am asking is to enter the high school in a commonly decent, suitable dress; to enter our dining room as a daughter; to enter a workroom decently equipped for my convenience. You needn't be surprised if you hear some changes going on in the billiard room and see some changes going on in the library. And if I feel that I can muster the nerve to drive the runabout, it's my car, it's up to me."

"Linda!" wailed Eileen, "how can you think of such a thing? You wouldn't dare."

"Because I haven't dared till the present is no reason why I should deprive myself of every single pleasure in life," said Linda. "You spend your days doing exactly what you please; driving that runabout for Father was my one soul-satisfying diversion. Why shouldn't I do the thing I love most, if I can muster the nerve?"

Linda arose, and walking over to a table, picked up a magazine lying among some small packages that Eileen evidently had placed there on entering her room.

"Are you subscribing to this?" she asked.

She turned in her hands and leafed through the pages of a most attractive magazine, Everybody's Home. It was devoted to poetry, good fiction, and everything concerning home life from beef to biscuits, and from rugs to roses.

"I saw it on a newsstand," said Eileen. "I was at lunch with some girls who had a copy and they were talking about some articles by somebody named something—Meredith, I think it was—Jane Meredith, maybe she's a Californian, and she is advocating the queer idea that we go back to nature by trying modern cooking on the food the aborigines ate. If we find it good then she recommends that we specialize on the growing of these native vegetables for home use and for export—as a new industry."

"I see," said Linda. "Out-Burbanking Burbank, as it were."

"No, not that," said Eileen. "She is not proposing to evolve new forms. She is proposing to show us how to make delicious dishes for luncheon or dinner from wild things now going to waste. What the girls said was so interesting that I thought I'd get a copy and if I see anything good I'll turn it over to Katy."

"And where's Katy going to get the wild vegetables?" asked Linda sceptically.

"Why you might have some of them in your wild garden, or you could easily find enough to try— all the prowling the canyons you do ought to result in something."

"So it should," said Linda. "I quite agree with you. Did I understand you to say that I should be ready to go to the bank with you to arrange about my income next week?"

Again the color deepened in Eileen's face, again she made a visible effort at self-control.

"Oh, Linda," she said, "what is the use of being so hard? You will make them think at the bank that I have not treated you fairly."

"I?" said Linda, "I will make them think? Don't you think it is YOU who will make them think? Will you kindly answer my question?"

"If I show you the books," said Eileen, "if I divide what is left after the bills are paid so that you say yourself that it is fair, what more can you ask?" .

Linda hesitated.

"What I ought to do is exactly what I have said I would do," she said tersely, "but if you are going to put it on that basis I have no desire to hurt you or humiliate you in public. If you do that, I can't see that I have any reason to complain, so we'll call it a bargain and we'll say no more about it until the first of the month, unless the spirit moves you, after taking a good square look at me, to produce some shoes and a school dress instanter."

"I'll see what I can do," answered Eileen.

"All right then," said Linda. "See you at dinner."

She went to her own room, slipped off her school dress, brushed her hair, and put on the skirt and blouse she had worn the previous evening, these being the only extra clothing she possessed. As she straightened her hair she looked at herself intently.

"My, aren't you coming on!" she said to the figure in the glass. "Dressing for dinner! First thing you know you'll be a perfect lady."

CHAPTER VI. Jane Meredith

When Eileen came down to dinner that evening Linda understood at a glance that an effort was to be made to efface thoroughly from the mind of John Gilman all memory of the Eileen of the previous evening. She had decided on redressing her hair, while she wore one of her most becoming and attractive gowns. To Linda and Katy during the dinner she was simply charming. Having said what she wanted to say and received the assurance she desired, Linda accepted her advances cordially and displayed such charming proclivities herself that Eileen began covertly to watch her, and as she watched there slowly grew in her brain the conviction that something had happened to Linda. At once she began studying deeply in an effort to learn what it might be. There were three paramount things in Eileen's cosmos that could happen to a girl: She could have lovely clothing. Linda did not have it. She could have money and influential friends. Since Marian's going Linda had practically no friend; she was merely acquainted with almost everyone living in Lilac Valley. She could have a lover. Linda had none. But stay! Eileen's thought halted at the suggestion. Maybe she had! She had been left completely, to her own devices when she was not wanted about the house. She had been mingling with hundreds of boys and girls in high school. She might have met some man repeatedly on the street cars, going to and from school. In school she might have attracted the son of some wealthy and influential family; which was the only kind of son Eileen chose to consider in connection with Linda. Through Eileen's brain ran bits of the conversation of the previous evening. She recalled that the men she had intended should spend the evening waiting on her and paying her pretty compliments had spent it eating like hungry men, laughing and jesting with Linda and Marian, giving every evidence of a satisfaction with their entertainment that never had been evinced with the best brand of attractions she had to offer.

Eileen was willing to concede that Marian Thorne had been a beautiful girl, and she had known, previous to the disaster, that it was quite as likely that any man might admire Marian's flashing dark beauty as her blonde loveliness. Between them then it would have been merely a question of taste on the part of the man. Since Marian's dark head had turned ashen, Eileen had simply eliminated her at one sweep. That white hair would brand Marian anywhere as an old woman. Very likely no man ever would want to marry her. Eileen was sure she would not want to if she were a man. No wonder John Gilman had ceased to be attracted by a girl's face with a grandmother setting.

As for Linda, Eileen never had considered her at all except as a convenience to serve her own purposes. Last night she had learned that Linda had a brain, that she had wit, that she could say things to which men of the world listened with interest. She began to watch Linda. She appraised with deepest envy the dark hair curling naturally on her temples. She wondered how hair that curled naturally could be so thick and heavy, and she thought what a crown of glory would adorn Linda's head when the day came to coil those long dark braids around it and fasten them with flashing pins. She drew some satisfaction from the sunburned face and lean figure before her, but it was not satisfaction of soul-sustaining quality. There was beginning to be something disquieting about Linda. A roundness was creeping over her lean frame; a glow was beginning to color her lips and cheek bones; a dewy look could be surprised in her dark eyes occasionally. She had the effect of a creature with something yeasty bottled inside it that was beginning to ferment and might effervesce at any minute. Eileen had been so surprised the previous evening and again before dinner, that she made up her mind that hereafter one might expect almost anything from Linda. She would no longer follow a suggestion unless the suggestion accorded with her sense of right and justice. It was barely possible that it might be required to please her inclinations. Eileen's mind worked with unbelievable swiftness. She tore at her subject like a vulture tearing at a feast, and like a vulture she reached the vitals swiftly. She prefaced her question with a dry laugh. Then she leaned forward and asked softly: "Linda, dear, why haven't you told me?"

Linda's eyes were so clear and honest as they met Eileen's that she almost hesitated.

"A little more explicit, please," said the girl quietly.

"WHO IS HE?" asked Eileen abruptly.

"Oh, I haven't narrowed to an individual," said Linda largely "You have noticed a flock of boys following me from school and hanging around the front door? I have such hosts to choose from that it's going to take a particularly splendid knight on a snow-white charger—I think 'charger' is the proper word—to capture my young affections."

Eileen was satisfied. There wasn't any he. She might for a short time yet cut Linda's finances to the extreme limit. Whenever a man appeared on the horizon she would be forced to make a division at least approaching equality.

Linda followed Eileen to the living room and sat down with a book until John Gilman arrived. She had a desire to study him for a few minutes. She was going to write Marian a letter that night. She wanted to know if she could honestly tell her that Gilman appeared lonely and seemed to miss her. Katy had no chance to answer the bell when it rang. Eileen was in the hall. Linda could not tell

21

what was happening from the murmur of voices. Presently John and Eileen entered the room, and as Linda greeted him she did have the impression that he appeared unusually thoughtful and worried. She sat for half an hour, taking slight part in the conversation. Then she excused herself and went to her room, and as she went she knew that she could not honestly write Marian what she had hoped, for in thirty minutes by the clock Eileen's blandishments had worked, and John Gilman was looking at her as if she were the most exquisite and desirable creature in existence.

Slowly Linda climbed the stairs and entered her room. She slid the bolt of her door behind her, turned on the lights, unlocked a drawer, and taking from it a heap of materials she scattered them over a small table, and picking up her pencil, she sat gazing at the sheet before her for some time. Then slowly she began writing:

It appeals to me that, far as modern civilization has gone in culinary efforts, we have not nearly reached the limits available to us as I pointed out last month. We consider ourselves capable of preparing and producing elaborate banquets, yet at no time are we approaching anything even to compare in lavishness and delicacy with the days of Lucullus. We are not feasting on baked swans, peacock tongues and drinking our pearls. I am not recommending that we should revive the indulgence of such lavish and useless expenditure, but I would suggest that if we tire with the sameness of our culinary efforts, we at least try some of the new dishes described in this department, established for the sole purpose of their introduction. In so doing we accomplish a multiple purpose. We enlarge the resources of the southwest. We tease stale appetites with a new tang. We offer the world something different, yet native to us. We use modern methods on Indian material and the results are most surprising. In trying these dishes I would remind you that few of us cared for oysters, olives, celery—almost any fruit or vegetable one could mention on first trial. Try several times and be sure you prepare dishes exactly right before condemning them as either fad or fancy. These are very real, nourishing and delicious foods that are being offered you. Here is a salad that would have intrigued the palate of Lucullus, himself. If you do not believe me, try it. The vegetable is slightly known by a few native mountaineers and ranchers. Botanists carried it abroad where under the name of winter-purslane it is used in France and England for greens or salad, while remaining practically unknown at home. Boiled and seasoned as spinach it makes equally good greens. But it is in salad that it stands pre-eminent.

Go to any canyon—I shall not reveal the name of my particular canyon—and locate a bed of miner's lettuce (Montia perfoliata). Growing in rank beds beside a cold, clean stream, you will find these pulpy, exquisitely shaped, pungent round leaves from the center of which lifts a tiny head of misty white lace, sending up a palate-teasing, spicy perfume. The crisp, pinkish stems snap in the fingers. Be sure that you wash the leaves carefully so that no lurking germs cling to them. Fill your salad bowl with the crisp leaves, from which the flowerhead has been plucked. For dressing, dice a teacup of the most delicious bacon you can obtain and fry it to a crisp brown together with a small sliced onion. Add to the fat two tablespoons of sugar, half a teaspoon of mustard; salt will scarcely be necessary the bacon will furnish that. Blend the fat, sugar, and mustard, and pour in a measure of the best apple vinegar, diluted to taste. Bring this mixture to the boiling point, and when it has cooled slightly pour it over the lettuce leaves, lightly turning with a silver fork. Garnish the edge of the dish with a deep border of the fresh leaves bearing their lace of white bloom intact, around the edge of the bowl, and sprinkle on top the sifted yolks of two hard-boiled eggs, heaping the diced whites in the center.

Linda paused and read this over carefully.

"That is all right," she said. "I couldn't make that much better."

She made a few corrections here and there, and picking up a colored pencil, she deftly sketched in a head piece of delicate sprays of miners' lettuce tipped at differing angles, fringy white with bloom. Below she printed: "A delicious Indian salad. The second of a series of new dishes to be offered made from materials used by the Indians. Compounded and tested in her own diet kitchen by the author."

Swiftly she sketched a tail piece representing a table top upon which sat a tempting-looking big salad bowl filled with fresh green leaves, rimmed with a row of delicate white flowers, from which you could almost scent a teasing delicate fragrance arising; and beneath, in a clear, firm hand, she stroked in the name, Jane Meredith. She went over her work carefully, then laid it flat on a piece of cardboard, shoved it into an envelope, directed it to the editor of Everybody's Home, laid it inside her geometry, and wrote her letter to Marian before going to bed.

In the morning on her way to the street car she gaily waved to a passing automobile going down Lilac Valley, in which sat John Gilman and Peter Morrison and his architect, and as they were driving in the direction from which she had come, Linda very rightly surmised that they were going to pick up Eileen and make a tour of the valley, looking for available building locations; and she wondered why Eileen had not told her that they were coming. Linda had been right about the destination of the car. It turned in at the Strong driveway and stopped at the door. John Gilman went to ring the bell and learn if Eileen were ready. Peter followed him. Henry Anderson stepped from the car and wandered over the lawn, looking at the astonishing array of bushes, vines, flowers, and trees.

From one to another he went, fingering the waxy leaves, studying the brilliant flower faces. Finally turning a corner and crossing the wild garden, to which he paid slight attention, he started down the other side of the house. Here an almost overpowering odor greeted his nostrils, and he went over to a large tree covered with rough, dark green, almost brownish, lance-shaped leaves, each branch terminating in a heavy spray of yellowish-green flowers, whose odor was of cloying sweetness. The bees were buzzing over it. It was not a tree with which he was familiar, and stepping back, he looked at it carefully. Then at its base, wind-driven into a crevice between the roots, his attention was attracted to a crumpled sheet of paper, upon which he could see lines that would have attracted the attention of any architect. He went forward instantly, picked up the sheet, and straightening it out he stood looking at it.

"Holy smoke!" he breathed softly. "What a find!"

He looked at the reverse of the sheet, his face becoming more intent every minute. When he heard Peter Morrison's voice calling him he hastily thrust the paper into his coat pocket; but he had gone only a few steps when he stopped, glanced keenly over the house and lawn, turned his back, and taking the sheet from his pocket, he smoothed it out, folded it carefully, and put it in an inside pocket. Then he joined the party.

At once they set out to examine the available locations that yet remained in Lilac Valley. Nature provided them a wonderful day of snappy sunshine and heady sea air. Spring favored them with lilac walls at their bluest, broken here and there with the rose-misted white mahogany. The violet nightshade was beginning to add deeper color to the hills in the sunniest wild spots. The panicles of mahonia bloom were showing their gold color. Wild flowers were lifting leaves of feather and lace everywhere, and most agreeable on the cool morning air was a faint breath of California sage. Up one side of the valley, weaving in and out, up and down, over the foothills they worked their way. They stopped for dinner at one of the beautiful big hotels, practically filled with Eastern tourists. Eileen never had known a prouder moment than when she took her place at the head of the table and presided over the dinner which was served to three most attractive specimens of physical manhood, each of whom was unusually well endowed with brain, all flattering her with the most devoted attention. This triumph she achieved in a dining room seating hundreds of people, its mirror-lined walls reflecting her exquisite image from many angles, to the click of silver, and the running accompaniment of many voices. What she had expected to accomplish in her own dining room had come to her before a large audience, in which, she had no doubt, there were many envious women. Eileen rayed loveliness like a Mariposa lily, and purred in utter contentment like a deftly stroked kitten.

When they parted in the evening Peter Morrison had memoranda of three locations that he wished to consider. That he might not seem to be unduly influenced or to be giving the remainder of Los Angeles County its just due, he proposed to motor around for a week before reaching an ultimate decision, but in his heart he already had decided that somewhere near Los Angeles he would build his home, and as yet he had seen nothing nearly so attractive as Lilac Valley.

CHAPTER VII. Trying Yucca

On her way to school that morning Linda stopped at the post office and pasted the required amount of stamps upon the package that she was mailing to New York. She hurried from her last class that afternoon to the city directory to find the street and number of James Brothers, figuring that the firm with whom Marian dealt would be the proper people for her to consult. She had no difficulty in finding the place for which she was searching, and she was rather agreeably impressed with the men to whom she talked. She made arrangements with their buyer to call at her home in Lilac Valley at nine o'clock the following Saturday morning to appraise the articles with which she wished to part.

Then she went to one of the leading book stores of the city and made inquiries which guided her to a reliable second-hand book dealer, and she arranged to be ready to receive his representative at ten o'clock on Saturday.

Reaching home she took a note book and pencil, and studied the billiard room and the library, making a list of the furniture which she did not actually need. After that she began on the library shelves, listing such medical works as were of a technical nature. Books of fiction, history, art, and biography, and those books written by her father she did not include. She found that she had a long task which would occupy several evenings. Her mind was methodical and she had been with her father through sufficient business transactions to understand that in order to drive a good bargain she must know how many volumes she had to offer and the importance of their authors as medical authorities; she should also know the exact condition of each set of books. Since she had made up her mind to let them go, and she knew the value of many of the big, leather-bound volumes, she determined that she would not sell them until she could secure the highest possible price for them.

Two months previously she would have consulted John Gilman and asked him to arrange the transaction for her. Since he had allowed himself to be duped so easily—or at least it had seemed easy to Linda; for, much as she knew of Eileen, she could not possibly know the weeks of secret plotting, the plans for unexpected meetings, the trumped-up business problems necessary to discuss, the deliberate flaunting of her physical charms before him, all of which had made his conquest extremely hard for Eileen, but Linda, seeing only results, had thought it contemptibly easy—she would not ask John Gilman anything. She would go ahead on the basis of her agreement with Eileen and do the best she could alone.

She counted on Saturday to dispose of the furniture. The books might go at her leisure. Then the first of the week she could select such furniture as she desired in order to arrange the billiard room for her study. If she had a suitable place in which to work in seclusion, there need be no hurry about the library. She conscientiously prepared all the lessons required in her school course for the next day and then, stacking her books, she again unlocked the drawer opened the previous evening, and taking from it the same materials, set to work. She wrote:

Botanists have failed to mention that there is any connection between asparagus, originally a product of salt marshes, and Yucca, a product of the alkaline desert. Very probably there is no botanical relationship, but these two plants are alike in flavor. From the alkaline, sunbeaten desert where the bayonet plant thrusts up a tender bloom head six inches in height, it slowly increases in stature as it travels across country more frequently rain washed, and winds its way beside mountain streams to where in more fertile soil and the same sunshine it develops magnificent specimens from ten to fifteen and more feet in height. The plant grows a number of years before it decides to flower. When it reaches maturity it throws up a bloom stem as tender as the delicate head of asparagus, thick as one's upper arm, and running to twice one's height. This bloom stem in its early stages is colored the pale pink of asparagus, with faint touches of yellow, and hints of blue. At maturity it breaks into a gorgeous head of lavender-tinted, creamy pendent flowers covering the upper third of its height, billowing out slightly in the center, so that from a distance the waxen torch takes on very much the appearance of a flaming candle. For this reason, in Mexico, where the plant flourishes in even greater abundance than in California, with the exquisite poetry common to the tongue and heart of the Spaniard, Yucca Whipplei has been commonly named "Our Lord's Candle." At the most delicate time of their growth these candlesticks were roasted and eaten by the Indians. Based upon this knowledge, I would recommend two dishes, almost equally delicious, which may be prepared from this plant.

Take the most succulent young bloom stems when they have exactly the appearance of an asparagus head at its moment of delicious perfection. With a sharp knife, cut them in circles an inch in depth. Arrange these in a shallow porcelain baking dish, sprinkle with salt, dot them with butter, add enough water to keep them from sticking and burning. Bake until thoroughly tender. Use a pancake turner to slide the rings to a hot platter, and garnish with circles of hard-boiled egg. This you will find an extremely delicate and appetizing dish.

The second recipe I would offer is to treat this vegetable precisely as you would creamed asparagus. Cut the stalks in six-inch lengths, quarter them to facilitate cooking and handling, and boil in salted water. Drain, arrange in a hot dish, and pour over a carefully made cream sauce. I might add that one stalk would furnish sufficient material for several families. This dish should be popular in southwestern states where the plant grows profusely; and to cultivate these plants for shipping to Eastern markets would be quite as feasible as the shipping of asparagus, rhubarb, artichokes, or lettuce.

I have found both these dishes peculiarly appetizing, but I should be sorry if, in introducing Yucca as a food, I became instrumental in the extermination of this universal and wonderfully beautiful plant. For this reason I have hesitated about including Yucca among these articles; but when I see the bloom destroyed ruthlessly by thousands who cut it to decorate touring automobiles and fruit and vegetable stands beside the highways, who carry it from its native location and stick it in the parching sun of the seashore as a temporary shelter, I feel that the bloom stems might as well be used for food as to be so ruthlessly wasted.

The plant is hardy in the extreme, growing in the most unfavorable places, clinging tenaciously to sheer mountain and canyon walls. After blooming and seeding the plant seems to have thrown every particle of nourishment it contains into its development, it dries out and dies (the spongy wood is made into pincushions for the art stores); but from the roots there spring a number of young plants, which, after a few years of growth, mature and repeat their life cycle, while other young plants develop from the widely scattered seeds. The Spaniards at times call the plant Quiota. This word seems to be derived from quiotl, which is the Aztec name for Agave, from which plant a drink not unlike beer is produced, and suggests the possibility that there might have been a time when the succulent flower stem of the Yucca furnished drink as well as food for the Indians.

After carefully re-reading and making several minor corrections, Linda picked up her pencil, and across the top of a sheet of heavy paper sketched the peaks of a chain of mountains. Across the base she drew a stretch of desert floor, bristling with the thorns of many different cacti brilliant with their gold, pink, and red bloom, intermingled with fine grasses and desert flower faces.

At the left she painstakingly drew a huge plant of yucca with a perfect circle of bayonets, from the center of which uprose the gigantic flower stem the length of her page, and on the misty bloom of the flaming tongue she worked quite as late as Marian Thorne had ever seen a light burning in her window. When she had finished her drawing she studied it carefully a long time, adding a touch here and there, and then she said softly: "There, Daddy, I feel that even you would think that a faithful reproduction Tomorrow night I'll paint it."

John Gilman saw the light from Linda's window when he brought Eileen home that night, and when he left he glanced that way again, and was surprised to see the room still lighted, and the young figure bending over a worktable. He stood very still for a few minutes, wondering what could keep Linda awake so far into the night, and while his thoughts were upon her he wondered, too, why she did not care to have beautiful clothes such as Eileen wore; and then he went further and wondered why, when she could be as entertaining as she had been the night she joined them at dinner, she did not make her appearance oftener; and then, because the mind is a queer thing, and he had wondered about a given state of affairs, he went a step further, and wondered whether the explanation lay in Linda's inclinations or in Eileen's management, and then his thought fastened tenaciously upon the subject of Eileen's management.

He was a patient man. He had allowed his reason and better judgment to be swayed by Eileen's exquisite beauty and her blandishments. He did not regret having discovered before it was too late that Marian Thorne was not the girl he had thought her. He wanted a wife cut after the clinging-vine pattern. He wanted to be the dominating figure in his home. It had not taken Eileen long to teach him that Marian was self-assertive and would do a large share of dominating herself. He had thought that he was perfectly satisfied and very happy with Eileen; yet that day he repeatedly had felt piqued and annoyed with her. She had openly cajoled and flirted with Henry Anderson past a point which was agreeable for any man to see his sweetheart go with another man With Peter Morrison she had been unspeakably charming in a manner with which John was very familiar.

He turned up his coat collar, thrust his hands in his pockets, and swore softly. Looking straight ahead of him, he should have seen a stretch of level sidewalk, bordered on one hand by lacy, tropical foliage, on the other, by sheets of level green lawn, broken everywhere by the uprising boles of great trees, clumps of rare vines, and rows of darkened homes, attractive in architectural 'design' vine covered, hushed for the night. What he really saw was a small plateau, sun illumined, at the foot of a mountain across the valley, where the lilac wall was the bluest, where the sun shone slightly more golden than anywhere else in the valley, where huge live oaks outstretched rugged arms, where the air had a tang of salt, a tinge of sage, an odor of orange, shot through with snowy coolness, thrilled with bird song, and the laughing chuckle of a big spring breaking from the foot of the mountain. They had left the road and followed a narrow, screened path by which they came unexpectedly into this opening. They had stood upon it in wordless enchantment, looking down the slope beneath it, across the peace of the valley, to the blue ranges beyond.

"Just where are we?" Peter Morrison had asked at last.

John Gilman had been looking at a view which included Eileen. She lifted her face, flushed and exquisite, to Peter Morrison and answered in a breathless undertone, yet John had distinctly heard her:

"How wonderful it would be if we were at your house. Oh, I envy the woman who shares this with you!"

It had not been anything in particular, yet all day it had teased John Gilman's sensibilities. He felt ashamed of himself for not being more enthusiastic as he searched records and helped to locate the owner of that particular spot. To John, there was a new tone in Peter's voice, a possessive light in his eyes as he studied the location, and made excursions in several directions, to fix in his mind the exact position of the land.

He had indicated what he considered the topographical location for a house—stood on it facing the valley, and stepped the distance suitably far away to set a garage and figured on a short private road down to the highway. He very plainly was deeply prepossessed with a location John Gilman blamed himself for not having found first. Certainly nature had here grown and walled a dream garden in which to set a house of dreams. So, past midnight, Gilman stood in the sunshine, looking at the face of the girl he had asked to marry him and who had said that she would; and a small doubt crept into his heart, and a feeling that perhaps life might be different for him if Peter Morrison decided to come to Lilac Valley to build his home. Then the sunlight faded, night closed in, but as he went his homeward way John Gilman was thinking, thinking deeply and not at all happily.

CHAPTER VIII. The Bear Cat

"Friday's child is loving and giving,
But Saturday's child must work for a living,"

Linda was chanting happily as she entered the kitchen early Saturday morning.

"Katy, me blessing," she said gaily, "did I ever point out to you the interesting fact that I was born on Saturday? And a devilish piece of luck it was, for I have been hustling ever since. It's bad enough to have been born on Monday and spoiled wash day, but I call Saturday the vanishing point, the end of the extreme limit."

Katy laughed, and, as always, turned adoring eyes on Linda.

"I am not needing ye, lambie," she said. "Is it big business in the canyon ye're having today? Shall I be ready to be cooking up one of them God-forsaken Red Indian messes for ye when ye come back?"

Linda held up a warning finger.

"Hiss, Katy," she said. "That is a dark secret. Don't you be forgetting yourself and saying anything like that before anyone, or I would be ruined entirely."

"Well, I did think when ye began it," said Katy, "that of all the wild foolishness ye and your pa had ever gone through with, that was the worst, but that last mess ye worked out was so tasty to the tongue that I thought of it a lot, and I'm kind o' hankering for more."

Linda caught Katy and swung her around the kitchen in a wild war dance. Her gayest laugh bubbled clear from the joy peak of her soul.

"Katy," she said, "if you had lain awake all night trying to say something that would particularly please me, you couldn't have done better. That was a quaint little phrase and a true little phrase, and I know a little spot that it will fit exactly. What am I doing today? Well, several things, Katy. First, anything you need about the house. Next, I am going to empty the billiard room and sell some of the excess furniture of the library, and with the returns I am going to buy me a rug and a table and some tools to work with, so I won't have to clutter up my bedroom with my lessons and things I bring in that I want to save. And then I am going to sell the technical stuff from the library and use that money where it will be of greatest advantage to me. And then, Katy, I am going to manicure the Bear Cat and I am going to drive it again."

Linda hesitated. Katy stood very still, thinking intently, but finally she said: "That's all right; ye have got good common sense; your nerves are steady; your pa drilled ye fine. Many's the time he has bragged to me behind your back what a fine little driver he was making of ye. I don't know a girl of your age anywhere that has less enjoyment than ye. If it would be giving ye any happiness to be driving that car, ye just go ahead and drive it, lambie, but ye promise me here and now that ye will be mortal careful. In all my days I don't think I have seen a meaner-looking little baste of a car."

"Of course I'll be careful, Katy," said Linda. "That car was not bought for its beauty. Its primal object in this world was to arrive. Gee, how we shot curves, and coasted down the canyons, and gassed up on the level when some poor soul went batty from nerve strain! The truth is, Katy, that you can't drive very slowly. You have got to go the speed for which it was built. But I have had my training. I won't forget. I adore that car, Katy, and I don't know how I have ever kept my fingers off it this long. Today it gets a bath and a facial treatment, and when I have thought up some way to meet my big problem, you're going to have a ride, Katy, that will quite uplift your soul. We'll go scooting through the canyons, and whizzing around the mountains, and roaring along the beach, as slick as a white sea swallow."

"Now, easy, lambie, easy," said Katy. "Ye're planning to speed that thing before ye've got it off the jacks."

"No, that was mere talk," said Linda. "But, Katy, this is my great day. I feel in my bones that I shall have enough money by night to get me some new tires, which I must have before I can start out in safety."

"Of course ye must, honey. I would just be tickled to pieces to let ye have what ye need."

Linda slid her hand across Katy's lips and gathered her close in her arms.

"You blessed old darling," she said. "Of course you would, but I don't need it, Katy. I can sit on the floor to work, if I must, and instead of taking the money from the billiard table to buy a worktable, I can buy tires with that. But here's another thing I want to tell you, Katy. This afternoon a male biped is coming to this house, and he's not coming to see Eileen. His name is Donald Whiting, and when he tells you it is, and stands very straight and takes off his hat, and looks you in the eye and says, 'Calling on Miss Linda Strong,' walk him into the living room, Katy, and seat him in the best chair and put a book beside him and the morning paper; and don't you forget to do it with a flourish. He is nothing but a high-school kid, but he's the first boy that ever in all my days asked to come to see me so it's a big event; and I wish to my soul I had something decent to wear."

"Well, with all the clothes in this house," said Katy; and then she stopped and shut her lips tight and looked at Linda with belligerent Irish eyes.

"I know it," nodded Linda in acquiescence; "I know what you think; but never mind. Eileen has agreed to make me a fair allowance the first of the month, and if that isn't sufficient, I may possibly figure up some way to do some extra work that will bring me a few honest pennies, so I can fuss up enough to look feminine at times, Katy. In the meantime, farewell, oh, my belovedest. Call me at half-past eight, so I will be ready for business at nine."

Then Linda went to the garage and began operations. She turned the hose on the car and washed the dust from it carefully. Then she dried it with the chamois skins as she often had done before. She carefully examined the cushioning, and finding it dry and hard, she gave it a bath of olive oil and wiped and manipulated it. She cleaned the engine with extreme care. At one minute she was running to Katy for kerosene to pour through the engine to loosen the carbon. At another she was telephoning for the delivery of oil, gasoline, and batteries for which she had no money to pay, so she charged them to Eileen, ordering the bill to be sent on the first of the month. It seemed to her that she had only a good start when Katy came after her.

The business of appraising the furniture was short, and Linda was well satisfied with the price she was offered for it. After the man had gone she showed Katy the pieces she had marked to dispose of, and told her when they would be called for. She ate a few bites of lunch while waiting for the book man, and the results of her business with him quite delighted Linda. She had not known that the value of books had risen with the price of everything else. The man with whom she dealt had known her father. He had appreciated the strain in her nature which made her suggest that he should number and appraise the books, but she must be allowed time to go through each volume in order to remove any scraps of paper or memoranda which her father so frequently left in books to which he was referring. He had figured carefully and he had made Linda a far higher price than could have been secured by a man. As the girl went back to her absorbing task in the garage, she could see her way clear to the comforts and conveniences and the material that she needed for her work. When she reached the car she patted it as if it had been a living creature.

"Cheer up, nice old thing," she said gaily. "I know how to get new tires for you, and you shall drink all the gasoline and oil your tummy can hold. Now let me see. What must I do next? I must get you off your jacks; and oh, my gracious there are the grease cups, and that's a nasty job, but it must be done; and what is the use of Saturday if I can't do it? Daddy often did."

Linda began work in utter absorption. She succeeded in getting the car off the jacks. She was lying on her back under it, filling some of the most inaccessible grease cups, and she was softly singing as she worked:

"The shoes I wear are common-sense shoes—"

At that minute Donald Whiting swung down the street, turned in at the Strong residence, and rang the bell. Eileen was coming down the stairs, dressed for the street. She had inquired for Linda, and Katy had told her that she thought Miss Linda had decided to begin using her car, and that she was in the garage working on it. To Eileen's credit it may be said that she had not been told that a caller was expected. Linda never before had had a caller and, as always, Eileen was absorbed in her own concerns. Had she got the rouge a trifle brighter on one cheek than on the other? Was the powder evenly distributed? Would the veil hold the handmade curls in exactly the proper place? When the bell rang her one thought might have been that some of her friends were calling for her. She opened the door, and when she learned that Linda was being asked for, it is possible that she mistook the clean, interesting, and well-dressed youngster standing before her for a mechanic. What she said was: "Linda's working on her car. Go around to the left and you will find her in the garage, and for heaven's sake, get it right before you let her start out, for we've had enough horror in this family from motor accidents."

Then she closed the door before him and stood buttoning her gloves; a wicked and malicious smile spreading over her face.

"Just possibly," she said, "that youngster is from a garage, but if he is, he's the best imitation of the real thing that I have seen in these chaotic days."

Donald Whiting stopped at the garage door and looked in, before Linda had finished her grease cups, and in time to be informed that he might wear common-sense shoes if he chose. At his step, Linda rolled her black head on the cement floor and raised her eyes. She dropped the grease cup, and her face reddened deeply.

"Oh, my Lord!" she gasped breathlessly. "I forgot to tell Katy when to call me!"

In that instant she also forgot that the stress of the previous four years had accustomed men to seeing women do any kind of work in any kind of costume; but soon Linda realized that Donald

Whiting was not paying any particular attention either to her or to her occupation. He was leaning forward, gazing at the car with positively an enraptured expression on his eager young face.

"Shades of Jehu!" he cried. "It's a Bear Cat!"

Linda felt around her head for the grease cup.

"Why, sure it's a Bear Cat," she said with the calmness of complete recovery. "And it's just about ready to start for its very own cave in the canyon."

Donald Whiting pitched his hat upon the seat, shook off his coat, and sent it flying after the hat. Then he began unbuttoning and turning back his sleeves.

"Here, let me do that," he said authoritatively. "Gee! I have never yet ridden in a Bear Cat. Take me with you, will you, Linda?"

"Sure," said Linda, pressing the grease into the cup with a little paddle and holding it up to see if she had it well filled. "Sure, but there's no use in you getting into this mess, because I have only got two more. You look over the engine. Did you ever grind valves, and do you think these need it?"

"Why, they don't need it," said Donald, "if they were all right when it was jacked up."

"Well, they were," said Linda. "It was running like a watch when it went to sleep. But do we dare take it out on these tires?"

"How long has it been?" asked Donald, busy at the engine.

"All of four years," answered Linda.

Donald whistled softly and started a circuit of the car, kicking the tires and feeling them.

"Have you filled them?" he asked.

"No," said Linda. "I did not want to start the engine until I had finished everything else."

"All right," he said, "I'll look at the valves first and then, if it is all ready, there ought to be a garage near that we can run to carefully, and get tuned up."

"There is," said Linda. "There is one only a few blocks down the street where Dad always had anything done that he did not want to do himself."

"That's that, then," said Donald.

Linda crawled from under the car and stood up, wiping her hands on a bit of waste.

"Do you know what tires cost now?" she asked anxiously.

"They have 'em at the garage," answered Donald, "and if I were you, I wouldn't get a set; I would get two. I would-put them on the rear wheels. You might be surprised at how long some of these will last. Anyway, that would be the thing to do."

"Of course," said Linda, in a relieved tone. "That would be the thing to do."

"Now," she said, "I must be excused a few minutes till I clean up so I am fit to go on the streets. I hope you won't think I forgot you were coming."

Donald laughed drily.

"When 'shoes' was the first word I heard," he said, "I did not for a minute think you had forgotten."

"No, I didn't forget," said Linda. "What I did do was to become so excited about cleaning up the car that I let time go faster than I thought it could. That was what made me late."

"Well, forget it!" said Donald. "Run along and jump into something, and let us get our tires and try Kitty out."

Linda reached up and released the brakes. She stepped to one side of the car and laid her hands on it.

"Let us run it down opposite the kitchen door," she said, "then you go around to the front, and I'll let you in, and you can read something a few minutes till I make myself presentable."

"Oh, I'll stay out here and look around the yard and go over the car again," said the boy. "What a bunch of stuff you have got growing here; I don't believe I ever saw half of it before." "It's Daddy's and my collection," said Linda. "Some day I'll show you some of the things, and tell you how we got them, and why they are rare. Today I just naturally can't wait a minute until I try my car."

"Is it really yours?" asked Donald enviously.

"Yes," said Linda. "It's about the only thing on earth that is peculiarly and particularly mine. I haven't a doubt there are improved models, but Daddy had driven this car only about nine months. It was going smooth as velvet, and there's no reason why it should not keep it up, though I suspect that by this time there are later models that could outrun it."

"Oh, I don't know," said the boy. "It looks like some little old car to me. I bet it can just skate."

"I know it can," said Linda, "if I haven't neglected something. We'll start carefully, and we'll have the inspector at the salesrooms look it over."

Then Linda entered the kitchen door to find Katy with everything edible that the house afforded spread before her on the table.

"Why, Katy, what are you doing?" she asked.

"I was makin' ready," explained Katy, "to fix ye the same kind of lunch I would for Miss Eileen. Will ye have it under the live oak, or in the living room?"

"Neither," said Linda. "Come upstairs with me, and in the storeroom you'll find the lunch case and the thermos bottles and don't stint yourself, Katy. This is a rare occasion. It never happened before. Probably it will never happen again. Let's make it high altitude while we are at it."

"I'll do my very best with what I happen to have," said Katy; "but I warn you right now I am making a good big hole in the Sunday dinner."

"I don't give two whoops," said Linda, "if there isn't any Sunday dinner. In memory of hundreds of times that we have eaten bread and milk, make it a banquet, Katy, and we'll eat bread and milk tomorrow."

Then she took the stairway at a bound, and ran to her room. In a very short time she emerged, clad in a clean blouse and breeches' her climbing boots, her black hair freshly brushed and braided.

"I ought to have something," said Linda, "to shade my eyes. The glare's hard on them facing the sun."

Going down the hall she came to the storeroom, opened a drawer' and picked out a fine black felt Alpine hat that had belonged to her father. She carried it back to her room and, standing at the glass, tried it on, pulling it down on one side, turning it up at the other, and striking a deep cleft across the crown. She looked at herself intently for a minute, and then she reached up and deliberately loosened the hair at her temples.

"Not half bad, all things considered, Linda," she said. "But, oh, how you do need a tich of color."

She ran down the hall and opened the door to Eileen's room, and going to her chiffonier, pulled out a drawer containing an array of gloves, veils, and ribbons. At the bottom of the ribbon stack, her eye caught the gleam of color for which she was searching, and she deftly slipped out a narrow scarf of Roman stripes with a deep black fringe at the end. Sitting down, she fitted the hat over her knee, picked up the dressing-table scissors, and ripped off the band. In its place she fitted the ribbon, pinning it securely and knotting the ends so that the fringe reached her shoulder. Then she tried the hat again. The result was blissfully satisfactory. The flash of orange, the blaze of red, the gleam of green, were what she needed.

"Thank you very much, sister mine," she said, "I know you I would be perfectly delighted to loan me this."

CHAPTER IX. One Hundred Per Cent Plus

Then she went downstairs and walked into the kitchen, prepared for what she would see, by what she heard as she approached.

With Katy's apron tied around his waist, Donald Whiting was occupied in squeezing orange, lemon, and pineapple juice over a cake of ice in a big bowl, preparatory to the compounding of Katy's most delicious brand of fruit punch. Without a word, Linda stepped to the bread board and began slicing the bread and building sandwiches, while Katy hurried her preparations for filling the lunch box. A few minutes later Katy packed them in the car, kissed Linda good-bye, and repeatedly cautioned Donald to make her be careful.

As the car rolled down the driveway and into the street, Donald looked appraisingly at the girl beside him.

"Is it the prevailing custom in Lilac Valley for young ladies to kiss the cook?" inquired Donald laughingly.

"Now, you just hush," said Linda. "Katy is NOT the cook, alone. Katy's my father, and my mother, and my family, and my best friend—"

"Stop right there," interposed Donald. "That is quite enough for any human to be. Katy's a multitude. She came out to the car with the canteen, and when I offered to help her, without any 'polly foxin',' she just said: 'Sure. Come in and make yourself useful.' So I went, and I am expecting amazing results from the job she gave me."

"Come to think of it," said Linda, "I have small experience with anybody's cooking except Katy's and my own, but so far as I know, she can't very well be beaten."

Carefully she headed the car into the garage adjoining the salesrooms. There she had an ovation. The manager and several of the men remembered her. The whole force clustered around the Bear Cat and began to examine it, and comment on it, and Linda climbed out and asked to have the carburetor adjusted, while the mechanic put on a pair of tires. When everything was satisfactory, she backed to the street, and after a few blocks of experimental driving, she headed for the Automobile Club to arrange for her license and then turned straight toward Multiflores Canyon, but she did not fail to call Donald Whiting's attention to every beauty of Lilac Valley as they passed through. When they had reached a long level stretch of roadway leading to the canyon, Linda glanced obliquely at the boy beside her.

"It all comes back as natural as breathing," she said. "I couldn't forget it any more than I could forget how to walk, or to swim. Sit tight. I am going to step on the gas for a bit, just for old sake's sake."

"That's all right," said Donald, taking off his hat and giving his head a toss so that the wind might have full play through his hair. "But remember our tires are not safe. Better not go the limit until we get rid of these old ones, and have a new set all around."

Linda settled back in her seat, took a firm grip on the wheel, and started down the broad, smooth highway, gradually increasing the speed. The color rushed to her cheeks. Her eyes were gleaming.

"Listen to it purr!" she cried to Donald. "If you hear it begin to growl, tell me."

And then for a few minutes they rode like birds on the path of the wind. When they approached the entrance to the canyon, gradually Linda slowed down. She turned an exultant flashing face to Donald Whiting.

"That was a whizzer," said the boy. "I'll tell you I don't know what I'd give to have a car like this for my very own. I'll bet not another girl in Los Angeles has a car that can go like that."

"And I don't believe I have any business with it," said Linda; "but since circumstances make it mine, I am going to keep it and I am going to drive it."

"Of course you are," said Donald emphatically. "Don't you ever let anybody fool you out of this car, because if they wanted to, it would be just because they are jealous to think they haven't one that will go as fast."

"There's not the slightest possibility of my giving it up so long as I can make the engine turn over," she said. "I told you how Father always took me around with him, and there's nothing in this world I am so sure of as I am sure that I am spoiled for a house cat. I have probably less feminine sophistication than any girl of my age in the world, and I probably know more about camping and fishing and the scientific why and wherefore of all outdoors than most of them. I just naturally had such a heavenly time with Daddy that it never has hurt my feelings to be left out of any dance or party that ever was given. The one thing that has hurt is the isolation. Since I lost Daddy I haven't anyone but Katy. Sometimes, when I see a couple of nice, interesting girls visiting with their heads together, a great feeling of envy wells up in my soul, and I wish with all my heart that I had such a friend."

"Ever try to make one?" asked Donald. "There are mighty fine girls in the high school."

"I have seen several that I thought I would like to be friends with," said Linda, "but I am so lacking in feminine graces that I haven't known how to make advances, in the first place, and I haven't had the courage, in the second."

"I wish my sister were not so much older than you," said Donald.

"How old is your sister?" inquired Linda.

"She will be twenty-three next birthday," said Donald; "and of all the nice girls you ever saw, she is the queen."

"Yes," she assented, "I am sure I have heard your sister mentioned. But didn't you tell me she had been reared for society?"

"No, I did not," said Donald emphatically. "I told you Mother j believed in dressing her as the majority of other girls were dressed, but I didn't say she had been reared for society. She has been reared with an eye single to making a well-dressed, cultured, and gracious woman."

"I call that fine," said Linda. "Makes me envious of you. Now forget everything except your eyes and tell me what you see. Have you ever been here before?"

"I have been through a few times before, but seems to me I | never saw it looking quite so pretty."

Linda drove carefully, but presently Donald uttered an exclamation as she swerved from the road and started down what appeared to be quite a steep embankment and headed straight for the stream.

"Sit tight," she said tersely. "The Bear Cat just loves its cave. It knows where it is going."

She broke through a group of young willows and ran the car! into a tiny plateau, walled in a circle by the sheer sides of the! canyon reaching upward almost out of sight, topped with great jagged overhanging boulders. Crowded to one side, she stopped the car and sat quietly, smiling at Donald Whiting.

"How about it?" she asked in a low voice.

The boy looked around him, carefully examining the canyon walls, and then at the level, odorous floor where one could not step without crushing tiny flowers of white, cerise, blue, and yellow. Big ferns grew along the walls, here and there "Our Lord's Candles" lifted high torches not yet lighted, the ambitious mountain stream skipped and circled and fell over its rocky bed, while many canyon wrens were singing.

"Do you think," she said, "that anyone driving along here at an ordinary rate of speed would see that car?"

"No," said Donald, getting her idea, "I don't believe they would."

"All right, then," said Linda. "Toe up even and I'll race YoU to the third curve where you see the big white sycamore."

Donald had a fleeting impression of a flash of khaki, a gleam of red, and a wave of black as they started. He ran with all the speed he had ever attained at a track meet. He ran with all his might. He ran until his sides strained and his breath came short; but the creature beside him was not running; she was flying; and long before they neared the sycamore he knew he was beaten, so he laughingly cried to her to stop it. Linda turned to him panting and laughing.

"I make that dash every time I come to the canyon, to keep my muscle up, but this is the first time I have had anyone to race with in a long time."

Then together they slowly walked down the smooth black floor between the canyon walls. As they crossed a small bridge Linda leaned over and looked down.

"Anyone at your house care about 'nose twister'?" she asked lightly.

"Why, isn't that watercress?" asked Donald.

"Sure it is," said Linda. "Anyone at your house like it?"

"Every one of us," answered Donald. "We're all batty about cress salad—and, say, that reminds me of something! If you know so much about this canyon and everything in it, is there any place in it where a fellow could find a plant, a kind of salad lettuce, that the Indians used to use?"

"Might be," said Linda carelessly. "For why?"

"Haven't you heard of the big sensation that is being made in feminine circles by the new department in Everybody's Home?" inquired Donald. "Mother and Mary Louise were discussing it the other day at lunch, and they said that some of the recipes for dishes to be made from stuff the Indians used sounded delicious. One reminded them of cress, and when we saw the cress I wondered if I could get them some of the other."

"Might," said Linda drily, "if you could give me a pretty good idea of what it is that you want."

"When you know cress, it's queer that you wouldn't know other things in your own particular canyon," said Donald.

Linda realized that she had overdone her disinterestedness a trifle.

"I suspect it's miners' lettuce you want," she said. "Of course I know where there's some, but you will want it as fresh as possible if you take any, so we'll finish our day first and gather it the last thing before we leave."

How it started neither of them noticed, but they had not gone far before they were climbing the walls and hanging to precarious footings. Her cheeks flushed, her eyes brilliant, her lips laughing, Linda was showing Donald thrifty specimens of that Cotyledon known as "old hen and chickens," telling him of the rare Echeveria of the same family, and her plunge down the canyon side while trying to uproot it, exulting that she had brought down the plant without a rift in the exquisite bloom on its leaves.

Linda told about her fall, and the two men who had passed at that instant, and how she had met them later, and who they were, and what they were doing. Then Donald climbed high for a bunch of larkspur, and Linda showed him how to turn his back to the canyon wall and come down with the least possible damage to his person and clothing. When at last both of them were tired they went back to the car. Linda spread an old Indian blanket over the least flower-grown spot she could select, brought out the thermos bottles and lunch case, and served their lunch. With a glass of fruit punch in one hand and a lettuce sandwich in the other, Donald smiled at Linda.

"I'll agree about Katy. She knows how," he said appreciatively.

"Katy is more than a cook," said Linda quietly. "She is a human being. She has the biggest, kindest heart. When anybody's sick or in trouble she's the greatest help. She is honest; she has principles; she is intelligent. In her spare time she reads good books and magazines. She knows what is going on in the world. She can talk intelligently on almost any subject. It's no disgrace to be a cook. If it were, Katy would be unspeakable. Fact is, at the present minute there's no one in all the world so dear to me as Katy. I always talk Irish with her."

"Well, I call that rough on your sister," said Donald.

"Maybe it is," conceded Linda. "I suspect a lady wouldn't have i said that, but Eileen and I are so different. She never has made the slightest effort to prove herself lovable to me, and so I have never learned to love her. Which reminds me—how did you happen to come to the garage?"

"The very beautiful young lady who opened the door mistook me for a mechanic. She told me I would find you working on your car and for goodness' sake to see that it was in proper condition before you drove it."

Linda looked at him with wide, surprised eyes in which a trace of indignation was plainly discernible.

"Now listen to me," she said deliberately. "Eileen is a most sophisticated young lady. If she saw you, she never in this world, thought you were a mechanic sent from a garage presenting yourself at our front door."

"There might have been a spark of malice in the big blue-gray I eyes that carefully appraised me," said Donald.

"Your choice of words is good," said Linda, refilling the punch glass. "'Appraise' fits Eileen like her glove. She appraises every thing on a monetary basis, and when she can't figure that it's going to be worth an appreciable number of dollars and cents to her—'to the garage wid it,' as Katy would say."

When they had finished their lunch Linda began packing the box and Donald sat watching her.

"At this point," said Linda, "Daddy always smoked. Do you smoke?"

There was a hint of deeper color in the boy's cheeks.

"I did smoke an occasional cigarette," he said lightly, "up to the day, not a thousand years ago, when a very emphatic young lady who should have known, insinuated that it was bad for the nerves, and going on the presumption that she knew, I haven't smoked a cigarette since and I'm not going to until I find out whether I can do better work without them."

Linda folded napkins and packed away accessories thoughtfully. Then she looked into the boy's eyes.

"Now we reach the point of our being here together," she said. "It's time to fight, and I am sorry we didn't go at it gas and bomb the minute we met. You're so different from what I thought you were. If anyone had told me a week ago that you would take off your coat and mess with my automobile engine, or wear Katy's apron and squeeze lemons in our kitchen I would have looked him over for Daddy's high sign of hysteria, at least. It's too bad to I have such a good time as I have had this afternoon, and then end with a fight."

"That's nothing," said Donald. "You couldn't have had as good a time as I have had. You're like another boy. A fellow can be just a fellow with you, and somehow you make everything you touch mean something it never meant before. You have made me feel that I would be about twice the man I am if I had spent the time I have wasted in plain jazzing around, hunting Cotyledon or trap-door spiders' nests."

"I get you," said Linda. "It's the difference between a girl reared in an atmosphere of georgette and rouge, and one who has grown up in the canyons with the oaks and sycamores. One is natural and the other is artificial. Most boys prefer the artificial."

"I thought I did myself," said Donald, "but today has taught me that I don't. I think, Linda, that you would make the finest friend a fellow ever had. I firmly and finally decline to fight with you; but for God's sake, Linda, tell me how I can beat that little cocoanut-headed Jap."

Linda slammed down the lid to the lunch box. Her voice was smooth and even but there was battle in her eyes and she answered decisively: "Well, you can't beat him calling him names. There is only one way on God's footstool that you can beat him. You can't beat him legislating against him. You can't beat him boycotting him. You can't beat him with any tricks. He is as sly as a cat and he has got a whole bag full of tricks of his own, and he has proved right here in Los Angeles that he has got a brain that is hard to beat. All you can do, and be a man commendable to your own soul, is to take his subject and put your brain in to such purpose that you cut pigeon wings around him. What are you studying in your classes, anyway?"

"Trigonometry, Rhetoric, Ancient History, Astronomy," answered Donald.

"And is your course the same as his?" inquired Linda.

"Strangely enough it is," answered Donald. "We have been in the same classes all through high school. I think the little monkey—"

"Man, you mean," interposed Linda.

"'Man,'" conceded Donald. "Has waited until I selected my course all the way through, and then he has announced what he would take. He probably figured that I had somebody with brains back of the course I selected, and that whatever I studied would be suitable for him."

"I haven't a doubt of it," said Linda. "They are quick; oh! they are quick; and they know from their cradles what it is that they have in the backs of their heads. We are not going to beat them driving them to Mexico or to Canada, or letting them monopolize China. That is merely temporizing. That is giving them fertile soil on which to take the best of their own and the level best of ours, and by amalgamating the two, build higher than we ever have. There is just one way in all this world that we can beat Eastern civilization and all that it intends to do to us eventually. The white man has dominated by his color so far in the history of the world, but it is written in the Books that when the men of color acquire our culture and combine it with their own methods of living and rate of production, they are going to bring forth greater numbers, better equipped for the battle of life, than we are. When they have got our last secret, constructive or scientific, they will take it, and living in a way that we would not, reproducing in numbers we don't, they will beat us at any game we start, if we don't take warning while we are in the ascendancy, and keep there."

"Well, there is something to think about," said Donald Whiting, staring past Linda at the side of the canyon as if he had seen the same handwriting on the wall that dismayed Belshazzar at the feast that preceded his downfall.

"I see what you're getting at," he said. "I had thought that there might be some way to circumvent him."

"There is!" broke in Linda hastily. "There is. You can beat him, but you have got to beat him in an honorable way and in a way that is open to him as it is to you."

"I'll do anything in the world if you will only tell me how," said Donald. "Maybe you think it isn't grinding me and humiliating me properly. Maybe you think Father and Mother haven't warned me. Maybe you think Mary Louise isn't secretly ashamed of me. How can I beat him, Linda?"

Linda's eyes were narrowed to a mere line. She was staring at the wall back of Donald as if she hoped that Heaven would intercede in her favor and write thereon a line that she might translate to the boy's benefit.

"I have been watching pretty sharply," she said. "Take them as a race, as a unit—of course there are exceptions, there always are—but the great body of them are mechanical. They are imitative. They are not developing anything great of their own in their own country. They are spreading all over the world and carrying home sewing machines and threshing machines and automobiles and cantilever bridges and submarines and aeroplanes—anything from eggbeaters to telescopes. They are not creating one single thing. They are not missing imitating everything that the white man can do anywhere else on earth. They are just like the Germans so far as that is concerned."

"I get that, all right enough," said Donald. "Now go on. What is your deduction? How the devil am I to beat the best? He is perfect, right straight along in everything."

The red in Linda's cheeks deepened. Her eyes opened their widest. She leaned forward, and with her closed fist, pounded the blanket before him.

"Then, by gracious," she said sternly, "you have got to do something new. You have got to be perfect, PLUS."

"'Perfect, plus?'" gasped Donald.

"Yes, sir!" said Linda emphatically. "You have got to be perfect, plus. If he can take his little mechanical brain and work a thing out till he has got it absolutely right, you have got to go further than that and discover something pertaining to it not hitherto thought of and start something NEW. I tell you you must use your brains. You should be more than an imitator. You must be a creator!"

Donald started up and drew a deep breath.

"Well, some job I call that," he said. "Who do you think I am, the Almighty?"

"No," said Linda quietly, "you are not. You are merely His son, created in His own image, like Him, according to the Book, and you have got to your advantage the benefit of all that has been learned down the ages. We have got to take up each subject in your course, and to find some different books treating this same subject. We have got to get at it from a new angle. We must dig into higher authorities. We have got to coach you till, when you reach the highest note possible for the parrot, you can go ahead and embellish it with a few mocking-bird flourishes. All Oka Sayye knows how to do is to learn the lesson in his book perfectly, and he is 100 per cent. I have told you what you must do to add the plus, and you can do it if you are the boy I take you for. People have talked about the 'yellow peril' till it's got to be a meaningless phrase. Somebody must wake up to the realization that it's the deadliest peril that ever has menaced white civilization. Why shouldn't you have your hand in such wonderful work?"

"Linda," said the boy breathlessly, "do you realize that you have been saying 'we'? Can you help me? Will you help me?"

"No," said Linda, "I didn't realize that I had said 'we.' I didn't mean two people, just you and me. I meant all the white boys and girls of the high school and the city and the state and the whole world. If we are going to combat the 'yellow peril' we must combine against it. We have got to curb our appetites and train our brains and enlarge our hearts till we are something bigger and finer and numerically greater than this yellow peril. We can't take it and pick it up and push it into the sea. We are not Germans and we are not Turks. I never wanted anything in all this world worse than I want to see you graduate ahead of Oka Sayye. And then I want to see the white boys and girls of Canada and of England and of Norway and Sweden and Australia, and of the whole world doing exactly what I am recommending that you do in your class and what I am doing personally in my own. I have had Japs in my classes ever since I have been in school, but Father always told me to study them, to play the game fairly, but to BEAT them in some way, in some fair way, to beat them at the game they are undertaking."

"Well, there is one thing you don't take into consideration," said Donald. "All of us did not happen to be fathered by Alexander Strong. Maybe we haven't all got your brains."

"Oh, posher!" said Linda. "I know of a case where a little Indian was picked up from a tribal battlefield in South America and brought to this country and put into our schools, and there was

33

nothing that any white pupil in the school could do that he couldn't, so long as it was imitative work. You have got to be constructive. You have got to work out some way to get ahead of them; and if you will take the history of the white races and go over their great achievements in mechanics, science, art, literature—anything you choose—when a white man is constructive, when he does create, he can simply cut circles around the colored races. The thing is to get the boys and girls of today to understand what is going on in the world, what they must do as their share in making the world safe for their grandchildren. Life is a struggle. It always has been. It always will be. There is no better study than to go into the canyons or the deserts and efface yourself and watch life. It's an all-day process of the stronger annihilating the weaker. The one inexorable thing in the world is Nature. The eagle dominates the hawk; the hawk, the falcon; the falcon, the raven; and so on down to the place where the hummingbird drives the moth from his particular trumpet flower. The big snake swallows the little one. The big bear appropriates the desirable cave."

"And is that what you are recommending people to do?"

"No," said Linda, "it is not. That is wild. We go a step ahead of the wild, or we ourselves become wild. We have brains, and with our brains we must do in a scientific way what Nature does with tooth and claw. In other words, and to be concrete, put these things in the car while I fold the blanket. We'll gather our miners' lettuce and then we'll go home and search Daddy's library and see if there is anything bearing in a higher way on any subject you are taking, so that you can get from it some new ideas, some different angle, some higher light, something that will end in speedily prefacing Oka Sayye's perfect with your pluperfect!"

CHAPTER X. Katy to the Rescue

Linda delivered Donald Whiting at his door with an armload of books and a bundle of miners' lettuce and then drove to her home in Lilac Valley—in the eye of the beholder on the floor-level macadam road; in her own eye she scarcely grazed it. The smooth, easy motion of the car, the softly purring engine were thrilling. The speed at which she was going was like having wings on her body. The mental stimulus she had experienced in concentrating her brain on Donald Whiting's problem had stimulated her imagination. The radiant color of spring; the chilled, perfumed, golden air; the sure sense of having found a friend, had ruffled the plumes of her spirit. On the home road Donald had plainly indicated that he would enjoy spending the morrow with her, and she had advised him to take the books she had provided and lock himself in his room and sweat out some information about Monday's lessons which would at least arrest his professor's attention, and lead his mind to the fact that something was beginning to happen. And then she had laughingly added: "Tomorrow is Katy's turn. I told the old dear I would take her as soon as I felt the car was safe. Every day she does many things that she hopes will give me pleasure. This is one thing I can do that I know will delight her."

"Next Saturday, then?" questioned Donald. And Linda nodded.

"Sure thing. I'll be thinking up some place extra interesting. Come in the morning if you want, and we'll take a lunch and go for the day. Which do you like best, mountains or canyons or desert or sea?"

"I like it best wherever what you're interested in takes you," said Donald simply.

"All right, then," answered Linda, "we'll combine business and pleasure."

So they parted with another meeting arranged.

When she reached home she found Katy tearfully rejoicing, plainly revealing how intensely anxious she had been. But when Linda told her that the old tires had held, that the car ran wonderfully, that everything was perfectly safe, that she drove as unconsciously as she breathed, and that tomorrow Katy was to go for a long ride, her joy was incoherent.

Linda laughed. She patted Katy and started down the hallway, when she called back: "What is this package?"

"A delivery boy left it special only a few minutes ago. Must be something Miss Eileen bought and thought she would want tomorrow, and then afterward she got this invitation and went on as she was."

Linda stood gazing at the box. It did look so suspiciously like a dress box.

"Katy," she said, "I have just about got an irresistible impulse to peep. I was telling Eileen last night of a dress I saw that I thought perfect. It suited me better than any other dress I ever did see. It was at 'The Mode.' This box is from 'The Mode.' Could there be a possibility that she sent it up specially for me?"

"I think she would put your name on it if she meant it for ye," said Katy.

"One peep would show me whether it is my dress or not," said Linda, "and peep I'm going to." She began untying the string.

"There's one thing," said Katy, "Miss Eileen's sizes would never fit ye."

"Might," conceded Linda. "I am taller than she is, but I could wear her waists if I wanted to, and she always alters her skirts herself to save the fees. Glory be! This is my dress, and there's a petticoat and stockings to match it. Why, the nice old thing! I suggested hard enough, but in my heart I hardly thought she would do it. Oh, dear, now if I only had some shoes, and a hat."

Linda was standing holding the jacket in one hand, the stockings in the other, her face flaming. Katy drew herself to full height. She reached over and picked the things from Linda's fingers.

"If ye know that is your dress, lambie," she said authoritatively, "ye go right out and get into that car and run to town and buy ye a pair of shoes."

"But I have no credit anywhere and I have no money, yet," said Linda.

"Well, I have," said Katy, "and this time ye're going to stop your stubbornness and take enough to get ye what you need. Ye go to the best store in Los Angeles and come back here with a pair of shoes that just match those stockings, and ye go fast, before the stores close. If ye've got to speed a little, do it in the country and do it judacious."

"Katy, you're arriving!" cried Linda. "'Judicious speeding' is one thing I learned better than any other lesson about driving a motor car. Three fourths of the driving Father and I did we were speeding judiciously."

Katy held the skirt to Linda's waist.

"Well, maybe it's a little shorter than any you have been wearing, but it ain't as short as Eileen and all the rest of the girls your age have them, so that's all right, honey. Slip on your coat."

Katy's fingers were shaking as she lifted the jacket and Linda slipped into it.

"Oh, Lord," she groaned, "ye can't be wearing that! The sleeves don't come much below your elbows."

"You will please to observe," said Linda, "that they are flowing sleeves and they are not intended to come below the elbows; but it's a piece of luck I tried it on, for it reminds me that it's a jacket suit and I must have a blouse. When you get the shoe money, make it enough for a blouse—two blouses, Katy, one for school and one to fuss up in a little."

Without stopping to change her clothing, Linda ran to the garage and hurried back to the city. It was less than an hour's run, but she made it in ample time to park her car and buy the shoes. She selected a pair of low oxfords of beautiful color, matching the stockings. Then she hurried to one of the big drygoods stores and bought the two waists and an inexpensive straw hat that would harmonize with the suit; a hat small enough to stick, in the wind, with brim enough to shade her eyes. In about two hours she was back with Katy and they were in her room trying on the new clothing.

"It dumbfounds me," said Linda, "to have Eileen do this for me."

She had put on the shoes and stockings, a plain georgette blouse of a soft, brownish wood-gray, with a bit of heavy brown silk embroidery decorating the front, and the jacket. The dress was of silky changeable tricolette, the skirt plain. Where a fold lifted and was strongly lighted, it was an exquisite silver-gray; where a shadow fell deeply it was green-brown. The coat reached half way to the knees. It had a rippling skirt with a row of brown embroidery around it, a deep belt with double buttoning at the waistline, and collar and sleeves in a more elaborate pattern of the same embroidery as the skirt. Linda perched the hat on her head, pulled it down securely, and faced Katy.

"Now then!" she challenged.

"And it's a perfect dress!" said Katy proudly, "and you're just the colleen to wear it. My, but I wisht your father could be seeing ye the now."

With almost reverent hands Linda removed the clothing and laid it away. Then she read a letter from Marian that was waiting for her, telling Katy scraps of it in running comment as she scanned the sheets.

"She likes her boarding place. There are nice people in it. She has got a wonderful view from the windows of her room. She is making friends. She thinks one of the men at Nicholson and Snow's is just fine; he is helping her all he can, on the course she is taking. And she wants us to look carefully everywhere for any scrap of paper along the hedge or around the shrubbery on the north side of the house. One of her three sheets of plans is missing. I don't see where in the world it could have gone, Katy."

Katy spread out her hands in despair.

"There was not a scrap of a sheet of paper in the room when I cleaned it," she said, "not a scrap. And if I had seen a sheet flying around the yard I would have picked it up. She just must be mistaken about having lost it here. She must have opened her case on the train and lost it there."

Linda shook her head.

"I put that stuff in the case myself," she said, "and the clothes on top of it, and she wouldn't have any reason for taking those things out on the train. I can't understand, but she did have three rough sketches. She had her heart set on winning that prize and it would be a great help to her, and certainly it was the most comprehensive and convenient plan for a house of that class that I ever have seen. If I ever have a house, she is going to plan it, even if she doesn't get to plan John Gilman's as he always used to say that she should. And by the way, Katy, isn't it kind of funny for Eileen to go away over Sunday when it's his only holiday?"

"Oh, she'll telephone him," said Katy, "and very like, he'll go down, or maybe he is with her. Ye needn't waste any sympathy on him. Eileen will take care that she has him so long as she thinks she wants him."

Later it developed that Eileen had secured the invitation because she was able to produce three most eligible men. Not only was John Gilman with the party, but Peter Morrison and Henry Anderson were there as well. It was in the nature of a hastily arranged celebration, because the deal for three acres of land that Peter Morrison most coveted on the small plateau, mountain walled, in Lilac Valley, was in escrow. He had made a payment on it. Anderson was working on his plans. Contractors had been engaged, and on Monday work would begin. The house was to be built as soon as possible, and Peter Morrison had arranged that the garage was to be built first. This he meant to occupy as a residence so that he could be on hand to superintend the construction of the new home and to protect, as far as possible, the natural beauty and the natural growth of the location.

Early Sunday morning Linda and Katy, with a full lunch box and a full gasoline tank, slid from the driveway and rolled down the main street of Lilac Valley toward the desert.

"We'll switch over and strike San Fernando Road," said Linda, "and I'll scout around Sunland a bit and see if I can find anything that will furnish material for another new dish."

That day was wonderful for Katy. She trotted after Linda over sandy desert reaches, along the seashore, up mountain trails, and through canyons connected by long stretches of motoring that was more like flying than riding. She was tired but happy when she went to bed. Monday morning she was an interested spectator as Linda dressed for school.

"Sure, and hasn't the old chrysalis opened up and let out the nicest little lady-bird moth, Katy?" inquired Linda as she smoothed her gray-gold skirts. "I think myself that this dress is a trifle too good for school. When I get my allowance next week I think I'll buy me a cloth skirt and a couple of wash waists and save this for better; but it really was good of Eileen to take so much pains and send it to me, when she was busy planning a trip."

Katy watched Linda go, and she noted the new light in her eyes, the new lift of her head, and the proud sureness of her step, and she wondered if a new dress could do all that for a girl, she scarcely believed that it could. And, too, she had very serious doubts about the dress. She kept thinking of it during the day, and when Eileen came, in the middle of the afternoon, at the first words on her lips: "Has my dress come?" Katy felt a wave of illness surge through her. She looked at Eileen so helplessly that that astute reader of human nature immediately Suspected something.

"I sent it special," she said, "because I didn't know at the time that I was going to Riverside and I wanted to work on it. Isn't it here yet?"

Then Katy prepared to do battle for the child of her heart.

"Was the dress ye ordered sent the one Miss Linda was telling ye about?" she asked tersely.

"Yes, it was," said Eileen. "Linda has got mighty good taste. Any dress she admired was sure to be right. She said there was a beautiful dress at 'The Mode'. I went and looked, and sure enough there was, a perfect beauty."

"But she wanted the dress for herself," said Katy.

"It was not a suitable dress for school," said Eileen.

"Well, it strikes me," said Katy, "that it was just the spittin' image of fifty dresses I've seen ye wear to school."

"What do you know about it?" demanded Eileen.

"I know just this," said Katy with determination. "Ye've had one new dress in the last few days and you're not needin' another. The blessed Virgin only knows when Miss Linda's had a dress. She thought ye'd done yourself proud and sent it for her, and she put it on, and a becoming and a proper thing it was too! I advanced her the money myself and sent her to get some shoes to match it since she had her car fixed and could go in a hurry. A beautiful dress it is, and on her back this minute it is!"

Eileen was speechless with anger. Her face was a sickly white and the rouge spots on her cheeks stood a glaring admission.

"Do you mean to tell me—" she gasped.

"Not again," said the daughter of Erin firmly, "because I have already told ye wance. Linda's gone like a rag bag since the Lord knows when. She had a right to the dress, and she thought it was hers, and she took it. And if ye ever want any more respect or obedience or love from the kiddie, ye better never let her know that ye didn't intend it for her, for nothing was ever quite so fair and right as that she should have it; and while you're about it you'd better go straight to the store and get her what she is needin' to go with it, or better still, ye had better give her a fair share of the money of which there used to be such a plenty, and let her get her things herself, for she's that tasty nobody can beat her when she's got anything to do with."

Eileen turned on Katy in a gust of fury.

"Katherine O'Donovan," she said shrilly, "pack your trunk and see how quick you can get out of this house. I have stood your insolence for years, and I won't endure it a minute longer!"

Katy folded her red arms and lifted her red chin, and a steel-blue light flashed from her steel-gray eyes.

"Humph!" she said, "I'll do nothing of the sort. I ain't working for ye and I never have been no more than I ever worked for your mother. Every lick I ever done in this house I done for Linda and Doctor Strong and for nobody else. Half of this house and everything in it belongs to Linda, and it's a mortal short time till she's of age to claim it. Whichever is her half, that half I'll be staying in, and if ye manage so as she's got nothing to pay me, I'll take care of her without pay till the day comes when she can take care of me. Go to wid ye, ye triflin', lazy, self-possessed creature. Ten years I have itched to tell ye what I thought of ye, and now ye know it."

As Katy's rage increased, Eileen became intimidated. Like every extremely selfish person she was a coward in her soul.

"If you refuse to go on my orders," she said, "I'll have John Gilman issue his."

Then Katy set her left hand on her left hip, her lower jaw shot past the upper, her doubled right fist shook precious near the tip of Eileen's exquisite little nose.

"I'm darin' ye," she shouted. "I'm just darin' ye to send John Gilman in the sound of my voice. If ye do, I'll tell him every mean and selfish thing ye've done to me poor lambie since the day of the Black Shadow. Send him to me? Holy Mither, I wish ye would! If ever I get my chance at him, don't ye think I won't be tellin' him what he has lost, and what he has got? And as for taking orders from him, I am taking my orders from the person I am working for, and as I told ye before, that's Miss Linda. Be off wid ye, and primp up while I get my supper, and mind ye this, if ye tell Miss Linda ye didn't mean that gown for her and spoil the happy day she has had, I won't wait for ye to send John Gilman to me; I'll march straight to him. Put that in your cigarette and smoke it! Think I've lost me nose as well as me sense?"

Then Katy started a triumphal march to the kitchen and cooled down by the well-known process of slamming pots and pans for half an hour. Soon her Irish sense of humor came to her rescue.

"Now, don't I hear myself telling Miss Linda a few days ago to kape her temper, and to kape cool, and to go aisy. Look at the aise of me when I got started. By gracious, wasn't I just itching to wallop her?"

Then every art that Katy possessed was bent to the consummation of preparing a particularly delicious dinner for the night.

Linda came in softly humming something to herself about the kind of shoes that you might wear if you chose. She had entered the high school that morning with an unusually brilliant color. Two or three girls, who never had noticed her before, had nodded to her that morning, and one or two had said: "What a pretty dress you have!" She had caught the flash of approval in the eyes of Donald Whiting, and she had noted the flourish with which he raised his hat when he saw her at a distance, and she knew what he meant when he held up a book, past the covers of which she could see protruding a thick fold of white paper. He had foresworn whatever pleasure he might have thought of for Sunday. He had prepared notes on some subject that he thought would further him. The lift of his head, the flourish of his hat, and the book all told Linda that he had struggled and that he felt the struggle had brought an exhilarating degree of success. That had made the day particularly bright for Linda. She had gone home with a feeling of uplift and exultation in her heart. As she closed the front door she cried up the stairway: "Eileen, are you there?"

"Yes," answered a rather sulky voice from above.

Linda ascended, two steps at a bound.

"Thank you over and over, old thing!" she cried as she raced down the hallway. "Behold me! I never did have a more becoming dress, and Katy loaned me money, till my income begins, to get shoes and a little scuff hat to go with it. Aren't I spiffy?"

She pirouetted in the doorway. Eileen gripped the brush she was wielding, tight.

"You have good taste," she said. "It's a pretty dress, but You're always howling about things being suitable. Do you call that suitable for school?"

"It certainly is an innovation for me," said Linda, "but there are dozens of dresses of the same material, only different cut and colors in the high school today. As soon as I get my money I'll buy a skirt and some blouses so I won't have to wear this all the time; but I surely do thank you very much, and I surely have had a lovely day. Did you have a nice time at Riverside?"

Eileen slammed down the brush and turned almost a distorted face to Linda. She had temper to vent. In the hour's reflection previous to Linda's coming, she realized that she had reached the limit with Katy. If she antagonized her by word or look, she would go to John Gilman, and Eileen dared not risk what she would say.

"No, I did not have a lovely time," she said. "I furnished the men for the party and I expected to have a grand time, but the first thing we did was to run into that inflated egotist calling herself Mary Louise Whiting, and like a fool, Janie Brunson introduced her to Peter Morrison. I had paired him with Janie on purpose to keep my eye on him."

Linda tried hard but she could not suppress a chuckle: "Of course you would!" she murmured softly.

Eileen turned her back. That had been her first confidence to Linda. She was so aggrieved at that moment that she could have told unanswering walls her tribulations. It would have been better if she had done so. She might have been able to construe silence as sympathy. Linda's laughter she knew exactly how to interpret. "Served you right," was what it meant.

"I hadn't the least notion you would take an interest in anything concerning me," she said. "People can talk all they please about Mary Louise Whiting being a perfect lady but she is a perfect beast. I have met her repeatedly and she has always ignored me, and yesterday she singled out for her special attention the most desirable man in my party—"

"'Most desirable,'" breathed Linda. "Poor John! I see his second fiasco. Lavender crystals, please!"

Eileen caught her lip in mortification. She had not intended to say what she thought.

"Well, you can't claim," she hurried on to cover her confusion, "that it was not an ill-bred, common trick for her to take possession of a man of my party, and utterly ignore me. She has everything on earth that I want; she treats me like a dog, and she could give me a glorious time by merely nodding her head."

"I am quite sure you are mistaken," said Linda. "From what I've heard of her, she wouldn't mistreat anyone. Very probably what she does is merely to feel that she is not acquainted with you. You have an unfortunate way, Eileen, of defeating your own ends. If you wanted to attract Mary Louise Whiting, you missed the best chance you ever could have had, at three o'clock Saturday afternoon, when you maliciously treated her only brother as you would a mechanic, ordered him to our garage, and shut our door in his face."

Eileen turned to Linda. Her mouth fell open. A ghastly greenish white flooded her face.

"What do you mean?" she gasped.

"I mean," said Linda, "that Donald Whiting was calling on me, and you purposely sent him to the garage."

Crash down among the vanities of Eileen's dressing table went her lovely head, and she broke into deep and violent sobs. Linda stood looking at her a second, slowly shaking her head. Then she turned and went to her room.

Later in the evening she remembered the Roman scarf and told Eileen of what she had done, and she was unprepared for Eileen's reply: "That scarf always was too brilliant for me. You're welcome to it if you want it."

"Thank you," said Linda gravely, "I want it very much indeed."

CHAPTER XI. Assisting Providence

Linda went to the library to see to what state of emptiness it had been reduced by the removal of several pieces of furniture she had ordered taken away that day. As she stood on the threshold looking over the room as usual, a throb of loving appreciation of Katy swept through her heart. Katy had been there before her. The room had been freshly swept and dusted, the rugs had been relaid, the furniture rearranged skilfully, and the table stood at the best angle to be lighted either by day or night. On the table and the mantel stood big bowls of lovely fresh flowers. Linda was quite certain that anyone entering the room for the first time would have felt it completely furnished, and she doubted if even Marian would notice the missing pieces. Cheered in her heart, she ran up to the billiard room, and there again Katy had preceded her. The windows were shining. The walls and floor had been cleaned. Everything was in readiness for the new furniture. Her heart full of gratitude, Linda went to her room, prepared her lessons for the next day, and then drew out her writing materials to answer Marian's letter. She wrote:

I have an acute attack of enlargement of the heart. So many things have happened since your leaving. But first I must tell you about your sketch. We just know you did not leave it here. Katy says there was not a scrap in our bedroom when she cleaned it; and as she knows you make plans and how precious they are to you, I guarantee she would have saved it if she had found anything looking like a parallelogram on a piece of paper. And I have very nearly combed the lawn, not only the north side, but the west, south, and east; and then I broke the laws and went over to your house and crawled through a basement window and worked my way up, and I have hunted every room in it, but there is nothing there. You must have lost that sketch after you reached San Francisco. I hope to all that's peaceful you did not lay it down in the offices of Nicholson and Snow, or where you take your lessons. I know nothing about architecture, but I do know something about comfort in a home, and I thought that was the most comfortable and convenient-looking house I ever had seen.

Now I'll go on and tell you all the news, and I don't know which is the bigger piece to burst on you first. Would you be more interested in knowing that Peter Morrison has bought three acres on the other side of the valley from us and up quite a way, or in the astonishing fact that I have a new dress, a perfect love of a dress, really too good for school? You know there was blood in my eye when you left, and I didn't wait long to start action. I have managed to put the fear of God into Eileen's heart so that she has agreed to a reasonable allowance for me from the first of next month; but she must have felt at least one small wave of contrition when I told her about a peculiarly enticing dress I had seen at The Mode. She sent it up right away, and Katy, blessed be her loving footprints, loaned me money to buy a blouse and some shoes to match, so I went to school today looking very like the Great General Average, minus rouge, lipstick, hairdress, and French heels.

I do hope you will approve of two things I have done.

Then Linda recounted the emptying of the billiard room, the inroads in the library, the listing of the technical books, and what she proposed to do with the money. And then, her face slightly pale and her fingers slightly trembling, she wrote:

And, Marian dear, I hope you won't be angry with me when I tell you that I have put the Bear Cat into commission and driven it three times already. It is running like the feline it is, and I am being as careful as I can. I know exactly how you will feel. It is the same feeling that has held me all these months, when I wouldn't even let myself think of it. But something happened at school one day, Marian. You know the Whitings? Mary Louise Whiting's brother is in the senior class. He is a six-footer, and while he is not handsome he is going to be a real man when he is fully developed, and steadied down to work. One day last week he made it his business to stop me in the hall and twit me about my shoes, and incidentally to ask me why I didn't dress like the other girls; and some way it came rougher than if it had been one of the girls. The more I thought about it the more wronged I felt, so I ended in a young revolution that is to bring me an income, a suitable place to work in and has brought me such a pretty dress. I think it has brought Eileen to a sense of at least partial justice about money, and it brought me back the Bear Cat. You know the proudest moment of my life was when Father would let me drive the little beast, and it all came back as natural as breathing. Please don't worry, Marian. Nothing shall happen, I promise you.

It won't be necessary to tell you that Katy is her darling old self, loyal and steadfast as the sun, and quite as necessary and as comforting to me. And I have a couple of other interests in life that are going to—I won't say make up for your absence, because nothing could do that— but they are going to give me something interesting to think about, something agreeable to work at, while you are gone. But, oh, Marian, do hurry. Work all day and part of the night. Be Saturday's child yourself if you must, just so you get home quick, and where your white head makes a beacon light for the truest, lovingest pal you will ever have,

LINDA.

Linda laid down the pen, slid down in her chair, and looked from the window across the valley, and she wondered if in her view lay the location that had been purchased by Peter Morrison. She glanced back at her letter and sat looking at the closing lines and the signature.

"Much good that will do her," she commented. "When a woman loves a man and loves him with all her heart, as Marian loved John, and when she loses him, not because she has done a single unworthy thing herself, but because he is so rubber spined that he will let another woman successfully intrigue him, a lot of comfort she is going to get from the love of a schoolgirl!"

Linda's eyes strayed to the window again, and traveled down to the city and up the coast, all the way to San Francisco, and out of the thousands of homes there they pictured a small, neat room, full of Marian's belongings, and Marian herself bending over a worktable, absorbed in the final draft of her precious plans. Linda could see Marian as plainly as she ever had seen her, but she let her imagination run, and she fancied that when Marian was among strangers and where no one knew of John Gilman's defection, that hers might be a very heavy heart, that hers might be a very sad face. Then she went to planning. She had been desolate, heart hungry, and isolated herself. First she had endured, then she had fought; the dawn of a new life was breaking over her hill. She had found work she was eager to do. She could put the best of her brain, the skill of her fingers, the creative impulse of her heart, into it.

She was almost sure that she had found a friend. She had a feeling that when the coming Saturday had been lived Donald Whiting would be her friend. He would want her advice and her help in his work. She would want his companionship and the stimulus of his mind, in hers. What Linda had craved was a dear friend among the girls, but no girl had offered her friendship. This boy had, so she would accept what the gods of time and circumstance provided. It was a very wonderful thing that had happened to her. Now why could not something equally wonderful happen to Marian? Linda wrinkled her brows and thought deeply.

"It's the worst thing in all this world to work and work with nobody to know about it and nobody to care," thought Linda. "Marian could break a record if she thought John Gilman cared now as he used to. It's almost a necessary element to her success. If he doesn't care, she ought to be made to feel that somebody cares. This thing of standing alone, since I have found a friend, appeals to me as almost insupportable. Let me think."

It was not long until she had worked out a scheme for putting an interest in Marian's life and giving her something for which to work, until a more vital reality supplanted it. The result was that she took some paper, went down to the library, and opening the typewriter, wrote a letter. She read it over, making many changes and corrections, and then she copied it carefully. When she came to addressing it she was uncertain, but at last she hit upon a scheme of sending it in the care of Nicholson and Snow because Marian had told her that she meant to enter their contest immediately she reached San Francisco, and she would have left them her address. On the last reading of the letter she had written, she decided that it was a manly, straightforward production, which should interest and attract any girl. But how was she to sign it? After thinking deeply for a long time, she wrote "Philip Sanders, General Delivery," and below she added a postscript:

To save you the trouble of inquiring among your friends as to who Philip Sanders is, I might as well tell you in the beginning that he isn't. He is merely an assumption under which I shall hide my personality until you let me know whether it is possible that you could become even slightly interested in me, as a small return for the very deep and wholesome interest abiding in my heart for you.

"Abiding," said Linda aloud. "It seems to me that there is nothing in all the world quite so fine as a word. Isn't 'abiding' a good word? Doesn't it mean a lot? Where could you find one other word that means being with you and also means comforting you and loving you and sympathizing with you and surrounding you with firm walls and a cushioned floor and a starry roof? I love that word. I hope it impresses Marian with all its wonderful meaning."

She went back to her room, put both letters into her Geometry, and in the morning mailed them. She stood a long time hesitating with the typewritten letter in her hand, but finally dropped it in the letter box also.

"It will just be something," she said, "to make her think that some man appreciates her lovely face and doesn't care if her hair is white, and sees how steadfast and fine she is."

And then she slowly repeated, "'steadfast,' that is another fine word. It has pearls and rubies all over it."

After school that evening she visited James Brothers' and was paid the full amount of the appraisement of her furniture. Then she went to an art store and laid in a full supply of the materials she needed for the work she was trying to do. Her fingers were trembling as she handled the boxes of water colors and selected the brushes and pencils for her work, and sheets of drawing paper upon which she could do herself justice. When the transaction was finished, she had a few dollars remaining. As she put them in her pocket she said softly:

"That's gasoline. Poor Katy! I'm glad she doesn't need her money, because she is going to have to wait for the allowance or the sale of the books or on Jane Meredith. But it's only a few days now, so that'll be all right."

CHAPTER XII. The Lay of the Land

Linda entered the street car for her daily ride to Lilac Valley. She noticed Peter Morrison and Henry Anderson sitting beside each other, deeply engrossed in a drawing. She had been accustomed to ride in the open section of the car as she liked the fresh air. She had a fleeting thought of entering the body of the car and sitting where they would see her; and then a perverse spirit in Linda's heart said to her:

"That is precisely what Eileen would do. You sit where you belong."

Whereupon Linda dropped into the first vacant seat she could reach, but it was only a few moments before Peter Morrison, looking up from the plans he was studying, saw her, and lifting his hat, beckoned her to come and sit with him. They made room for her between them and spreading the paper across her lap, all three of them began to discuss the plans for the foundation for Peter's house. Anderson had roughly outlined the grounds, sketching in the trees that were to be saved, the spring, and the most available route for reaching the road. The discussion was as to where the road should logically enter the grounds, and where the garage should stand.

"Which reminds me," said Linda—"haven't you your car with you? Or was that a hired one you were touring in?"

"Mine," said Peter Morrison, "but we toured so far, it's in the shop for a general overhauling today."

"That being the case," said Linda, "walk home with me and I'll take you to your place in mine and bring you back to the cars, if you only want to stay an hour or two."

"Why, that would be fine," said Peter. "You didn't mention, the other evening, that you had a car."

"No," said Linda, "I had been trying to keep cars out of my thought for a long time, but I could endure it no longer the other day, so I got mine out and tuned it up. If you don't mind stacking up a bit, three can ride in it very comfortably."

That was the way it happened that Linda walked home after school that afternoon between Peter Morrison and his architect, brought out the Bear Cat, and drove them to Peter's location.

All that day, workmen had been busy under the management of a well-instructed foreman, removing trees and bushes and stones and clearing the spot that had been selected for the garage and approximately for the house.

The soft brownish gray of Linda's dress was exactly the color to intensify the darker brown of her eyes. There was a fluctuating red in her olive cheeks, a brilliant red framing her even white teeth. Once dressed so that she was satisfied with the results, Linda immediately forgot her clothes, and plunged into Morrison's plans.

"Peter," she said gravely, with Peter perfectly cognizant of the twinkle in her dark eyes, "Peter, you may save money in a straight-line road, but you're going to sin against your soul if you build it. You'll have to economize in some other way, and run your road around the base of those boulders, then come in straight to the line here, and then you should swing again and run out on this point, where guests can have one bewildering glimpse of the length of our blue valley, and then whip them around this clump of perfumy lilac and elders, run them to your side entrance, and then scoot the car back to the garage. I think you should place the front of your house about here." Linda indicated where. "So long as you're buying a place like this you don't want to miss one single thing; and you do want to make the very most possible out of every beauty you have. And you mustn't fail to open up and widen the runway from that energetic, enthusiastic spring. Carry it across your road, sure. It will cost you another little something for a safe bridge, but there's nothing so artistic as a bridge with a cold stream running under it. And think what a joyful time I'll have, gathering specimens for you of every pretty water plant that grows in my particular canyon. Any time when you're busy in your library and you hear my car puffing up the incline and around the corner and rattling across the bridge, you'll know that I am down here giving you a start of watercress and miners' lettuce and every lovely thing you could mention that likes to be nibbled or loved-up, while it dabbles its toes in the water."

Peter Morrison looked at Linda reflectively. He looked for such a long moment that Henry Anderson reached a nebulous conclusion. "Fine!" he cried. "Every one of those suggestions is valuable to an inexperienced man. Morrison, shan't I make a note of them?"

"Yes, Henry, you shall," said Peter. "I am going to push this thing as fast as possible, so far as building the garage is concerned and getting settled in it. After that I don't care if I live on this spot until we know each other by the inch, before I begin building my home. At the present minute it appeals to me that 'home' is about the best word in the language of any nation. I have a feeling that what I build here is going to be my home, very possibly the only one I shall ever have. We must find the spot on which the Lord intended that a house should grow on this hillside, and then we must build that house so that it has a room suitable for a workshop in which I may strive, under the best conditions possible, to get my share of the joy of life and to earn the money that I shall require to support me and entertain my friends; and that sounds about as selfish as anything possibly could. It seems to be mostly 'me' and 'mine,' and it's not the real truth concerning this house. I don't believe there is a healthy, normal man living who has not his dream. I have no hesitation whatever in admitting that I have mine. This house must be two things. It has got to be a concrete workshop for me, and it has got to be an abstract abiding place for a dream. It's rather difficult to build a dream house for a dream lady, so I don't know what kind of a fist I am going to make of it."

Linda sat down on a boulder and contemplated her shoes for a minute. Then she raised her ever-shifting, eager, young eyes to Peter, and it seemed to him as he looked into them that there were little gold lights flickering at the bottom of their darkness.

"Why, that's just as easy," she said. "A home is merely a home. It includes a front porch and a back porch and a fireplace and a bathtub and an ice chest and a view and a garden around it; all the rest is incidental. If you have more money, you have more incidentals. If you don't have so much, you use your imagination and think you have just as much on less."

"Now, I wonder," said Peter, "when I find my dream lady, if she will have an elastic imagination."

"Haven't you found her yet?" asked Linda casually.

"No," said Peter, "I haven't found her, and unfortunately she hasn't found me. I have had a strenuous time getting my start in life. It's mostly a rush from one point of interest to another, dropping at any wayside station for refreshment and the use of a writing table. Occasionally I have seen a vision that I have wanted to follow, but I never have had time. So far, the lady of this house is even more of a dream than the house."

"Oh, well, don't worry," said Linda comfortingly. "The world is full of the nicest girls. When you get ready for a gracious lady I'll find you one that will have an India-rubber imagination and a great big loving heart and Indian-hemp apron strings so that half a dozen babies can swing from them."

Morrison turned to Henry Anderson.

"You hear, Henry?" he said. "I'm destined to have a large family. You must curtail your plans for the workroom and make that big room back of it into a nursery."

"Well, what I am going to do," said Henry Anderson, "is to build a place suitable for your needs. If any dream woman comes to it, she will have to fit herself to her environment."

Linda frowned.

"Now, that isn't a bit nice of you," she said, "and I don't believe Peter will pay the slightest attention to you. He'll let me make you build a lovely room for the love of his heart, and a great big bright nursery on the sunny side for his small people."

"I never believed," said Henry Anderson, "in counting your chickens before they are hatched. There are a couple of acres around Peter's house, and he can build an addition as his needs increase."

"Messy idea," said Linda promptly. "Thing to do, when you build a house, is to build it the way you want it for the remainder of your life, so you don't have to tear up the scenery every few years, dragging in lumber for expansion. And I'll tell you another thing. If the homemakers of this country don't get the idea into their heads pretty soon that they are not going to be able to hold their own with the rest of the world, with no children, or one child in the family, there's a sad day of reckoning coming. With the records at the patent office open to the world, you can't claim that the brain of the white man is not constructive. You can look at our records and compare them with those of countries ages and ages older than we are, which never discovered the beauties of a Dover egg-beater or a washing machine or a churn or a railroad or a steamboat or a bridge. We are head and shoulders above other nations in invention, and just as fast as possible, we are falling behind in the birth rate. The red man and the yellow man and the brown man and the black man can look at our egg-beaters and washing machines and bridges and big guns, and go home and copy them; and use them while rearing even bigger families than they have now. If every home in Lilac Valley had at least six sturdy boys and girls growing up in it with the proper love of country and the proper realization of the white man's right to supremacy, and if all the world now occupied by white men could make an equal record, where would be the talk of the yellow peril? There wouldn't be any yellow peril. You see what I mean?"

Linda lifted her frank eyes to Peter Morrison.

"Yes, young woman," said Peter gravely, "I see what you mean, but this is the first time I ever heard a high-school kid propound such ideas. Where did you get them?"

"Got them in Multiflores Canyon from my father to start with," said Linda, "but recently I have been thinking, because there is a boy in high school who is making a great fight for a better scholarship record than a Jap in his class. I brood over it every spare minute, day or night, and when I say my prayers I implore high Heaven to send him an idea or to send me one that I can pass on to him, that will help him to beat that Jap."

"I see," said Peter Morrison. "We'll have to take time to talk this over. It's barely possible I might be able to suggest something."

"You let that kid fight his own battles," said Henry Anderson roughly. "He's no proper bug-catcher. I feel it in my bones."

For the first time, Linda's joy laugh rang over Peter Morrison's possession.

"I don't know about that," she said gaily. "He's a wide-awake specimen; he has led his class for four years when the Jap didn't get ahead of him. But, all foolishness aside, take my word for it, Peter, you'll be sorry if you don't build this house big enough for your dream lady and for all the little dreams that may spring from her heart."

"Nightmares, you mean," said Henry Anderson. "I can't imagine a bunch of kids muddying up this spring and breaking the bushes and using slingshots on the birds."

"Yes," said Linda with scathing sarcasm, "and wouldn't our government be tickled to death to have a clear spring and a perfect bush and a singing bird, if it needed six men to go over the top to handle a regiment of Japanese!"

Then Peter Morrison laughed.

"Well, your estimate is too low, Linda," he said in his nicest drawling tone of voice. "Believe me, one U. S. kid will never march in a whole regiment of Japanese. They won't lay down their guns and walk to surrender as bunches of Germans did. Nobody need ever think that. They are as good fighters as they are imitators. There's nothing for you to do, Henry, but to take to heart what Miss Linda has said. Plan the house with a suite for a dream lady, and a dining room, a sleeping porch and a nursery big enough for the six children allotted to me."

"You're not really in earnest?" asked Henry Anderson in doubting astonishment.

"I am in the deepest kind of earnest," said Peter Morrison. "What Miss Linda says is true. As a nation, our people are pampering themselves and living for their own pleasures. They won't take the trouble or endure the pain required to bear and to rear children; and the day is rolling toward us, with every turn of the planet one day closer, when we are going to be outnumbered by a combination of peoples who can take our own tricks and beat us with them. We must pass along the good word that the one thing America needs above every other thing on earth is HOMES AND HEARTS BIG ENOUGH FOR CHILDREN, as were the homes of our grandfathers, when no joy in life equaled the joy of a new child in the family, and if you didn't have a dozen you weren't doing your manifest duty."

"Well, if that is the way you see the light, we must enlarge this house. As designed, it included every feminine convenience anyway. But when I build my house I am going to build it for myself."

"Then don't talk any more about being my bug-catcher," said Linda promptly, "because when I build my house it's going to be a nest that will hold six at the very least. My heart is perfectly set on a brood of six."

Linda was quite unaware that the two men were studying her closely, but if she had known what was going on in their minds she would have had nothing to regret, because both of them found her very attractive, and both of them were wondering how anything so superficial as Eileen could be of the same blood as Linda.

"Are we keeping you too late?" inquired Peter.

"No," said Linda, "I am as interested as I can be. Finish everything you want to do before we go. I hope you're going to let me come over often and watch you with your building. Maybe I can get an idea for some things I want to do. Eileen and I have our house divided by a Mason and Dixon line. On her side is Mother's suite, the dining room, the living room and the front door. On mine there's the garage and the kitchen and Katy's bedroom and mine and the library and the billiard room. At the present minute I am interested in adapting the library to my requirements instead of Father's, and I am emptying the billiard room and furnishing it to make a workroom. I have a small talent with a brush and pencil, and I need some bare walls to tack my prints on to dry, and I need numerous places for all the things I am always dragging in from the desert and the canyons; and since I have the Bear Cat running, what I have been doing in that line with a knapsack won't be worthy of mention."

"How did it come," inquired Henry Anderson, "that you had that car jacked up so long?"

"Why, hasn't anybody told you," asked Linda, "about our day of the Black Shadow?"

"John Gilman wrote me when it happened," said Peter softly, "but I don't believe it has been mentioned before Henry. You tell him."

Linda turned to Henry Anderson, and with trembling lips and paling cheeks, in a few brief sentences she gave him the details. Then she said to Peter Morrison in a low voice: "And that is the why of Marian Thorne's white head. Anybody tell you that?"

"That white head puzzled me beyond anything I ever saw," he said. "I meant to ask John about it. He used to talk to me and write to me often about her, and lately he hasn't; when I came I saw the reason, and so you see I felt reticent on the subject."

"Well, there's nothing the matter with my tongue," said Linda. "It's loose at both ends. Marian was an expert driver. She drove with the same calm judgment and precision and graceful skill that she does everything else, but the curve was steep and something in the brakes was defective. It broke with a snap and there was not a thing she could do. Enough was left of the remains of the car to prove that. Ten days afterward her head was almost as white as snow. Before that it was as dark as mine. But her body is just as young and her heart is just as young and her face is even more beautiful. I do think that a white crown makes her lovelier than she was before. I have known Marian ever since I can remember, and I don't know one thing about her that I could not look you straight in the eye and tell you all about. There is not a subterfuge or an evasion or a small mean deceit in her soul. She is the brainiest woman and the biggest woman I know."

"I haven't a doubt of it," said Peter Morrison. "And while you are talking about nice women, we met a mighty fine one at Riverside on Sunday. Her name is Mary Louise Whiting. Do you know her?"

"Not personally," said Linda. "I don't recall that I ever saw her. I know her brother, Donald. He is the high-school boy who is having the wrestle with the Jap."

"I liked her too," said Henry Anderson. "And by the way, Miss Linda, haven't bug-catchers any reputation at all as nest builders? Is it true that among feathered creatures the hen builds the home?"

"No, it's not," said Linda promptly. "Male birds make a splendid record carrying nest material. What is true is that in the majority of cases the female does the building."

43

"Well, what I am getting at," said Henry Anderson, "is this. Is there anything I can do to help you with that billiard room that you're going to convert to a workroom? What do you lack in it that you would like to have? Do you need more light or air, or a fireplace, or what? When you take us to the station, suppose you drive us past your house and give me a look at that room and let me think over it a day or two. I might be able to make some suggestion that would help you."

"Now that is positively sweet of you," said Linda. "I never thought of such a thing as either comfort or convenience. I thought I had to take that room as it stands and do the best I could with it, but since you mention it, it's barely possible that more air might be agreeable and also more light, and if there could be a small fireplace built in front of the chimney where it goes up from the library fireplace, it certainly would be a comfort, and it would add something to the room that nothing else could.

"No workroom really has a soul if you can't smell smoke and see red when you go to it at night."

"You little outdoor heathen," laughed Peter Morrison. "One would think you were an Indian."

"I am a fairly good Indian," said Linda. "I have been scouting around with my father a good many years. How about it, Peter? Does the road go crooked?"

"Yes," said Peter, "the road goes crooked."

"Does the bed of the spring curve and sweep across the lawn and drop off to the original stream below the tree-tobacco clump there?"

"If you say so, it does," said Peter.

"Including the bridge?" inquired Linda.

"Including the bridge," said Peter. "I'll have to burn some midnight oil, but I can visualize the bridge."

"And is this house where you 'set up your rest,' as you so beautifully said the other night at dinner, going to lay its corner stone and grow to its roof a selfish house, or is it going to be generous enough for a gracious lady and a flight of little footsteps?"

Peter Morrison took off his hat. He turned his face toward the length of Lilac Valley and stood, very tall and straight, looking far away before him. Presently he looked down at Linda.

"Even so," he said softly. "My shoulders are broad enough; I have a brain; and I am not afraid to work. If my heart is not quite big enough yet, I see very clearly how it can be made to expand."

"I have been told," said Linda in a low voice, "that Mary Louise Whiting is a perfect darling."

Peter looked at her from the top of her black head to the tips of her brown shoes. He could have counted the freckles bridging her nose. The sunburn on her cheeks was very visible; there was something arresting in the depth of her eyes, the curve of her lips, the lithe slenderness of her young body; she gave the effect of something smoldering inside that would leap at a breath.

"I was not thinking of Miss Whiting," he said soberly.

Henry Anderson was watching. Now he turned his back and commenced talking about plans, but in his heart he said: "So that's the lay of the land. You've got to hustle yourself, Henry, or you won't have the ghost of a show."

Later, when they motored down the valley and stopped at the Strong residence, Peter refused to be monopolized by Eileen. He climbed the two flights of stairs with Henry Anderson and Linda and exhausted his fund of suggestions as to what could be done to that empty billiard room to make an attractive study of it. Linda listened quietly to all their suggestions, and then she said:

"It would be fine to have another window, and a small skylight would be a dream, and as for the fireplace you mention, I can't even conceive how great it would be to have that; but my purse is much more limited than Peter's, and while I have my school work to do every day, my earning capacity is nearly negligible. I can only pick up a bit here and there with my brush and pencil—place cards and Easter cards and valentines, and once or twice magazine covers, and little things like that. I don't see my way clear to lumber and glass and bricks and chimney pieces."

Peter looked at Henry, and Henry looked at Peter, and a male high sign, ancient as day, passed between them.

"Easiest thing in the world," said Peter. "It's as sure as shooting that when my three or four fireplaces, which Henry's present plans call for, are built, there is going to be all the material left that can be used in a light tiny fireplace such as could be built on a third floor, and when the figuring for the house is done it could very easily include the cutting of a skylight and an extra window or two here, and getting the material in with my stuff, it would cost you almost nothing."

Linda's eyes opened wide and dewy with surprise and pleasure.

"Why, you two perfectly nice men!" she said. "I haven't felt as I do this minute since I lost Daddy. It's wonderful to be taken care of. It's better than cream puffs with almond flavoring."

Henry Anderson looked at Linda keenly.

"You're the darndest kid!" he said. "One minute you're smacking your lips over cream puffs, and the next you're going to the bottom of the yellow peril. I never before saw your combination in one girl. What's the explanation?" For the second time that evening Linda's specialty in rapture floated free.

"Bunch all the component parts into the one paramount fact that I am Saturday's child," she said, "so I am constantly on the job of working for a living, and then add to that the fact that I was reared by a nerve specialist."

Then they went downstairs, and the men refused both Eileen's and Linda's invitation to remain for dinner. When they had gone Eileen turned to Linda with a discontented and aggrieved face.

"In the name of all that's holy, what are you doing or planning to do?" she demanded.

"Not anything that will cost you a penny beyond my natural rights," said Linda quietly.

"That is not answering my question," said Eileen. "You're not of age and you're still under the authority of a guardian. If you can't answer me, possibly you can him. Shall I send John Gilman to ask what I want to know of you?"

"When did I ever ask you any questions about what you chose to do?" asked Linda. "I am merely following the example that you have previously set me. John Gilman and I used to be great friends. It might help both of us to have a family reunion. Send him by all means."

"You used to take pride," suggested Eileen, "in leading your class."

"And has anyone told you that I am not leading my class at the present minute?" asked Linda.

"No," said Eileen, "but what I want to point out to you is that the minute you start running with the boys you will quit leading your class."

"Don't you believe it," said Linda quietly. "I'm not built that way. I shan't concentrate on any boy to the exclusion of chemistry and geometry, never fear it."

Then she thoughtfully ascended the stairs and went to work.

Eileen went to her room and sat down to think; and the more she thought, the deeper grew her anger and chagrin; and to the indifference that always had existed in her heart concerning Linda was added in that moment a new element. She was jealous of her. How did it come that a lanky, gangling kid in her tees had been paid a visit by the son of possibly the most cultured and influential family of the city, people of prestige, comfortable wealth, and unlimited popularity? For four years she had struggled to gain an entrance in some way into Louise Whiting's intimate circle of friends, and she had ended by shutting the door on the only son of the family. And why had she ever allowed Linda to keep the runabout? It was not proper that a young girl should own a high powered car like that. It was not proper that she should drive it and go racing around the country, heaven knew where, and with heaven knew whom. Eileen bit her lip until it almost bled. Her eyes were hateful and her hands were nervous as she reviewed the past week. She might think any mean thing that a mean brain could conjure up, but when she calmed down to facts she had to admit that there was not a reason in the world why Linda should not drive the car she had driven for her father, or why she should not take with her Donald Whiting or Peter Morrison or Henry Anderson. The thing that rankled was that the car belonged to Linda. The touring car which she might have owned and driven, had she so desired, lay in an extremely slender string of pearls around her neck at that instant. She reflected that if she had kept her car and made herself sufficiently hardy to drive it, she might have been the one to have taken Peter Morrison to his home location and to have had many opportunities for being with him.

"I've been a fool," said Eileen, tugging at the pearls viciously. "They are nothing but a little bit of a string that looks as if I were trying to do something and couldn't, at best. What I've got to do is to think more of myself. I've got to plan some way to prevent Linda from being too popular until I really get my mind made up as to what I want to do."

CHAPTER XIII. Leavening the Bread of Life

"'A house that is divided against itself cannot stand,'" quoted Linda. "I must keep in mind what Eileen said, not that there is the slightest danger, but to fall behind in my grades is a thing that simply must not happen. If it be true that Peter and Henry can so easily and so cheaply add a few improvements in my workroom in connection with Peter's building, I can see no reason why they shouldn't do it, so long as I pay for it. I haven't a doubt but that there will be something I can do for Peter, before he finishes his building, that he would greatly appreciate, while, since I'm handy with my pencil, I MIGHT be able to make a few head and tail pieces for some of his articles that would make them more attractive. I don't want to use any friend of mine: I don't want to feel that I am not giving quite as much as I get, but I think I see my way clear, between me and the Bear Cat, to pay for all the favors I would receive in altering my study.

"First thing I do I must go through Father's books and get the money for them, so I'll know my limitation when I come to select furniture. And I don't know that I am going to be so terribly modest when it comes to naming the sum with which I'll be satisfied for my allowance. Possibly I shall exercise my age-old prerogative and change my mind; I may just say 'half' right out loud and stick to it. And there's another thing. Since the editor of Everybody's Home has started my department and promised that if it goes well he will give it to me permanently, I can certainly depend on something from that. He has used my Introduction and two instalments now. I should think it might be fair to talk payments pretty soon. He should give me fifty dollars for a recipe with its perfectly good natural history and embellished with my own vegetable and floral decorations.

"In the meantime I think I might buy my worktable and possibly an easel, so I can have real room to spread out my new material and see how it would feel to do one drawing completely unhampered. I'll order the table tonight, and then I'll begin on the books, because I must have Saturday free; and I must be thinking about the most attractive and interesting place I can take Donald to. I just have to keep him interested until he gets going of his own accord, because he shall beat Oka Sayye. I wouldn't let Donald say it but I don't mind saying myself to myself with no one present except myself that in all my life I have never seen anything so masklike as the stolid little square head on that Jap. I have never seen anything I dislike more than the oily, stiff, black hair standing up on it like menacing bristles. I have never had but one straight look deep into his eyes, but in that look I saw the only thing that ever frightened me in looking into a man's eyes in my whole life. And there is one thing that I have to remember to caution Donald about. He must carry on this contest in a perfectly open, fair, and aboveboard way, and he simply must not antagonize Oka Sayye. There are so many of the Japs. They all look so much alike, and there's a blood brotherhood between them that will make them protect each other to the death against any white man. It wouldn't be safe for Donald to make Oka Sayye hate him. He had far better try to make him his friend and put a spirit of honest rivalry into his heart; but come to think of it, there wasn't anything like that in my one look into Oka Sayye's eyes. I don't know what it was, but whatever it was it was something repulsive."

With this thought in her mind Linda walked slowly as she approached the high school the next time. Far down the street, over the walks and across the grounds, her eyes were searching eagerly for the tall slender figure of Donald Whiting. She did not see him in the morning, but at noon she encountered him in the hall.

"Looking for you," he cried gaily when he saw her. "I've got my pry in on Trig. The professor's interested. Dad fished out an old Trig that he used when he was a boy and I have some new angles that will keep my esteemed rival stirring up his gray matter for some little time."

"Good for you! Joyous congratulations! You've got the idea!" cried Linda. "Go to it! Start something all along the line, but make it something founded on brains and reason and common sense. But, Donald, I was watching for you. I wanted to say a word."

Donald Whiting bent toward her. The faintest suspicion of a tinge of color crept into his cheeks.

"That's fine," he said. "What was it you wanted?"

"Only this," she said in almost a breathless whisper. "There is nothing in California I am afraid of except a Jap, and I am afraid of them, not potentially, not on account of what all of us know they are planning in the backs of their heads for the future, but right here and now, personally and physically. Don't antagonize Oka Sayye. Don't be too precipitate about what you're trying to do. Try to make it appear that you're developing ideas for the interest and edification of the whole class. Don't incur his personal enmity. Use tact."

"You think I am afraid of that little jiu-jitsu?" he scoffed. "I can lick him with one hand."

"I haven't a doubt of it," said Linda, measuring his height and apparent strength and fitness. "I haven't a doubt of it. But let me ask you this confidentially: Have you got a friend who would slip in and stab him in the back in case you were in an encounter and he was getting the better of you?"

Donald Whiting's eyes widened. He looked at Linda amazed.

"Wouldn't that be going rather far?" he asked. "I think I have some fairly good friends among the fellows, but I don't know just whom I would want to ask to do me that small favor."

"That is precisely the point," cried Linda. "You haven't a friend you would ask; and you haven't a friend who would do it, if you did. But don't believe for one second that Oka Sayye hasn't half a dozen who would make away with you at an unexpected time and in a secluded place, and vanish, if it would in any way further Oka Sayye's ambition, or help establish the supremacy of the Japanese in California."

"Um-hm," said Donald Whiting.

He was looking far past Linda and now his eyes were narrowed in thought. "I believe you're RIGHT about it."

"I've thought of you so often since I tried to spur you to beat Oka Sayye," said Linda. "I feel a sort of responsibility for you. It's to the honor and glory of all California, and the United States, and the white race everywhere for you to beat him, but if any harm should come to you I would always feel that I shouldn't have urged it."

"Now that's foolishness," said Donald earnestly. "If I am such a dub that I didn't have the ambition to think up some way to beat a Jap myself, no matter what happens you shouldn't regret having been the one to point out to me my manifest duty. Dad is a Harvard man, you know, and that is where he's going to send me, and in talking about it the other night I told him about you, and

46

what you had said to me. He's the greatest old scout, and was mightily interested. He went at once and opened a box of books in the garret and dug out some stuff that will be a big help to me. He's going to keep posted and see what he can do; he said even worse things to me than you did; so you needn't feel that you have any responsibility; besides that, it's not proved yet that I can beat Oka Sayye."

"Yes, it is!" said Linda, sending a straight level gaze deep into his eyes. "Yes, it is! Whenever a white man makes up his mind what he's going to do, and puts his brain to work, he beats any man, of any other color. Sure you're going to beat him."

"Fat chance I have not to," said Donald, laughing ruefully. "If I don't beat him I am disgraced at home, and with you; before I try very long in this highly specialized effort I am making, every professor in the high school and every member of my class is bound to become aware of what is going on. You're mighty right about it. I have got to beat him or disgrace myself right at the beginning of my nice young career."

"Of course you'll beat him," said Linda.

"At what hour did you say I should come, Saturday?"

"Oh, come with the lark for all I care," said Linda. "Early morning in the desert is a mystery and a miracle, and the larks have been there just long enough to get their voices properly tuned for their purest notes."

Then she turned and hurried away. Her first leisure minute after reaching home she went to the library wearing one of Katy's big aprons, and carrying a brush and duster. Beginning at one end of each shelf, she took down the volumes she intended to sell, carefully dusted them, wiped their covers, and the place on which they had stood, and then opened and leafed through them so that no scrap of paper containing any notes or memoranda of possible value should be overlooked. It was while handling these volumes that Linda shifted several of the books written by her father, to separate them from those with which she meant to part. She had grown so accustomed to opening each book she handled and looking through it, that she mechanically opened the first one she picked up and from among its leaves there fell a scrap of loose paper. She picked it up and found it was a letter from the publishers of the book. Linda's eyes widened suddenly as she read:

MY DEAR STRONG:

Sending you a line of congratulations. You have gone to the head of the list of "best sellers" among medical works, and the cheque I draw you for the past six months' royalties will be considerably larger than that which goes to your most esteemed contemporary on your chosen subject.

Very truly yours,

The signature was that of Frederic Dickman, the editor of one of the biggest publishing houses of the country.

"Hm," she said to herself softly. "Now that is a queer thing. That letter was written nearly five years ago. I don't know why I never thought of royalties since Daddy went. I frequently heard him mention them before. I suppose they're being paid to John Gilman as administrator, or to the Consolidated Bank, and cared for with Father's other business. There's no reason why these books should not keep on selling. There are probably the same number of young men, if not a greater number, studying medicine every year. I wonder now, about these royalties. I must do some thinking."

Then Linda began to examine books more carefully than before. The letter she carried with her when she went to her room; but she made a point of being on the lawn that evening when John Gilman came, and after talking to him a few minutes, she said very casually: "John, as Father's administrator, does a royalty from his medical books come to you?"

"No," said Gilman. "It is paid to his bank."

"I don't suppose," said Linda casually, "it would amount to enough to keep one in shoes these inflated days."

"Oh, I don't know about that," said John testily. "I have seen a few of those cheques in your Father's time. You should be able to keep fairly well supplied with shoes."

"So I should," said Linda drily. "So I should."

Then she led him to the back of the house and talked the incident out of his mind as cleverly as possible by giving him an intensive botanical study of Cotyledon. But she could not interest him quite so deeply as she had hoped, for presently he said: "Eileen tells me that you're parting with some of the books."

"Only technical ones for which I could have no possible use," said Linda. "I need clothes, and have found that had I a proper place to work in and proper tools to work with, I could earn quite a bit with my brush and pencil, and so I am trying to get enough money together to fit up the billiard room for a workroom, since nobody uses it for anything else."

"I see," said John Gilman. "I suppose running a house is extremely expensive these days, but even so the income from your estate should be sufficient to dress a schoolgirl and provide for anything you would want in the way of furnishing a workroom."

"That's what I have always thought myself," said Linda; "but Eileen doesn't agree with me, and she handles the money. When the first of the month comes, we are planning to go over things together, and she is going to make me a proper allowance."

"That is exactly as it should be," said Gilman. "I never realized till the other night at dinner that you have grown such a great girl, Linda. That's fine! Fix your workroom the way you would like to have it, and if there's anything I can do to help you in any way, you have only to command me. I haven't seen you often lately."

"No," said Linda, "but I don't feel that it is exactly my fault. Marian and I were always pals. When I saw that you preferred Eileen, I kept with Marian to comfort her all I could. I don't suppose she cared, particularly. She couldn't have, or she would at least have made some effort to prevent Eileen from monopolizing you. She probably was mighty glad to be rid of you; but since you had been together so much, I thought she might miss you, so I tried to cover your defection."

John Gilman's face flushed. He stood very still, while he seemed deeply thoughtful.

"Of course you were free to follow your inclinations, or Eileen's machinations, whichever you did follow," Linda said lightly, "but 'them as knows' could tell you, John, as Katy so well puts it, that you have made the mistake of your young life."

Then she turned and went to the garage, leaving John to his visit with Eileen.

The Eileen who took possession of John was an Eileen with whom he was not acquainted. He had known, the night of the dinner party, that Eileen was pouting, but there had been no chance to learn from her what her grievance was, and by the next time they met she was a bundle of flashing allurement, so he ignored the occurrence. This evening, for the first time, it seemed to him that Eileen was not so beautiful a woman as he had thought her. Something had roiled the blood in her delicate veins until it had muddied the clear freshness of her smooth satiny skin. There was discontent in her eyes, which were her most convincing attraction. They were big eyes, wide open and candid. She had so trained them through a lifetime of practice that she could meet other eyes directly while manipulating her most dextrous evasion. Whenever Eileen was most deceptively subtle, she was looking straight at her victim with the innocent appeal of a baby in her gaze.

John Gilman had had his struggle. He had succeeded. He had watched, and waited, and worked incessantly, and when his opportunity came he was ready. Success had come to such a degree that in a short time he had assured himself of comfort for any woman he loved. He knew that his appearance was quite as pleasing as that of his friend. He knew that in manner and education they were equals. He was now handling large business affairs. He had made friends in high places. Whenever Eileen was ready, he would build and furnish a home he felt sure would be equal, if not superior, to what Morrison was planning. Why had Eileen felt that she would envy any woman who shared life with Peter Morrison?

All that day she had annoyed him, because there must have been in the very deeps of his soul "a still, small voice" whispering to him that he had not lived up to the best traditions of a gentleman in his course with Marian. While no definite plans had been made, there had been endless assumption. Many times they had talked of the home they would make together. When he reached the point where he decided that he never had loved Marian as a man should love the woman he marries, he felt justified in turning to Eileen, but in his heart he knew that if he had been the man he was pleased to consider himself, he would have gone to Marian Thorne and explained, thereby keeping her friendship, while he now knew that he must have earned her contempt.

The day at Riverside had been an enigma he could not solve. Eileen was gay to a degree that was almost boisterous. She had attracted attention and comment which no well-bred woman would have done.

The growing discontent in John's soul had increased under Linda's direct attack. He had known Linda since she was four years old and had been responsible for some of her education. He had been a large influence in teaching Linda from childhood to be a good sport, to be sure she was right and then go ahead, and if she hurt herself in the going, to rub the bruise, but to keep her path.

A thing patent to the eye of every man who turned an appraising look upon Linda always had been one of steadfast loyalty. You could depend upon her. She was the counterpart of her father; and Doctor Strong had been loved by other men. Wherever he had gone he had been surrounded. His figure had been one that attracted attention. When he had spoken, his voice and what he had to say had commanded respect. And then there had emanated from him that peculiar physical charm which gives such pleasing and distinguished personality to a very few people in this world. This gift too had descended to Linda. She could sit and look straight at you with her narrow, interested eyes, smile faintly, and make you realize what she thought and felt without opening her lips. John did not feel very well acquainted with the girl who had dominated the recent dinner party, but he did see that she was attractive, that both Peter Morrison and Henry Anderson had been greatly amused and very much entertained by her. He had found her so interesting himself that he had paid slight attention to Eileen's pouting.

Tonight he was forced to study Eileen, for the sake of his own comfort to try to conciliate her. He was uncomfortable because he was unable to conduct himself as Eileen wished him to, without a small sickening disgust creeping into his soul. Before the evening was over he became exasperated, and ended by asking flatly: "Eileen, what in the dickens is the matter with you?"

It was a new tone and a new question on nerves tensely strung.

"If you weren't blind you'd know without asking," retorted Eileen hotly.

"Then I am 'blind,' for I haven't the slightest notion. What have I done?"

"Isn't it just barely possible," asked Eileen, "that there might be other people who would annoy and exasperate me? I have not hinted that you have done anything, although I don't know that it's customary for a man calling on his betrothed to stop first for a visit with her sister."

"For the love of Mike!" said John Gilman. "Am I to be found fault with for crossing the lawn a minute to see how Linda's wild garden is coming on? I have dug and helped set enough of those plants to justify some interest in them as they grow."

"And the garden was your sole subject of conversation?" inquired Eileen, implied doubt conveyed nicely.

"No, it was not," answered Gilman, all the bulldog in his nature coming to the surface.

"As I knew perfectly," said Eileen. "I admit that I'm not feeling myself. Things began going wrong recently, and everything has gone wrong since. I think it all began with Marian Thorne's crazy idea of selling her home and going to the city to try to ape a man."

"Marian never tried to ape a man in her life," said John, instantly yielding to a sense of justice. "She is as strictly feminine as any woman I ever knew."

"Do you mean to say that you think studying architecture is a woman's work?" sneered Eileen.

"Yes, I do," said Gilman emphatically. "Women live in houses. They're in them nine tenths of the time to a man's one tenth. Next to rocking a cradle I don't know of any occupation in this world more distinctly feminine than the planning of comfortable homes for homekeeping people."

Eileen changed the subject swiftly. "What was Linda saying to you?" she asked.

"She was showing me a plant, a rare Echeveria of the Cotyledon family, that she tobogganed down one side of Multiflores Canyon and delivered safely on the roadway without its losing an appreciable amount of 'bloom' from its exquisitely painted leaves."

Eileen broke in rudely. "Linda has missed Marian. There's not a possible thing to make life uncomfortable for me that she is not doing. You needn't tell me you didn't see and understand her rude forwardness the other night!"

"No, I didn't see it," said John, "because the fact is I thought the kid was positively charming, and so did Peter and Henry because both of them said so. There's one thing you must take into consideration, Eileen. The time has come when she should have clothes and liberty and opportunity to shape her life according to her inclinations. Let me tell you she will attract attention in georgette and laces."

"And where are the georgette and laces to come from?" inquired Eileen sarcastically. "All outgo and no income for four years is leaving the Strong finances in mighty precarious shape, I can tell you."

"All right," said Gilman, "I'm financially comfortable now. I'm ready. Say the word. We'll select our location and build our home, and let Linda have what there is of the Strong income till she is settled in life. You have pretty well had all of it for the past four years."

"Yes," said Eileen furiously, "I have 'pretty well' had it, in a few little dresses that I have altered myself and very frequently made entirely. I have done the best I could, shifting and skimping, and it's not accomplished anything that I have really wanted. According to men, the gas and the telephone and the electric light and the taxes and food and cook pay for themselves. All a woman ever spends money on is clothes!"

"Eileen," chuckled John Gilman, "this sounds exactly as if we were married, and we're not, yet."

"No," said Eileen, "thank heaven we're not. If it's come to the place where you're siding with everybody else against me, and where you're more interested in what my kid sister has to say to you than you are in me, I don't think we ever shall be."

Then, from stress of nerve tension and long practice, some big tears gushed up and threatened to overflow Eileen's lovely eyes. That never should happen, for tears are salt water and they cut little rivers through even the most carefully and skillfully constructed complexion, while Eileen's was looking its worst that evening. She hastily applied her handkerchief, and John Gilman took her into his arms; so the remainder of the evening it was as if they were not married. But when John returned to the subject of a home and begged Eileen to announce their engagement and let him begin work, she evaded him, and put him off, and had to have time to think, and she was not ready, and there were many excuses, for none of which Gilman could see any sufficient reason. When he left Eileen that night, it was with a heavy heart.

CHAPTER XIV. Saturday's Child

Throughout the week Linda had worked as never during her life previously, in order to save Saturday for Donald Whiting. She ran the Bear Cat down to the garage and had it looked over once more to be sure that everything was all right. Friday evening, on her way from school, she stopped at a grocery where she knew Eileen kept an account, and for the first time ordered a few groceries. These she carried home with her, and explained to Katy what she wanted.

Katy fully realized that Linda was still her child, with no thought in her mind save standing at the head of her classes, carrying on the work she had begun with her father, keeping up her nature study, and getting the best time she could out of life in the open as she had been taught to do from her cradle.

Katy had not the slightest intention of opening her lips to say one word that might put any idea into the head of her beloved child, but she saw no reason why she herself should not harbor all the ideas she pleased.

Whereupon, actuated by a combination of family pride, love, ambition in her chosen profession, Katy made ready to see that on the morrow the son of Frederick Whiting should be properly nourished on his outing with Linda.

At six o'clock Saturday morning Linda ran the Bear Cat to the back door, where she and Katy packed it. Before they had finished, Donald Whiting came down the sidewalk, his cheeks flushed with the exercise of walking, his eyes bright with anticipation, his cause forever won—in case he had a cause—with Katy, because she liked the wholesome, hearty manner in which he greeted Linda, and she was dumbfounded when he held out his hand to her and said laughingly: "Blessed among women, did you put in a fine large consignment of orange punch?"

"No," said Katy, "I'll just tell ye flat-footed there ain't going to be any punch, but, young sir, you're eshcortin' a very capable young lady, and don't ye bewail the punch, because ye might be complimenting your face with something ye would like a hape better."

"Can't be done, Katy," cried Donald.

"Ye must have a poor opinion of us," laughed Katy, "if ye are thinking ye can get to the end of our limitations in one lunch. Fourteen years me and Miss Linda's been on this lunch-box stunt. Don't ye be thinkin' ye can exhaust us in any wan trip, or in any wan dozen."

So they said good-bye to Katy and rolled past Eileen's room on the way to the desert. Eileen stood at the window watching them, and never had her heart been so full of discontent and her soul the abiding place of such envy or her mind so busy. Just when she had thought life was going to yield her what she craved, she could not understand how or why things should begin to go wrong.

As the Bear Cat traversed Lilac Valley, Linda was pointing out Peter Morrison's location. She was telling Donald Whiting where to find Peter's articles, and what a fine man he was, and that he had promised to think how he could help with their plan to make of Donald a better scholar than was Oka Sayye.

"Well, I call that mighty decent of a stranger," said Donald.

"But he is scarcely more of a stranger than I am," answered Linda. "He is a writer. He is interested in humanity. It's the business of every man in this world to reach out and help every boy with whom he comes in contact into the biggest, finest manhood possible. He only knows that you're a boy tackling a big job that means much to every white boy to have you succeed with, and for that reason he's just as interested as I am. Maybe, when we come in this evening, I'll run up to his place, and you can talk it over with him. If your father helped you at one angle, it's altogether probable that Peter Morrison could help you at another."

Donald Whiting rubbed his knee reflectively. He was sitting half turned in the wide seat so that he might watch Linda's hands and her face while she drove.

"Well, that's all right," he said heartily. "You can write me down as willing and anxious to take all the help I can get, for it's going to be no microscopic job, that I can tell you. One week has waked up the Jap to the fact that there's something doing, and he's digging in and has begun, the last day or two, to speak up in class and suggest things himself. Since I've been studying him and watching him, I have come to the conclusion that he is much older than I am. Something he said in class yesterday made me think he had probably had the best schooling Japan could give him before he came here. The next time you meet him look for a suspicion of gray hairs around his ears. He's too blamed comprehensive for the average boy of my age. You said the Japs were the best imitators in the world and I have an idea in the back of my head that before I get through with him, Oka Sayye is going to prove your proposition."

Linda nodded as she shot the Bear Cat across the streetcar tracks and headed toward the desert. The engine was purring softly as it warmed up. The car was running smoothly. The sun of early morning was shining on them through bracing, salt, cool air, and even in the valley the larks were busy, and the mockingbirds, and from every wayside bush the rosy finches were singing. All the world was coming to the exquisite bloom of a half-tropical country. Up from earth swept the heavy odors of blooming citrus orchards, millions of roses, and the overpowering sweetness of gardens and cultivated flowers; while down from the mountains rolled the delicate breath of the misty blue lilac, the pungent odor of California sage, and the spicy sweet of the lemonade bush. They were two young things, free for the day, flying down a perfect road, adventuring with Providence. They had only gone a few miles when Donald Whiting took off his hat, stuffed it down beside him, and threw back his head, shaking his hair to the wind in a gesture so soon to become familiar to Linda. She glanced across at him and found him looking at her. A smile broke over her lips. One of her most spontaneous laughs bubbled up in her throat.

"Topping, isn't it!" she cried gaily.

"It's the best thing that ever happened to me," answered Donald Whiting instantly. "Our car is a mighty good one and Dad isn't mean about letting me drive it. I can take it frequently and can have plenty of gas and take my crowd; but lordy, I don't believe there's a boy or girl living that doesn't just positively groan when they see one of these little gray Bear Cats go loping past. And I never even had a ride in one before. I can't get over the fact that it's yours. It wouldn't seem so funny if it belonged to one of the fellows."

With steady hand and gradually increasing speed, Linda put the Bear Cat over the roads of early morning. Sometimes she stopped in the shade of pepper, eucalyptus, or palm, where the larks were specializing in their age-old offertory. And then again they went racing until they reached the real desert. Linda ran the car under the shade of a tall clump of bloom-whitened alders. She took off her hat, loosened the hair at her temples, and looked out across the long morning stretch of desert.

"It's just beginning to be good," she said. She began pointing with her slender hand. "That gleam you see over there is the gold of a small clump of early poppies. The purple beyond it is lupin. All these exquisite colors on the floor are birds'-eyes and baby blue eyes, and the misty white here and there is forget-me-not. It won't be long til thousands and thousands of yucca plants will light their torches all over the desert and all the alders show their lacy mist. Of course you know how exquisitely the Spaniards named the yucca 'Our Lord's Candles.' Isn't that the prettiest name for a flower, and isn't it the prettiest thought?"

"It certainly is," answered Donald.

"Had any experience with the desert?" Linda asked lightly.

"Hunted sage hens some," answered Donald.

"Oh, well, that'll be all right," said Linda. "I wondered if you'd go murdering yourself like a tenderfoot."

"What's the use of all this artillery?" inquired Donald as he stepped from the car.

"Better put on your hat. You're taller than most of the bushes; you'll find slight shade," cautioned Linda. "The use is purely a matter of self-protection. The desert has got such a devil of a fight for existence, without shade and practically without water, that it can't afford to take any other chance of extermination, and so it protects itself with needles here and spears there and sabers at other places and roots that strike down to China everywhere. First thing we are going to get is some soap."

"Great hat!" exclaimed Donald. "If you wanted soap why didn't you bring some?"

"For all you know," laughed Linda, "I may be going to education you up a little. Dare you to tell me how many kinds of soap I can find today that the Indians used, and where I can find it."

"Couldn't tell you one to save my life," said Donald.

"And born and reared within a few miles of the desert!" scoffed Linda. "Nice Indian you'd make. We take our choice today between finding deer-brush and digging for amole, because the mock oranges aren't ripe enough to be nice and soapy yet. I've got the deer-brush spotted, and we'll pass an amole before we go very far. Look for a wavy blue-green leaf like a wide blade of grass and coming up like a lily."

So together they went to the deer-brush and gathered a bunch of flowers that Linda bound together with some wiry desert grass and fastened to her belt. It was not long before Donald spied an amole, and having found one, discovered many others growing near. Then Linda led the way past thorns and brush, past impenetrable beds of cholla, until they reached a huge barrel cactus that she had located with the glasses. Beside this bristling monstrous growth Linda paused, and reached for the axe, which Donald handed to her. She drew it lightly across the armor protecting the plant.

"Short of Victrola needles?" she inquired. "Because if you are, these make excellent ones. A lot more singing quality to them than the steel needles, not nearly so metallic."

"Well, I am surely going to try that," said Donald. "Never heard of such a thing."

51

Linda chopped off a section of plant. Then she picked one of the knives from the bucket and handed it to him.

"All right, you get what you want," she said, "while I operate on the barrel."

She set her feet firmly in the sand, swung the axe, and with a couple of deft strokes sliced off the top of the huge plant, and from the heart of it lifted up half a bucketful of the juicy interior, with her dipper.

"If we didn't have drink, here is where we would get it, and mighty good it is," she said, pushing down with the dipper until she formed a small pool in the heart of the plant which rapidly filled. "Have a taste."

"Jove, that is good!" said Donald. "What are you going to do with it?"

"Show you later," laughed Linda. "Think I'll take a sip myself."

Then by a roundabout route they started on their return to the car. Once Linda stopped and gathered a small bunch of an extremely curious little plant spreading over the ground, a tiny reddish vine with quaint round leaves that looked as if a drop of white paint rimmed with maroon had fallen on each of them.

"I never saw that before," said Donald. "What are you going to do with it?"

"Use it on whichever of us gets the first snake bite," said Linda. "That is rattlesnake weed and if a poisonous snake bites you, score each side of the wound with the cleanest, sharpest knife you have and then bruise the plant and bind it on with your handkerchief, and forget it."

"Is that what you do?" inquired Donald.

"Why sure," said Linda, "that is what I would do if a snake were so ungallant as to bite me, but there doesn't seem to be much of the antagonistic element in my nature. I don't go through the desert exhaling the odor of fright, and so snakes lie quiescent or slip away so silently that I never see them."

"Now what on earth do you mean by that?" inquired Donald.

"Why that is the very first lesson Daddy ever taught me when he took me to the mountains and the desert. If you are afraid, your system throws off formic acid, and the animals need only the suspicion of a scent of it to make them ready to fight. Any animal you encounter or even a bee, recognizes it. One of the first things that I remember about Daddy was seeing him sit on the running board of the runabout buckling up his desert boots while he sang to me,

'Let not your heart be troubled
Neither let it be afraid,'

as he got ready to take me on his back and go into the desert for our first lesson; he told me that a man was perfectly safe in going to the forest or the desert or anywhere he chose among any kind of animals if he had sufficient self-control that no odor of fear emanated from him. He said that a man was safe to make his way anywhere he wanted to go, if he started his journey by recognizing a blood brotherhood with anything living he would meet on the way; and I have heard Enos Mills say that when he was snow inspector of Colorado he traveled the crest of the Rockies from one end of the state to the other without a gun or any means of self-defense."

"Now, that is something new to think about," said Donald.

"And it's something that is very true," said Linda. "I have seen it work times without number. Father and I went quietly up the mountains, through the canyons, across the desert, and we would never see a snake of any kind, but repeatedly we would see men with guns and dogs out to kill, to trespass on the rights of the wild, and they would be hunting for sticks and clubs and firing their guns where we had passed never thinking of lurking danger. If you start out in accord, at one with Nature, you're quite as safe as you are at home, sometimes more so. But if you start out to stir up a fight, the occasion is very rare on which you can't succeed."

"And that reminds me," said Donald, with a laugh, "that a week ago I came to start a fight with you. What has become of that fight we were going to have, anyway?"

"You can search me," laughed Linda, throwing out her hands in a graceful gesture. "There's not a scrap of fight in my system concerning you, but if Oka Sayye were having a fight with you and I were anywhere around, you'd have one friend who would help you to handle the Jap."

Donald looked at Linda thoughtfully.

"By the great hocus-pocus," he said, "you know, I believe you. If two fellows were having a pitched battle most of the girls I know would quietly faint or run, but I do believe that you would stand by and help a fellow if he needed it."

"That I surely would," said Linda; "but don't you say 'most of the girls I know' and then make a statement like that concerning girls, because you prove that you don't know them at all. A few years ago, I very distinctly recall how angry many women were at this line in one of Kipling's poems:

The female of the species is more deadly than the male,

and there was nothing to it save that a great poet was trying to pay womanhood everywhere the finest compliment he knew how. He always has been fundamental in his process of thought. He gets right back to the heart of primal things. When he wrote that line he was not really thinking that there was a nasty poison in the heart of a woman or death in her hands. What he was thinking was that in the jungle the female lion or tiger or jaguar must go and find a particularly secluded cave and bear her young and raise them to be quite active kittens before she leads them out, because there is danger of the bloodthirsty father eating them when they are tiny and helpless. And if perchance a male finds the cave of his mate and her tiny young and enters it to do mischief, then there is no recorded instance I know of in which the female, fighting in defense of her young, has not been 'more deadly than the male.' And that is the origin of the much-discussed line concerning the female of the species, and it holds good fairly well down the line of the wild. It's even true among such tiny things as guinea pigs and canary birds. There is a mother element in the heart of every girl. Daddy used to say that half the women in the world married the men they did because they wanted to mother them. You can't tell what is in a woman's heart by looking at her. You must bring her face to face with an emergency before you can say what she'll do, but I would be perfectly willing to stake my life on this: There is scarcely a girl you know who would see you getting the worst of a fight, say with Oka Sayye, or someone who meant to kill you or injure you, who would not pick up the first weapon she could lay her hands on, whether it was an axe or a stick or a stone, and go to your defense, and if she had nothing else to fight with, I have heard of women who put up rather a tidy battle with their claws. Sounds primitive, doesn't it?"

"It sounds true," said Donald reflectively. "I see, young lady, where one is going to have to measure his words and think before he talks to you."

"Pretty thought!" said Linda lightly. "We'll have a great time if you must stop to consider every word before you say it."

"Well, anyway," said Donald, "when are we going to have that fight which was the purpose of our coming together?"

"Why, we're not ever going to have it," answered Linda. "I have got nothing in this world to fight with you about since you're doing your level best to beat Oka Sayye. I have watched your head above the remainder of your class for three years and wanted to fight with you on that point."

"Now that's a queer thing," said Donald, "because I have watched you for three years and wanted to fight with you about your drygoods, and now since I've known you only such a short while, I don't care two whoops what you wear. It's a matter of perfect indifference to me. You can wear French heels or baby pumps, or go barefoot. You would still be you."

"Is it a truce?" asked Linda.

"No, ma'am," said Donald, "it's not a truce. That implies war and we haven't fought. It's not armed neutrality; it's not even watchful waiting. It's my friend, Linda Strong. Me for her and her for me, if you say so."

He reached out his hand. Linda laid hers in it, and looking into his eyes, she said: "That is a compact. We'll test this friendship business and see what there is to it. Now come on; let's run for the canyon."

It was only a short time until the Bear Cat followed its trail of the previous Saturday, and, rushing across the stream, stopped at its former resting place, while Linda and Donald sat looking at the sheer-walled little room before them.

"I can see," said Linda, "a stronger tinge in the green. There are more flowers in the carpet. There is more melody in the birds' song. We are going to have a better time than we had last Saturday. First let's fix up our old furnace, because we must have a fire today."

So they left the car, and under Linda's direction they reconstructed the old fireplace at which the girl and her father had cooked when botanizing in Multiflores. In a corner secluded from wind, using the wall of the canyon for a back wall, big boulders the right distance apart on each side, and small stones for chinking, Linda superintended the rebuilding of the fireplace.

She unpacked the lunch box, set the table, and when she had everything in readiness she covered the table, and taking a package, she carried it on a couple of aluminium pie pans to where her fire was burning crisply. With a small field axe she chopped a couple of small green branches, pointed them to her liking, and peeled them. Then she made a poker from one of the saplings they had used to move the rocks, and beat down her fire until she had a bright bed of deep coals. When these were arranged exactly to her satisfaction, she pulled some sprays of deer weed bloom from her bundle and, going down to the creek, made a lather and carefully washed her hands, tucking the towel she used in drying them through her belt. Then she came back to the fire and, sitting down beside it, opened the package and began her operations. On the long, slender sticks she strung a piece of tenderloin beef, about three inches in circumference and one fourth of an inch in thickness, then half a slice of bacon, and then a slice of onion. This she repeated until her skewer would bear no more weight. Then she laid it across the rocks walling her fire, occasionally turning it while she filled the second skewer. Then she brought from the car the bucket of pulp she had taken from the barrel cactus, transferred it to a piece of cheesecloth and deftly extracted the juice. To this she added the contents of a thermos bottle containing a pint of sugar that had been brought to the boiling point with a pint of water and poured over some chopped spearmint to which had been added the juice of half a dozen lemons and three or four oranges. From a small, metal-lined compartment, Linda took a chunk of ice and dropped it into this mixture.

She was sitting on the ground, one foot doubled under her, the other extended. She had taken off her hat; the wind and the bushes had roughened her hair. Exercise had brought deep red to her cheeks and her lips. Happiness had brought a mellow glow to her dark eyes. She had turned back her sleeves, and her slender hands were fascinatingly graceful in their deft handling of everything she touched. They were a second edition of the hands with which Alexander Strong had felt out defective nerve systems and made delicate muscular adjustments. She was wholly absorbed in what she was doing. Sitting on the blanket across from her Donald Whiting was wholly absorbed in her and he was thinking. He was planning how he could please her, how he could earn her friendship. He was admitting to himself that he had very little, if anything, to show for hours of time that he had spent in dancing, at card games, beach picnics, and races. All these things had been amusing. But he had nothing to show for the time he had spent or the money he had wasted. Nothing had happened that in any way equipped him for his battle with Oka Sayye. Conversely, this girl, whom he had resented, whom he had criticized, who had claimed his notice only by her radical difference from the other girls, had managed, during the few minutes he had first talked with her in the hall, to wound his pride, to spur his ambition, to start him on a course that must end in lasting and material benefit to him even if he failed in making a higher record of scholarship than Oka Sayye. It was very certain that the exercise he was giving his brain must be beneficial. He had learned many things that were intensely interesting to him and he had not even touched the surface of what he could see that she had been taught by her father or had learned through experience and personal investigation. She had been coming to the mountains and the canyons alone, for four years doing by herself what she would have done under her father's supervision had he lived. That argued for steadfastness and strength of character. She would not utter one word of flattery. She would say nothing she did not mean. Watching her intently, Donald Whiting thought of all these things. He thought of what she had said about fighting for him, and he wondered if it really was true that any girl he knew would fight for him. He hardly believed it when he remembered some of his friends, so entirely devoted to personal adornment and personal gratification. But Linda had said that all women were alike in their hearts. She knew about other things. She must know about this. Maybe all women would fight for their young or for their men, but he knew of no other girl who could drive a Bear Cat with the precision and skill with which Linda drove. He knew no other girl who was master of the secrets of the desert and the canyons and the mountains. Certainly he knew no other girl who would tug at great boulders and build a fireplace and risk burning her fingers and scorching her face to prepare a meal for him. So he watched Linda and so he thought.

At first he thought she was the finest pal a boy ever had, and then he thought how he meant to work to earn and keep her friendship; and then, as the fire reddened Linda's cheeks and she made running comments while she deftly turned her skewers of brigand beefsteak, food that half the Boy Scouts in the country had been eating for four years, there came an idea with which he dallied until it grew into a luring vision.

"Linda," he asked suddenly, "do you know that one of these days you're going to be a beautiful woman?"

Linda turned her skewers with intense absorption. At first he almost thought she had not heard him, but at last she said quietly: "Do you really think that is possible, Donald?"

"You're lovely right now!" answered the boy promptly.

"For goodness' sake, have an eye single to your record for truth and veracity," said Linda. "Doesn't this begin to smell zippy?"

"It certainly does," said Donald. "It's making me ravenous. But honest, Linda, you are a pretty girl."

"Honest, your foot!" said Linda scornfully. "I am not a pretty girl. I am lean and bony and I've got a beak where I should have a nose. Speaking of pretty girls, my sister, Eileen, is a pretty girl. She is a downright beautiful girl."

"Yes," said Donald, "she is, but she can't hold a candle to you. How did she look when she was your age?"

"I can't remember Eileen," said Linda, "when she was not exquisitely dressed and thinking more about taking care of her shoes than anything else in the world. I can't remember her when she was not curled, and even when she was a tiny thing Mother put a dust of powder on her nose. She said her skin was so delicate that it could not bear the sun. She never could run or play or motor much or do anything, because she has always had to be saved for the sole purpose of being exquisitely beautiful. Talk about lilies of the field, that's what Eileen is! She is an improvement on the original lily of the field—she's a lily of the drawing room. Me, now, I'm more of a Joshua tree."

Donald Whiting laughed, as Linda intended that he should.

A minute afterward she slid the savory food from a skewer upon one of the pie pans, tossed back the cover from the little table, stacked some bread-and-butter sandwiches beside the meat and handed the pan to Donald.

"Fall to," she said, "and prove that you're a man with an appreciative tummy. Father used to be positively ravenous for this stuff. I like it myself."

She slid the food from the second skewer to a pan for herself, settled the fire to her satisfaction and they began their meal. Presently she filled a cup from the bucket beside her and handed it to Donald. At the same time she lifted another for herself.

"Here's to the barrel cactus," she said. "May the desert grow enough of them so that we'll never lack one when we want to have a Saturday picnic."

Laughingly they drank this toast; and the skewers were filled a second time. When they could eat no more they packed away the lunch things, buried the fire, took the axe and the field glasses, and started on a trip of exploration down the canyon. Together they admired delicate and exquisite ferns growing around great gray boulders. Donald tasted hunters' rock leek, and learned that any he found while on a hunting expedition would furnish a splendid substitute for water. Linda told him of rare flowers she lacked and what they were like and how he would be able to identify what she wanted in case he should ever find any when he was out hunting or with his other friends. They peeped into the nesting places of canyon wrens and doves and finches, and listened to the exquisite courting songs of the birds whose hearts were almost bursting with the exuberance of spring and the joy of home making. When they were tired out they went back to the dining room and after resting a time, they made a supper from the remnants of their dinner. When they were seated in the car and Linda's hand was on the steering wheel, Donald reached across and covered it with his own.

"Wait a bit," he said. "Before we leave here I want to ask you a question and I want you to make me a promise."

"All right," said Linda. "What's your question?"

"What is there," said Donald, "that I can do that would give you such pleasure as you have given me?"

Linda could jest on occasions, but by nature she was a serious person. She looked at Donald reflectively.

"Why, I think," she said at last, "that having a friend, having someone who understands and who cares for the things I do, and who likes to go to the same places and to do the same things, is the biggest thing that has happened to me since I lost my father. I don't see that you are in any way in my debt, Donald."

"All right then," said the boy, "that brings me to the promise I want you to make me. May we always have our Saturdays together like this?"

"Sure!" said Linda, "I would be mightily pleased. I'll have to work later at night and scheme, maybe. By good rights Saturday belongs to me anyway because I am born Saturday's child."

"Well, hurrah for Saturday! It always was a grand old day," said Donald, "and since I see what it can do in turning out a girl like you, I've got a better opinion of it than ever. We'll call that settled. I'll always ask you on Friday at what hour to come, and hereafter Saturday is ours."

"Ours it is," said Linda.

Then she put the Bear Cat through the creek and on the road and, driving swiftly as she dared, ran to Lilac Valley and up to Peter Morrison's location.

She was amazed at the amount of work that had been accomplished. The garage was finished. Peter's temporary work desk and his cot were in it. A number of his personal belongings were there. The site for his house had been selected and the cellar was being excavated.

Linda descended from the Bear Cat and led Donald before Peter.

"Since you're both my friends," she said, "I want you to know each other. This is Donald Whiting, the Senior I told you about, Mr. Morrison. You know you said you would help him if you could."

"Certainly," said Peter. "I am very glad to know any friend of yours, Miss Linda. Come over to my workroom and let's hear about this."

"Oh, go and talk it over between yourselves," said Linda. "I am going up here to have a private conversation with the spring. I want it to tell me confidentially exactly the course it would enjoy running so that when your house is finished and I come to lay out your grounds I will know exactly how it feels about making a change."

"Fine!" said Peter. "Take your time and become extremely confidential, because the more I look at the location and the more I hear the gay chuckling song that that water sings, the more I am in love with your plan to run it across the lawn and bring it around the boulder."

"It would be a downright sin not to have that water in a convenient place for your children to play in, Peter," said Linda.

"Then that's all settled," said Peter. "Now, Whiting, come this way and we'll see whether I can suggest anything that will help you with your problem."

"Whistle when you are ready, Donald," called Linda as she turned away.

Peter Morrison glanced after her a second, and then he led Donald Whiting to a nail keg in the garage and impaled that youngster on the mental point of a mental pin and studied him as carefully as any scientist ever studied a rare specimen. When finally he let him go, his mental comment was: "He's a mighty fine kid. Linda is perfectly safe with him."

CHAPTER XV. Linda's Hearthstone

Early the following week Linda came from school one evening to find a load of sand and a heap of curiously marked stones beside the back door.

"Can it possibly be, Katy," she asked, "that those men are planning to begin work on my room so soon? I am scared out of almost seven of my five senses. I had no idea they would be ready to begin work until after I had my settlement with Eileen or was paid for the books."

"Don't ye be worried," said Katy. "There's more in me stocking than me leg, and you're as welcome to it as the desert is welcome to rain, an' nadin' it 'most as bad."

"Anyway," said Linda, "it will surely take them long enough so that I can pay by the time they finish."

But Linda was not figuring that back of the projected improvements stood two men, each of whom had an extremely personal reason for greatly desiring to please her. Peter Morrison had secured a slab of sandstone. He had located a marble cutter to whom he meant to carry it, and was spending much thought that he might have been using on an article in trying to hit upon exactly the right line or phrase to build in above Linda's fire—something that would convey to her in a few words a sense of friendship and beauty.

While Peter gazed at the unresponsive gray sandstone and wrote line after line which he immediately destroyed, Henry Anderson explored the mountain and came in, red faced and perspiring, from miles of climbing with a bright stone in each hand, or took the car to bring in small heaps too heavy to carry that he had collected near the roads. They were two men striving for the favor of the same girl. How Linda would have been amused had she understood the situation, or how Eileen would have been provoked, neither of the men knew nor did they care.

The workmen came after Linda left and went before her return. Having been cautioned to silence, Katy had not told her when work actually began; and so it happened that, going to her room one evening, she unlocked the door and stepped inside to face the completed fireplace. The firebox was not very large but ample. The hearthstone was a big sheet of smooth gray sandstone. The sides and top were Henry's collection of brilliant boulders, carefully and artistically laid in blue mortar, and over the firebox was set Peter's slab of gray sandstone. On it were four deeply carved lines. The quaint Old English lettering was filled even to the surface with a red mortar, while the capitals were done in dull blue. The girl slowly read:

Voiceless stones, with Flame-tongues Preach
Sermons struck from Nature's Lyre;
Notes of Love and Trust and Hope
Hourly sing in Linda's Fire.

In the firebox stood a squat pair of black andirons, showing age and usage. A rough eucalyptus log waited across them while the shavings from the placing of the mantel and the cutting of the windows were tucked beneath it. Linda stood absorbed a minute. She looked at the skylight, flooding the room with the light she so needed coming from the right angle. She went over to the new window that gave her a view of the length of the valley she loved and a most essential draft. When she turned back to the fireplace her hands were trembling.

"Now isn't that too lovely of them?" she said softly. "Isn't that altogether wonderful? How I wish Daddy were here to sit beside my fire and share with me the work I hope to do here."

In order to come as close to him as possible she did the next best thing. She sat down at her table and wrote a long letter to Marian, telling her everything she could think of that would interest her. Then she re-read with extreme care the letter she had found at the Post Office that day in reply to the one she had written Marian purporting to come from an admirer. Writing slowly and thinking deeply, she answered it. She tried to imagine that she was Peter Morrison and she tried to say the things in that letter that she thought Peter would say in the circumstances, because she felt sure that Marian would be entertained by such things as Peter would say. When she finished, she read it over carefully, and then copied it with equal care on the typewriter, which she had removed to her workroom.

When she heard Katy's footstep outside her door, she opened it and drew her in, slipping the bolt behind her. She led her to the fireplace and recited the lines.

"Now ain't they jist the finest gentlemen?" said Katy. "Cut right off of a piece of the same cloth as your father. Now some way we must get together enough money to get ye a good-sized rug for under your worktable, and then ye've got to have two bits of small ones, one for your hearthstone and one for your aisel; and then ye're ready, colleen, to show what ye can do. I'm so proud of ye when I think of the grand secret it's keepin' for ye I am; and less and less are gettin' me chances for the salvation of me soul, for every night I'm a-sittin' starin' at the magazines ye gave me when I ought to be tellin' me beads and makin' me devotions. Ain't it about time the third was comin' in?"

"Any day now," said Linda in a whisper. "And, Katy, you'll be careful? That editor must think that 'Jane Meredith' is full of years and ripe experience. I probably wouldn't get ten cents, no not even a for-nothing chance, if he knew those articles were written by a Junior."

"Junior nothing!" scoffed Katy. "There was not a day of his life that your pa did not spend hours drillin' ye in things the rest of the girls in your school never heard of. 'Tain't no high-school girl that's written them articles. It's Alexander Strong speakin' through the medium of his own flesh and blood."

"Why, so it is, Katy!" cried Linda delightedly. "You know, I never thought of that. I have been so egoistical I thought I was doing them myself."

"Paid ye anything yet?" queried Katy.

"No," said Linda, "they haven't. It seems that the amount of interest the articles evoke is going to decide what I am to be paid for them, but they certainly couldn't take the recipe and the comments and the sketch for less than twenty-five or thirty dollars, unless recipes are like poetry. Peter said the other day that if a poet did not have some other profession to support him, he would starve to death on all he was paid for writing the most beautiful things that ever are written in all this world. Peter says even an effort to write a poem is a beautiful thing."

"Well, maybe that used to be the truth," said Katy as she started toward the door, "but I have been reading some things labeled 'poetry' in the magazines of late, and if the holy father knows what they mean, he's even bigger than ever I took him to be."

"Katy," said Linda, "we are dreadful back numbers. We are letting this world progress and roll right on past us without a struggle. We haven't either one been to a psychoanalyst to find out the color of our auras."

"Now God forbid," said Katy. "I ain't going to have one of them things around me. The colors I'm wearin' satisfy me entoirely."

"And mine are going to satisfy me very shortly, now," laughed Linda, "because tomorrow is my big day with Eileen. Next time we have a minute together, old dear, I'll have started my bank account."

"Right ye are," said Katy, "jist exactly right. You're getting such a great girl it's the proper thing ye should be suitably dressed, and don't ye be too modest."

"The unfortunate thing about that, Katy, is that I intimated the other day that I would be content with less than half, since she is older and she should have her chance first."

"Now ain't that jist like ye?" said Katy. "I might have known ye would be doing that very thing."

"After I have gone over the accounts," said Linda, "I'll know better what to demand. Now fly to your cooking, Katy, and let me sit down at this table and see if I can dig out a few dollars of honest coin; but I'm going to have hard work to keep my eyes on the paper with that fireplace before me. Isn't that red and blue lettering the prettiest thing, Katy, and do you notice that tiny 'P. M.' cut down in the lower left-hand corner nearly out of sight? That, Katy, stands for 'Peter Morrison,' and one of these days Peter is going to be a large figure on the landscape. The next Post he has an article in I'll buy for you."

"It never does," said Katy, "to be makin' up your mind in this world so hard and fast that ye can't change it. In the days before John Gilman got bewitched out of his senses I did think, barrin' your father, that he was the finest man the Lord ever made; but I ain't thought so much of him of late as I did before."

"Same holds good for me," said Linda.

"I've studied this Peter," continued Katy, "like your pa used to study things under his microscope. He's the most come-at-able man. He's got such a kind of a questionin' look on his face, and there's a bit of a stoop to his shoulders like they had been whittled out for carryin' a load, and there's a kind of a whimsy quiverin' around his lips that makes me heart stand still every time he speaks to me, because I can't be certain whether he is going to make me laugh or going to make me cry, and when what he's sayin' does come with that little slow drawl, I can't be just sure whether he's meanin' it or whether he's jist pokin' fun at me. He said the quarest thing to me the other day when he was here fiddlin' over the makin' of this fireplace. He was standin' out beside your desert garden and I come aven with him and I says to him: 'Them's the rare plants Miss Linda and her pa have been goin' to the deserts and the canyons, as long as he lived, to fetch in; and then Miss Linda went alone, and now the son of Judge Whiting, the biggest lawyer in Los Angeles, has begun goin' with her. Ain't it the brightest, prettiest place?' I says to him. And he stood there lookin', and he says to me: 'No, Katy, that is a graveyard.' Now what in the name of raison was the man meanin' by that?"

Linda stared at the hearth motto reflectively.

"A graveyard!" she repeated. "Well, if anything could come farther from a graveyard than that spot, I don't know how it would do it. I haven't the remotest notion what he meant. Why didn't you ask him?"

"Well, the truth is," said Katy, "that I proide myself on being able to kape me mouth shut when I should."

"I'll leave to think over it," said Linda. "At present I have no more idea than you in what respect my desert garden could resemble a graveyard. Oh! yes, there's one thing I wanted to ask you, Katy. Has Eileen been around while this room was being altered?"

"She came in yesterday," answered Katy, "when the hammerin' and sawin' was goin' full blast."

"What I wanted to find out" said Linda, "was whether she had been here and seen this room or not, because if she hasn't and she wants to see it, now is her time. After I get things going here and these walls are covered with drying sketches this room is going to be strictly private. You see that you keep your key where nobody gets hold of it."

"It's on a string round me neck this blessed minute," said Katy. "I didn't see her come up here, but ye could be safe in bettin' anything ye've got that she came."

"Yes, I imagine she did," said Linda. "She would be sufficiently curious that she would come to learn how much I have spent if she had no other interest in me."

She looked at the fireplace reflectively.

"I wonder," she said, "what Eileen thought of that and I wonder if she noticed that little 'P. M.' tucked away down there in the corner."

"Sure she did," said Katy. "She has got eyes like a cat. She can see more things in a shorter time than anybody I ever knew." So that evening at dinner Linda told Eileen that the improvements she had made for her convenience in the billiard room were finished, and asked her if she would like to see them.

"I can't imagine what you want to stick yourself off up there alone for," said Eileen. "I don't believe I am sufficiently interested in garret skylights and windows to climb up to look at them. What everybody in the neighborhood can see is that you have absolutely ruined the looks of the back part of the house."

"Good gracious!" said Linda. "Have I? You know I never thought of that."

"Of course! But all you've got to do is go on the cast lawn and take a look at that side and the back end of the house to see what you have done," said Eileen. "Undoubtedly you've cut the selling price of the house one thousand, at least. But it's exactly like you not to have thought of what chopping up the roof and the end of the house as you have done, would make it look like. You have got one of those single-track minds, Linda, that can think of only one thing at a time, and you never do think, when you start anything, of what the end is going to be."

"Very likely there's a large amount of truth in that," said Linda soberly. "Perhaps I do get an idea and pursue it to the exclusion of everything else. It's an inheritance from Daddy, this concentrating with all my might on one thing at a time. But I am very sorry if I have disfigured the house."

"What I want to know," said Eileen, "is how in this world, at present wages and cost of material, you're expecting to pay men for the work you have had done."

"I can talk more understandingly about that," said Linda quietly, "day after tomorrow. I'll get home from school tomorrow as early as I can, and then we'll figure out our financial situation exactly."

Eileen made no reply.

CHAPTER XVI. Producing the Evidence

When Linda hurried home the next evening, her first word to Katy was to ask if Eileen were there.

"No, she isn't here," said Katy, "and she's not going to be."

"Not going to be!" cried Linda, her face paling perceptibly.

"She went downtown this morning and she telephoned me about three sayin' she had an invoitation to go with a motor party to Pasadena this afternoon, an' she wasn't knowin' whether she could get home the night or not."

"I don't like it," said Linda. "I don't like it at all."

She liked it still less when Eileen came home for a change of clothing the following day, and again went to spend the night with a friend, without leaving any word whatever.

"I don't understand this," said Linda, white lipped and tense. "She does not want to see me. She does not intend to talk business with me if she can possibly help it. She is treating me as if I were a four-year-old instead of a woman with as much brain as she has. If she appears while I am gone tomorrow and starts away again, you tell her Come to think of it, you needn't tell her anything; I'll give you a note for her."

So Linda sat down and wrote:

DEAR EILEEN:

It won't be necessary to remind you of our agreement night before last to settle on an allowance from Father's estate for me. Of course I realize that you are purposely avoiding seeing me, for what reason I can't imagine; but I give you warning, that if you have been in this house and have read this note, and are not here with your figures ready to meet me when I get home tomorrow night, I'll take matters into my own hands, and do exactly what I think best without the slightest reference to what you think about it. If you don't want something done that you will dislike, even more than you dislike seeing me, you had better heed this warning.

LINDA.

She read it over slowly: "My, that sounds melodramatic!" she commented. "It's even got a threat in it, and it's a funny thing to threaten my own sister. I don't think that it's a situation that occurs very frequently, but for that matter I sincerely hope that Eileen isn't the kind of sister that occurs frequently."

Linda went up to her room and tried to settle herself to work, but found that it was impossible to fix her attention on what she was doing. Her mind jumped from one thing to another in a way that totally prohibited effective work of any kind. A sudden resolve came into her heart. She would not wait any longer. She would know for herself just how she was situated financially. She wrote a note to the editor of Everybody's Home, asking him if it would be convenient to let her know what reception her work was having with his subscribers, whether he desired her to continue the department in his magazines, and if so, what was the best offer he could make her for the recipes, the natural history comments accompanying them, and the sketches. Then she went down to the telephone book and looked up the location of the Consolidated Bank. She decided that she would stop there on her way from school the next day and ask to be shown the Strong accounts.

While she was meditating these heroic measures the bell rang and Katy admitted John Gilman. Strangely enough, he was asking for Linda, not for Eileen. At the first glimpse of him Linda knew that something was wrong; so without any prelude she said abruptly: "What's the matter, John? Don't you know where I Eileen is either?"

"Approximately," he answered. "She has 'phoned me two or three times, but I haven't seen her for three days. Do you know where she is or exactly why she is keeping away from home as she is?"

"Yes," said Linda, "I do. I told you the other day the time had come when I was going to demand a settlement of Father's estate and a fixed income. That time came three days ago and I have not seen Eileen since."

They entered the living room. As Linda passed the table, propped against a candlestick on it, she noticed a note addressed to herself.

"Oh, here will be an explanation," she said. "Here is a note for me. Sit down a minute till I read it."

She seated herself on the arm of a chair, tore open the note, and instantly began reading aloud. "Dear little sister—"

"Pathetic," interpolated Linda, "in consideration of the fact that I am about twice as big as she is. However, we'll let that go, and focus on the enclosure." She waved a slender slip of paper at Gilman. "I never was possessed of an article like this before in all my tender young life, but it seems to me that it's a cheque, and I can't tell you quite how deeply it amuses me. But to return to business, at the present instant I am:

DEAR LITTLE SISTER:

It seems that all the friends I have are particularly insistent on seeing me all at once and all in a rush. I don't think I ever had quite so many invitations at one time in my life before, and the next two or three days seem to be going to be equally as full. But I took time to run into the bank and go over things carefully. I find that after the payment of taxes and insurance and all the household expenses, that by wearing old clothes I have and making them over I can afford to turn over at least seventy-five dollars a month to you for your clothing and personal expenses. As I don't know exactly when I can get home, I am enclosing a cheque which is considerably larger than I had supposed I could make it, and I can only do this by skimping myself; but of course you are getting such a big girl and beginning to attract attention, so it is only right that you should have the very best that I can afford to do for you. I am not taking the bill from The Mode into consideration. I paid that with last month's expenses.

With love,

EILEEN.

Linda held the letter in one hand, the cheque in the other, and stared questioningly at John Gilman.

"What do you think of that?" she inquired tersely.

"It seems to me," said Gilman, "that a more pertinent question would be, what do you think of it?"

"Rot!" said Linda tersely. "If I were a stenographer in your office I would think that I was making a fairly good start; but I happen to be the daughter of Alexander Strong living in my own home with my only sister, who can afford to flit like the flittingest of social butterflies from one party to another as well dressed as, and better dressed than, the Great General Average. You have known us, John, ever since Eileen sat in the sun to dry her handmade curls, while I was leaving a piece of my dress on every busk in Multiflores Canyon. Right here and now I am going to show you something!"

Linda started upstairs, so John Gilman followed her. She went to the door of Eileen's suite and opened it.

"Now then," she said, "take a look at what Eileen feels she can afford for herself. You will observe she has complete and exquisite furnishings and all sorts of feminine accessories on her dressing table. You will observe that she has fine rugs in her dressing room and bathroom. Let me call your attention to the fact that all these drawers are filled with expensive comforts and conveniences."

Angrily Linda began to open drawers filled with fancy feminine apparel, daintily and neatly folded, everything in perfect order: gloves, hose, handkerchiefs, ribbons, laces, all in separate compartments She pointed to the high chiffonier, the top decorated with candlesticks and silver-framed pictures. Here the drawers revealed heaps of embroidered underclothing and silken garments. Then she walked to the closet and threw the door wide.

She pushed hangers on their rods, sliding before the perplexed and bewildered man dress after dress of lace and georgette, walking suits of cloth, street dresses of silk, and pretty afternoon gowns, heavy coats, light coats, a beautiful evening coat. Linda took this down and held it in front of John Gilman.

"I see things marked in store windows," she said. "Eileen paid not a penny less than three hundred for this one coat. Look at the rows of shoes, and pumps, and slippers, and what that box is or I don't know."

Linda slid to the light a box screened by the hanging dresses, and with the toe of her shoe lifted the lid, disclosing a complete smoking outfit—case after case of cigarettes. Linda dropped the lid and shoved the box back. She stood silent a second, then she looked at John Gilman.

"That is the way things go in this world," she said quietly. "Whenever you lose your temper, you always do something you didn't intend to do when you started. I didn't know that, and I wouldn't have shown it to you purposely if I had known it; but it doesn't alter the fact that you should know it. If you did know it no harm's done but if you didn't know it, you shouldn't be allowed to marry Eileen without knowing as much about her as you did about Marian, and there was nothing about Marian that you didn't know. I am sorry for that, but since I have started this I am going through with it. Now give me just one minute more."

Then she went down the hall, threw open the door to her room, and walking in said: "You have seen Eileen's surroundings; now take a look at mine. There's my bed; there's my dresser and toilet articles; and this is my wardrobe."

She opened the closet door and exhibited a pair of overalls in which she watered her desert garden. Next ranged her khaki breeches and felt hat. Then hung the old serge school dress, beside it the extra skirt and orange blouse. The stack of underclothing on the shelves was pitifully small, visibly dilapidated. Two or three outgrown gingham dresses hung forlornly on the opposite wall. Linda stood tall and straight before John Gilman.

"What I have on and one other waist constitute my wardrobe," she said, "and I told Eileen where to get this dress and suggested it before I got it."

Gilman looked at her in a dazed fashion.

"I don't understand," he said slowly. "If that isn't the dress I saw Eileen send up for herself, I'm badly mistaken. It was the Saturday we went to Riverside. It surely is the very dress."

Linda laughed bleakly.

"That may be," she said. "The one time she ever has any respect for me is in a question of taste. She will agree that I know when colors are right and a thing is artistic. Now then, John, you are the administrator of my father's estate; you have seen what you have seen. What are you going to do about it?"

"Linda," he said quietly, "what my heart might prompt me to do in consideration of the fact that I am engaged to marry Eileen, and what my legal sense tells me I must do as executor of your father's wishes, are different propositions. I am going to do exactly what you tell me to. What you have shown me, and what I'd have realized, if I had stopped to think, is neither right nor just."

Then Linda took her tun at deep thought.

"John," she said at last, "I am feeling depressed over what I have just done. I am not sure that in losing my temper and bringing you up here I have played the game fairly. You don't need to do anything. I'll manage my affairs with Eileen myself. But I'll tell you before you go, that you needn't practice any subterfuges. When she reaches the point where she is ready to come home, I'll tell her that you were here, and what you have seen. That is the best I can do toward squaring myself with my own conscience."

Slowly they walked down the hall together. At the head of the stairs Linda took the cheque that she carried and tore it into bits. Stepping across the hall, she let the little heap slowly flutter to the rug in front of Eileen's door. Then she went back to her room and left John Gilman to his own reflections.

CHAPTER XVII. A Rock and a Flame

The first time Linda entered the kitchen after her interview with Gilman, Katy asked in deep concern, "Now what ye been doing, lambie?"

"Doing the baby act, Katy," confessed Linda. "Disgracing myself. Losing my temper. I wish I could bring myself to the place where I would think half a dozen times before I do a thing once."

"Now look here," said Katy, beginning to bristle, "ain't it the truth that ye have thought for four years before ye did this thing once?"

"Quite so," said Linda. "But since I am the daughter of the finest gentleman I ever knew, I should not do hasty, regrettable things. On the living-room table I found a note sweeter than honey, and it contained a cheque for me that wouldn't pay Eileen's bills for lunches, candy, and theaters for a month; so in undue heat I reduced it to bits and decorated the rug before her door. But before that, Katy, I led my guardian into the room, and showed him everything. I meant to tell him that, since he had neglected me for four years, he could see that I had justice now, but when I'd personally conducted him from Eileen's room to mine, and when I took a good look at him there was something on his face, Katy, that I couldn't endure. So I told him to leave it to me; that I would tell Eileen myself what I had done, and so I will. But I am sorry I did it, Katy; I am awfully sorry. You always told me to keep my temper and I lost it completely. From now on I certainly will try to behave myself more like a woman than a spoiled child. Now give me a dust cloth and brushes. I am almost through with my job in the library and I want to finish, because I shall be forced to use the money from the books to pay for my skylight and fireplace."

Linda went to the library and began work, efficiently, carefully, yet with a precise rapidity habitual to her. Down the long line of heavy technical books, she came to the end of the shelf. Three books from the end she noticed a difference in the wall behind the shelf. Hastily removing the other two volumes, she disclosed a small locked door having a scrap of paper protruding from the edge which she pulled out and upon which she read:

In the event of my passing, should anyone move these books and find this door, these lines are to inform him that it is to remain untouched. The key to it is in my safety-deposit vault at the Consolidated Bank. The Bank will open the door and attend to the contents of the box at the proper time.

Linda fixed the paper back exactly as she had found it. She stood looking at the door a long time, then she carefully wiped it, the wall around it, and the shelf. Going to another shelf, she picked out the books that had been written by her father and, beginning at the end of the shelf, she ranged them in a row until they completely covered the opening. Then she finished filling the shelf with other books that she meant to keep, but her brain was working, milling over and over the question of what that little compartment contained and when it was to be opened and whether John Gilman knew about it, and whether the Consolidated Bank would remember the day specified, and whether it would mean anything important to her.

She carried the dusters back to Katy, and going to her room, concentrated resolutely upon her work; but she was unable to do anything constructive. Her routine lessons she could prepare, but she could not even sketch a wild rose accurately. Finally she laid down her pencil, washed her brushes, put away her material, and locking her door, slipped the key into her pocket. Going down to the garage she climbed into the Bear Cat and headed straight for Peter Morrison. She drove into his location and blew the horn. Peter stepped from the garage, and seeing her, started in her direction. Linda sprang down and hurried toward him. He looked at her intently as she approached and formed his own conclusions.

"Sort of restless," said Linda. "Couldn't evolve a single new idea with which to enliven the gay annals of English literature and Greek history. A personal history seems infinitely more insistent and unusual. I ran away from my lessons, and my work, and came to you, Peter, because I had a feeling that there was something you could give me, and I thought you would."

Peter smiled a slow curious smile.

"I like your line of thought, Linda," he said quietly. "It greatly appeals to me. Any time an ancient and patriarchal literary man named Peter Morrison can serve as a rock upon which a young thing can rest, why he'll be glad to be that rock."

"What were you doing?" asked Linda abruptly.

"Come and see," said Peter.

He led the way to the garage. His worktable and the cement floor around it were littered with sheets of closely typed paper.

"I'll have to assemble them first," said Peter, getting down on his knees and beginning to pick them up.

Linda sat on a packing case and watched him. Already she felt comforted. Of course Peter was a rock, of course anyone could trust him, and of course if the tempest of life beat upon her too strongly she could always fly to Peter.

"May I?" she inquired, stretching her hand in the direction of a sheet.

"Sure," said Peter.

"What is it?" inquired Linda lightly. "The bridge or the road or the playroom?"

"Gad!" he said slowly. "Don't talk about me being a rock! Rocks are stolid, stodgy unresponsive things. I thought I was struggling with one of the biggest political problems of the day from an economic and psychological standpoint. If I'd had sense enough to realize that it was a bridge I was building, I might have done the thing with some imagination and subtlety. If you want a rock and you say I am a rock, a rock I'll be, Linda. But I know what you are, and what you will be to me when we really become the kind of friends we are destined to be."

"I wonder now," said Linda, "if you are going to say that I could be any such lovely thing on the landscape as a bridge."

"No," said Peter slowly, "nothing so prosaic. Bridges are common in this world. You are going to be something uncommon. History records the experiences of but one man who has seen a flame in the open. I am a second Moses and you are going to be my burning bush. I intended to read this article to you."

Peter massed the sheets, straightened them on the desk, and deliberately ripped them across several times. Linda sprang to her feet and stretched out her hands.

"Why, Peter!" she cried in a shocked voice. "That is perfectly inexcusable. There are hours and hours of work on that, and I have not a doubt but that it was good work."

"Simple case of mechanism," said Peter, reducing the bits to smaller size and dropping them into the empty nail keg that served as his wastebasket. "A lifeless thing without a soul, mere clockwork. I have got the idea now. I am to build a bridge and make a road. Every way I look I can see a golden-flame tongue of inspiration burning. I'll rewrite that thing and animate it. Take me for a ride, Linda."

Linda rose and walked to the Bear Cat. Peter climbed in and sat beside her. Linda laid her hands on the steering wheel and started the car. She ran it down to the highway and chose a level road leading straight down the valley through cultivated country. In all the world there was nothing to equal the panorama that she spread before Peter that evening. She drove the Bear Cat past orchards, hundreds of acres of orchards of waxen green leaves and waxen white bloom of orange, grapefruit, and lemon. She took him where seas of pink outlined peach orchards, and other seas the more delicate tint of the apricots. She glided down avenues lined with palm and eucalyptus, pepper and olive, and through unbroken rows, extending for miles, of roses, long stretches of white, again a stretch of pink, then salmon, yellow, and red. Nowhere in all the world are there to be found so many acres of orchard bloom and so many miles of tree-lined, rose-decorated roadway as in southern California. She sent the little car through the evening until she felt that it was time to go home, and when at last she stopped where they had started, she realized that neither she nor Peter had spoken one word. As he stepped from the car she leaned toward him and reached out her hand.

"Thank you for the fireplace, Peter," she said.

Peter took the hand she extended and held it one minute in both his own. Then very gently he straightened it out in the palm of one of his hands and with the other hand turned back the fingers and laid his lips to the heart of it.

"Thank you, Linda, for the flame," he said, and turning abruptly, he went toward his workroom.

Stopping for a bite to eat in the kitchen, Linda went back to her room. She sat down at the table and picking up her pencil, began to work, and found that she could work. Every stroke came true and strong. Every idea seemed original and unusual. Quite as late as a light ever had shone in her window, it shone that night, the last thing she did being to write another anonymous letter to Marian, and when she reread it Linda realized that it was an appealing letter. She thought it certainly would comfort Marian and surely would make her feel that someone worth while was interested in her and in her work. She loved some of the whimsical little touches she had put into it, and she wondered if she had made it so much like Peter Morrison that it would be suggestive of him to Marian. She knew that she had no right to do that and had no such intention. She merely wanted a model to copy from and Peter seemed the most appealing model at hand.

After school the next day Linda reported that she had finished going through the books and was ready to have them taken. Then, after a few minutes of deep thought, she made her way to the Consolidated Bank. At the window of the paying teller she explained that she wished to see the person connected with the bank who had charge of the safety-deposit boxes and who looked after the accounts pertaining to the estate of Alexander Strong. The teller recognized the name. He immediately became deferential.

"I'll take you to the office of the president," he said. "He and Doctor Strong were very warm friends. You can explain to him what it is you want to know."

Before she realized what was happening, Linda found herself in an office that was all mahogany and marble. At a huge desk stacked with papers sat a man, considerably older than her father. Linda remembered to have seen him frequently in their home, in her father's car, and she recalled one fishing expedition to the Tulare Lake region where he had been a member of her father's party.

"Of course you have forgotten me, Mr. Worthington," she said as she approached his desk. "I have grown such a tall person during the past four years."

The white-haired financier rose and stretched out his hand.

"You exact replica of Alexander Strong," he said laughingly, "I couldn't forget you any more than I could forget your father. That fine fishing trip where you proved such a grand little scout is bright in my memory as one of my happiest vacations. Sit down and tell me what I can do for you."

Linda sat down and told him that she was dissatisfied with the manner in which her father's estate was being administered.

He listened very carefully to all she had to say, then he pressed a button and gave a few words of instruction to the clerk who answered it. When several ledgers and account books were laid before him, with practiced hand he turned to what he wanted. The records were not complicated. They covered a period of four years. They showed exactly what monies had been paid into the bank for the estate. They showed what royalties had been paid on the books. Linda sat beside him and watched his pencil running up and down columns, setting down a list of items, and making everything plain. Paid cheques for household expenses I and drygoods bills were all recorded and deducted. With narrow, alert eyes, Linda was watching, and her brain was keenly alive. As she realized the discrepancy between the annual revenue from the estate and the totaling of the expenses, she had an inspiration. Something she never before had thought of occurred to her. She looked the banker in the eye and said very quietly: "And now, since she is my sister and I am going to be of age very shortly and these things must all be gone into and opened up, would it be out of place for me to ask you this afternoon to let me have a glimpse at the private account of Miss Eileen Strong?"

The banker drew a deep breath and looked at Linda keenly.

"That would not be customary," he said slowly.

"No?" said Linda. "But since Father and Mother went out at the same time and there was no will and the property would be legally divided equally between us upon my coming of age, would my sister be entitled to a private account?"

"Had she any sources of obtaining money outside the estate?"

"No," said Linda. "At least none that I know of. Mother had I some relatives in San Francisco who were very wealthy people, but they never came to see us and we never went there. I know nothing about them. I never had any money from them and I am quite sure Eileen never had."

Linda sat very quietly a minute and then she looked at the banker.

"Mr. Worthington," she said, "the situation is slightly peculiar. My guardian, John Gilman, is engaged to marry my sister Eileen. She is a beautiful girl, as you no doubt recall, and he is very much in love with her. Undoubtedly she has been able, at least recently, to manage affairs very much in her own way. She is more than four years my senior, and has always had charge of the household accounts and the handling of the bank accounts. Since there is such a wide discrepancy between the returns from the property and the expenses that these books show, I am forced to the conclusion that there must be upon your books, or the books of some other bank in the city, a private account in Eileen's name or in the name of the Strong estate."

"That I can very easily ascertain," said Mr. Worthington, reaching again toward the button on his desk. A few minutes later the report came that there was a private account in the name of Miss Eileen Strong. Again Linda was deeply thoughtful.

"Is there anything I can do," she inquired, "to prevent that account from being changed or drawn out previous to my coming of age?"

Then Mr. Worthington grew thoughtful.

"Yes," he said at last. "If you are dissatisfied, if you feel that you have reason to believe that money rightfully belonging to you is being diverted to other channels, you have the right to issue an injunction against the bank, ordering it not to pay out any further money on any account nor to honor any cheques drawn by Miss Strong until the settlement of the estate. Ask your guardian to execute and deliver such an injunction, or merely ask him, as your guardian and the administrator of the estate, to give the bank a written order to that effect."

"But because he is engaged to Eileen, I told him I would not bring him into this matter," said Linda. "I told him that I would do what I wanted done, myself."

"Well, how long is it until this coming birthday of yours?" inquired Mr. Worthington.

"Less than two weeks," answered Linda.

For a time the financier sat in deep thought, then he looked at Linda. It was a keen, searching look. It went to the depths of her eyes; it included her face and hair; it included the folds of her dress, the cut of her shoe, and rested attentively on the slender hands lying quietly in her lap.

"I see the circumstances very clearly," he said. "I sympathize with your position. Having known your father and being well acquainted with your guardian, would you be satisfied if I should take the responsibility of issuing to the clerks an order not to allow anything to be drawn from the private account until the settlement of the estate?"

"Perfectly satisfied," said Linda.

"It might be," said Mr. Worthington, "managing matters i that way, that no one outside of ourselves need ever know of il Should your sister not draw on the private account in the mean time, she would be free to draw household cheques on the monthly income and if in the settlement of the estate she turns in this private account or accounts, she need never know of the restriction concerning this fund."

"Thank you very much," said Linda. "That will fix everything finely."

On her way to the street car, Linda's brain whirled.

"It's not conceivable," she said, "that Eileen should be enriching herself at my expense. I can't imagine her being dishonest in money affairs, and yet I can recall scarcely a circumstance in life in which Eileen has ever hesitated to be dishonest when a lie served her purpose better than the truth. Anyway, matters are safe now."

The next day the books were taken and a cheque for their value was waiting for Linda when she reached home. She cashed this cheque and went straight to Peter Morrison for his estimate of the expenses for the skylight and fireplace. When she asked for the bill Peter hesitated.

"You wouldn't accept this little addition to your study as a gift from Henry and me?" he asked lightly. "It would be a great pleasure to us if you would."

"I could accept stones that Henry Anderson had gathered from the mountains and canyons, and I could accept a verse carved on stone, and be delighted with the gift; but I couldn't accept hours of day labor at the present price of labor, so you will have to give me the bill, Peter."

Peter did not have the bill, but he had memoranda, and when Linda paid him she reflected that the current talk concerning the inflated price of labor was greatly exaggerated.

For two evenings as Linda returned from school and went to her room she glanced down the hall and smiled at the decoration remaining on Eileen's rug. The third evening it was gone, so that she knew Eileen was either in her room or had been there. She did not meet her sister until dinnertime. She was prepared to watch Eileen, to study her closely. She was not prepared to admire her, but in her heart she almost did that very thing. Eileen had practiced subterfuges so long, she was so accomplished, that it would have taken an expert to distinguish reality from subterfuge. She entered the dining room humming a gay tune. She was carefully dressed and appealingly beautiful. She blew a kiss to Linda and waved gaily to Katy.

"I was rather afraid," she said lightly, "that I might find you two in mourning when I got back. I never stayed so long before, did I? Seemed as if every friend I had made special demand on my time all at once. Hope you haven't been dull without me."

"Oh, no," said Linda quietly. "Being away at school all day, of course I wouldn't know whether you were at home or not, and I have grown so accustomed to spending my evenings alone that I don't rely on you for entertainment at any time."

"In other words," said Eileen, "it doesn't make any difference to you where I am."

"Not so far as enjoying your company is concerned," said Linda. "Otherwise, of course it makes a difference. I hope you had a happy time."

"Oh, I always have a happy time," answered Eileen lightly. "I certainly have the best friends."

"That's your good fortune," answered Linda.

At the close of the meal Linda sat waiting. Eileen gave Katy instructions to have things ready for a midnight lunch for her and John Gilman and then, humming her tune again, she left the dining room and went upstairs. Linda stood looking after her.

"Now or never," she said at last. "I have no business to let her meet John until I have recovered my self-respect. But the Lord help me to do the thing decently!"

64

So she followed Eileen up the stairway. She tapped at the door, and without waiting to hear whether she was invited or not, opened it and stepped inside. Eileen was sitting before the window, a big box of candy beside her, a magazine in her fingers.

Evidently she intended to keep her temper in case the coming interview threatened to become painful.

"I was half expecting you," she said, "you silly hothead. I found the cheque I wrote you when I got home this afternoon. That was a foolish thing to do. Why did you tear it up? If it were too large or if it were not enough why didn't you use it and ask for another? Because I had to be away that was merely to leave you something to go on until I got back."

Then Linda did the most disconcerting thing possible. In her effort at self-control she went too far. She merely folded her hands in her lap and sat looking straight at Eileen without saying one word. It did not show much on the surface, but Eileen really had a conscience, she really had a soul; Linda's eyes, resting rather speculatively on her, were honest eyes, and Eileen knew what she knew. She flushed and fidgeted, and at last she broke out impatiently: "Oh, for goodness' sake, Linda, don't play 'Patience-on-a-monument.' Speak up and say what it is that you want. If that cheque was not big enough, what will satisfy you?"

"Come to think of it," said Linda quietly, "I can get along with what I have for the short time until the legal settlement of our interests is due. You needn't bother any more about a cheque."

Eileen was surprised and her face showed it; and she was also relieved. That too her face showed.

"I always knew," she said lightly, "that I had a little sister with a remarkably level head and good common sense. I am glad that you recognize the awful inflation of prices during the war period, and how I have had to skimp and scheme and save in order to make ends meet and to keep us going on Papa's meager income."

All Linda's good resolutions vanished. She was under strong nervous tension. It irritated her to have Eileen constantly referring to their monetary affairs as if they were practically paupers, as if their father's life had been a financial failure, as if he had not been able to realize from achievements recognized around the world a comfortable living for two women.

"Oh, good Lord!" she said shortly. "Bluff the rest of the world like a professional, Eileen, but why try it with me? You're right about my having common sense. I'll admit that I am using it now. I will be of age in a few days, and then we'll take John Gilman and go to the Consolidated Bank, and if it suits your convenience to be absent for four or five days at that period, I'll take John Gilman and we'll go together."

Eileen was amazed. The receding color in her cheeks left the rouge on them a ghastly, garish thing.

"Well, I won't do anything of the sort," she said hotly, "and neither will John Gilman."

"Unfortunately for you," answered Linda, "John Gilman is my guardian, not yours. He'll be forced to do what the law says he must, and what common decency tells him he must, no matter what his personal feelings are; and I might as well tell you that your absence has done you no good. You'd far better have come home, as you agreed to, and gone over the books and made me a decent allowance, because in your absence John came here to ask me where you were, and I know that he was anxious."

"He came here!" cried Eileen.

"Why, yes," said Linda. "Was it anything unusual? Hasn't he been coming here ever since I can remember? Evidently you didn't keep him as well posted this time as you usually do. He came here and asked for me."

"And I suppose," said Eileen, an ugly red beginning to rush into her white cheeks, "that you took pains to make things uncomfortable for me."

"I am very much afraid," said Linda, "that you are right. You have made things uncomfortable for me ever since I can remember, for I can't remember the time when you were not finding fault with me, putting me in the wrong and getting me criticized and punished if you possibly could. It was a fair understanding that you should be here, and you were not, and I was seeing red about it; and just as John came in I found your note in the living room and read it aloud.'

"Oh, well, there was nothing in that," said Eileen in a relieved tone.

"Nothing in the wording of it, no," said Linda, "but there was everything in the intention back of it. Because you did not live up to your tacit agreement, and because I had been on high tension for two or three days, I lost my temper completely. I brought John Gilman up here and showed him the suite of rooms in which you have done for yourself, for four years. I gave him rather a thorough inventory of your dressing table and drawers, and then I opened the closet door and called his attention to the number and the quality of the garments hanging there. The box underneath them I thought was a shoe box, but it didn't prove to be exactly that; and for that I want to tell you, as I have already told John, I am sorry. I wouldn't have done that if I had known what I was doing."

"Is that all?" inquired Eileen, making a desperate effort at self-control.

"Not quite," said Linda. "When I finished with your room, I took him back and showed him mine in even greater detail than I showed him yours. I thought the contrast would be more enlightening than anything either one of us could say."

"And I suppose you realize," said Eileen bitterly, "that you lost me John Gilman when you did it."

"I?" said Linda. "I lost you John Gilman when I did it? But I didn't do it. You did it. You have been busy for four years doing it. If you hadn't done it, it wouldn't have been there for me to show him. I can't see that this is profitable. Certainly it's the most distressing thing that ever has occurred for me. But I didn't feel that I could let you meet John Gilman tonight without telling you what he knows. If you have any way to square your conscience and cleanse your soul before you meet him, you had better do it, for he's a mighty fine man and if you lose him you will have lost the best chance that is likely ever to come to you."

Linda sat studying Eileen. She saw the gallant effort she was making to keep her self-possession, to think with her accustomed rapidity, to strike upon some scheme whereby she could square herself. She rose and started toward the door.

"What you'll say to John I haven't the faintest notion," she said. "I told him very little. I just showed him."

Then she went out and closed the door after her. At the foot of the stairs she met Katy admitting Gilman. Without any preliminaries she said: "I repeat, John, that I'm sorry for what happened the other day. I have just come from Eileen. She will be down as soon as Katy tells her you're here, no doubt. I have done what I told you I would. She knows what I showed you so you needn't employ any subterfuges. You can be frank and honest with each other."

"I wish to God we could," said John Gilman.

Linda went to her work. She decided that she would gauge what happened by the length of time John stayed. If he remained only a few minutes it would indicate that there had been a rupture. If he stayed as long as he usually did, the chances were that Eileen's wit had triumphed as usual.

At twelve o'clock Linda laid her pencils in the box, washed the brushes, and went down the back stairs to the ice chest for a glass of milk. The living room was still lighted and Linda thought Eileen's laugh quite as gay as she ever had heard it. Linda closed her lips very tight and slowly climbed the stairs. When she entered her room she walked up to the mirror and stared at herself in the glass for a long time, and then of herself she asked this question:

"Well, how do you suppose she did it?"

CHAPTER XVIII. Spanish Iris

Just as Linda was most deeply absorbed with her own concerns there came a letter from Marian which Linda read and reread several times; for Marian wrote:

MY DEAREST PAL:

Life is so busy up San Francisco way that it makes Lilac Valley look in retrospection like a peaceful sunset preliminary to bed time.

But I want you to have the consolation and the comfort of knowing that I have found at least two friends that I hope will endure. One is a woman who has a room across the hall from mine in my apartment house. She is a newspaper woman and life is very full for her, but it is filled with such intensely interesting things that I almost regret having made my life work anything so prosaic as inanimate houses; but then it's my dream to enliven each house I plan with at least the spirit of home. This woman—her name is Dana Meade—enlivens every hour of her working day with something concerning the welfare of humanity. She is a beautiful woman in her soul, so extremely beautiful that I can't at this minute write you a detailed description of her hair and her eyes and her complexion, because this nice, big, friendly light that radiates from her so lights her up and transfigures her that everyone says how beautiful she is, and yet I have a vague recollection that her nose is what you would call a "beak," and I am afraid her cheek bones are too high for good proportion, and I know that her hair is not always so carefully dressed as it should be, but what is the difference when the hair is crowned with a halo? I can't swear to any of these things; they're sketchy impressions. The only thing I am absolutely sure about is the inner light that shines to an unbelievable degree. I wish she had more time and I wish I had more time and that she and I might become such friends as you and I are. I can't tell you, dear, how much I think of you. It seems to me that you're running a sort of undercurrent in my thoughts all day long.

You will hardly credit it, Linda, but a few days ago I drove a car through the thickest traffic, up a steep hill, and round a curve. I did it, but practically collapsed when it was over. The why of it was this: I think I told you before that in the offices of Nicholson and Snow there is a man who is an understanding person. He is the junior partner and his name is Eugene Snow. I happened to arrive at his desk the day I came for my instructions and to make my plans for entering their contest. He was very kind to me and went out of his way to smooth out the rough places. Ever since, he makes a point of coming to me and talking a few minutes when I am at the office or when he passes me on my way to the drafting rooms where I take my lessons. The day I mention I had worked late and hard the night before. I had done the last possible thing to the plans for my dream house. At the last minute, getting it all on paper, working at the specifications, at which you know I am wobbly, was nervous business; and when I came from the desk after having turned in my plans, perhaps I showed fatigue. Anyway, he said to me that his car was below. He said also that he was a lonely person, having lost his wife two years ago, and not being able very frequently to see his little daughter who is in the care of her grandmother, there were times when he was hungry for the companionship he had lost. He asked me if I would go with him for a drive and I told him that I would. I am rather stunned yet over what happened. The runabout he led me to was greatly like yours, and, Linda, he stopped at a florist's and came out with an armload of bloom—exquisite lavender and pale pink and faint yellow and waxen white—the most enticing armload of spring. For one minute I truly experienced a thrill. I thought he was going to give that mass of flowers to me, but he did not. He merely laid it across my lap and said: "Edith adored the flowers from bulbs. I never see such bloom that my heart does not ache with a keen, angry ache to think that she should be taken from the world, and the beauty that she so loved, so early and so ruthlessly. We'll take her these as I would take them to her were she living."

So, Linda dear, I sat there and looked at color and drank in fragrance, and we whirled through the city and away to a cemetery on a beautiful hill, and filled a vase inside the gates of a mausoleum with these appealing flowers. Then we sat down, and a man with a hurt heart told me about his hurt, and what an effort he was making to get through the world as the woman he loved would have had him; and before I knew what I was doing, Linda, I told him the tellable part of my own hurts. I even lifted my turban and bowed my white head before him. This hurt—it was one of the inexorable things that come to people in this world—I could talk about. That deeper hurt, which has put a scar that never will be effaced on my soul, of course I could not tell him about. But when we went back to the car he said to me that he would help me to get back into the sunlight. He said the first thing I must do to regain self-confidence was to begin driving again. I told him I could not, but he said I must, and made me take the driver's seat of a car I had never seen and take the steering wheel of a make of machine I had never driven, and tackle two or three serious problems for a driver. I did it all right, Linda, because I couldn't allow myself to fail the kind of a man Mr. Snow is, when he was truly trying to help me, but in the depths of my heart I am afraid I am a coward forever, for there is a ghastly illness takes possession of me as I write these details to you. But anyway, put a red mark on your calendar beside the date on which you get this letter, and joyfully say to yourself that Marian has found two real, sympathetic friends.

In a week or ten days I shall know about the contest. If I win, as I really have a sneaking hope that I shall, since I have condensed the best of two dozen houses into one and exhausted my imagination on my dream home, I will surely telegraph, and you can make it a day of jubilee. If I fail, I will try to find out where my dream was not true and what can be done to make it materialize properly; but between us, Linda girl, I am going to be dreadfully disappointed. I could use the material value that prize represents. I could start my life work which I hope to do in Lilac Valley on the prestige and the background that it would give me. I don't know, Linda, whether you ever learned to pray or not, but I have, and it's a thing that helps when the black shadow comes, when you reach the land of "benefits forgot and friends remembered not."

And this reminds me that I should not write to my very dearest friend who has her own problems and make her heart sad with mine; so to the joyful news of my two friends add a third, Linda, for I am going to tell you a secret because it will make you happy. Since I have been in San Francisco some man, who for a reason of his own does not tell me his name, has been writing me extremely attractive letters. I have had several of them and I can't tell you, Linda, what they mean to me or how they help me. There is a touch of whimsy about them. I can't as yet connect them with anybody I ever met, but to me they are taking the place of a little lunch on the bread of life. They are such real, such vivid, such alive letters from such a real person that I have been doing the very foolish and romantic thing of answering them as my heart dictates and signing my own name to them, which on the surface looks unwise when the man in the case keeps his identity in the background; but since he knows me and knows my name it seems useless to do anything else: and answer these letters I shall and must; because every one of them is to me a strong light thrown on John Gilman. Every time one of these letters comes to me I have the feeling that I would like to reach out through space and pick up the man who is writing them and dangle him before Eileen and say to her: "Take HIM. I dare you to take HIM." And my confidence, Linda, is positively supreme that she could not do it.

You know, between us, Linda, we regarded Eileen as a rare creature, a kind of exotic thing, made to be kept in a glass house with tempered air and warmed water; but as I go about the city and at times amuse myself at concerts and theaters, I am rather dazed to tell you, honey, that the world is chock full of Eileens. On the streets, in the stores, everywhere I go, sometimes half a dozen times in a day I say to myself: "There goes Eileen." I haven't a doubt that Eileen has a heart, if it has not become so calloused that nobody could ever reach it, and I suspect she has a soul, but the more I see of her kind the more I feel that John Gilman may have to breast rather black water before he finds them.

With dearest love, be sure to remember me to Katherine O'Donovan. Hug her tight and give her my unqualified love. Don't let her forget me.

As ever,

MARIAN.

This was the letter that Linda read once, then she read it again and then she read it a third time, and after that she lost count and reread it whenever she was not busy doing something else, for it was a letter that was the next thing to laying hands upon Marian. The part of the letter concerning the unknown man who was writing Marian, Linda pondered over deeply.

"That is the best thing I ever did in my life," she said in self-commendation. "It's doing more than I hoped it would. It's giving Marian something to think about. It's giving her an interest in life. It's distracting her attention. Without saying a word about John Gilman it is making her see for herself the weak spots in him through the very subtle method of calling her attention to the strength that may lie in another man. For once in your life, Linda, you have done something strictly worth while. The thing for you to do is to keep it up, and in order to keep it up, to make each letter fresh and original, you will have to do a good deal of sticking around Peter Morrison's location and absorbing rather thoroughly the things he says. Peter doesn't know he is writing those letters but he is in them till it's a wonder Marian does not hear him drawl and see the imps twisting his lips as she reads them. Before I write another single one I'll go see Peter. Maybe he will have that article written. I'll take a pencil, and as he reads I'll jot down the salient points and then I'll come home and work out a head and tail piece for him to send in with it, and in that way I'll ease my soul about the skylight and the fireplace."

So Linda took pad and pencils, raided Katy for everything she could find that was temptingly edible, climbed into the Bear Cat, and went to see Peter as frankly as she would have crossed the lawn to visit Marian. He was not in the garage when she stopped her car before it, but the workmen told her that he had strolled up the mountain and that probably he would return soon. Learning that he had been gone but a short time Linda set the Bear Cat squalling at the top of its voice. Then she took possession of the garage, and clearing Peter's worktable spread upon it the food she had brought, and then started out to find some flowers for decorations. When Peter came upon the scene he found Linda, flushed and brilliant eyed, holding before him a big bouquet of alder bloom, the last of the lilacs she had found in a cool, shaded place, pink filaree, blue lupin, and white mahogany panicles. "Peter," she cried. "you can't guess what I have been doing!"

Peter glanced at the flowers.

"Isn't it obvious?" he inquired.

"No, it isn't," said Linda, "because I am capable of two processes at once. The work of my hands is visible; with it I am going to decorate your table. You won't have to go down to the restaurant for your supper tonight because I have brought my supper up to share with you, and after we finish, you're going to read me your article as you have rewritten it. I am going to decorate it and we are going to make a hit with it that will be at least a start on the road to greater fame. What you see is material. You can pick it up, smell it, admire it and eat it. But what I have truly been doing is setting Spanish iris for yards down one side of the bed of your stream. When I left it was a foot and a half high Peter, and every blue that the sky ever knew in its loveliest moments, and a yellow that is the concentrated essence of the best gold from the heart of California. Oh, Peter, there is enchantment in the way I set it. There are irregular deep beds, and there are straggly places where there are only one or two in a ragged streak, and then it runs along the edge in a fringy rim, and then it stretches out in a marshy place that is going to have some other wild things, arrowheads, and orchids, and maybe a bunch of paint brush on a high, dry spot near by. I wish you could see it!"

Peter looked at Linda reflectively and then he told her that he could see it. He fold her that he adored it, that he was crazy about her straggly continuity and her fringy border, but there was not one word of truth in what he said, because what he saw was a slender thing, willowy, graceful; roughened wavy black hair hanging half her length in heavy braids, dark eyes and bright cheeks, a vivid red line of mouth, and a bright brown line of freckles bridging a prominent and aristocratic nose. What he was seeing was a soul, a young thing, a thing he coveted with every nerve and fiber of his being. And while he glibly humored her in her vision of decorating his brook, in his own consciousness he was saying to himself: "Is there any reason why I should not try for her?"

And then he answered himself. "There is no reason in your life. There is nothing ugly that could offend her or hurt her. The reason, the real reason, probably lies in the fact that if she were thinking of caring for anyone it would be for that attractive young schoolmate she brought up here for me to exercise my wits upon. It is very likely that she regards me in the light of a grandfatherly person to whom she can come with her joys or her problems, as frankly as she has now."

So Peter asked if the irises crossed the brook and ran down both sides. Linda sat on a packing case and concentrated on the iris, and finally she announced that they did. She informed him that his place was going to be natural, that Nature evolved things in her own way. She did not grow irises down one side of a brook and arrowheads down the other. They waded across and flew across and visited back and forth, riding the water or the wind or the down of a bee or the tail of a cow. As she served the supper she had brought she very gravely informed him that there would be iris on both sides of his brook, and cress and miners' lettuce under the bridge; and she knew exactly where the wild clematis grew that would whiten his embankment after his workmen had extracted the last root of poison oak.

"It may not scorch you, Peter," she said gravely, "but you must look out for the Missus and the little things. I haven't definitely decided on her yet, but she looks a good deal like Mary Louise Whiting to me. I saw her the other day. She came to school after Donald. I liked her looks so well that I said to myself: 'Everybody talks about how fine she is. I shouldn't wonder if I had better save her for Peter'; but if I decide to, you should act that poison stuff out, because it's sure as shooting to attack any one with the soft, delicate skin that goes with a golden head."

"Oh, let's leave it in," said Peter, "and dispense with the golden head. By the time you get that stream planted as you're planning, I'll have become so accustomed to a dark head bobbing up and down beside it that I won't take kindly to a sorrel top." "That is positively sacrilegious," said Linda, lifting her hands to her rough black hair. "Never in my life saw anything lovelier than the rich gold on Louise Whiting's bare head as she bent to release her brakes and start her car. A black head looks like a cinder bed beside it; and only think what a sunburst it will be when Mary Louise kneels down beside the iris."

When they had finished their supper Linda gathered up the remnants and put them in the car, then she laid a notebook and pencil on the table.

"Now I want to hear that article," she said. "I knew you would do it over the minute I was gone, and I knew you would keep it to read to me before you sent it."

"Hm," said Peter. "Is it second sight or psychoanalysis or telepathy, or what?"

"Mostly 'what'," laughed Linda. "I merely knew. The workmen are gone and everything is quiet now, Peter. Begin. I am crazy to get the particular angle from which you 'make the world safe for democracy.' John used to call our attention to your articles during the war. He said we had not sent another man to France who could write as humanely and as interestingly as you did. I wish I had kept those articles; because I didn't get anything from them to compare with what I can get since I have a slight acquaintance with the procession that marches around your mouth. Peter, you will have to watch that mouth of yours. It's an awfully betraying feature. So long as it's occupied with politics and the fads and the foibles and the sins and the foolishness and the extravagances of humanity, it's all very well. But if you ever get in trouble or if ever your heart hurts, or you get mad enough to kill somebody, that mouth of yours is going to be a most awfully revealing feature, Peter. You will have hard work to settle it down into hard-and-fast noncommittal lines."

Peter looked at the girl steadily.

"Have you specialized on my mouth?" he asked.

"Huh-umph!" said Linda, shaking her head vigorously. "When I specialize I use a pin and a microscope and go right to the root of matters as I was taught. This is superficial. I am extemporizing now."

"Well, if this is extemporizing," said Peter, "God help my soul if you ever go at me with a pin and a microscope."

"Oh, but I won't!" cried Linda. "It wouldn't be kind to pin your friends on a setting board and use a microscope on them. You might see things that were strictly private. You might see things they wouldn't want you to see. They might not be your friends any more if you did that. When I make a friend I just take him on trust like I did Donald. You're my friend, aren't you, Peter?"

"Yes, Linda," said Peter soberly. "Put me to any test you can think of if you want proof."

"But I don't believe in PROVING friends, either," said Linda. "I believe in nurturing them. I would set a friend in my garden and water his feet and turn the sunshine on him and tell him to stay there and grow. I might fertilize him, I might prune him, and I might use insecticide on him. I might spray him with rather stringent solutions, but I give you my word I would not test him. If he flourished under my care I would know it, and if he did not I would know it, and that would be all I would want to know. I have watched Daddy search for the seat of nervous disorders, and sometimes he had to probe very deep to find what developed nerves unduly but he didn't ever do any picking and raveling and fringing at the soul of a human being merely for the sake of finding out what it was made of; and everyone says I am like him."

"I wish I might have known him," said Peter.

"Don't I wish it!" said Linda. "Now then, Peter, go ahead. Read your article."

Peter opened a packing case, picked out a sheaf of papers, and sitting opposite Linda, began to read. He was dumbfounded to find that he, a man who had read and talked extemporaneously before great bodies of learned men, should have cold feet and shaking hands and a hammering heart because he was trying to read an article on America for Americans before a high-school Junior. But presently, as the theme engrossed him, he forgot the vision of Linda interesting herself in his homemaking, and saw instead a vision of his country threatened on one side by the red menace of the Bolshevik, on the other by the yellow menace of the Jap, and yet on another by the treachery of the Mexican and the slowly uprising might of the black man, and presently he was thundering his best-considered arguments at Linda until she imperceptibly drew back from him on the packing case, and with parted lips and wide eyes she listened in utter absorption. She gazed at a transformed Peter with aroused eyes and a white light of patriotism on his forehead, and a conception even keener than anything that the war had brought her young soul was burning in her heart of what a man means when he tries to express his feeling concerning the land of his birth. Presently, without realizing what she was doing, she reached for her pad and pencils and rapidly began sketching a stretch of peaceful countryside over which a coming storm of gigantic proportions was gathering. Fired by Peter's article, the touch of genius in Linda's soul became creative and she fashioned huge storm clouds wind driven, that floated in such a manner as to bring the merest suggestion of menacing faces, black faces, yellow faces, brown faces, and under the flash of lightning, just at the obscuring of the sun, a huge, evil, leering red face. She swept a stroke across her sheet and below this she began again, sketching the same stretch of country she had pictured above, strolling in cultivated fields, dotting it with white cities, connecting it with smooth roadways, sweeping the sky with giant planes. At one side, winging in from the glow of morning, she drew in the strong-winged flight of a flock of sea swallows, peacefully homing toward the far-distant ocean. She was utterly unaware when Peter stopped reading. Absorbed, she bent over her work. When she had finished she looked up.

"Now I'll take this home," she said. "I can't do well on color with pencils. You hold that article till I have time to put this on water-color paper and touch it up a bit here and there, and I believe it will be worthy of starting and closing your article."

She pushed the sketches toward him.

"You little wonder!" said Peter softly.

"Yes, 'little' is good," scoffed Linda, rising to very nearly his height and reaching for the lunch basket. "'Little' is good, Peter. If I could do what I like to myself I would get in some kind of a press and squash down about seven inches."

"Oh, Lord!" said Peter. "Forget it. What's the difference what the inches of your body are so long as your brain has a stature worthy of mention?"

"Good-bye!" said Linda. "On the strength of that I'll jazz that sketch all up, bluey and red-purple and jade-green. I'll make it as glorious as a Catalina sunset."

As she swung the car around the sharp curve at the boulders she looked back and laughingly waved her hand at Peter, and Peter experienced a wild desire to shriek lest she lose control of the car and plunge down the steep incline. A second later, when he saw her securely on the road below, he smiled to himself.

"Proves one thing," he said conclusively. "She is over the horrors. She is driving unconsciously. Thank God she knew that curve so well she could look the other way and drive it mentally."

CHAPTER XIX. The Official Bug-Catcher

Not a mile below the exit from Peter's grounds, Linda perceived a heavily laden person toiling down the roadway before her and when she ran her car abreast and stopped it, Henry Anderson looked up at her with joyful face.

"Sorry I can't uncover, fair lady," he said, "but you see I am very much otherwise engaged."

What Linda saw was a tired, disheveled man standing in the roadway beside her car, under each arm a boulder the size of her head, one almost jet-black, shot through with lines of white and flying figures of white crossing between these bands that almost reminded one of winged dancers. The other was a combination stone made up of matrix thickly imbedded with pebbles of brown, green, pink, and dull blue.

"For pity's sake!" said Linda. "Where are you going and why are you personally demonstrating a new method of transporting rock?"

"I am on my way down Lilac Valley to the residence of a friend of mine," said Henry Anderson. "I heard her say the other day that she saved every peculiarly marked boulder she could find to preserve coolness and moisture in her fern bed."

Linda leaned over and opened the car door.

"All well and good," she said; "but why in the cause of reason didn't you leave them at Peter's and bring them down in his car?"

Henry Anderson laid the stones in the bottom of the car, stepped in and closed the door behind him. He drew a handkerchief from his pocket and wiped his perspiring face and soiled hands.

"I had two sufficient personal reasons," he said. "One was that the car at our place is Peter Morrison's car, not mine; and the other was that it's none of anybody's business but my own if I choose to 'say it' with stones."

Linda started the car, being liberal with gas—so liberal that it was only a few minutes till Henry Anderson protested.

"This isn't the speedway," he said. "What's your hurry?"

"Two reasons seem to be all that are allowed for things at the present minute," answered Linda. "One of mine is that you can't drive this beast slow, and the other is that my workroom is piled high with things I should be doing. I have two sketches I must complete while I am in the mood, and I have had a great big letter from my friend, Marian Thorne, today that I want to answer before I go to bed tonight."

"In other words," said Henry Anderson bluntly, "you want me to understand that when I have reached your place and dumped these stones I can beat it; you have no further use for me."

"You said that," retorted Linda.

"And who ever heard of such a thing," said Henry, "as a young woman sending away a person of my numerous charms and attractions in order to work, or to write a letter to another woman?"

"But you're not taking into consideration," said Linda, "that I must work, and I scarcely know you, while I have known Marian ever since I was four years old and she is my best friend."

"Well, she has no advantage over me," said Henry instantly, "because I have known you quite as long as Peter Morrison has at least, and I'm your official bug-catcher."

"I had almost forgotten about the bugs," said Linda.

"Well, don't for a minute think I am going to give you an opportunity to forget," said Henry Anderson.

He reached across and laid his hand over Linda's on the steering gear. Linda said nothing, neither did she move. She merely added more gas and put the Bear Cat forward at a dizzy whirl. Henry laughed.

"That's all right, my beauty," he said. "Don't you think for a minute that I can't ride as fast as you can drive."

A dull red mottled Linda's cheeks. As quickly as it could be done she brought the Bear Cat to a full stop. Then she turned and looked at Henry Anderson. The expression in her eyes was disconcerting even to that cheeky young individual—he had not borne her gaze a second until he removed his hand.

"Thanks," said Linda in a dry drawl. "And you will add to my obligation if in the future you will remember not to deal in assumptions. I am not your 'beauty,' and I'm not anyone's beauty; while the only thing in this world that I am interested in at present is to get the best education I can and at the same time carry on work that I love to do. I have a year to finish my course in the high school and when I finish I will only have a good beginning for whatever I decide to study next."

"That's nothing," said the irrepressible Henry. "It will take me two years to catch a sufficient number of gold bugs to be really serious, but there wouldn't be any harm in having a mutual understanding and something definite to work for, and then we might be able, you know, to cut out some of that year of high-school grinding. If the plans I have submitted in the Nicholson and Snow contest should just happen to be the prize winners, that would put matters in such a shape for young Henry that he could devote himself to crickets and tumble-bugs at once."

"Don't you think," said Linda quietly, "that you would better forget that silly jesting and concentrate the best of your brains on improving your plans for Peter Morrison's house?"

"Why, surely I will if that's what you command me to do," said Henry, purposely misunderstanding her.

"You haven't mentioned before," said Linda, "that you had submitted plans in that San Francisco contest."

"All done and gone," said Henry Anderson lightly. "I had an inspiration one day and I saw a way to improve a house with comforts and conveniences I never had thought of before. I was enthusiastic over the production when I got it on paper and figured it. It's exactly the house that I am going to build for Peter, and when I've cut my eye teeth on it I am going to correct everything possible and build it in perfection for you."

"Look here," said Linda soberly, "I'm not accustomed to this sort of talk. I don't care for it. If you want to preserve even the semblance of friendship with me you must stop it, and get to impersonal matters and stay there."

"All right," he agreed instantly, "but if you don't like my line of talk, you're the first girl I ever met that didn't."

"You have my sympathy," said Linda gravely. "You have been extremely unfortunate."

Then she started the Bear Cat, and again running at undue speed she reached her wild-flower garden. Henry Anderson placed the stones as she directed and waited for an invitation to come in, but the invitation was not given. Linda thanked him for the stones. She told him that in combination with a few remaining from the mantel they would make all she would require, and excusing herself she drove to the garage. When she came in she found the irrepressible Henry sitting on the back steps explaining to Katy the strenuous time he had had finding and carrying down the stones they had brought. Katy had a plate of refreshments ready to hand him when Linda laughingly passed them and went to her room.

When she had finished her letter to Marian she took a sheet of drawing paper, and in her most attractive lettering sketched in the heading, "A Palate Teaser," which was a direct quotation from Katy. Below she wrote:

You will find Tunas in the cacti thickets of any desert, but if you are so fortunate as to be able to reach specimens which were brought from Mexico and set as hedges around the gardens of the old missions, you will find there the material for this salad in its most luscious form. Naturally it can be made from either Opuntia Fiscus-Indica or Opuntia Tuna, but a combination of these two gives the salad an exquisite appearance and a tiny touch more delicious flavor, because Tuna, which is red, has to my taste a trifle richer and fuller flavor than Indica, which is yellow. Both fruits taste more like the best well-ripened watermelon than any other I recall.

Bring down the Tunas with a fishing rod or a long pole with a nail in the end. With anything save your fingers roll them in the sand or in tufts of grass to remove the spines. Slice off either end, score the skin down one side, press lightly, and a lush globule of pale gold or rosy red fruit larger than a hen's egg lies before you. With a sharp knife, beginning with a layer of red and ending with one of yellow, slice the fruits thinly, stopping to shake out the seeds as you work. In case you live in San Diego County or farther south, where it is possible to secure the scarlet berries of the Strawberry Cactus—it is the Mammillaria Goodridgei species that you should use—a beautiful decoration for finishing your salad can be made from the red strawberries of these. If you live too far north to find these, you may send your salad to the table beautifully decorated by cutting fancy figures from the red Tuna, or by slicing it lengthwise into oblong pieces and weaving them into a decoration over the yellow background.

For your dressing use the juice of a lemon mixed with that of an orange, sweetened to taste, into which you work, a drop at a time, four tablespoons of the best Palermo olive oil. If the salad is large more oil and more juice should be used.

To get the full deliciousness of this salad, the fruit must have been on ice, and the dressing made in a bowl imbedded in cracked ice, so that when ready to blend both are ice-cold, and must be served immediately.

Gigantic specimens of fruit-bearing Cacti can be found all over the Sunland Desert near to the city, but they are not possessed of the full flavor of the cultivated old mission growths, so that it is well worth your while to make a trip to the nearest of these for the fruit with which to prepare this salad. And if, as you gather it, you should see a vision of a white head, a thin, ascetic, old face, a lean figure trailing a brown robe, slender white hands clasping a heavy cross; if you should hear the music of worship ascending from the throats of Benedictine fathers leading a clamoring choir of the blended voices of Spaniard, Mexican, and Indian, combining with the music of the bells and the songs of the mocking birds, nest making among the Tunas, it will be good for your soul in the line of purging it from selfishness, since in this day we are not asked to give all of life to the service of others, only a reasonable part of it.

Linda read this over, working in changes here and there, then she picked up her pencil and across the top of her sheet indicated an open sky with scarcely a hint of cloud. Across the bottom she outlined a bit of Sunland Desert she well remembered, in the foreground a bed of flat-leaved nopal, flowering red and yellow, the dark red prickly pears, edible, being a near relative of the fruits she had used in her salad. After giving the prickly pear the place of honor to the left, in higher growth she worked in the slender, cylindrical, jointed stems of the Cholla, shading the flowers a paler, greenish yellow. On the right, balancing the Cholla, she drew the oval, cylindrical columns of the hedgehog cactus, and the color touch of the big magenta flowers blended exquisitely with the color she already had used. At the left, the length of her page, she drew a gigantic specimen of Opuntia Tuna, covered with flowers, and well-developed specimens of the pears whose coloring ran into the shades of the hedgehog cactus.

She was putting away her working materials when she heard steps and voices on the stairs, so knew that Eileen and John Gilman were coming. She did not in the least want them, yet she could think of no excuse for refusing them admission that would not seem ungracious. She hurried to the wall, snatched down the paintings for Peter Morrison, and looked around to see how she could dispose of them. She ended by laying one of them in a large drawer which she pushed shut and locked. The other she placed inside a case in the wall which formerly had been used for billiard cues. At their second tap she opened the door. Eileen was not at her best. There was a worried look across her eyes, a restlessness visible in her movements, but Gilman was radiant.

"What do you think, Linda?" he cried. "Eileen has just named the day!"

"I did no such thing," broke in Eileen.

"Your pardon, fair lady, you did not," said Gilman. "That was merely a figure of speech. I meant named the month. She has definitely promised in October, and I may begin to hunt a location and plan a home for us. I want the congratulations of my dear friend and my dearer sister."

Linda held out her hand and smiled as bravely as she could.

"I am very glad you are so pleased, John," she said quietly, "and I hope that you will be as happy as you deserve to be."

"Now exactly what do you mean by that?" he asked.

"Oh, Linda prides herself on being deep and subtle and conveying hidden meanings," said Eileen. "She means what a thousand people will tell you in the coming months: merely that they hope you will be happy."

"Of course," Linda hastened to corroborate, wishing if possible to avoid any unpleasantness.

"You certainly have an attractive workroom here," said John, "much as I hate to see it spoiled for billiards."

"It's too bad," said Linda, "that I have spoiled it for you for billiards. I have also spoiled the outside appearance of the house for Eileen."

"Oh, I don't know," said John. "I looked at it carefully the other day as I came up, and I thought your changes enhanced the value of the property."

"I am surely glad to hear that," said Linda. "Take a look through my skylight and my new window. Imagine you see the rugs I am going to have and a few more pieces of furniture when I can afford them; and let me particularly point out the fireplace that Henry Anderson and your friend Peter designed and had built for me. Doesn't it add a soul and a heart to my study?"

John Gilman walked over and looked at the fireplace critically. He read the lines aloud, then he turned to Eileen.

"Why, that is perfectly beautiful," he said. "Let's duplicate it in our home."

"You bungler!" scoffed Eileen.

"I think you're right," said Gilman reflectively, "exactly right. Of course I would have no business copying Linda's special fireplace where the same people would see it frequently; and if I had stopped to think a second, I might have known that you would prefer tiling to field stone."

"Linda seems very busy tonight," said Eileen. "Perhaps we are bothering her."

"Yes," said John, "we'll go at once. I had to run up to tell our good news; and I wanted to tell you too, Linda dear, that I think both of us misjudged Eileen the other day. You know, Linda, you have always dressed according to your father's ideas, which were so much simpler and plainer than the manner in which your mother dressed Eileen, that she merely thought that you wished to continue in his way. She had no objection to your having any kind of clothes you chose, if only you had confided in her, and explained to her what you wanted."

Linda stood beside her table, one lean hand holding down the letter she had been writing. She stood very still, but she was powerless to raise her eyes to the face of either John or Eileen. Above everything she did not wish to go any further in revealing Eileen to John Gilman. If he knew what he knew and if he felt satisfied, after what he had seen, with any explanation that Eileen could trump up to offer, Linda had no desire to carry the matter further. She had been ashamed of what she already had done. She had felt angry and dissatisfied with herself, so she stood before them downcast and silent.

"And it certainly was a great joke on both of us," said John jovially, "what we thought about that box of cigarettes, you know. They were a prize given by a bridge club at an 'Ambassador' benefit for the Good Samaritan Hospital. Eileen, the little card shark she is, won it, and she was keeping it hidden away there to use as a gift for my birthday. Since we disclosed her plans prematurely, she gave it to me at once, and I'm having a great time treating all my friends."

At that instant Linda experienced a revulsion. Previously she had not been able to raise her eyes. Now it would have been quite impossible to avoid looking straight into Eileen's face. But Eileen had no intention of meeting anyone's gaze at that minute. She was fidgeting with a sheet of drawing paper.

"Careful you don't bend that," cautioned Linda. Then she looked at John Gilman. He BELIEVED what he was saying; he was happy again. Linda evolved the best smile she could.

"How stupid of us not to have guessed!" she said.

Closing the door behind them, Linda leaned against it and looked up through the skylight at the creep blue of the night, the low-hung stars. How long she stood there she did not know. Presently she went to her chair, picked up her pencil, and slowly began to draw. At first she scarcely realized what she was doing, then she became absorbed in her work. Then she reached for her color box and brushes, and shortly afterward tacked against the wall an extremely clever drawing of a greatly enlarged wasp. Skillfully she had sketched a face that was recognizable round the big insect eyes. She had surmounted the face by a fluff of bejewelled yellow curls, encased the hind legs upon which the creature stood upright in pink velvet Turkish trousers and put tiny gold shoes on the feet. She greatly exaggerated the wings into long trails and made them of green gauze with ruffled edges. All the remainder of the legs she had transformed into so many braceleted arms, each holding a tiny fan, or a necklace, a jewel box, or a handkerchief of lace. She stood before this sketch, studying it for a few minutes, then she walked over to the table and came back with a big black pencil. Steadying her hand with a mahl stick rested against the wall, with one short sharp stroke she drew a needle-pointed stinger, so screened by the delicate wings that it could not be seen unless you scrutinized the picture minutely. After that, with careful, interested hands she brought out Peter Morrison's drawings and replaced them on the wall to dry.

CHAPTER XX. The Cap Sheaf

Toward the last of the week Linda began to clear the mental decks of her ship of life in order that she might have Saturday free for her promised day with Donald. She had decided that they would devote that day to wave-beaten Laguna. It was a long drive but delightful. It ran over the old King's Highway between miles of orange and lemon orchards in full flower, bordered by other miles of roses in their prime.

Every minute when her mind was not actively occupied with her lessons or her recipes Linda was dreaming of the King's Highway. Almost unconsciously she began to chant:

"All in the golden weather, forth let us ride today, You and I together on the King's Highway, The blue skies above us, and below the shining sea; There's many a road to travel, but it's this road for me."

You must have ridden this road with an understanding heart and the arm of God around you to know the exact degree of disappointment that swelled in Linda's heart when she answered the telephone early Saturday morning and heard Donald Whiting's strained voice speaking into it. He was talking breathlessly in eager, boyish fashion.

"Linda, I am in a garage halfway downtown," he was saying, "and it looks to me as if to save my soul I couldn't reach you before noon. I have had the darnedest luck. Our Jap got sick last week and he sent a new man to take his place. There wasn't a thing the matter with our car when I drove it in Friday night. This morning Father wanted to use it on important business, and it wouldn't run. He ordered me to tinker it up enough to get it to the shop. I went at it and when it would go, I started You can imagine the clip I was going, and the thing went to pieces. I don't know yet how it comes that I saved my skin. I'm pretty badly knocked out, but I'll get there by noon if it's a possible thing."

"Oh, that's all right," said Linda, fervently hoping that the ache in her throat would not tincture her voice.

It was half-past eleven when Donald came. Linda could not bring herself to give up the sea that day. She found it impossible to drive the King's Highway. It seemed equally impossible not to look on the face of the ocean, so she compromised by skirting Santa Monica Bay, and taking the foothill road she ran it to the north end of the beach drive. When they had spread their blankets on the sand, finished their lunch and were resting, Linda began to question Donald about what had happened. She wanted to know how long Whitings' gardener had been in their employ; if they knew where he lived and about his family; if they knew who his friends were, or anything concerning him. She inquired about the man who had taken his place, and wanted most particularly to know what the garage men had found the trouble with a car that ran perfectly on Friday night and broke down in half a dozen different places on Saturday morning. Finally Donald looked at her, laughingly quizzical.

"Linda," he said, "you're no nerve specialist and no naturalist. You're the cross examiner for the plaintiff. What are you trying to get at? Make out a case against Yogo Sani?"

"Of course it's all right," said Linda, watching a distant pelican turn head down and catapult into the sea. "It has to be all right, but you must admit that it looks peculiar. How have you been getting along this week?"

Donald waved his hand in the direction of a formation of stone the size of a small house.

"Been rolling that to the top of the mountain," he said lightly. Linda's eyes narrowed, her face grew speculative. She looked at Donald intently.

"Is it as difficult as that?" she asked in a lowered voice as if the surf and the sea chickens might hear.

"It is just as difficult as that," said Donald. "While you're talking about peculiar things, I'll tell you one. In class I came right up against Oka Sayye on the solution of a theorem in trigonometry. We both had the answer, the correct answer, but we had arrived at it by widely different routes, and it was up to me to prove that my line of reasoning was more lucid, more natural, the inevitable one by which the solution should be reached. We got so in earnest that I am afraid both of us were rather tense. I stepped over to his demonstration to point out where I thought his reasoning was wrong. I got closer to the Jap than I had ever been before; and by gracious, Linda! scattered, but nevertheless still there, and visible, I saw a sprinkling of gray hairs just in front of and over his ears. It caught me unawares, and before I knew what I was doing, before the professor and the assembled classroom I blurted it out: 'Say, Oka Sayye, how old are you?' If the Jap had had any way of killing me, I believe he would have done it. There was a look in his eyes that was what I would call deadly. It was only a flash and then, very courteously, putting me in the wrong, of course, he remarked that he was 'almost ninekleen'; and it struck me from his look and the way he said it that it was a lie. If he truly was the average age of the rest of the class there was nothing for him to be angry about. Then I did take a deliberate survey. From the settled solidity of his frame and the shape of his hands and the skin of his face and the set of his eyes in his head, I couldn't see that much youth. I'll bet he's thirty if he's a day, and I shouldn't be a bit surprised if he has graduated at the most worthwhile university in Japan, before he ever came to this country to get his English for nothing."

Linda was watching a sea swallow now, and slowly her lean fingers were gathering handfuls of sand and sifting them into a little pyramid she was heaping beside her. Again almost under her breath she spoke.

"Donald, do you really believe that?" she asked. "Is it possible that mature Jap men are coming here and entering our schools and availing themselves of the benefits that the taxpayers of California provide for their children?"

"Didn't you know it?" asked Donald. "I hadn't thought of it in connection with Oka Sayye, but I do know cases where mature Japs have been in grade schools with children under ten."

"Oh, Donald!" exclaimed Linda. "If California is permitting that or ever has permitted it, we're too easy. We deserve to become their prey if we are so careless."

"Why, I know it's true," said Donald. "I have been in the same classes with men more than old enough to be my father."

"I never was," said Linda, industriously sifting sand. "I have been in classes with Japs ever since I have been at school, but it was with girls and boys of our gardeners and fruit dealers and curio-shop people, and they were always of my age and entitled to be in school, since our system includes the education of anybody who happens to be in California and wants to go to school."

"Did my being late spoil any particular plan you had made, Linda?"

"Yes," said Linda, "it did."

"Oh, I am so sorry!" cried Donald. "I certainly shall try to see that it doesn't occur again. Could we do it next Saturday?"

"I am hoping so," said Linda.

"I told Dad," said Donald, "where I wanted to go and what I wanted to do, and he was awfully sorry but he said it was business and it would take only a few minutes and he thought I could do it and be on time. If he had known I would be detained I don't believe he would have asked it of me. He's a grand old peter, Linda."

"Yes, I know," said Linda. "There's not much you can tell me about peters of the grand sort, the real, true flesh-and-blood, bighearted, human-being fathers, who will take you to the fields and the woods and take the time to teach you what God made and how He made it and why He made it and what we can do with it, and of the fellowship and brotherhood we can get from Nature by being real kin. The one thing that I have had that was the biggest thing in all this world was one of these real fathers."

Donald watched as she raised the pyramid higher and higher.

"Did you tell your father whom you were to go with?" she asked.

"Sure I did," said Donald. "Told the whole family at dinner last night. Told 'em about all the things I was learning, from where to get soap off the bushes to the best spot for material for wooden legs or instantaneous relief for snake bite."

"What did they say?" Linda inquired laughingly.

"Unanimously in favour of continuing the course," he said. "I had already told Father about you when I asked him for books and any help that he could give me with Oka Sayye. Since I had mentioned you last night he told Mother and Louise about that, and they told me to bring you to the house some time. All of them are crazy to know you. Mother says she is just wild to know whether a girl who wears boots and breeches and who knows canyons and the desert and the mountains as you do can be a feminine and lovable person."

"If I told her how many friends I have, she could have speedily decided whether I am lovable or not," said Linda; "but I would make an effort to convince her that I am strictly feminine."

"You would convince her of that without making the slightest effort. You're infinitely more feminine than any other girl I have ever known."

"How do you figure that?" asked Linda.

"Well," said Donald, "it's a queer thing about you, Linda. I take any liberty I pretty nearly please with most of the girls I have been associated with. I tie their shoes and pull their hair—down if I want to—and hand them round 'most any way the notion takes me, and they just laugh and take the same liberties with me, which proves that I am pretty much a girl with them or they are pretty much boys with me. But it wouldn't occur to me to touch your hair or your shoe lace or the tips of your fingers; which proves that you're more feminine than any other girl I know, because if you were not I would be treating you more like another boy. I thought, the first day we were together, that you were like a boy, and I said so, and I thought it because you did not tease me and flirt with me, but since I have come to know you better, you're less like a boy than any other girl I ever have known."

"Don't get psychological, Donald," said Linda. "Go on with the Jap. I haven't got an answer yet to what I really want to know. Have you made the least progress this week? Can you beat him?"

Donald hesitated, studying over the answer.

"Beat him at that trig proposition the other day," he said. "Got an open commendation before the class. There's not a professor in any of my classes who isn't 'hep' to what I'm after by this time, and if I would cajole them a little they would naturally be on my side, especially if their attention were called to that incident of yesterday; but you said I have to beat him with my brains, by doing better work than he does; so about the biggest thing I can honestly tell you is that I have held my own. I have only been ahead of him once this week, but I haven't failed in anything that he has accomplished. I have been able to put some additional touches to some work that he has done for which he used to be marked A which means your One Hundred. Double A which means your plus I made in one instance. And you needn't think that Oka Sayye does not realize what I am up to as well as any of the rest of the class, and you needn't think that he is not going to give me a run for my brain. All I've got will be needed before we finish this term."

"I see," said Linda, slowly nodding her head.

"I wish," said Donald, "that we had started this thing two years ago, or better still, four. But of course you were not in the high school four years ago and there wasn't a girl in my class or among my friends who cared whether I beat the Jap or not. They greatly preferred that I take them motoring or to a dance or a picture show or a beach party. You're the only one except Mother and Louise who ever inspired me to get down to business."

Linda laid her palm on the top of the sand heap and pressed it flat. She looked at Donald with laughing eyes.

"Symbolical," she announced. "That sand was the Jap." She stretched her hand toward him. "That was you. Did you see yourself squash him?"

Donald's laugh was grim.

"Yes, I saw," he said. "I wish it were as easy as that."

"That was not easy," said Linda; "make a mental computation of all the seconds that it took me to erect that pyramid and all the millions of grains of sand I had to gather."

Donald was deeply thoughtful, yet a half smile was playing round his lips.

"Of all the queer girls I ever knew, you're the cap sheaf, Linda," he said.

Linda rose slowly, shook the sand from her breeches and stretched out her hand.

"Let's hotfoot it down to the African village and see what the movies are doing that is interesting today," she proposed.

CHAPTER XXI. Shifting the Responsibility

On her pillow that night before dropping to almost instantaneous sleep Linda reflected that if you could not ride the King's Highway, racing the sands of Santa Monica was a very excellent substitute. It had been a wonderful day after all. When she had left Donald at the Lilac Valley end of the car line he had held her hand tight an instant and looked into her face with the most engaging of clear, boyish smiles.

"Linda, isn't our friendship the nicest thing that ever happened to us?" he demanded.

"Yes," answered Linda promptly, "quite the nicest. Make your plans for all day long next Saturday."

"I'll be here before the birds are awake," promised Donald.

At the close of Monday's sessions, going down the broad walk from the high school, Donald overtook Linda and in a breathless whisper he said: "What do you think? I came near Oka Sayye again this morning in trig, and his hair was as black as jet, dyed to a midnight, charcoal finish, and I am not right sure that he had not borrowed some girl's lipstick and rouge pot for the benefit of his lips and cheeks. Positively he's hectically youthful today. What do you know about that?"

Then he hurried on to overtake the crowd of boys he had left, Linda's heart was racing in her breast.

Turning, she re-entered the school building, and taking a telephone directory she hunted an address, and then, instead of going to the car line that took her to Lilac Valley she went to the address she had looked up. With a pencil she wrote a few lines on a bit of scratch paper in one of her books. That note opened a door and admitted her to the presence of a tall, lean, gray-haired man with quick, blue-gray eyes and lips that seemed capable of being either grave or gay on short notice. With that perfect ease which Linda had acquired through the young days of her life in meeting friends of her father, she went to the table beside which this man was standing and stretched out her hand.

"Judge Whiting?" she asked.

"Yes," said the Judge.

"I am Linda Strong, the younger daughter of Alexander Strong. I think you knew my father."

"Yes," said the Judge, "I knew him very well indeed, and I have some small acquaintance with his daughter through very interesting reports that my son brings home."

"Yes, it is about Donald that I came to see you," said Linda.

If she had been watching as her father would have watched, Linda would have seen the slight uplift of the Judge's figure, the tensing of his muscles, the narrowing of his eyes in the swift, speculative look he passed over her from the crown of her bare, roughened black head down the gold-brown of her dress to her slender, well-shod feet. The last part of that glance Linda caught. She slightly lifted one of the feet under inspection, thrust it forward and looked at the Judge with a gay challenge in her dark eyes.

"Are you interested in them too?" she asked.

The Judge was embarrassed. A flush crept into his cheeks. He was supposed to be master of any emergency that might arise, but one had arisen in connection with a slip of a schoolgirl that left him wordless.

"It is very probable," said Linda, "that if my shoes had been like most other girls' shoes I wouldn't be here today. I was in the same schoolroom with your son for three years, and he never saw me or spoke to me until one day he stopped me to inquire why I wore the kind of shoes I did. He said he had a battle to wage with me because I tried to be a law to myself, and he wanted to know why I wasn't like other girls. And I told him I had a crow to pick with HIM because he had the kind of brain that would be content to let a Jap beat him in his own school, in his own language and in his own country; so we made an engagement to fight to a finish, and it ended by his becoming the only boy friend I have and the nicest boy friend a girl ever had, I am very sure. That's why I'm here."

Linda lifted her eyes and Judge Whiting looked into them till he saw the same gold lights in their depths that Peter Morrison had seen. He came around the table and placed a big leather chair for Linda. Then he went back and resumed his own.

"Of course," said the Judge in his most engaging manner. "I gather from what Donald has told me that you have a reason for being here, and I want you to understand that I am intensely interested in anything you have to say to me. Now tell me why you came."

"I came," said Linda, "because I started something and am afraid of the possible result. I think very likely if, in retaliation for what Donald said to me about my hair and my shoes, I had not twitted him about the use he was making of his brain and done everything in my power to drive him into competition with Oka Sayye in the hope that a white man would graduate with the highest honors, he would not have gone into this competition, which I am now certain has antagonized Oka Sayye."

Linda folded her slim hands on the table and leaned forward.

"Judge Whiting," she said earnestly, "I know very little about men. The most I know was what I learned about my father and the men with whom he occasionally hunted and fished. They were all such fine men that I must have grown up thinking that every man was very like them, but one day I came in direct contact with the Jap that Donald is trying to beat, and the thing I saw in his face put fear into my heart and it has been there ever since. I have almost an unreasoning fear of that Jap, not because he has said anything or done anything. It's just instinctive. I may be wholly wrong in having come to you and in taking up your time, but there are two things I wanted to tell you. I could have told Donald, but if I did and his mind went off at a tangent thinking of these things he wouldn't be nearly so likely to be in condition to give his best thought to his studies. If I really made him see what I think I have seen, and fear what I know I fear, he might fail where I would give almost anything to see him succeed; so I thought I would come to you and tell you about it and ask you please to think it over, and to take extra care of him, because I really believe that he may be in danger; and if he is I never shall be able to rid myself of a sense of responsibility."

"I see," said Judge Whiting. "Now tell me, just as explicitly as you have told me this, exactly what it is that you fear."

"Last Saturday," said Linda, "Donald told me that while standing at the board beside Oka Sayye, demonstrating a theorem, he noticed that there were gray hairs above the Jap's ears, and he bluntly asked him, before the professor and the class, how old he was. In telling me, he said he had the feeling that if the Jap could have done so in that instant, he would have killed him. He said he was nineteen, but Donald says from the matured lines of his body, from his hands and his face and his hair, he is certain that he is thirty or more, and he thinks it very probable that he may have graduated at home before he came here to get his English for nothing from our public schools. I never before had the fact called to my attention that this was being done, but Donald told me that he had been in classes with matured men when he was less than ten years of age. That is not fair, Judge Whiting; it is not right. There should be an age specified above which people may not be allowed to attend public school."

"I quite agree with you," said the Judge. "That has been done in the grades, but there is nothing fair in bringing a boy under twenty in competition with a man graduated from the institutions of another country, even in the high schools. If this be the case—"

"You can be certain that it is," said Linda, "because Donald whispered to me as he passed me half an hour ago, coming from the school building, that TODAY Oka Sayye's hair is a uniform, shining black, and he also thought that he had used a lipstick and rouge in an effort at rejuvenation. Do you think, from your knowledge of Donald, that he would imagine that?"

"No," said Judge Whiting, "I don't think such a thing would occur to him unless he saw it."

"Neither do I," said Linda. "From the short acquaintance I have with him I should not call him at all imaginative, but he is extremely quick and wonderfully retentive. You have to show him but once from which cactus he can get Victrola needles and fishing hooks, or where to find material for wooden legs."

The Judge laughed. "Doesn't prove much," he said. "You wouldn't have to show me that more than once either. If anyone were giving me an intensive course on such interesting subjects, I would guarantee to remember, even at my age."

Linda nodded in acquiescence. "Then you can regard it as quite certain," she said, "that Oka Sayye is making up in an effort to appear younger than he is which means that he doesn't want his right questioned to be in our schools, to absorb the things that we are taught, to learn our language, our government, our institutions, our ideals, our approximate strength and our only-too-apparent weakness."

The Judge leaned forward and waited attentively.

"The other matter," said Linda, "was relative to Saturday. There may not be a thing in it, but sometimes a woman's intuition proves truer than what a man thinks he sees and knows. I haven't SEEN a thing, and I don't KNOW a thing, but I don't believe your gardener was sick last week. I believe he had a dirty job he wanted done and preferred to save his position and avoid risks by getting some other Jap who had no family and no interests here, to do it for him. I don't BELIEVE that your car, having run all right Friday night, was shot to pieces Saturday morning so that Donald went smash with it in a manner that might very easily have killed him, or sent him to the hospital for months, while Oka Sayye carried off the honors without competition I want to ask you to find out whether your regular gardener truly was ill, whether he has a family and interests to protect here, or whether he is a man who could disappear in a night as Japs who have leased land and have families cannot. I want to know about the man who took your gardener's place, and I want the man who is repairing your car interviewed very carefully as to what he found the trouble with it."

Linda paused. Judge Whiting sat in deep thought, then he looked at Linda.

"I see," he said at last. "Thank you very much for coming to me. All these things and anything that develops from them shall be handled carefully. Of course you know that Donald is my only son and you can realize what he is to me and to his mother and sister."

"It is because I do realize that," said Linda, "that I am here. I appreciate his friendship, but it is not for my own interests that I am asking to have him taken care of while he wages his mental war with this Jap. I want Donald to have the victory, but I want it to be a victory that will be an inspiration to any boy of white blood among any of our allies or among peoples who should be our allies. There's a showdown coming between the white race and a mighty aggregation of colored peoples one of these days, and if the white man doesn't realize pretty soon that his supremacy is not only going to be contested but may be lost, it just simply will be lost; that is all there is to it."

The Judge was studying deeply now. Finally he said: "Young lady, I greatly appreciate your coming to me. There may be NOTHING in what you fear. It MIGHT be a matter of national importance. In any event, it shows that your heart is in the right place. May Mrs. Whiting and I pay you a visit some day soon in your home?"

"Of course," said Linda simply. "I told Donald to bring his mother the first time he came, but he said he did not need to be chaperoned when he came to see me, because my father's name was a guarantee to his mother that my home would be a proper place for him to visit."

"I wonder how many of his other girl friends invited him to bring his mother to see them," said the Judge.

"Oh, he probably grew up with the other girls and was acquainted with them from tiny things," said Linda.

"Very likely," conceded the Judge. "I think, after all, I would rather have an invitation to make one of those trips with you to the desert or the mountains. Is there anything else as interesting as fish hooks and Victrola needles and wooden legs to be learned?"

"Oh, yes," said Linda, leaning farther forward, a lovely color sweeping up into her cheeks, her eyes a-shine. She had missed the fact that the Judge was jesting. She had thought him in sober, scientific earnest.

"It's an awfully nice thing if you dig a plant or soil your hands in hunting, or anything like that, to know that there are four or five different kinds of vegetable soap where you can easily reach them, if you know them. If you lose your way or have a long tramp, it's good to know which plants will give you drink and where they are. And if you're short of implements, you might at any time need a mescal stick, or an arrow shaft or an arrow, even. If Donald were lost now, he could keep alive for days, because he would know what wood would make him a bow and how he could take amole fiber and braid a bow string and where he could make arrows and arrow points so that he could shoot game for food. I've taught him to make a number of snares, and he knows where to find and how to cook his greens and potatoes and onions and where to find his pickles and how to make lemonade and tea, and what to use for snake bite. It's been such fun, Judge Whiting, and he has been so interested."

"Yes, I should think he would be," said the Judge. "I am interested myself. If you would take an old boy like me on a few of those trips, I would be immensely pleased."

"You'd like brigand beefsteak," suggested Linda, "and you'd like cress salad, and I am sure you'd like creamed yucca."

"Hm," said the Judge. "Sounds to me like Jane Meredith."

Linda suddenly sat straight. A dazed expression crossed her face. Presently she recovered.

"Will you kindly tell me," she said, "what a great criminal judge knows about Jane Meredith?"

"Why, I hear my wife and daughter talking about her," said the Judge.

"I wonder," said Linda, "if a judge hears so many secrets that he forgets what a secret is and couldn't possibly keep one to save his life."

"On the other hand," said Judge Whiting, "a judge hears so many secrets that he learns to be a very secretive person himself, and if a young lady just your size and so like you in every way as to be you, told me anything and told me that it was a secret, I would guarantee to carry it with me to my grave, if I said I would."

One of Linda's special laughs floated out of the windows. Her right hand slipped across the table toward the Judge.

"Cross your heart and body?" she challenged.

The Judge took the hand she offered in both of his own.

"On my soul," he said, "I swear it."

"All right," bubbled Linda. "Judge Whiting, allow me to present to you Jane Meredith, the author and originator of the Aboriginal Cookery articles now running in Everybody's Home."

Linda stood up as she made the presentation and the Judge arose with her. When she bowed her dark head before him the Judge bowed equally as low, then he took the hand he held and pressed it against his lips.

"I am not surprised," he said. "I am honored, deeply honored, and I am delighted. For a high school girl that is a splendid achievement."

"But you realize, of course," said Linda, "that it is vicarious. I really haven't done anything. I am just passing on to the world what Alexander Strong found it interesting to teach his daughter, because he hadn't a son."

"I certainly am fortunate that my son is getting the benefit of this," said Judge Whiting earnestly. "There are girls who make my old-fashioned soul shudder, but I shall rest in great comfort whenever I know that my boy is with you."

"Sure!" laughed Linda. "I'm not vamping him. I don't know the first principles. We're not doing a thing worse than sucking 'hunters' rock leek' or roasting Indian potatoes or fishing for trout with cactus spines. I have had such a lovely time I don't believe that I'll apologize for coming. But you won't waste a minute in making sure about Oka Sayye?"

"I won't waste a minute," said the Judge.

CHAPTER XXII. The End of Marian's Contest

Coming from school a few days later on an evening when she had been detained, Linda found a radiant Katy awaiting her.

"What's up, old dear?" cried Linda. "You seem positively illumined."

"So be," said Katy. "It's a good time I'm havin'. In the first place the previous boss of this place ain't nowise so bossy as sue used to be, an' livin' with her is a dale aisier. An' then, when Miss Eileen is around these days, she is beginning to see things, and she is just black with jealousy of ye. Something funny happened here the afternoon, an' she was home for once an' got the full benefit of it. I was swapin' the aist walk, but I know she was inside the window an' I know she heard. First, comes a great big loaded automobile drivin' up, and stopped in front with a flourish an' out hops as nice an' nate a lookin' lad as ever you clapped your eyes on, an' up he comes to me an' off goes his hat with a swape, an' he hands me that bundle an' he says: 'Here's something Miss Linda is wantin' bad for her wild garden.'"

Katy handed Linda a bundle of newspaper, inside which, wrapped in a man's handkerchief, she found several plants, carefully lifted, the roots properly balled, the heads erect, crisp, although in full flower.

"Oh, Katy!" cried Linda. "Look, it's Gallito, 'little rooster'!" "Now ain't them jist yellow violets?" asked Katy dubiously.

"No," said Linda, "they are not. They are quite a bit rarer. They are really a wild pansy. Bring water, Katy, and help me."

"But I've something else for ye," said Katy.

"I don't care what you have," answered Linda. "I am just compelled to park these little roosters at once."

"What makes ye call them that ungodly name?" asked Katy.

"Nothing ungodly about it," answered Linda. "It's funny. Gallito is the Spanish name for these violets, and it means 'little rooster.'"

Linda set the violets as carefully as they had been lifted and rinsed her hands at the hydrant.

"Now bring on the remainder of the exhibit," she ordered.

"It's there on the top of the rock pile, which you notice has incrased since ye last saw it."

"So it has!" said Linda. "So it has! And beautifully colored specimens those are too. My fern bed will lift up its voice and rejoice in them. And rocks mean Henry Anderson. The box I do not understand."

Linda picked it up, untied the string, and slipped off the wrapping. Katy stared in wide-mouthed amazement.

"I was just tickled over that because Miss Eileen saw a good-looking and capable young man leave a second package, right on the heels of young Whiting," she said. "Whatever have ye got, lambie? What does that mean?"

Linda held up a beautiful box of glass, inside of which could be seen swarming specimens of every bug, beetle, insect, and worm that Henry Anderson had been able to collect in Heaven only knew what hours of search. Linda opened the box. The winged creatures flew, the beetles tumbled, the worms went over the top. She set it on the ground and laughed to exhaustion. Her eyes were wet as she looked up at Katy.

"That first night Henry Anderson and Peter Morrison were here to dinner, Katy," she said, "Anderson made a joke about being my bug-catcher when I built my home nest, and several times since he has tried to be silly about it, but the last time I told him it was foolishness to which I would listen no more, so instead of talking, he has taken this way of telling me that he is fairly expert as a bug-catcher. Really, it is awfully funny, Katy."

Katy was sober. She showed no appreciation of the fun.

"Ye know, lambie," she said, her hands on her hips, her elbows wide-spread, her jaws argumentative, "I've done some blarneying with that lad, an' I've fed him some, because he was doin' things that would help an' please ye, but now I'm tellin' ye, just like I'll be tellin' ye till I die, I ain't STRONG for him. If ever the day comes when ye ask me to take on that Whiting kid for me boss, I'll bow my head an' I'll fly at his bidding, because he is real, an' he's goin' to come out a man lots like your pa, or hisn. An' if ever the day comes when ye will be telling me ye want me to serve Pater Morrison, I'll well nigh get on my knees to him. I think he'd be the closest we'd ever come to gettin' the master back. But I couldn't say I'd ever take to Anderson. They's something about him, I can't just say what, but he puts me back up amazin'."

"Don't worry, ancient custodian of the family," said Linda. "That same something in Henry Anderson that antagonizes you, affects me in even stronger degree. You must not get the foolish notion that any man has a speculative eye on me, because it is not true. Donald Whiting is only a boy friend, treating me as a brother would, and Peter Morrison is much too sophisticated and mature to pay any serious attention to a girl with a year more high school before her. I want to be decent to Henry Anderson, because he is Peter's architect, and I'm deeply interested in Peter's house and the lady who will live in it. Sometimes I hope it will be Donald's sister, Mary Louise. Anyway, I am going to get acquainted with her and make it my business to see that she and Peter get their chance to know each other well. My job for Peter is to help run his brook at the proper angle, build his bridge, engineer his road, and plant his grounds; so don't be dreaming any foolish dreams, Katy."

Katy folded her arms, tilted her chin at an unusually aspiring angle, and deliberately sniffed.

"Don't ye be lettin' yourself belave your own foolishness," she said. "I ain't done with me exhibit yet. On the hall table ye will find a package from the Pater Morrison man that Miss Eileen had the joy of takin' in and layin' aside for ye, an atop of it rists a big letter that I'm thinkin' might mean Miss Marian."

"Oh," cried Linda. "Why are you wasting all this time? If there is a letter from Marian it may mean that the competition is decided; but if it is, she loses, because she was to telegraph if she won."

Linda rushed into the house and carried her belongings to her workroom. She dropped them on the table and looked at them.

"I'll get you off my mind first," she said to the Morrison package, which enclosed a new article entitled "How to Grow Good Citizens." With it was a scrawled line, "I'm leaving the head and heels of the future to you."

"How fine!" exulted Linda. "He must have liked the head and tail pieces I drew for his other article, so he wants the same for this, and if he is well paid for his article, maybe in time, after I've settled for my hearth motto, he will pay me something for my work. Gal-lum-shus!"

As she opened the letter from Marian she slowly shook her head.

"Drat the luck," she muttered, "no good news here."

Slowly and absorbedly she read:

DEAREST LINDA:

No telegram to send. I grazed the first prize and missed the second because Henry Anderson wins with plans so like mine that they are practically duplicates. I have not seen the winning plans. Mr. Snow told me as gently as he could that the judges had ruled me out entirely. The winning plans are practically a reversal of mine, more professionally drawn, and no doubt the specifications are far ahead of mine, as these are my weak spot, although I have worked all day and far into the night on the mathematics of house building. Mr. Snow was very kind, and terribly cut up about it. I made what I hope was a brave fight, I did so believe in those plans that I am afraid to say just how greatly disappointed I am. All I can do is to go to work again and try to find out how to better my best, which I surely put into the plans I submitted. I can't see how Henry Anderson came to hit upon some of my personal designs for comforts and conveniences. I had hoped that no man would think of my especial kitchen plans. I rather fancied myself as a benefactor to my sex, an emancipator from drudgery, as it were. I had a concealed feeling that it required a woman who had expended her strength combating the construction of a devilish kitchen, to devise some of my built-in conveniences, and I worked as carefully on my kitchen table, as on any part of the house. If I find later that the winning plans include these things I shall believe that Henry Anderson is a mind reader, or that lost plans naturally gravitate to him. But there is no use to grouch further. I seem to be born a loser. Anyway, I haven't lost you and I still have Dana Meade.

I have nothing else to tell you except that Mr. Snow has waited for me two evenings out of the week ever since I wrote you, and he has taken me in his car and simply forced me to drive him for an hour over what appeals to me to be the most difficult roads he could select. So far I have not balked at anything but he has had the consideration not to direct me to the mountains. He is extremely attractive, Linda, and I do enjoy being with him, but I dread it too, because his grief is so deep and so apparent that it constantly keeps before me the loss of my own dear ones, and those things to which the hymn books refer as "aching voids" in my own life.

But there is something you will be glad to hear. That unknown correspondent of mine is still sending letters, and I am crazy about them. I don't answer one now until I have mulled over it two or three days and I try to give him as good as he sends.

I judge from your letters that you are keeping at least even with Eileen, and that life is much happier for you. You seem to be broadening. I am so glad for the friendship you have formed with Donald Whiting. My mother and Mrs. Whiting were friends. She is a charming woman and it has seemed to me that in her daughter Louise she has managed a happy compound of old-fashioned straightforwardness and unswerving principle, festooned with happy trimmings of all that is best in the present days. I hope that you do become acquainted with her. She is older than you, but she is the kind of girl I know you would like.

Don't worry because I have lost again, Linda dear. Today is my blue day. Tomorrow I shall roll up my sleeves and go at it again with all my might, and by and by it is written in the books that things will come right for me. They cannot go wrong for ever. With dearest love,

MARIAN.

Linda looked grim as she finished the letter.

81

"Confound such luck," she said emphatically. "I do not understand it. How can a man like Henry Anderson know more about comforts and conveniences in a home than a woman with Marian's experience and comprehension? And she has been gaining experience for the past ten years. That partner of his must be a six-cylinder miracle."

Linda went to the kitchen, because she was in pressing need of someone to whom to tell her troubles, and there was no one except Katy. What Katy said was energetic and emphatic, but it comforted Linda, because she agreed with it and what she was seeking at the minute was someone who agreed with her. As she went back upstairs, she met Eileen on her way to the front door. Eileen paused and deliberately studied Linda's face, and Linda stopped and waited quietly until she chose to speak.

"I presume," said Eileen at last, "that you and Katy would call the process through which you are going right now, 'taking the bit in your teeth,' or some poetic thing like that, but I can't see that you are getting much out of it. I don't hear the old laugh or the clatter of gay feet as I did before all this war of dissatisfaction broke out. This minute if you haven't either cried, or wanted to, I miss my guess."

"You win," said Linda. "I have not cried, because I make it a rule never to resort to tears when I can help it; so what you see now is unshed tears in my heart. They in no way relate to what you so aptly term my 'war of dissatisfaction'; they are for Marian. She has lost again, this time the Nicholson and Snow prize in architecture."

"Serves her right," said Eileen, laughing contemptuously. "The ridiculous idea of her trying to compete in a man's age-old occupation! As if she ever could learn enough about joists and beams and girders and installing water and gas and electricity to build a house. She should have had the sense to know she couldn't do it."

"But," said Linda quietly, "Marian wasn't proposing to be a contractor, she only wants to be an architect. And the man who beat her is Peter Morrison's architect, Henry Anderson, and he won by such a narrow margin that her plans were thrown out of second and third place, because they were so very similar to his. Doesn't that strike you as curious?"

"That is more than curious," said Eileen slowly. "That is a very strange coincidence. They couldn't have had anything from each other, because they only met at dinner, before all of us, and Marian went away the next morning; it does seem queer." Then she added with a flash of generosity and justice, "It looks pretty good for Marian, at that. If she came so near winning that she lost second and third because she was too near first to make any practical difference, I must be wrong and she must be right."

"You are wrong," said Linda tersely, "if you think Marian cannot make wonderful plans for houses. But going back to what my 'war of dissatisfaction' is doing to me, it's a pale affair compared with what it is doing to you, Eileen. You look a debilitated silhouette of the near recent past. Do you feel that badly about giving up a little money and authority?"

"I never professed to have the slightest authority over you," said Eileen very primly, as she drew back in the shadows. "You have come and gone exactly as you pleased. All I ever tried to do was to keep up a decent appearance before the neighbors and make financial ends meet."

"That never seemed to wear on you as something seems to do now," said Linda. "I am thankful that this week ends it. I was looking for you because I wanted to tell you to be sure not to make any date that will keep you from meeting me at the office of the president of the Consolidated Bank Thursday afternoon. I am going to arrange with John to be there and it shouldn't take fifteen minutes to run through matters and divide the income in a fair way between us. I am willing for you to go on paying the bills and ordering for the house as you have been."

"Certainly you are," sneered Eileen. "You are quite willing for all the work and use the greater part of my time to make you comfortable."

Linda suddenly drew back. Her body seemed to recoil, but her head thrust forward as if to bring her eyes in better range to read Eileen's face.

"That is utterly unjust, Eileen," she cried.

Then two at a time she rushed the stairs in a race for her room.

CHAPTER XXIII. The Day of Jubilee

Linda started to school half an hour earlier Wednesday morning because that was the day for her weekly trip to the Post Office for any mail which might have come to her under the name of Jane Meredith. She had hard work to keep down her color when she recognized the heavy gray envelope used by the editor of Everybody's Home. As she turned from the window with it in her fingers she was trembling slightly and wondering whether she could have a minute's seclusion to face the answer which her last letter might have brought. There was a small alcove beside a public desk at one side of the room. Linda stepped into this, tore open the envelope and slipped out the sheet it contained.

Dazedly she stared at the slip that fell from it. Slowly the color left her cheeks and then came rushing back from her surcharged heart until her very ears were red, because that slip was very manifestly a cheque for five hundred dollars. Mentally and physically Linda shook herself, then she straightened to full height, tensing her muscles and holding the sheet before her with a hand on each side to keep it from shaking, while she read:

MY DEAR MADAM:

I sincerely apologize for having waited so long before writing you of the very exceptional reception which your articles have had. I think one half their attraction has been the exquisite and appealing pictures you have sent for their illustration. At the present minute they are forming what I consider the most unique feature in the magazine. I am enclosing you a cheque for five hundred dollars as an initial payment on the series. Just what the completed series should be worth I am unable to say until you inform me how many months you can keep it up at the same grade of culinary and literary interest and attractive illustration; but I should say at a rough estimate that you would be safe in counting upon a repetition of this cheque for every three articles you send in. This of course includes payment for the pictures also, which are to me if anything more attractive than the recipes, since the local color and environment they add to the recipe and the word sketch are valuable in the extreme.

If you feel that you can continue this to the extent of even a small volume, I shall be delighted to send you a book contract. In considering this proposition, let me say that if you could not produce enough recipes to fill a book, you could piece it out to the necessary length most charmingly and attractively by lengthening the descriptions of the environment in which the particular fruits and vegetables you deal with are to be found; and in book form you might allow yourself much greater latitude in the instructions concerning the handling of the fruits and the preparation of the recipes. I think myself that a wonderfully attractive book could be made from this material, and hope that you will agree with me. Trusting that this will be satisfactory to you and that you will seriously consider the book proposition before you decline it, I remain, my dear madam, Very truly yours,

HUGH THOMPSON,
Editor, Everybody's Home.

Gripping the cheque and the letter, Linda lurched forward against the window casement and shut her eyes tight, because she could feel big, nervous gulps of exultation and rejoicing swelling up in her throat. She shifted the papers to one hand and surreptitiously slipped the other to her pocket. She tried to keep the papers before her and looked straight from the window to avoid attracting attention. The tumult of exultation in her heart was so wild that she did not surely know whether she wanted to sink to the floor, lay her face against the glass, and indulge in what for generations women have referred to as "a good cry," or whether she wanted to leap from the window and sport on the wind like a driven leaf.

Then she returned the letter and cheque to the envelope, and slipped it inside her blouse, and started on her way to school. She might as well have gone to Multiflores Canyon and pitted her strength against climbing its walls for the day, for all the good she did in her school work. She heard no word of any recitation by her schoolmates. She had no word ready when called on for a recitation herself. She heard nothing that was said by any of the professors. On winged feet she was flying back and forth from the desert to the mountains, from the canyons to the sea. She was raiding beds of amass and devising ways to roast the bulbs and make a new dish. She was compounding drinks from mescal and bisnaga. She was hunting desert pickles and trying to remember whether Indian rhubarb ever grew so far south. She was glad when the dismissal hour came that afternoon. With eager feet she went straight to the Consolidated Bank and there she asked again to be admitted to the office of the president. Mr. Worthington rose as she came in.

"Am I wrong in my dates?" he inquired. "I was not expecting you until tomorrow."

"No, you're quite right," said Linda. "At this hour tomorrow. But, Mr. Worthington, I am in trouble again."

Linda looked so distressed that the banker pushed a chair to the table's side for her, and when she had seated herself, he said quietly: "Tell me all about it, Linda. We must get life straightened out as best we can."

"I think I must tell you all about it," said Linda, "because I know just enough about banking to know that I have a proposition that I don't know how to handle. Are bankers like father confessors and doctors and lawyers?"

"I think they are even more so," laughed Mr. Worthington. "Perhaps the father confessor takes precedence, otherwise I believe people are quite as much interested in their financial secrets as in anything else in all this world. Have you a financial secret?"

"Yes," said Linda, "I have what is to me a big secret, and I don't in the least know how to handle it, so right away I thought about you and that you would be the one to tell me what I could do."

"Go ahead," said Mr. Worthington kindly. "I'll give you my word of honor to keep any secret you confide to me."

Linda produced her letter. She opened it and without any preliminaries handed it and the cheque to the banker. He looked at the cheque speculatively, and then laid it aside and read the letter. He gave every evidence of having read parts of it two or three times, then he examined the cheque again, and glanced at Linda.

"And just how did you come into possession of this, young lady?" he inquired. "And what is it that you want of me?"

"Why, don't you see?" said Linda. "It's my letter and my cheque; I'm 'Jane Meredith.' Now how am I going to get my money."

For one dazed moment Mr. Worthington studied Linda; then he threw back his head and laughed unrestrainedly. He came around the table and took both Linda's hands.

"Bully for you!" he cried exultantly. "How I wish your father could see the seed he has sown bearing its fruit. Isn't that fine? And do you want to go on with this anonymously?"

"I think I must," said Linda. "I have said in my heart that no Jap, male or female, young or old, shall take first honors in a class from which I graduate; and you can see that if people generally knew this, it would make it awfully hard for me to go on with my studies, and I don't know that the editor who is accepting this work would take it if he knew it were sent him by a high-school Junior. You see the dignified way in which he addresses me as 'madam'?"

"I see," said Mr. Worthington reflectively.

"I'm sure," said Linda with demure lips, though the eyes above them were blazing and dancing at high tension, "I'm sure that the editor is attaching a husband, and a house having a well-ordered kitchen, and rather wide culinary experience to that 'dear madam.'"

"And what about this book proposition?" asked the banker gravely. "That would be a big thing for a girl of your age. Can you do it, and continue your school work?"

"With the background I have, with the unused material I have, and with vacation coming before long, I can do it easily," said Linda. "My school work is not difficult for me. It only requires concentration for about two hours in the preparation that each day brings. The remainder of the time I could give to amplifying and producing new recipes."

"I see," said the banker. "So you have resolved, Linda, that you don't want your editor to know your real name."

"Could scarcely be done," said Linda.

"But have you stopped to think," said the banker, "that you will be asked for personal history and about your residence, and no doubt a photograph of yourself. If you continue this work anonymously you're going to have trouble with more matters than cashing a cheque."

"But I am not going to have any trouble cashing a cheque," she said, "because I have come straight to the man whose business is cheques."

"True enough," he said; "I SHALL have to arrange the cheque; there's not a doubt about that; and as for your other bugbears."

"I refuse to be frightened by them," interposed Linda.

"Have you ever done any business at the bank?"

"No," said Linda.

"None of the clerks know you?"

"Not that I remember," said Linda. "I might possibly be acquainted with some of them. I have merely passed through the bank on my way to your room twice."

"Then," said the banker, "we'll have to risk it. After this estate business is settled you will want to open an account in your name."

"Quite true," said Linda.

"Then I would advise you," said Mr. Worthington, "to open this account in your own name. Endorse this cheque 'Jane Meredith' and make it payable to me personally. Whenever one of these comes, bring it to me and I'll take care of it for you. One minute."

He left Linda sitting quietly reading and rereading her letter, and presently returned and laid a sheaf of paper money before her.

"Take it to the paying teller. Tell him that you wish to deposit it, and ask him to give you a bank book and a cheque book," he said. "Thank you very much for coming to me and for confiding in me."

Linda gathered up the money, and said good-bye to the banker. Just as she started forward she recognized Eileen at the window of the paying teller. It was an Eileen she never before had seen. Her face was strained to a ghastly gray. Her hat was not straight and her hands were shaking. Without realizing that she was doing it, Linda stepped behind one of the huge marble pillars supporting the ceiling and stood there breathlessly, watching Eileen. She could gather that she was discussing the bank ledger which lay before the teller and that he was refusing something that Eileen was imploring him to do. Linda thought she understood what it was. Then very clearly Eileen's voice, sharp and strained, reached her ears.

"You mean that you are refusing to pay me my deposits on my private account?" she cried; and Linda could also hear the response.

"I am very sorry if it annoys or inconveniences you, Miss Strong, but since the settlement of the estate takes place tomorrow, our orders are to pay out no funds in any way connected with the estate until after that settlement has been arranged."

"But this is my money, my own private affair," begged Eileen. "The estate has nothing to do with it."

"I am sorry," repeated the teller. "If that is the case, you will have no difficulty in establishing the fact in a few minutes' time."

Eileen turned and left the bank, and it seemed that she was almost swaying. Linda stood a second with narrowed eyes, in deep thought.

"I think," she said at last, deep down in her heart, "that it looks precious much as if there had been a bit of transgression in this affair. It looks, too, as if 'the way of the transgressor' were a darned hard way. Straight ahead open and aboveboard for you, my girl!"

Then she went quietly to the desk and transacted her own business; but her beautiful day was clouded. Her heart was no longer leaping exultantly. She was sickened and sorrowful over the evident nerve strain and discomfort which Eileen seemed to have brought upon herself. She dreaded meeting her at dinner that night, and she wondered all the way home where Eileen had gone from the bank and what she had been doing. What she felt was a pale affair compared with what she would have felt if she could have seen Eileen leave the bank and enter a near-by store, go to a telephone booth and put in a long-distance call for San Francisco. Her eyes were brilliant, her cheeks by nature redder than the rouge she had used upon them. She squared her shoulders, lifted her head, as if she irrevocably had made a decision and would not be thwarted in acting upon it. While she waited she straightened her hat, and tucked up her pretty hair, once more evincing concern about her appearance. After a nervous wait she secured her party.

"Am I speaking with Mr. James Heitman?" she asked.

"Yes," came the answer.

"Well, Uncle Jim, this is Eileen."

"Why, hello, girlie," was the quick response. "Delighted that you're calling your ancient uncle. Haven't changed the decision in the last letter I had from you, have you?"

"Yes," said Eileen, "I have changed it. Do you and Aunt Caroline still want me, Uncle Jim?"

"YOU BET WE WANT YOU!" roared the voice over the 'phone. "Here we are, with plenty of money and not a relation on earth but you to leave it to. You belong to us by rights. We'd be tickled to death to have you, and for you to have what's left of the money when we get through with it. May I come after you? Say the word, and I'll start this minute."

"Oh, Uncle Jim, could you? Would you?" cried Eileen.

"Well, I'd say I could. We'd be tickled to death, I tell you!"

"How long would it take you to get here?" said Eileen.

"Well, I could reach you by noon tomorrow. Eleven something is the shortest time it's been made in; that would give me thirteen—more than enough. Are you in that much of a hurry?"

"Yes," gasped Eileen, "yes, I am in the biggest kind of a hurry there is, Uncle Jim. This troublesome little estate has to be settled tomorrow afternoon. There's going to be complaint about everything that I have seen fit to do. I've been hounded and harassed till I am disgusted with it. Then I've promised to marry John Gilman as I wrote you, and I don't believe you would think that was my best chance with the opportunities you could give me. It seems foolish to stay here, abused as I have been lately, and as I will be tomorrow. You have the house number. If you come and get me out of it by noon tomorrow, I'll go with you. You may take out those adoption papers you have always entreated me to agree to and I'll be a daughter that you can be proud of. It will be a relief to have some real money and some real position, and to breathe freely and be myself once more."

"All right for you, girlie!" bellowed the great voice over the line. "Pick up any little personal bits you can put in a suitcase, and by twelve o'clock tomorrow I'll whisk you right out of that damn mess."

Eileen walked from the telephone booth with her head high, triumph written all over her face and figure. They were going to humiliate her. She would show them!

She went home immediately. Entering her room, she closed the door and stood looking at her possessions. How could she get her trunk from the garret? How could she get it to the station? Would it be possible for Uncle James to take it in his car? As she pondered these things Eileen had a dim memory of a day in her childhood when her mother had gone on business to San Francisco and had taken her along. She remembered a huge house, all turrets and towers and gables, all turns and twists and angles, closed to the light of day and glowing inside with shining artificial lights. She remembered stumbling over deep rugs. One vivid impression was of walls covered with huge canvases, some of them having frames more than a foot wide. She remembered knights in armor, and big fireplaces, and huge urns and vases. It seemed to her like the most wonderful bazaar she ever had been in. She remembered, too, that she had been glad when her mother had taken her out into the sunshine again and from the presence of two ponderous people who had objected strongly to everything her mother had discussed with them. She paused one instant, contemplating this picture. The look of triumph on her face toned down considerably. Then she comforted herself aloud.

"I've heard Mother say," she said softly, "that everybody overdid things and did not know how to be graceful with immense fortunes got from silver and gold mines, and lumber. It will be different now. Probably they don't live in the same house, even. There is a small army of servants, and there is nothing I can think of that Uncle Jim won't gladly get me. I've been too big a fool for words to live this way as long as I have. Crush me, will they? I'll show them! I won't even touch these things I have strained so to get."

Eileen jerked from her throat the strand of pearls that she had worn continuously for four years and threw it contemptuously on her dressing table.

"I'll make Uncle Jim get me a rope with two or three strands in it that will reach to my waist. 'A suitcase!' I don't know what I would fill a suitcase with from here. The trunk may stay in the garret, and while I am leaving all this rubbish, I'll just leave John Gilman with it. Uncle Jim will give me an income that will buy all the cigarettes I want without having to deceive anyone; and I can have money if I want to stake something at bridge without being scared into paralysis for fear somebody may find it out or the accounts won't balance. I'll put on the most suitable thing I have to travel in, and just walk out and leave everything else."

That was what Eileen did. At noon the next day her eyes were bright with nervousness. Her cheeks alternately paled with fear and flooded red with anxiety. She had dressed herself carefully, laid out her hat and gloves and a heavy coat in case the night should be chilly. Once she stood looking at the dainty, brightly colored dresses hanging in her wardrobe A flash of regret passed over her face.

"Tawdry little cheap things and makeshifts," she said. "If Linda feels that she has been so terribly defrauded, she can help herself now!"

By twelve o'clock she found herself standing at the window, straining her eyes down Lilac Valley. She was not looking at its helpful hills, at its appealing curves, at its brilliant colors. She was watching the roadway. When Katy rang to call her to lunch, she told her to put the things away; she was expecting people who had taken her out to lunch presently. In the past years she had occasionally written to her uncle. Several times when he had had business in Los Angeles she had met him at his hotel and dined with him. She reasoned that he would come straight to the house and get her, and then they would go to one of the big hotels for lunch before they started.

"I shan't feel like myself," said Eileen, "until we are well on the way to San Francisco."

At one o'clock she was walking the floor. At two she was almost frantic. At half past she almost wished that she had had the good sense to have some lunch, since she was very hungry and under tense nerve strain. Once she paused before the glass, but what she saw frightened her. Just when she felt that she could not endure the strain another minute, grinding brakes, the blast of a huge Klaxon, and the sound of a great voice arose from the street. Eileen rushed to the window. She took one look, caught up the suitcase and raced down the stairs. At the door she met a bluff, big man, gross from head to foot. It seemed to Eileen strange that she could see in him even a trace of her mother, and yet she could. Red veins crossed his cheeks and glowed on his nose. His tired eyes were watery; his thick lips had an inclination to sag; but there was heartiness in his voice and earnestness in the manner in which he picked her up.

"What have they been doing to you down here?" he demanded. "Never should have left you this long. Ought to have come down and taken you and showed you what you wanted, and then you would have known whether you wanted it or not."

At this juncture a huge woman, gross in a feminine way as her husband was in his, paddled up the walk.

"I'm comin' in and rest a few minutes," she said. "I'm tired to death and I'm pounded to pieces." Her husband turned toward her. He opened his lips to introduce Eileen. His wife forestalled him.

"So this is the Eileen you have been ravin' about for years," she said. "I thought you said she was a pretty girl."

Eileen's soul knew one sick instant of recoil. She looked from James Heitman to Caroline, his wife, and remembered that he had a habit of calling her "Callie." All that paint and powder and lipstick and brilliantine could do to make the ponderous, big woman more ghastly had been done, but in the rush of the long ride through which her husband had forced her, the colors had mixed and slipped, the false waves were displaced. She was not in any condition to criticize the appearance of another woman. For one second Eileen hesitated, then she lifted her shaking hands to her hat.

"I have been hounded out of my senses," she said apologetically, "and have been so terribly anxious for fear you wouldn't get here on time. Please, Aunt Caroline, let us go to a hotel, some place where we can straighten up comfortably."

"Well, what's your hurry?" said Aunt Caroline coolly. "You're not a fugitive from justice, are you? Can't a body rest a few minutes and have a drink, even? Besides, I am going to see what kind of a place you've been living in, and then I'll know how thankful you'll be for what we got to offer."

Eileen turned and threw open the door. The big woman walked in. She looked down the hall, up the stairway, and went on to the living room. She gave it one contemptuous glance, and turning, came back to the door.

"All right, Jim," she said brusquely. "I have seen enough. If you know the best hotel in the town, take me there. And then, if Eileen's in such a hurry, after we have had a bite we'll start for home."

"Thank you, Aunt Caroline, oh, thank you!" cried Eileen.

"You needn't take the trouble to 'aunt' me every time you speak to me," said the lady. "I know you're my niece, but I ain't goin' to remind you of it every time I speak to you. It's agein', this 'auntie' business. I don't stand for it, and as for a name, I am free to confess I always like the way Jim calls me 'Callie.' That sounds younger and more companionable than 'Caroline.'"

James Heitman looked at Eileen and winked.

"You just bet, old girl!" he said. "They ain't any of them can beat you, not even Eileen at her best. Let's get her out of here. Does this represent your luggage, girlie?"

"You said not to bother with anything else," said Eileen.

"So I did," said Uncle Jim, "and I meant just what I said if it's all right with you. I suppose I did have, in the back of my head, an idea that there might be a trunk or a box—some things that belonged to your mother, mebby, and your 'keepsakes.'"

"Oh, never mind," interrupted Eileen. "Do let's go. It's nearly four o'clock. Any minute they may send for me from the bank, and I'd be more than glad to be out of the way."

"Well, I'm not accustomed to being the porter, but if time's that precious, here we go," said Uncle Jim.

He picked up the suitcase with one hand and took his wife's arm with the other.

"Scoot down there and climb into that boat," he said proudly to Eileen. "We'll have a good dinner in a private room when we get to the hotel. I won't even register. And then we'll get out of here when we have rested a little."

"Can't we stay all night and go in the morning?" panted his wife.

"No, ma'am, we can't," said James Heitman authoritatively. "We'll eat a bite because we need to be fed up, and I sincerely hope they's some decent grub to be had in this burg. The first place we come to outside of here, that looks like they had a decent bed, we'll stop and make up for last night. But we ain't a-goin' to stay here if Eileen wants us to start right away, eh, Eileen?"

"Yes, please!" panted Eileen. "I just don't want to meet any of them. It's time enough for them to know what has happened after I am gone."

"All right then," said Uncle James. "Pile in and we'll go."

So Eileen started on the road to the unlimited wealth her soul had always craved.

CHAPTER XXIV. Linda's First Party

At the bank Linda and John Gilman waited an hour past the time set for Eileen's appearance. Then Linda asserted herself.

"I have had a feeling for some time," she said quietly, "that Eileen would not appear today, and if she doesn't see fit to come, there is no particular reason why she should. There is nothing to do but go over the revenue from the estate. The books will show what Eileen has drawn monthly for her expense budget. That can be set aside and the remainder divided equally between us. It's very simple. Here is a letter I wrote to the publishers of Father's books asking about royalties. I haven't even opened it. I will turn it in with the remainder of the business."

They were in the office with the president of the bank. He rang for the clerk he wanted and the books he required, and an hour's rapid figuring settled the entire matter, with the exception of the private account, amounting to several thousands, standing in Eileen's name. None of them knew any source of separate income she might have. At a suggestion from Linda, the paying teller was called in and asked if he could account for any of the funds that had gone into the private account.

"Not definitely," he said, "but the amounts always corresponded exactly with the royalties from the books. I strongly suspect that they constitute this private account of Miss Eileen's."

But he did not say that she had tried to draw it the day previous.

John Gilman made the suggestion that they should let the matter rest until Eileen explained about it. Then Linda spoke very quietly, but with considerable finality in her tone.

"No," she said, "I know that Eileen HAD no source of private income. Mother used to mention that she had some wealthy relatives in San Francisco, but they didn't approve of her marriage to what they called a 'poor doctor,' and she would never accept, or allow us to accept, anything from them. They never came to see us and we never went to see them. Eileen knows no more about them than I do. We will work upon the supposition that everything that is here belonged to Father. Set aside to Eileen's credit the usual amount for housekeeping expenses. Turn the private account in with the remainder. Start two new bank books, one for Eileen and one for me. Divide the surplus each month exactly in halves. And I believe this is the proper time for the bank to turn over to me a certain key, specified by my father as having been left in your possession to be delivered to me on my coming of age."

With the key in her possession, Linda and John Gilman left the bank. As they stood for a moment in front of the building, Gilman removed his hat and ran his hands through his hair as if it were irritating his head.

"Linda," he said in a deeply wistful tone, "I don't understand this. Why shouldn't Eileen have come today as she agreed? What is there about this that is not according to law and honor and the plain, simple rights of the case?"

"I don't know," said Linda; "but there is something we don't understand about it. And I am going to ask you, John, as my guardian, closing up my affairs today, to go home with me to be present when I open the little hidden door I found at the back of a library shelf when I was disposing of Daddy's technical books. There was a slip of paper at the edge of it specifying that the key was in possession of the Consolidated Bank and was to be delivered to me, in the event of Daddy's passing, on my coming of age. I have the key, but I would like to have you with me, and Eileen if she is in the house, when I open that door. I don't know what is behind it, but there's a certain feeling that always has been strong in my heart and it never was so strong as it is at this minute."

So they boarded the street car and ran out to Lilac Valley. When Katy admitted them Linda put her arm around her and kissed her. She could see that the house was freshly swept and beautifully decorated with flowers, and her trained nostrils could scent whiffs of delicious odors from food of which she was specially fond. In all her world Katy was the one person who was celebrating her birthday. She seemed rather surprised when Linda and Gilman came in together.

"Where is Eileen?" inquired Linda.

"She must have made some new friends," said Katy. "About four o'clock, the biggest car that ever roared down this street rolled up, and the biggest man and woman that I ever see came puffin' and pantin' in. Miss Eileen did not tell me where she was goin' or when she would be back, but I know it won't be the night, because she took her little dressin' case with her. Belike it's another of them trips to Riverside or Pasadena."

"Very likely," said Linda quietly. "Katy, can you spare a few minutes?"

"No, lambie, I jist can't," said Katy, "because a young person that's the apple of me eye is havin' a birthday the day and I have got me custard cake in the oven and the custard is in the makin', and after Miss Eileen went and I didn't see no chance for nothin' special, I jist happened to look out, one of the ways ye do things unbeknownst to yourself, and there stood Mr. Pater Morrison moonin' over the 'graveyard,' like he called it, and it was lookin' like seein' graves he was, and I jist took the bull by the horns, and I sings out to him and I says: 'Mr. Pater Morrison, it's a good friend ye were to the young missus when ye engineered her skylight and her beautiful fireplace, and this bein' her birthday, I'm takin' the liberty to ask ye to come to dinner and help me celebrate.' And he said he would run up to the garage and get into his raygimentals, whatever them might be, and he would be here at six o'clock. So ye got a guest for dinner, and if the custard's scorched and the cake's flat, it's up to ye for kapin' me here to tell ye all this."

Then Katy hurried to the kitchen. Linda looked at John Gilman and smiled.

"Isn't that like her?" she said.

Then she led the way to the library, pulled aside the books, fitted the key to the little door, and opened it. Inside lay a single envelope, sealed and bearing her name. She took the envelope, and walking to her father's chair beside his library table, sat down in it, and laying the envelope on the table, crossed her hands on top of it.

"John," she said, "ever since I have been big enough to think and reason and study things out for myself, there is a feeling I have had—I used to think it was unreasonable, then I thought it remote possibility. This minute I think it's extremely probable. Before I open this envelope I am going to tell you what I believe it contains. I have not the slightest evidence except personal conviction, but I believe that the paper inside this envelope is written by my father's hand and I believe it tells me that he was not Eileen's father and that I am not her sister. If it does not say this, then there is nothing in race and blood and inherited tendencies."

Linda picked up the paper cutter, ran it across the envelope, slipped out the sheet, and bracing herself she read:

MY DARLING LINDA:

These lines are to tell you that your mother went to her eternal sleep when you were born. Four years later I met and fell in love with the only mother you ever have known. At the time of our marriage we entered into a solemn compact that her little daughter by a former marriage and mine should be reared as sisters. I was to give half my earnings and to do for Eileen exactly as I did for you. She was to give half her love and her best attention to your interests.

I sincerely hope that what I have done will not result in any discomfort or inconvenience to you. With dearest love, as ever your father,

ALEXANDER STRONG.

Linda laid the sheet on the table and dropped her hands on top of it. Then she looked at John Gilman.

"John," she said, "I believe you had better face the fact that the big car and the big people that carried Eileen away today were her mother's wealthy relatives from San Francisco. She must have been in touch with them. I think very likely she sent for them after I saw her in the bank yesterday afternoon, trying with all her might to make the paying teller turn over to her the funds of the private account."

John Gilman sat very still for a long time, then he raised tired, disappointed eyes to Linda's face. "Linda," he said, "do you mean you think Eileen was not straight about money matters?"

"John," said Linda quietly, "I think it is time for the truth about Eileen between you and me. If you want me to answer that question candidly, I'll answer it."

"I want the truth," said John Gilman gravely.

"Well," said Linda, "I never knew Eileen to be honest about anything in all her life unless the truth served her better than an evasion. Her hair was not honest color and it was not honest curl. Her eyebrows were not so dark as she made them. Her cheeks and lips were not so red, her forehead and throat were not so white, her form was not so perfect. Her friends were selected because they could serve her. As long as you were poor and struggling, Marian was welcome to you. When you won a great case and became prosperous and fame came rapidly, Eileen took you. I believe what I told you a minute ago: I think she has gone for good. I think she went because she had not been fair and she would not be forced to face the fact before you and me and the president of the Consolidated today. I think you will have to take your heart home tonight and I think that before the night is over you will realize what Marian felt when she knew that in addition to having been able to take you from her, Eileen was not a woman who would make you happy. I am glad, deeply glad, that there is not a drop of her blood in my veins, sorry as I am for you and much as I regret what has happened. I won't ask you to stay tonight, because you must go through the same black waters Marian breasted, and you will want to be alone. Later, if you think of any way I can serve you, I will be glad for old sake's sake; but you must not expect me ever to love you or respect your judgment as I did before the shadow fell."

Then Linda rose, replaced the letter, turned the key in the lock, and quietly slipped out of the room.

When she opened her door and stepped into her room she paused in astonishment. Spread out upon the bed lay a dress of georgette with little touches of fur and broad ribbons of satin. In color it was like the flame of seasoned beechwood. Across the foot of the bed hung petticoat, camisole, and hose, and beside the dress a pair of satin slippers exactly matching the hose, and they seemed the right size. Linda tiptoed to the side of the bed and delicately touched the dress, and then she saw a paper lying on the waist front, and picking it up read:

Lambie, here's your birthday, from loving old Katy.

The lines were terse and to the point. Linda laid them down, and picking up the dress she walked to the mirror, and holding it under her chin glanced down the length of its reflection. What she saw almost stunned her.

"Oh, good Lord!" she said. "I can't wear that. That isn't me."

Then she tossed the dress on the bed and started in a headlong rush to the kitchen. As she came through the door, "You blessed old darling!" she cried. "What am I going to say to make you know how I appreciate your lovely, lovely gift?"

Katy raised her head. There was something that is supposed to be the prerogative of royalty in the lift of it. Her smile was complacent in the extreme.

"Don't ye be standin' there wastin' no time talkie'," she said.

"I have oodles of time," said Linda, "but I warn you, you won't know me if I put on that frock, Katy."

"Yes, I will, too," said Katy.

"Katy," said Linda, sobering suddenly, "would it make any great difference to you if I were the only one here for always, after this?"

Katy laughed contemptuously.

"Well, I'd warrant to survive it," she said coolly.

"But that is exactly what I must tell you, Katy," said Linda soberly. "You know I have told you a number of times through these years that I did not believe Eileen and I were sisters, and I am telling you now that I know it. She did not come to the bank today, and the settlement of Father's affairs developed the fact that I was my father's child and Eileen was her mother's; and I'm thinking, Katy, that the big car you saw and the opulent people in it were Eileen's mother's wealthy relatives from San Francisco. My guess is, Katy, that Eileen has gone with them for good. Lock her door and don't touch her things until we know certainly what she wants done with them."

Katy stood thinking intently, then she lifted her eyes to Linda's.

"Lambie," she whispered softly, "are we ixpected to go into mourning over this?"

A mischievous light leaped into Linda's eyes.

"Well, if there are any such expectations abroad, Katherine O'Donovan," she said soberly, "the saints preserve 'em, for we can't fulfill 'em, can we, Katy?"

"Not to be savin' our souls," answered Katy heartily. "I'm jist so glad and thankful that I don't know what to do, and it's such good news that I don't belave one word of it. And while you're talkie', what about John Gilman?"

"I think," said Linda quietly, "that tonight is going to teach him how Marian felt in her blackest hours."

"Well, he needn't be coming to me for sympathy," said Katy. "But if Miss Eileen has gone to live with the folks that come after her the day, ye might be savin' a wee crap o' sympathy for her, lambie. They was jist the kind of people that you'd risk your neck slidin' down a mountain to get out of their way."

"That is too bad," said Linda reflectively; "because Eileen is sensitive and constant contact with crass vulgarity certainly would wear on her nerves."

"Now you be goin' and gettin' into that dress, lambie," said Katy.

"Katherine O'Donovan," said Linda, "you're used to it; come again to confession. Tell me truly where and how did you get that dress?"

"'Tain't no rule of polite society to be lookin' gift horses in the mouth," said Katy proudly. "HOW I got it is me own affair, jist like ye got any gifts ye was ever makin' me, is yours. WHERE I got it? I went into the city on the strafe car and I went to the biggest store in the city and I got in the elevator and I says to the naygur: 'Let me off where real ladies buy ready-to-wear dresses.'

"And up comes a little woman, and her hair was jist as soft and curling round her ears, and brown and pretty was her eyes, and the pink that God made was in her cheeks, and in a voice like runnin' water she says: 'Could I do anything for you?' I told her what I wanted. And she says: 'How old is the young lady, and what's her size, and what's her color?' Darlin', ain't that dress the answer to what I told her?"

"Yes," said Linda. "If an artist had been selecting a dress for me he would probably have chosen that one. But, old dear, it's not suitable for me. It's not the kind of dress that I intended to wear for years and years yet. Do you think, if I put it on tonight, I'll ever be able to go back to boots and breeches again, and hunt the canyons for plants to cook for—you know what?"

Katy stood in what is commonly designated as a "brown study." Then she looked Linda over piercingly.

"Yes, ma'am," she said conclusively. "It's my judgment that ye will. I think ye'll maybe wrap the braids of ye around your head tonight, and I think ye'll put on that frock, and I think ye'll show Pater Morrison how your pa's daughter can sit at the head of his table and entertain her friends. Then I think ye'll hang it in your closet and put on your boots and breeches and go back to your old Multiflores and attind to your business, the same as before."

"All right, Katy," said Linda, "if you have that much faith in me I have that much faith in myself; but, old dear, I can't tell you how I LOVE having a pretty dress for tonight. Katy dear, the 'Day of Jubilee' has come. Before you go to sleep I'm coming to your room to tell you fine large secrets, that you won't believe for a minute, but I haven't the time to do it now."

Then Linda raced to her room and began dressing. She let down the mop of her hair waving below her waist and looked at it despairingly.

"That dress never was made for braids down your back," she said, glancing toward the bed where it lay shimmering in a mass of lovely color. "I am of age today; for state occasions I should be a woman. What shall I do with it?"

And then she recalled Katy's voice saying: "Braids round your head."

"Of course," said Linda, "that would be the thing to do. I certainly don't need anything to add to my height; I am far too tall now."

So she parted her hair in the middle, brushed it back, divided it in even halves, and instead of braiding it, she coiled it around her head, first one side and then the other.

She slipped into the dress and struggled with its many and intricate fastenings. Then she went to the guest room to stand before the full-length mirror there. Slowly she turned. Critically she examined herself.

"It's a bit shorter than I would have ordered it," she said, "but it reduces my height, it certainly gives wonderful freedom in walking, and it's not nearly so short as I see other girls wearing."

Again she studied herself critically.

"Need some kind of ornament for my hair," she muttered, "but I haven't got it, and neither do I own beads, bracelet, or a ring; and my ears are sticking right out in the air. I am almost offensively uncovered."

Then she went down to show herself to a delighted Katy. When the doorbell rang Linda turned toward the hall. Katy reached a detaining hand.

"You'll do nothing of the sort," she said. "I answered the bell for Miss Eileen. Answer the bell I shall for you."

Down the hall went Katy with the light of battle in her eyes and the air of a conqueror in the carriage of her head. She was well trained. Neither eyelid quivered as she flung the door wide to Peter Morrison. He stood there in dinner dress, more imposing than Katy had thought he could be. With quick, inner exultation she reached for two parcels he carried; over them her delight was so overpowering that Peter Morrison must have seen a hint of it. With a flourish Katy seated him, and carried the packages to Linda. She returned a second later for a big vase, and in this Linda arranged a great sheaf of radiant roses. As Katy started to carry them back to the room, Linda said "Wait a second," and selecting one half opened, she slipped it out, shortened the stem and tucked it among the coils of hair where she would have set an ornament. The other package was a big box that when opened showed its interior to be divided into compartments in each of which nestled an exquisite flower made of spun sugar. The petals, buds, and leaves were perfect. There were wonderful roses with pale pink outer petals and deeper-colored hearts. There were pink mallows that seemed as if they must have been cut from the bushes bordering Santa Monica road. There were hollyhocks of white and gold, and simply perfect tulips. Linda never before had seen such a treasure candy box. She cried out in delight, and hurried to show Katy. In her pleasure over the real flowers and the candy flowers Linda forgot her dress, but when she saw Peter Morrison standing tall and straight, in dinner dress, she stopped and looked the surprise and pleasure she felt. She had grown accustomed to Peter in khaki pottering around his building. This Peter she never before had seen. He represented something of culture, something of pride, a conformity to a nice custom and something more. Linda was not a psychoanalyst.

She could not see a wonderful aura of exquisite color enveloping Peter. But when Peter saw the girl approaching him, transformed into a woman whose shining coronet was jewelled with his living red rose, when he saw the beauty of her lithe slenderness clothed in a soft, flaming color, something emanated from his inner consciousness that Linda did see, and for an instant it disturbed her as she went forward holding out her hands.

"Peter," she said gaily, "do you know that this is my Day of Jubilee? I am a woman today by law, Peter. Hereafter I am to experience at least a moderate degree of financial freedom, and that I shall enjoy. But the greatest thing in life is friends."

Peter took both the hands extended to him and looked smilingly into her eyes.

"You take my breath," he said. "I knew, the first glimpse I ever had of you scrambling from the canyon floor, that this transformation COULD take place. My good fortune is beyond words that I have been first to see it. Permit me, fair lady."

Peter bent and kissed both her hands. He hesitated a second, then he turned the right hand and left one more kiss in its palm.

"To have and to hold!" he said whimsically.

"Thank you," said Linda, closing her fist over it and holding it up for inspection. "I'll see that it doesn't escape. And this minute I thank you for the candy, which I know is delicious, and for my very first sheaf of roses from any man. See what I have done with one of them?"

She turned fully around that he might catch the effect of the rose, and in getting that he also got the full effect of the costume, and the possibilities of the girl before him. And then she gave him a shock.

"Isn't it a lovely frock?" she said. "Another birthday gift from the Strong rock of ages. I have been making a collection of rocks for my fern bed, and I have got another collection that is not visible to anyone save myself. Katy's a rock, and you're a rock, and Donald is a rock, and Marian's a rock, and I am resting securely on all of you. I wish my father knew that in addition to Marian and Katy I have found two more such wonderful friends."

"And what about Henry Anderson?" inquired Peter. "Aren't you going to include him?"

Linda walked over to the chair in which she intended to seat herself.

"Peter," she said, "I wish you hadn't asked me that."

Peter's figure tensed suddenly.

"Look here, Linda," he said sternly, "has that rather bold youngster made himself in any way offensive to you?"

"Not in any way that I am not perfectly capable of handling myself," said Linda. She looked at Peter confidently.

"Do you suppose," she said, "that I can sit down in this thing without ruining it? Shouldn't I really stand up while I am wearing it?"

Peter laughed unrestrainedly.

"Linda, you're simply delicious," he said. "It seems to me that I have seen young ladies in like case reach round and gather the sash to one side and smooth out the skirt as they sit."

"Thank you, Peter, of course that would be the way," said Linda. "This being my first, I'm lacking in experience."

And thereupon she sat according to direction; while Peter sat opposite her.

"Now finish. Just one word more about Henry Anderson," he said. "Are you perfectly sure there is nothing I need do for you in that connection?"

"Oh, perfectly," said Linda lightly. "I didn't mean to alarm you. He merely carried that bug-catcher nonsense a trifle too far. I wouldn't have minded humoring him and fooling about it a little. But, Peter, do you know him quite well? Are you very sure of him?"

"No," said Peter, "I don't know him well at all. The only thing I am sure about him is that he is doing well in his profession. I chose him because he was an ambitious youngster and I thought I could get more careful attention from him than I could from some of the older fellows who had made their reputation. You see, there are such a lot of things I want to know about in this building proposition, and the last four years haven't been a time for any man to be careful about saving his money."

"Then," said Linda, "he is all right, of course. He must be. But I think I'm like a cat. I'm very complacent with certain people, but when I begin to get goose flesh and hair prickles my head a bit, I realize that there is something antagonistic around, something for me to beware of. I guess it's because I am such a wild creature."

"Do you mean to say," said Peter, "that these are the sensations that Henry gives you?"

Linda nodded.

"Now forget Henry," she said. "I have had such a big day I must tell you about it, and then we'll come to that last article you left me. I haven't had time to put anything on paper concerning it yet, but I believe I have an awfully good idea in the paint pot, and I'll find time in a day or two to work it out. Peter, I have just come from the bank, where I was recognized as of legal age, and my guardian discharged. And perhaps I ought to explain to you, Peter, that your friend, John Gilman, is not here because this night is going to be a bad one for him. When you knew him best he was engaged, or should have been, to Marian Thorne. When you met him this time he really was engaged to Eileen. I don't know what you think about Eileen. I don't feel like influencing anyone's thought concerning her, so I'll merely say that today has confirmed a conviction that always has been in my heart. Katy could tell you that long ago I said to her that I did not believe Eileen was my sister. Today has brought me the knowledge and proof positive that she is not, and today she has gone to some wealthy relatives of her mother in San Francisco. She expressed her contempt for what she was giving up by leaving everything, including the exquisite little necklace of pearls which has been a daily part of her since she owned them. I may be mistaken, but intuition tells me that with the pearls and the wardrobe she has also discarded John Gilman. I think your friend will be suffering tonight quite as deeply as my friend suffered when John abandoned her at a time when she had lost everything else in life but her money. I feel very sure that we won't see Eileen any more. I hope she will have every lovely thing in life."

"Amen," said Peter Morrison earnestly. "I loved John Gilman when we were in school together, but I have not been able to feel, since I located here, that he is exactly the same John; and what you have told me very probably explains the difference in him."

When Katy announced dinner Linda arose.

Peter Morrison stepped beside her and offered his arm. Linda rested her finger tips upon it and he led her to the head of the table and seated her. Then Katy served a meal that, if it had been prepared for Eileen, she would have described as a banquet. She gave them delicious, finely flavored food, stimulating, exquisitely compounded drinks that she had concocted from the rich fruits of California and mints and essences at her command. When, at the close of the meal, she brought Morrison some of the cigars Eileen kept for John Gilman, she set a second tray before Linda, and this tray contained two packages. Linda looked at Katy inquiringly, and Katy, her face beaming, nodded her sandy red head emphatically.

"More birthday gifts you've havin', me lady," she said in her mellowest Irish voice.

"More?" marveled Linda. She picked up the larger package, and opening it, found a beautiful book inscribed from her friend Donald, over which she passed caressing fingers.

"Why, how lovely of him!" she said. "How in this world did he know?"

Katherine O'Donovan could have answered that question, but she did not. The other package was from Marian. When she opened it Linda laughed unrestrainedly.

"What a joke!" she said. "I had promised myself that I would not touch a thing in Eileen's room, and before I could do justice to Katy's lovely dress I had to go there for pins for my hair and powder for my nose. This is Marian's way of telling me that I am almost a woman. Will you look at this?"

"Well, just what is it?" inquired Peter.

"Hairpins," laughed Linda, "and hair ornaments, and a box of face powder, and the little, feminine touches that my dressing table needs badly. How would you like, Peter, to finish your cigar in my workroom?"

"I would like it immensely," said Peter.

So together they climbed to the top of the house. Linda knelt and made a little ceremony of lighting the first fire in her fireplace. She pushed one of her chairs to one side for Peter, and taking the other for herself, she sat down and began the process of really becoming acquainted with him. Two hours later, as he was leaving her, Peter made a circuit of the room, scrutinizing the sketches and paintings that were rapidly covering the walls, and presently he came to the wasp. He looked at it so closely that he did not miss even the stinger. Linda stood beside him when he made his first dazed comment: "If that isn't Eileen, and true to the life!"

"I must take that down," said Linda. "I did it one night when my heart was full of bitterness."

"Better leave it," said Peter drily.

"Do you think I need it as a warning?" asked Linda.

Peter turned and surveyed her slowly.

"Linda," he said quietly, "what I think of you has not yet been written in any of the books."

CHAPTER XXV. Buena Moza

As soon as Peter had left her Linda took her box of candy flowers and several of her finest roses and went to Katy's room. She found Katy in a big rocking chair, her feet on a hassock, reading a story in Everybody's home. When her door opened and she saw her young mistress framed in it she tossed the magazine aside and sprang to her feet, but Linda made her resume her seat. The girl shortened the stems of the roses and put them in a vase on Katy's dresser.

"They may clash with your coloring a mite, Mother Machree," she said, "but by themselves they are very wonderful things, aren't they?"

Linda went over, and drawing her dress aside, sat down on the hassock and leaning against Katy's knee she held up the box of candy flowers for amazed and delighted inspection.

"Ah, the foine gintleman!" cried Katy. "Sure 'twas only a pape I had when ye opened the box, an' I didn't know how rare them beauties railly was."

"Choose the one you like best," said Linda.

But Katy would not touch the delicate things, so Linda selected a brushy hollyhock for her and then sat at her knee again.

"Katherine O'Donovan," she said solemnly, "it's up to a couple of young things such as we are, stranded on the shoals of the Pacific as we have been, to put our heads together and take counsel. You're a host, Katy, and while I am taking care of you, I'll be just delighted to have you go on looking after your black sheep; but it's going to be lonely, for all that. After Eileen has taken her personal possessions, what do you say to fixing up that room with the belongings that Marian kept, and inviting her to make that suite her home until such time as she may have a home of her own again?"

"Foine!" cried Katy. "I'd love to be havin' her. I'd agree to take orders from Miss Marian and to be takin' care of her jist almost the same as I do of ye, Miss Linda. The one thing I don't like about it is that it ain't fair nor right to give even Marian the best. Ye be takin' that suite yourself, lambie, and give Miss Marian your room all fixed up with her things, or, if ye want her nearer, give her the guest room and make a guest room of yours."

"I am willing to follow either of the latter suggestions for myself," said Linda; "it might be pleasant to be across the hall from Marian where we could call back and forth to each other. I wouldn't mind a change as soon as I have time to get what I'd need to make the change. I'll take the guest room for mine, and you may call in a decorator and have my room freshly done and the guest things moved into it."

Katy looked belligerent. Linda reached up and touched the frowning lines on her forehead.

"Brighten your lovely features with a smile, Katherine me dear," she said gaily. "Don't be forgetting that this is our Day of Jubilee. We are free—I hope we are free forever—from petty annoyances and dissatisfactions and little, galling things that sear the soul and bring out all the worst in human nature. I couldn't do anything to Eileen's suite, not even if I resorted to tearing out partitions and making it new from start to finish, that would eliminate Eileen from it for me. If Marian will give me permission to move and install her things in it, I think she can use it without any such feeling, but I couldn't. It's agreed then, Katy, I am to write to Marian and extend to her a welcome on your part as well as on mine?"

"That ye may, lambie," said Katy heartily. "And, as the boss used to be sabin', just to make assurance doubly sure, if YoU would address it for me I would be writin' a bit of a line myself, conveyin' to her me sentiments on the subject."

"Oh, fine, Katy; Marian would be delighted!" cried Linda, springing up.

"And, Katy dear, it won't make us feel any more like mourning for Eileen when I tell you that it developed at the bank yesterday and today, that since she has been managing household affairs she has deposited in a separate account all the royalties from Father's books. I had thought the matter closed at the bank when this fund was added to the remainder of the estate, the household expenses set aside to Eileen, and the remainder divided equally between us. I didn't get the proof that she was not my sister until after I came home. I think it means that I shall have to go back to the bank, have the matter reopened, and unless she can produce a will or something proving that she is entitled to it, it seems to me that what remains of my father's estate is legally mine. Of course, if it develops that he has made any special provision for her, she shall have it; otherwise, Katy, we'll be in a position to install you as housekeeper and put some light-footed, capable young person under you for a step-saver in any direction you want to use her. It means, too, that I shall be able to repay your loan immediately and to do the things that I wanted to do about the house."

"Now I ain't in any hurry about that money, lambie," said Katy; "and you understand of course that the dress you're wearin' I am given' ye."

"Of course, old dear, and you should have seen Peter Morrison light up and admire it. He thinks you have wonderful taste, Katy."

Katy threw up both her hands.

"Oh, my Lord, lambie!" she cried, aghast. "Was you tellin' him that the dress ye were wearin' was a present from your old cook?"

"Why, certainly I was," said Linda, wide eyed with astonish meet. "Why shouldn't I? I was proud to. And now, old dear, before I go, the biggest secret of all. I had a letter, Katy, from the editor of Everybody's Home, and people like our articles, Katy; they are something now and folk are letting the editor know about it, and he wants all I can send him. He likes the pictures I make; and, Katy, you won't believe it till I show you my little bank book, but for the three already published with their illustrations he pays me five hundred nice, long, smooth, beautifully decorated, paper dollars!"

"Judas praste!" cried Katy, her hands once more aloft. "Ye ain't manin' it, lambie?"

"Yes, I are," laughed Linda. "I've got the money; and for each succeeding three with their pictures I am to have that much more, and when I finish—now steady yourself, Katy, because this is going to be a shock—when I finish, blessed old dear heart, he is going to make them into a book! That will be my job for this summer, and you shall help me, and it will be a part of our great secret. Won't it be the most fun?"

"My soul!" said Katy. "You're jist crazy. I don't belave a word you're tellin' me."

"But I can prove it, because I have the letter and the bank book," said Linda.

Katy threw her arms around the girl and kissed the top of her head and cried over her and laughed at the same time and patted her and petted her and ended by saying: "Oh, lambie, if only the master could be knowin' it."

"But he does know, Katy," said Linda.

She went to her room, removed the beautiful dress and, arranging it on a hanger, left it in her closet. Slipping into an old dressing gown, she ran to her workroom and wrote a letter to Marian from herself. She tried not to tell Marian the big, vital thing that was throbbing in her heart all day concerning her work, the great secret that meant such a wonderful thing to her, the thing that was beating in her heart and fluttering behind her lips like a bird trying to escape its cage; but she could tell her in detail of Eileen's undoubted removal to San Francisco; she could tell her enough of the financial transactions of the day to make her understand what had been happening in the past; and she could tell of her latest interview with John Gilman. Once, as she sat with her pen poised, thinking how to phrase a sentence, Linda said to herself: "I wonder in my heart if he won't try to come crawfishing back to Marian now, and if he does, I wonder, oh, how I wonder, what she will do." Linda shut her lips very tight and stared up through her skylight to the stars, as she was fast falling into a habit of doing when she wanted inspiration.

"Well, I know one thing," she said to the shining things above her, "Marian will do as she sees fit, of course, but if it were I, and any man had discarded me as John Gilman discarded Marian, in case he ever wanted to pick me up again he would find I was not there. Much as I plan in my heart for the home and the man and the little people that I hope to have some day, I would give up all of them before I would be discarded and re-sought like that; and knowing Marian as I do, I have a conviction that she will feel the same way. From the things she is writing about this Snow man I think it is highly probable that he may awake some day to learn that he is not so deeply grieved but that he would like to have Marian to comfort him in his loneliness; and as for his little girl I don't see where he could find a woman who would rear her more judiciously and beautifully than Marian would."

She finished her letter, sealed and stamped it, and then, taking out a fresh sheet, she lettered in at the top of it, "INDIAN POTATOES" and continued:

And very good potatoes they are. You will find these growing everywhere throughout California, blooming from May to July, their six long, slender, white petals shading to gold at the base, grayish on the outside, a pollen-laden pistil upstanding, eight or ten gold-clubbed stamens surrounding it, the slender brown stem bearing a dozen or more of these delicate blooms, springing high from a base of leaves sometimes nearly two feet long and an inch broad, wave margined, spreading in a circle around it. In the soil of the plains and the dry hillsides you will find an amazingly large solid bulb, thickly enwrapped in a coat of brown fiber, the long threads of which can be braided, their amazing strength making them suitable for bow strings, lariats, or rope of any kind that must needs be improvised for use at the moment. The bulbs themselves have many uses. Crushed and rubbed up in water they make a delightful cleansing lather. The extracted juice, when cooked down, may be used as glue. Of the roasted bulbs effective poultices for bruises and boils may be made. It was an Indian custom to dam a small stream and throw in mashed Amole bulbs, the effect of which was to stupefy the fish so that they could be picked out by hand; all of which does not make it appear that the same bulb would serve as an excellent substitute for a baked potato; but we must remember how our grandmothers made starch from our potatoes, used them to break in the new ironware, and to purify the lard; which goes to prove that one vegetable may be valuable for many purposes. Amole, whose ponderous scientific name is Chlorogalum pomeridiarum, is at its best for my purposes when all the chlorophyll from flower and stem has been driven back to the bulb, and it lies ripe and fully matured from late August until December.

Remove the fibrous cover down to the second or third layer enclosing the bulb. These jackets are necessary as they keep the bulbs from drying out and having a hard crust. Roast them exactly as you would potatoes. When they can easily be pierced with a silver fork remove from the oven, and serve immediately with any course with which you would use baked potatoes.

"And gee, but they're good!" commented Linda as she reread what she had written.

After that she turned her attention to drawing a hillside whitened here and there with amole bloom showing in its purity against the warm grayish-tan background. The waving green leaves ran among big rocks and overlapped surrounding growth. At the right of her drawing Linda sketched in a fine specimen of monkey flower, deepening the yellow from the hearts of the amole lilies for the almost human little monkey faces. On the left one giant specimen of amole, reared from a base of exquisitely waving leaves, ran up the side of the drawing and broke into an airy and graceful head of gold-hearted white lilies. For a long time Linda sat with poised pencil, studying her foreground. What should she introduce that would be most typical of the location and gave her the desired splash of contrasting color that she used as a distinctive touch in the foreground of all her drawings?

Her pencil flew busily a few minutes while she sketched in a flatly growing bush of prickly phlox, setting the flower faces as closely as the overlapped scales of a fish, setting them even as they grow in nature; and when she resorted to the color box she painted these faces a wonderful pink that was not wild rose, not cerise, not lilac, but it made one think of all of them. When she could make no further improvement on this sketch, she carefully stretched it against the wall and tacked it up to dry.

Afterward she cleared her mental decks of all the work she could think of in order to have Saturday free, because Saturday was the day upon which she found herself planning in the back of her mind throughout the strenuous week, to save for riding the King's Highway with Donald Whiting. Several times she had met him on the walks or in the hallways, and always he had stopped to speak with her and several times he had referred to the high hope in which he waited for Saturday. Linda already had held a consultation with Katy on the subject of the lunch basket. That matter being satisfactorily arranged, there was nothing for her to do but to double on her work so that Saturday would be free. Friday evening Linda was called from the dinner table to the telephone. She immediately recognized the voice inquiring for her as that of Judge Whiting, and then she listened breathlessly while he said to her: "You will recognize that there is very little I may say over a telephone concerning a matter to which you brought my attention. I have a very competent man looking into the matter thoroughly, and I find that your fear is amply justified. Wherever you go or whatever you do, use particular care. Don't have anything to do with any stranger. Just use what your judgment and common sense tell you is a reasonable degree of caution in every direction no matter how trivial. You understand?"

"I do," said Linda promptly. "Would you prefer that we do not go on any more Saturday trips at present?"

The length of time that the Judge waited to answer proved that he had taken time to think.

"I can't see," he said finally, "that you would not be safer on such a trip where you are moving about, where no one knows who you are, than you would where you are commonly found."

"All right then," said Linda. "Ask the party we are considering and he will tell you where he will be tomorrow. Thank you very much for letting me know. If anything should occur, you will understand that it was something quite out of my range of fore-sight."

"I understand," said the Judge.

With all care and many loving admonitions Katy assisted in the start made early Saturday morning. The previous Saturday Linda had felt that all nature along the road she planned to drive would be at its best, but they had not gone far until she modified her decision. They were slipping through mists of early morning, over level, carefully made roads like pavilion floors. If any one objection could have been made, it would have been that the mists of night were weighting too heavily to earth the perfume from the blooming orchards and millions of flowers in gardens and along the roadside. At that hour there were few cars abroad. Linda was dressed in her outing suit of dark green. She had removed her hat and slipped it on the seat beside her. She looked at Donald, a whimsical expression on her most expressive young face.

"Please to 'scuse me," she said lightly, "if I step on the gas a mite while we have the road so much to ourselves and are so familiar with it. Later, when we reach stranger country and have to share with others, we'll be forced to go slower."

"Don't stint your speed on account of me," said Donald. "I am just itching to know what Kitty can do."

"All right, here's your chance," said Linda. "Hear her purr?"

She settled her body a trifle tensely, squared her shoulders, and gripped the steering wheel. Then she increased the gas and let the Bear Cat roll over the smooth road from Lilac Valley running south into Los Angeles. At a speed that was near to flying as a non-professional attains, the youngsters traveled that road. Their eyes were shining; their blood was racing. Until the point where rougher roads and approaching traffic forced them to go slower, they raced, and when they slowed down they looked at each other and laughed in morning delight.

"I may not be very wise," said Linda, "but didn't I do the smartest thing when I let Eileen have the touring car and saved the Bear Cat for us?"

"Nothing short of inspiration," said Donald. "The height of my ambition is to own a Bear Cat. If Father makes any mention of anything I would like particularly to have for a graduation present, I am cocked and primed as to what I shall tell him."

"You'd better save yourself a disappointment," said Linda soberly. "You will be starting to college this fall, and when you do you will be gone nine months out of the year, and I am fairly sure your father wouldn't think shipping a Bear Cat back and forth a good investment, or furnishing you one to take to school with you. He would fear you would never make a grade that would be a credit to him if he did."

"My!" laughed Donald, "you've got a long head on your shoulders!"

"When you're thrown on your own for four of the longest, lonesomest years of your life, you learn to think," said Linda soberly.

She was touching the beginning of Los Angeles traffic. Later she was on the open road again. The mists were thinning and lifting. The perfume was not so heavy. The sheeted whiteness of the orange groves was broken with the paler white of plum merging imperceptibly into the delicate pink of apricot and the stronger pink of peach, and there were deep green orchards of smooth waxen olive foliage and the lacy-leaved walnuts. Then came the citrus orchards again, and all the way on either hand running with them were almost uninterrupted miles of roses of every color and kind, and everywhere homes ranging from friendly mansions, all written over in adorable flower color with the happy invitation, "Come in and make yourself at home," to tiny bungalows along the wayside crying welcome to this gay pair of youngsters in greetings fashioned from white and purple wisteria, gold bignonia, every rose the world knows, and myriad brilliant annual and perennial flower faces gathered from the circumference of the tropical globe and homing enthusiastically on the King's Highway. Sometimes Linda lifted her hand from the wheel to wave a passing salute to a particularly appealing flower picture. Sometimes she whistled a note or cried a greeting to a mockingbird, a rosy finch, or a song sparrow.

"Look at the pie timber!" she cried to Donald, calling his attention to a lawn almost covered with red-winged blackbirds. "Four hundred and twenty might be baked in that pie," she laughed.

Then a subtle change began to creep over the world. The sun peered over the mountains inquiringly, a timid young thing, as if she were asking what degree of light and warmth they would like for the day. A new brilliancy tinged every flower face in this light, a throbbing ecstasy mellowed every bird note; the orchards dropped farther apart, meadows filled with grazing cattle flashed past them, the earthy scent of freshly turned fields mingled with flower perfume, and on their right came drifting in a cool salt breath from the sea. At mid-forenoon, as they neared Laguna, they ran past great hills, untouched since the days when David cried: "I will lift up mine eyes unto the hills from whence cometh my help." At one particularly beautiful range, draped with the flowing emerald of spring, decorated with beds of gold poppy, set with flowering madrona and manzanita, with the gold of yellow monkey flower or the rich red of the related species, with specimens of lupin growing in small trees, here and there adventurous streams singing and flashing their unexpected way to the mother breast of the waiting ocean very near to the road which at one surprising turn carried them to the never-ending wonder of the troubled sea, they drove as slowly as the Bear Cat would consent to travel, so that they might study great boulders, huge as many of the buildings they had passed, their faces scarred by the wrack of ages. Studying their ancient records one could see that they had been familiar with the star that rested over Bethlehem. On their faces had shone the same moon that opened the highways Journeying into Damascus. They had stood the storms that had beaten upon the world since the days when the floods subsided, the land lifted above the face of the waters in gigantic upheavals that had ripped the surface of the globe from north to south and forced up the hills, the foothills, and the mountains of the Coast Range. They had been born then, they had first seen the light of day, in glowing, molten, red-hot, high-piled streams of lava that had gushed forth in that awful evolution of birth.

Sometimes Linda stopped the car, they left it, and climbed over the faces of these mighty upheavals. Once Linda reached her hand to Donald and cried, half laughingly, half in tense earnest: "Oh, kid, we have got to hurry. Compared with the age of these, we've only a few minutes. It's all right to talk jestingly about 'the crack of doom' but you know there really was a crack of doom, and right here is where it cracked and spewed out the material that hardened into these very rocks. Beside them I feel as a shrimp must feel beside a whale, and I feel that we must hurry."

"And so we must," said Donald. "I'm hungry as Likeliest when he waited for them to find enough peacock tongues to satisfy his appetite."

"I wonder what brand of home-brew made him think of that," said Linda.

"Well, you know," said Donald, "the world was only a smallish place then. They didn't have to go far to find everything to which they had access, and it must have been rather a decent time in which to live. Awful lot of light and color and music and unique entertainment."

"You're talking," said Linda, "from the standpoint of the king or the master. Suppose you had lived then and had been the slave."

"There you go again," said Donald, "throwing a brick into the most delicate mechanism of my profound thought. You ought to be ashamed to round me up with something scientific and materialistic every time I go a-glimmering. Don't you think this would be a fine place to have lunch?"

"You wait and see where we lunch today, and you will have the answer to that," said Linda, starting back to the Bear Cat.

A few miles farther on they followed the road around the frowning menace of an overhanging rock and sped out directly to the panorama of the sea. The sun was shining on it, but, as always round the Laguna shore, the rip tide was working itself into undue fury. It came dashing up on the ancient rocks until one could easily understand why a poet of long ago wrote of sea horses. Some of the waves did suggest monstrous white chargers racing madly to place their feet upon the solid rock.

Through the village, up the steep inclines, past placid lakes, past waving yellow mustard beds, beside highways where the breastplate of Mother Earth gleamed emerald and ruby against the background of billions of tiny, shining diamonds of the iceplant, past the old ostrich tree reproduced by etchers of note the world over, with grinding brakes, sliding down the breathless declivity leading to the shore, Linda stopped at last where the rock walls lifted sheer almost to the sky. She led Donald to a huge circle carpeted with cerise sand verbena, with pink and yellow iceplant bloom, with jewelled iceplant foliage, with the running blue of the lovely sea daisy, with the white and pink of the sea fig, where the walls were festooned with ferns, lichens, studded all over with flaming Our Lord's Candles, and strange, uncanny, grotesque flower forms, almost human in their writhing turns as they twisted around the rocks and slipped along clinging to the sheer walls. Just where the vegetation met the white, sea-washed sand, Linda spread the Indian blanket, and Donald brought the lunch box. At their feet adventurous waves tore themselves to foam on the sharp rocks. On their left they broke in booming spray, tearing and fretting the base of cliffs that had stood impregnable through aeons of such ceaseless attack and repulse.

"I wonder," said Donald, "how it comes that I have lived all my life in California, and today it seems to me that most of the worthwhile things I know about her I owe to you. When I go to college this winter the things I shall be telling the boys will be how I could gain a living, if I had to, on the desert, in Death Valley, from the walls of Multiflores Canyon; and how the waves go to smash on the rocks of Laguna, not to mention cactus fish hooks, mescal sticks, and brigand beefsteak. It's no wonder the artists of all the world come here copying these pictures. It's no wonder they build these bungalows and live here for years, unsatisfied with their efforts to reproduce the pictures of the Master Painter of them all."

"I wonder," said Linda, "if anybody is very easily satisfied. I wonder today if Eileen is satisfied with being merely rich. I wonder if we are satisfied to have this golden day together. I wonder if the white swallows are satisfied with the sea. I wonder if those rocks are satisfied and proud to stand impregnable against the constant torment of the tide."

"I wonder, oh, Lord, how I wonder," broke in Donald, "about Katherine O'Donovan's lunch box. If you want a picture of per feet satisfaction, Belinda beloved, lead me to it!"

"Thank heaven you're mistaken," she said; "they spared me the 'Be'—. It's truly just 'Linda.'"

"Well, I'm not sparing you the 'Be—'," said Donald, busy with the fastenings of the lunch basket. "Did you hear where I used it?"

"Yes, child, and I like it heaps," said Linda casually. "It's fine to have you like me. Awfully proud of myself."

"You have two members of our family at your feet," said Donald soberly as he handed her packages from the box. "My dad is beginning to discourse on you with such signs of intelligence that I am almost led to believe, from some of his wildest outbursts, that he has had some personal experience in some way."

"And why not?" asked Linda lightly. "Haven't I often told you that my father constantly went on fishing and hunting trips, that he was a great collector of botanical specimens, that he frequently took his friends with him? You might ask your father if he does not recall me as having fried fish and made coffee and rendered him camp service when I was a slip of a thing in the dawn of my teens."

"Well, he didn't just mention it," said Donald, "but I can easily see how it might have been."

After they had finished one of Katy's inspired lunches, in which a large part of the inspiration had been mental on Linda's part and executive on Katy's, they climbed rock faces, skirted wave-beaten promontories, and stood peering from overhanging cliffs dipping down into the fathomless green sea, where the water boiled up in turbulent fury. Linda pointed out the rocks upon which she would sit, if she were a mermaid, to comb the seaweed from her hair. She could hear the sea bells ringing in those menacing depths, but Donald's ears were not so finely tuned. At the top of one of the highest cliffs they climbed, there grew a clump of slender pale green bushes, towering high above their heads with exquisitely cut blue-green leaves, lance shaped and slender. Donald looked at the fascinating growth appraisingly.

"Linda," he said, "do you know that the slimness and the sheerness and the audacious foothold and the beauty of that thing remind me of you? It is covered all over with the delicate frostbloom you taught me to see upon fruit. I find it everywhere but you have never told me what it is."

Linda laughingly reached up and broke a spray of greenish-yellow tubular flowers, curving out like clustered trumpets spilling melody from their fluted throats.

"You will see it everywhere. You will find these flowers every month of the year," she said, "and I am particularly gladsome that this plant reminds you of me. I love the bluish-green 'bloom' of its sheer foliage. I love the music these flower trumpets make to me. I love the way it has traveled, God knows how, all the way from the Argentine and spread itself over our country wherever it is allowed footing. I am glad that there is soothing in these dried leaves for those who require it. I shall be delighted to set my seal on you with it. There are two little Spanish words that it suggests to the Mexican—Buena moza—but you shall find out for yourself what they mean."

Encountering his father that night at his library door, Donald Whiting said to him: "May I come in, Dad? I have something I must look up before I sleep. Have you a Spanish lexicon, or no doubt you have this in your head."

"Well, I've a halting vocabulary," said the Judge. "What's your phrase?"

"Linda put this flower on me today," said Donald, "and she said she was pleased because I said the tall, slender bush it grew on reminded me of her. She gave me the Spanish name, but I don't know the exact significance of the decoration I am wearing until I learn the meaning of the phrase."

"Try me on it," said the Judge.

"'Buena moza,'" quoted Donald.

The Judge threw back his head and laughed heartily.

"Son," he said, "you should know that from the Latin you're learning. You should translate it instinctively. I couldn't tell you exactly whether a Spaniard would translate 'Buena' 'fine' or 'good.' Knowing their high-falutin' rendition of almost everything else I would take my chance on 'fine.' Son, your phrase means 'a fine girl.'"

Donald looked down at the flower in his buttonhole, and then he looked straight at his father.

"And only the Lord knows, Dad," he said soberly, "exactly how fine Linda-girl is."

CHAPTER XXVI. A Mouse Nest

LINDA DEAREST:

I am delighted that you had such a wonderful birthday. I would take a shot in air that anything you don't understand about it you might with reasonable safety charge to Katherine O'Donovan. I think it was great of her to have a suitable and a becoming dress waiting for you and a congenial man like Peter Morrison to dine with you. He appealed to me as being a rare character, highly original, and, I should think, to those who know him well he must be entertaining and lovable in the extreme. I never shall be worried about you so long as I know that he is taking care of you.

I should not be surprised if some day I meet Eileen somewhere, because Dana and I are going about more than you would believe possible. I heartily join with you in wishing her every good that life can bring her. I don't want to be pessimistic, but I can't help feeling, Linda, that she is taking a poor way to win the best, and I gravely doubt whether she finds it in the spending of unlimited quantities of the money of a coarse man who stumbled upon his riches accidentally, as has many a man of California and Colorado.

I intended, when I sat down to write, the very first thing I said, to thank you for your wonderful invitation, seconded so loyally and cordially by Katy, to make my home with you until the time comes—if it ever does come—when I shall have a home of my own again. And just as simply and wholeheartedly as you made the offer, I accept it. I am enclosing the address and the receipt for my furniture in storage, and a few lines ordering it delivered at your house and the bill sent to me. I only kept a few heirlooms and things of Mother's and Father's that are very precious to me. Whenever Eileen takes her things you can order mine in and let me know, and I'll take a day or two off and run down for a short visit.

Mentioning Eileen makes me think of John. I think of him more frequently than I intend or wish that I did, but I feel my ninth life is now permanently extinguished concerning him. I thought I detected in your letter, Linda dear, a hint of fear that he might come back to me and that I might welcome him. If you have any such feeling in your heart, abandon it, child, because, while I try not to talk about myself, I do want to say that I rejoice in a family inheritance of legitimate pride. I couldn't give the finest loyalty and comradeship I had to give to a man, have it returned disdainfully, and then furbish up the pieces and present it over again. If I can patch those same pieces and so polish and refine them that I can make them, in the old phrase, "as good as new," possibly in time— but, Linda, one thing is certain as the hills of morning. Never in my life will any man make any headway with me again with vague suggestions and innuendoes and hints. If ever any man wants to be anything in my life, he will speak plainly and say what he wants and thinks and hopes and intends and feels in not more than two-syllable English. I learned my lesson about the futility of building your house of dreams on a foundation of sand. Next time I erect a dream house, it is going to have a proper foundation of solid granite. And that may seem a queer thing for me to say when you know that I am getting the joy in my life, that I do not hesitate to admit I am, from letters written by a man whose name I don't know. It may be that I don't know the man, but I certainly am very well acquainted with him, and in some way he seems to me to be taking on more definite form. I should not be surprised if I were to recognize him the first time I met him face to face.

Linda looked through the skylight and cried out to the stars: "Good heavens! Have I copied Peter too closely?"

She sat thinking a minute and then she decided she had not.

And in this connection you will want to know how I am progressing in my friendship with the junior partner, and what kind of motorist I am making. I am still driving twice a week, and lately on Sundays in a larger car, taking Dana and a newspaper friend of hers along. I think I have driven every hazard that this part of California affords except the mountains; Mr. Snow is still merciful about them.

Linda dear, I know what you're dying to know. You want to know whether Mr. Snow is in the same depths of mourning as when our acquaintance first began. This, my dear child, is very reprehensible of you. Young girls with braids down their backs—and by the way, Linda, you did not tell me what happened "after the ball was over." Did you go to school the next morning with braids down your back, or wearing your coronet? Because on that depends what I have to say to you now; if you went with braids, you're still my little girl chum, the cleanest, finest kid I have ever known; but if you wore your coronet, then you're a woman and my equal and my dearest friend, far dearer than Dana even; and I tell you this, Linda, because I want you always to understand that you come first.

I have tried and tried to visualize you, and can't satisfy my mind as to whether the braids are up or down. Going on the assumption that they are up, and that life may in the near future begin to hold some interesting experiences for you, I will tell you this, beloved child: I don't think Mr. Snow is mourning quite so deeply as he was. I have not been asked, the last four or five trips we have been on, to carry an armload of exquisite flowers to the shrine of a departed love. I have been privileged to take them home and arrange them in my room and Dana's. And I haven't heard so much talk about loneliness, and I haven't seen such tired, sad eyes. It seems to me that a familiar pair of shoulders are squaring up to the world again, and a very kind pair of eyes are brighter with interest. I don't know how you feel about this; I don't know how I feel about it myself. I am sure that Eugene Snow is a man who, in the years to come, would line up beside your father and mine, and I like him immensely. It is merely a case of not liking him less, but of liking my unknown man more. I couldn't quite commit the sacrilege, Linda dear, of sending you a sample of the letters I am receiving, but they are too fanciful and charming for any words of mine to describe adequately. I don't know who this man is, or what he has to offer, or whether he intends to offer anything, but it is a ridiculous fact, Linda, that I would rather sit with him in a chimney corner of field boulders, on a pine floor, with a palm roof and an Ocotillo candle, than to glow in the parchment-shielded electric light of the halls of a rich man. In a recent letter, Linda, there was a reference to a woman who wore "a diadem of crystallized light." It was a beautiful thing and I could not help taking it personally. It was his way of telling me that he knew me, and knew my tragedy; and, as I said before, I am beginning to feel that I have him rather definitely located; and I can understand the fine strain in him that prompted his anonymity, and his reasons for it. Of course I am not sufficiently confident yet to say anything definite, but my heart is beginning to say things that I sincerely hope my lips never will be forced to deny.

Linda laid down the letter, folded her hands across it, and once more looked at the stars.

"Good gracious!" she said. "I am tincturing those letters with too much Peter. I'll have to tone down a bit. Next thing I know she will be losing her chance with that wonderful Snow man for a dream. In my efforts to comfort her I must have gone too far. It is all right to write a gushy love letter and stuff it full of Peter's whimsical nonsense, but, in the language of the poet, how am I going to 'deliver the goods'? Of course that talk about Louise Whiting was all well enough. Equally, of course, I outlined and planted the brook and designed the bridge for Marian, whether she knows it or Peter knows it, or not. If they don't know it, it's about time they were finding it out. I think it's my job to visit Peter more frequently and see if I can't invent some way to make him see the light. I will give Katy a hint in the morning. Tomorrow evening I'll go up and have supper with him and see if he has another article in the stewpan. I like this work with Peter. I like having him make me dream dreams and see pictures. I like the punch and the virility he puts into my drawings. It's all right reproducing monkey flowers and lilies for pastime, but for serious business, for real life work, I would rather do Peter's brainstorming, heart-thrilling pictures than my merely pretty ones. On the subject of Peter, I must remember in the morning to take those old books he gave me to Donald. I believe that from one of them he is going to get the very material he needs to down the Jap in philosophy. And they are not text books which proves that Peter must have been digging into the subject and hunted them up in some second-hand store, or even sent away an order for them."

In the hall the next morning Linda stopped Donald and gave him the books. In the early stages of their friendship she had looked at him under half-closed lids and waited to see whether he intended stopping to say a word with her when they passed each other or came down the halls together. She knew that their acquaintance would be noted and commented upon, and she knew how ready the other girls would be to say that she was bold and forward, so she was careful to let Donald make the advances, until he had called to her so often, and had dug flowers and left his friends waiting at her door while he delivered them, that she felt free to address him as she chose. He had shown any interested person in the high school that he was her friend, that he was speaking to her exactly as he did to girls he had known from childhood. He was very popular among the boys and girls of his class and the whole school. His friendship, coming at the time of Linda's rebellion on the subject of clothes, had developed a tendency to bring her other friendships. Boys who never had known she was in existence followed Donald's example in stopping her to say a word now and then. Girls who had politely ignored her now found things to say; and several invitations she had not had leisure to accept had been sent to her for afternoon and evening entertainments among the young people. Linda had laid out for herself something of a task in deciding to be the mental leader of her class. There were good brains in plenty among the other pupils. It was only by work, concentration, and purpose, only by having a mind keenly alert, by independent investigation and introducing new points of view that she could hold her prestige. Up to the receipt of her letter containing the offer to publish her book she had been able rigorously to exclude from her mind the personality and the undertakings of Jane Meredith. She was Linda Strong in the high school and for an hour or two at her studies. She was Jane Meredith over the desert, through the canyons, beside the sea, in her Multiflores kitchen or in Katherine O'Donovan's. But this book offer opened a new train of thought, a new series of plans. She could see her way—thanks to her father she had the material in her mind and the art in her finger tips—to materialize what she felt would be even more attractive in book form than anything her editor had been able to visualize from her material. She knew herself, she knew her territory so minutely. Frequently she smiled when she read statements in her botanies as to where plants and vegetables could be found. She knew the high home of the rare and precious snow plant. She knew the northern limit of the strawberry cactus. She knew where the white sea swallow nested. She knew where the Monarch butterfly went on his winter migration. She knew where the trap-door spider, with cunning past the cunning of any other architect of Nature, built his small, round, silken-lined tower and hinged his trap door so cleverly that only he could open it from the outside. She had even sat immovable and watched him erect his house, and she would have given much to see him weave its silver lining.

Linda was fast coming to the place where she felt herself to be one in an interested group of fellow workers. She no longer gave a thought to what kind of shoes she wore. Other girls were beginning to wear the same kind. The legislatures of half a dozen states were passing laws regulating the height of heel which might be worn within their boundaries. Manufacturers were promising for the coming season that suitable shoes would be built for street wear and mountain climbing, for the sands of the sea and the sands of the desert, and the sheer face of canyons. The extremely long, dirt-sweeping skirts were coming up; the extremely short, immodest skirts were coming down. A sane and sensible wave seemed to be sweeping the whole country. Under the impetus of Donald Whiting's struggles to lead his classes and those of other pupils to lead theirs a higher grade of scholarship was beginning to be developed throughout the high school. Pupils were thinking less of what they wore and how much amusement they could crowd in, and more about making grades that would pass them with credit from year to year. The horrors of the war and the disorders following it had begun to impress upon the young brains growing into maturity the idea that soon it would be their task to take over the problems that were now vexing the world's greatest statesmen and its wisest and most courageous women. A tendency was manifesting itself among young people to equip themselves to take a worthy part in the struggles yet to come. Classmates who had looked with toleration upon Linda's common-sense shoes and plain dresses because she was her father's daughter, now looked upon her with respect and appreciation because she started so many interesting subjects for discussion, because she was so rapidly developing into a creature well worth looking at. Always she would be unusual because of her extreme height, her narrow eyes, her vivid coloring. But a greater maturity, a fuller figure, had come to be a part of the vision with which one looked at Linda. In these days no one saw her as she was. Even her schoolmates had fallen into the habit of seeing her as she would be in the years to come.

Thus far she had been able to keep her identities apart without any difficulty; but the book proposition was so unexpected, it was such a big thing to result from her modest beginning, that Linda realized that she must proceed very carefully, she must concentrate with all her might, else her school work would begin to suffer in favor of the book. Recently so many things had arisen to distract her attention. Many days she had not been able to keep Eileen's face off her geometry papers; and again she saw Gilman's, anxious and pain-filled. Sometimes she found herself lifting her eyes from tasks upon which she was concentrating with all her might, and with no previous thought whatever she was searching for Donald Whiting, and when she saw him, coming into muscular and healthful manhood, she returned to her work with more strength, deeper vision, a quiet, assured feeling around her heart. Sometimes, over the edge of Literature and Ancient History, Peter Morrison looked down at her with gravely questioning eyes and dancing imps twisting his mouth muscles, and Linda paused a second to figure upon what had become an old problem with her. Why did her wild-flower garden make Peter Morrison think of a graveyard? What was buried there besides the feet of her rare flowers? She had not as yet found the answer.

This day her thoughts were on Peter frequently because she intended to see him that night. She was going to share with him a supper of baked ham and beans and bread and butter and pickled onions and little nut cakes, still warm from Katy's oven. She was going to take Katy with her in order that she might see Peter Morrison's location and the house for his dream lady, growing at the foot of the mountain like a gay orchid homing on a forest tree. To Linda it was almost a miracle, the rapidity with which a house could be erected in California. In a few weeks' time she had seen a big cellar scooped out of the plateau, had seen it lined and rising to foundation height above the surface in solid concrete, faced outside with cracked boulders. She had seen a framework erected, a rooftree set, and joists and rafters and beams swinging into place. Fretworks of lead and iron pipe were running everywhere, and wires for electricity. Soon shingles and flooring would be going into place, and Peter said that when he had finished acrobatic performances on beams and girders and really stepped out on solid floors where he might tread without fear of breaking any of his legs, he would perform a Peacock Dance all by himself.

"Peter, you sound like a centipede," said Linda.

"Dear child," said Peter, "when I enter my front door and get to the back on two-inch footing, I positively feel that I have numerous legs, and I ache almost as badly in the fear that I shall break the two I have, as I should if they were really broken."

And then he added a few words on a subject of which he had not before spoken to Linda.

"It was like that in France. When we really got into the heat of things and the work was actually being done, we were not afraid: we were too busy; we were 'supermen.' The time when we were all legs and arms and head, and all of them were being blown away wholesale was when the shells whined over while we had a rest hour and were trying to sleep, or in the cold, dim dawn when we stumbled out stiff, hungry, and sleepy. It's not the REAL THING when it's really occurring that gets one. It's the devils of imagination tormenting the soul. There is only one thing in this world can happen to me that is really going to be as bad as the things I dream."

Linda looked down Lilac Valley, her eyes absently focusing on Katy busily setting supper on a store box in front of the garage. Then she looked at Peter.

"Mind telling?" she inquired lightly.

Peter looked at her speculatively.

"And would a man be telling his heart's best secret to a kid like you?" he asked.

"Now, I call that downright mean," said Linda. "Haven't you noticed that my braids are up? Don't you see a maturity and a dignity and a general matronliness apparent all over me today?"

"Matronliness" was too much for Peter. You could have heard his laugh far down the blue valley. "That's good!" he cried.

"It is," agreed Linda. "It means that my braids are up to stay, so hereafter I'm a real woman."

She lingered over the word an instant, glancing whimsically at Peter, a trace of a smile on her lips, then she made her way down a slant declivity and presently returned with an entire flower plant, new to Peter and of unusual beauty.

"And because I am a woman I shall set my seal upon you," she said.

In the buttonhole of his light linen coat she placed a flower of satin face of purest gold, the five petals rounded, but sharply tipped, a heavy mass of silk stamens, pollen dusted in the heart. She pushed back the left side of his coat and taking one of the rough, hairy leaves of the plant she located it over Peter's heart, her slim, deft fingers patting down the leaf and flattening it out until it lay pasted smooth and tight. As she worked, she smiled at him challengingly. Peter knew he was experiencing a ceremony of some kind, the significance of which he must learn. It was the first time Linda had voluntarily touched him. He breathed lightly and held steady, lest he startle her.

"Lovely enough," he said, "to have come from the hills of the stars. Don't make me wait, Linda; help me to the interpretation."

"Buena Mujer," suggested Linda.

"Good woman," translated Peter.

Linda nodded, running a finger down the leaf over his heart.

"Because she sticks close to you," she explained. Then startled by the look in Peter's eyes, she cried in swift change: "Now we are all going to work for a minute. Katy's spreading the lunch. You take this pail and go to the spring for water and I shall tidy your quarters for you."

With the eye of experience Linda glanced over the garage deciding that she must ask for clean sheets for the cot and that the Salvation Army would like the heap of papers. Studying the writing table she heard a faint sound that untrained ears would have missed.

"Ah, ha, Ma wood mouse," said Linda, "nibbling Peter's dr. goods are you?"

Her cry a minute later answered the question. She came from the garage upon Katherine O'Donovan rushing to meet her, holding a man's coat at the length of her far-reaching arm.

"I wish you'd look at that pocket. I don't know how long this coat has been hanging there, but there is a nest of field mice in it," she said.

Katy promptly retreated to the improvised dining table, seated herself upon an end of it, and raised both feet straight into the air.

"Small help I'll be getting from you," said Linda laughingly.

She went to the edge of the declivity that cut back to the garage and with a quick movement reversed the coat catching it by the skirts and shaking it vigorously.

CHAPTER XXVII. The Straight and Narrow

This served exactly the purpose Linda had intended. It dislodged the mouse nest and dropped it three feet below her level, but it did something else upon which Linda had no time to count. It emptied every pocket in the coat and sent the contents scattering down the rough declivity.

"Oh my gracious!" gasped Linda. "Look what I have done! Katy, come help me quickly; I have to gather up this stuff; but it's no use; I'll have to take it to Peter and tell him. I couldn't put these things back in the pockets where his hand will reach for them, because I don't know which came from inside and which came from out."

Linda sprang down and began hastily gathering up everything she could see that had fallen from the coat pockets. She had almost finished when her fingers chanced upon a very soiled, befigured piece of paper whose impressed folds showed that it had been carried for some time in an inner pocket. As her fingers touched this paper her eyes narrowed, her breath came in a gasp. She looked at it a second, irresolute, then she glanced over the top of the declivity in the direction Peter had taken. He was standing in front of the building, discussing some matter with the contractor. He had not yet gone to the spring. Shielded by the embankment with shaking fingers Linda opened the paper barely enough to see that it was Marian's lost sheet of plans; but it was not as Marian had lost it. It was scored deeply here and there with heavy lines suggestive of alterations, and the margin was fairly covered with fine figuring. Linda did not know Peter Morrison's writing or figures. His articles had been typewritten and she had never seen his handwriting. She sat down suddenly on account of weakened knees, and gazed unseeingly down the length of Lilac Valley, her heart sick, her brain tormented. Suddenly she turned and studied the house.

"Before the Lord!" she gasped. "I THOUGHT there was something mighty familiar even about the skeleton of you! Oh, Peter, Peter, where did you get this, and how could you do it?"

For a while a mist blurred her eyes. She reached for the coat and started to replace the things she had gathered up, then she shut her lips tight.

"Best time to pull a tooth," she said tersely to a terra cotta red manzanita bush, "is when it aches."

When Peter returned from the spring he was faced by a trembling girl, colorless and trying hard to keep her voice steady. She held out the coat to him with one hand, the package of papers with the other, the folded drawing conspicuous on the top. With these she gestured toward the declivity.

"Mouse nest in your pocket, Peter," she said thickly. "Reversed the coat to shake it out, and spilled your stuff."

Then she waited for Peter to be confounded. But Peter was not in the faintest degree troubled about either the coat or the papers. What did trouble him was the face and the blazing eyes of the girl concerning whom he would not admit, even to himself, his exact state of feeling.

"The mouse did not get on you, Linda?" he asked anxiously.

Linda shook her head. Suddenly she lost her self-control.

"Oh, Peter," she wailed, "how could you do it?"

Peter's lean frame tensed suddenly.

"I don't understand, Linda," he said quietly. "Exactly what have I done?"

Linda thrust the coat and the papers toward him accusingly and stood there wordless but with visible pain in her dark eyes. peter smiled at her reassuringly.

"That's not my coat, you know. If there is anything distressing about it, don't lay it to me."

"Oh, Peter!" cried Linda, "tell the truth about it. Don't try any evasions. I am so sick of them."

A rather queer light sprang into Peter's eyes. He leaned forward suddenly and caught the coat from Linda's fingers.

"Well, if you need an alibi concerning this coat," he said, "I think I can furnish it speedily."

As he talked he whirled the garment around and shot his long arms into the sleeves. Shaking it into place on his shoulders, he slowly turned in front of Linda and the surprised Katy. The sleeves came halfway to his wrists and the shoulders slid down over his upper arms. He made such a quaint and ridiculous figure that Katy burst out laughing. She was very well trained, but she knew Linda was deeply distressed.

"Wake up, lambie!" she cried sharply. "That coat ain't belonging to Mr. Pater Morrison. That gairment is the property of that bug-catchin' architect of his."

Peter shook off the coat and handed it back to Linda.

"Am I acquitted?" he asked lightly; but his surprised eyes were searching her from braid to toe.

Linda turned from him swiftly. She thrust the packet into a side pocket and started to the garage with the coat. As she passed inside she slipped down her hand, slid the sheet of plans from the other papers, and slipped it into the front of her blouse. She hung the coat back where she had found it, then suddenly sat down on the side of Peter Morrison's couch, white and shaken. Peter thought he heard a peculiar gasp and when he strayed past the door, casually glancing inward, he saw what he saw, and it brought him to his knees beside Linda with all speed.

"Linda-girl," he implored, "what in this world has happened?"

Linda struggled to control her voice; but at last she buried her face in her hands and frankly emitted a sound that she herself would have described as "howling." Peter knelt back in wonder.

"Of all the things I ever thought about you, Linda," he said, "the one thing I never did think was that you were hysterical."

If there was one word in Linda's vocabulary more opprobrious than "nerves," which could be applied to a woman, it was "hysterics." The great specialist had admitted nerves; hysterics had no standing with him. Linda herself had no more use for a hysterical woman than she had for a Gila monster. She straightened suddenly, and in removing her hands from her face she laid one on each of Peter's shoulders.

"Oh, Peter," she wailed, "I am not a hysterical idiot, but I couldn't have stood it if that coat had been yours. Peter, I just couldn't have borne it!"

Peter held himself rigidly in the fear that he might disturb the hands that were gripping him.

"I see I have the job of educating these damned field mice as to where they may build with impunity," he said soberly.

But Linda was not to be diverted. She looked straight and deep into his eyes.

"Peter," she said affirmatively, "you don't know a thing about that coat, do you?"

"I do not," said Peter promptly.

"You never saw what was in its pockets, did you?"

"Not to my knowledge," answered Peter. "What was in the pockets, Linda?"

Linda thought swiftly. Peter adored his dream house. If she told him that the plans for it had been stolen by his architect, the house would be ruined for Peter. Anyone could see from the candor of his gaze and the lines that God and experience had graven on his face that Peter was without guile. Suddenly Linda shot her hands past Peter's shoulders and brought them together on the back of his neck. She drew his face against hers and cried: "Oh Peter, I would have been killed if that coat had been yours. I tell you I couldn't have endured it, Peter. I am just tickled to death!"

One instant she hugged him tight. If her lips did not brush his cheek, Peter deluded himself. Then she sprang up and ran from the garage. Later he took the coat from its nail, the papers from its pockets, and carefully looked them over. There was nothing among them that would give him the slightest clue to Linda's conduct. He looked again, penetratingly, searchingly, for he must learn from them a reason; and no reason was apparent. With the coat in one hand and the papers in the other he stepped outside.

"Linda," he said, "won't you show me? Won't you tell me? What is there about this to upset you?"

Linda closed her lips and shook her head. Once more Peter sought in her face, in her attitude the information he craved.

"Needn't tell me," he said, "that a girl who will face the desert and the mountains and the canyons and the sea is upset by a mouse."

"Well, you should have seen Katy sitting in the midst of our supper with her feet rigidly extended before her!" cried the girl, struggling to regain her composure. "Put back that coat and come to your supper. It's time for you to be fed now. The last workman has gone and we'll barely have time to finish nicely and show Katy your dream house before it's time to go."

Peter came and sat in the place Linda indicated. His mind was whirling. There was something he did not understand, but in her own time, in her own way, a girl of Linda's poise and self-possession would tell him what had occurred that could be responsible for the very peculiar things she had done. In some way she had experienced a shock too great for her usual self-possession. The hands with which she fished pickled onions from the bottle were still unsteady, and the corroboration Peter needed for his thoughts could be found in the dazed way in which Katy watched Linda as she hovered over her in serving her. But that was not the time. By and by the time would come. The thing to do was to trust Linda and await its coming. So Peter called on all the reserve wit and wisdom he had at command. He jested, told stories, and to Linda's satisfaction and Katy's delight, he ate his supper like a hungry man, frankly enjoying it, and when the meal was finished Peter took Katy over the house, explaining to her as much detail as was possible at that stage of its construction, while Linda followed with mute lips and rebellion surging in her heart. When leaving time came, while Katy packed the Bear Cat, Linda wandered across toward the spring, and Peter, feeling that possibly she might wish to speak with him, followed her. When he overtook her she looked at him straightly, her eyes showing the hurt her heart felt.

"Peter," she said, "that first night you had dinner with us, was Henry Anderson out of your presence one minute from the time you came into the house until you left it?"

Peter stopped and studied the ground at his feet intently. Finally he said conclusively: "I would go on oath, Linda, that he was not. We were all together in the living room, all together in the dining room. We left together at night and John was with us."

"I see," said Linda. "Well, then, when you came back the next morning after Eileen, before you started on your trip, to hunt a location, was he with you all the time?"

Again Peter took his time to answer.

"We came to your house with Gilman," he said. "John started to the front door to tell Miss Eileen that we were ready. I followed him. Anderson said he would look at the scenery. He must have made a circuit of the house, because when we came out ready to start, a very few minutes later, he was coming down the other side of the house."

"Ah," said Linda comprehendingly.

"Linda," said Peter quietly, "it is very obvious that something has worried you extremely. Am I in any way connected with it?"

104

Linda shook her head.

"Is there anything I can do?"

The negative was repeated. Then she looked at him.

"No, Peter," she said quietly, "I confess I have had a shock, but it is in no way connected with you and there is nothing you can do about it but forget my foolishness. But I am glad—Peter, you will never know how glad I am—that you haven't anything to do with it."

Then in the friendliest fashion imaginable she reached him her hand and led the way back to the Bear Cat, their tightly gripped hands swinging between them. As Peter closed the door he looked down on Linda.

"Young woman," he said, "since this country has as yet no nerve specialist to take the place of your distinguished father, if you have any waves to wave to me tonight, kindly do it before you start or after you reach the highway. If you take your hands off that steering wheel as you round the boulders and strike that declivity as I have seen you do heretofore, I won't guarantee that I shall not require a specialist myself."

Linda started to laugh, then she saw Peter's eyes and something in them stopped her suddenly.

"I did not realize that I was taking any risk," she said. "I won't do it again. I will say good-bye to you right here and now so I needn't look back."

So she shook hands with Peter and drove away. Peter slowly followed down the rough driveway, worn hard by the wheels of delivery trucks, and stood upon the highest point of the rocky turn, looking after the small gray car as it slid down the steep declivity. And he wondered if there could have been telepathy in the longing with which he watched it go, for at the level roadway that followed between the cultivated land out to the highway Linda stopped the car, stood up in it, and turning, looked back straight to the spot upon which Peter stood. She waved both hands to him, and then gracefully and beautifully, with outstretched, fluttering fingers she made him the sign of birds flying home. And with the whimsy in his soul uppermost, Peter reflected, as he turned back for a microscopic examination of Henry Anderson's coat and the contents of its pockets, that there was one bird above all others which made him think of Linda; but he could not at the moment feather Katherine O'Donovan. And then he further reflected as he climbed the hill that if it had to be done the best he could do would be a bantam hen contemplating domesticity.

Linda looked the garage over very carefully when she put away the Bear Cat. When she closed the garage doors she was particular about the locks. As she came through the kitchen she said to Katy, busy with the lunch box:

"Belovedest, have there been any strange Japs poking around here lately?"

She nearly collapsed when Katy answered promptly:

"A dale too many of the square-headed haythens. I am pestered to death with them. They used to come jist to water the lawn but now they want to crane the rugs; they want to do the wash. They are willing to crane house. They want to get into the garage; they insist on washing the car. If they can't wash it they jist want to see if it nades washin'."

Linda stood amazed.

"And how long has this been going on, Katy?" she finally asked.

"Well, I have had two good months of it," said Katy; "that is, it started two months ago. The past month has been workin' up and the last ten days it seemed to me they was a Jap on the back steps oftener than they was a stray cat, and I ain't no truck with ayther of them. They give me jist about the same falin'. Between the two I would trust the cat a dale further with my bird than I would the Jap."

"Have you ever unlocked the garage for them, Katy?" asked Linda.

"No," said Katy. "I only go there when I nade something about me work."

"Well, Katy," said Linda, "let me tell you this: the next time you go there for anything take a good look for Japs before you open the door. Get what you want and get out as quickly as possible and be sure, Katy, desperately sure, that you lock the door securely when you leave."

Katy set her hands on her hips, flared her elbows, and lifted her chin.

"What's any of them little haythen been coin' to scare ye, missy?" she demanded belligerently. "Don't you think I'm afraid of them! Comes any of them around me and I'll take my mopstick over the heads of them."

"And you'll break a perfectly good mopstick and not hurt the Jap when you do it," said Linda. "There's an undercurrent of something deep and subtle going on in this country right now, Katy. When Japan sends college professors to work in our kitchens and relatives of her greatest statesmen to serve our tables, you can depend on it she is not doing it for the money that is paid them. If California does not wake up very shortly and very thoroughly she is going to pay an awful price for the luxury she is experiencing while she pampers herself with the service of the Japanese, just as the South has pampered herself for generations with the service of the Negroes. When the Negroes learn what there is to know, then the day of retribution will be at hand. And this is not croaking, Katy. It

105

is the truest gospel that was ever preached. Keep your eyes wide open for Japs. Keep your doors locked, and if you see one prowling around the garage and don't know what he is after, go to the telephone and call the police."

Linda climbed the stairs to her workroom, plumped down at the table, set her chin in her palms, and lost herself in thought. For half an hour she sat immovable, staring at her caricature of Eileen through narrowed lids. Then she opened the typewriter, inserted a sheet and wrote:

MY DEAR Mr. SNOW:

I am writing as the most intimate woman friend of Marian Thorne. As such, I have spent much thought trying to figure out exactly the reason for the decision in your recent architectural competition; why a man should think of such a number of very personal, intimate touches that, from familiarity with them, I know that Miss Thorne had incorporated in her plans, and why his winning house should be her winning house, merely reversed.

Today I have found the answer, which I am forwarding to you, knowing that you will understand exactly what should be done. Enclosed you will find one of the first rough sketches Marian made of her plans. In some mysterious manner it was lost on a night when your prize-winning architect had dinner at our house where Miss Thorne was also a guest. Before retiring she showed to me and explained the plans with which she hoped to win your competition. In the morning I packed her suitcase and handed it to the porter of her train. When she arrived at San Francisco she found that the enclosed sheet was missing.

This afternoon tidying a garage in which Mr. Peter Morrison, the author, is living while Henry Anderson completes a residence he is building for him near my home, I reversed a coat belonging to Henry Anderson to dislodge from its pocket the nest of a field mouse. In so doing I emptied all the pockets, and in gathering up their contents I found this lost sheet from Marian's plans.

I think nothing more need be said on my part save that I understood the winning plan was to become the property of Nicholson and Snow. Without waiting to see whether these plans would win or not, Henry Anderson has them three fourths of the way materialized in Mr. Morrison's residence in Lilac Valley which is a northwestern suburb of Los Angeles.

You probably have heard Marian speak of me, and from her you may obtain any information you might care to have concerning my responsibility.

I am mailing the sketch to you rather than to Marian because I feel that you are the party most deeply interested in a business way, and I hope, too, that you will be interested in protecting my very dear friend from the disagreeable parts of this very disagreeable situation.

Very truly yours,
LINDA STRONG.

CHAPTER XXVIII. Putting It Up to Peter

When Peter Morrison finally gave up looking in the pockets of Henry Anderson's coat for enlightenment concerning Linda's conduct, it was with his mind settled on one point. There was nothing in the coat now that could possibly have startled the girl or annoyed her. Whatever had been there that caused her extremely peculiar conduct she had carried away with her. Peter had settled convictions concerning Linda. From the first instant he had looked into her clear young eyes as she stood in Multiflores Canyon triumphantly holding aloft the Cotyledon in one hand and with the other struggling to induce the skirt of her blouse to resume its proper location beneath the band of her trousers, he had felt that her heart and her mind were as clear and cool and businesslike as the energetic mountain stream hurrying past her. Above all others, "straight" was the one adjective he probably would have applied to her. Whatever she had taken from Henry's pockets was something that concerned her. If she took anything, she had a right to take it; of that Peter was unalterably certain. He remembered that a few days before she practically had admitted to him that Anderson had annoyed her, and a slow anger began to surge up in Peter's carefully regulated heart. His thoughts were extremely busy, but the thing he thought most frequently and most forcefully was that he would thoroughly enjoy taking Henry Anderson by the scruff of the neck, leading him to the sheerest part of his own particular share of the mountain, and exhaustively booting him down it.

"It takes these youngsters to rush in and raise the devil where there's no necessity for anything to happen if just a modicum of common sense had been used," growled Peter.

He mulled over the problem for several days, and then he decided he should see Linda, and with his first look into her straight-forward eyes, from the tones of her voice and the carriage of her head he would know whether the annoyance persisted. About the customary time for her to return from school Peter started on foot down the short cut between his home and the Strong residence. He was following a footpath rounding the base of the mountain, crossing and recrossing the enthusiastic mountain stream as it speeded toward the valley, when a flash of color on the farther side of the brook attracted him. He stopped, then hastily sprang across the water, climbed a few yards, and, after skirting a heavy clump of bushes, looked at Linda sitting beside them—a most astonishing Linda, appearing small and humble, very much tucked away, unrestrained tears rolling down her cheeks, a wet handkerchief wadded in one hand, a packet of letters in her lap. A long instant they studied each other.

"Am I intruding?" inquired Peter at last.

Linda shook her head vigorously and gulped down a sob.

"No, Peter," she sobbed, "I had come this far on my way to you when my courage gave out."

Peter rearranged the immediate landscape and seated himself beside Linda.

"Now stop distressing yourself," he said authoritatively. "You youngsters do take life so seriously. The only thing that could have happened to you worth your shedding a tear over can't possibly have happened; so stop this waste of good material. Tears are very precious things, Linda. They ought to be the most unusual things in life. Now tell me something. Were you coming to me about that matter that worried you the other evening?"

Linda shook her head.

"No," she said, "I have turned that matter over where it belongs. I have nothing further to do with it. I'll confess to you I took a paper from among those that fell from Henry Anderson's pocket. It was not his. He had no right to have it. He couldn't possibly have come by it honorably or without knowing what it was. I took the liberty to put it where it belongs, or at least where it seemed to me that it belongs. That is all over."

"Then something else has happened?" asked Peter. "Something connected with the package of letters in your lap?"

Linda nodded vigorously.

"Peter, I have done something perfectly awful," she confessed. "I never in this world meant to do it. I wouldn't have done it for anything. I have got myself into the dreadfullest mess, and I don't know how to get out. When I couldn't stand it another minute I started right to you, Peter, just like I'd have started to my father if I'd had him to go to."

"I see," said Peter, deeply interested in the toe of his shoe. "You depended on my age and worldly experience and my unconcealed devotion to your interests, which is exactly what you should do, my dear. Now tell me. Dry your eyes and tell me, and whatever it is I'll fix it all right and happily for you. I'll swear to do it if you want me to."

Then Linda raised her eyes to his face.

"Oh, Peter, you dear!" she cried. "Peter, I'll just kneel and kiss your hands if you can fix this for me."

Peter set his jaws and continued his meditations on shoe leather.

"Make it snappy!" he said tersely. "The sooner your troubles are out of your system the better you'll feel. Whose letters are those, and why are you crying over them?"

"Oh, Peter," quavered Linda, "you know how I love Marian. You have seen her and I have told you over and over."

"Yes," said Peter soothingly, "I know."

"I have told you how, after years of devotion to Marian, John Gilman let Eileen make a perfect rag of him and tie him into any kind of knot she chose. Peter, when Marian left here she had lost everything on earth but a little dab of money. She had lost a father who was fine enough to be my father's best friend. She had lost a mother who was fine enough to rear Marian to what she is. She had lost them in a horrible way that left her room for a million fancies and regrets: 'if I had done this,' or 'if I had done that,' or 'if I had taken another road.' And when she went away she knew definitely she had lost the first and only love of her heart; and I knew, because she was so sensitive and so fine, I knew, better than anybody living, how she COULD be hurt; and I thought if I could fix some scheme that would entertain her and take her mind off herself and make her feel appreciated only for a little while—I knew in all reason, Peter, when she got out in the world where men would see her and see how beautiful and fine she is, there would be somebody who would want her quickly. All the time I have thought that when she came back, YOU would want her. Peter, I fibbed when I said I was setting your brook for Louise Whiting. I was not. I don't know Louise Whiting. She is nothing to me. I was setting it for you and Marian. It was a WHITE head I saw among the iris marching down your creek bank, not a gold one, Peter."

Peter licked his dry lips and found it impossible to look at Linda.

"Straight ahead with it," he said gravely. "What did you do?"

"Oh, I have done the awfullest thing," wailed Linda, "the most unforgivable thing!"

She reached across and laid hold of the hand next her, and realizing that she needed it for strength and support, Peter gave it into her keeping.

"Yes?" he questioned. "Get on with it, Linda. What was it you did?"

"I had a typewriter: I could. I began writing her letters, the kind of letters that I thought would interest her and make her feel loved and appreciated."

"You didn't sign my name to them, did you, Linda?" asked Peter in a dry, breathless voice.

"No, Peter," said Linda, "I did not do that, I did worse. Oh, I did a whole lot worse!"

"I don't understand," said Peter hoarsely.

"I wanted to make them fine. I wanted to make them brilliant. I wanted to make them interesting. And of course I could not do it by myself. I am nothing but a copycat. I just quoted a lot of things I had heard you say; and I did worse than that, Peter. I watched the little whimsy lines around your mouth and I tried to interpret the perfectly lovely things they would make you say to a woman if you loved her and were building a dream house for her. And oh, Peter, it's too ghastly; I don't believe I can tell you."

"This is pretty serious business, Linda," said Peter gravely. "Having gone this far you are in honor bound to finish. It would not be fair to leave me with half a truth. What is the result of this impersonation?"

"Oh, Peter," sobbed Linda, breaking down again, "you're going to hate me; I know you're going to hate me and Marian's going to hate me; and I didn't mean a thing but the kindest thing in all the world."

"Don't talk like that, Linda," said Peter. "If your friend is all you say she is, she is bound to understand. And as for me, I am not very likely to misjudge you. But be quick about it. What did you do, Linda?"

"Why, I just wrote these letters that I am telling you about," said Linda, "and I said the things that I thought would comfort her and entertain her and help with her work; and these are the answers that she wrote me, and I don't think I realized till last night that she was truly attributing them to any one man, truly believing in them. Oh, Peter, I wasn't asleep a minute all last night, and for the first time I failed in my lessons today."

"And what is the culmination, Linda?" urged Peter.

"She liked the letters, Peter. They meant all I intended them to and they must have meant something I never could have imagined. And in San Francisco one of the firm where she studies—a very fine man she says he is, Peter; I can see that in every way he would be quite right for her; and I had a letter from her last night, and, Peter, he had asked her to marry him, to have a lifelong chance at work she's crazy about. He had offered her a beautiful home with everything that great wealth and culture and good taste could afford. He had offered her the mothering of his little daughter; and she refused him, Peter, refused him because she is in love, with all the love there is left in her disappointed, hurt heart, with the personality that these letters represent to her; and that personality is yours, Peter. I stole it from you. I copied it into those letters. I'm not straight. I'm not fair. I wasn't honest with her. I wasn't honest with you. I'll just have to take off front the top of the highest mountain or sink in the deepest place in the sea, Peter. I thought I was straight. I thought I was honorable I have made Donald believe that I was. If I have to tell him the truth about this he won't want to wear my flower any more. I shall know all the things that Marian has suffered, and a thousand times worse, because she was not to blame; she had nothing with which to reproach herself."

Peter put an arm across Linda's shoulders and drew her up to him. For a long, bitter moment he thought deeply, and then he said hoarsely: "Now calm down, Linda. You're making an extremely high mountain out of an extremely shallow gopher hole. You haven't done anything irreparable. I see the whole situation. You are sure your friend has finally refused this offer she has had on account of these letters you have written?"

Suddenly Linda relaxed. She leaned her warm young body against Peter. She laid her tired head on his shoulder. She slipped the top letter of the packet in her lap from under its band, opened it, and held it before him. Peter read it very deliberately, then he nodded in acquiescence.

"It's all too evident," he said quietly, "that you have taught her that there is a man in this world more to her liking than John Gilman ever has been. When it came to materializing the man, Linda, what was your idea? Were you proposing to deliver me?"

"I thought it would be suitable and you would be perfectly happy," sobbed Linda, "and that way I could have both of you."

"And Donald also?" asked Peter lightly.

"Donald of course," assented Linda.

And then she lifted her tear-spilling, wonderful eyes, wide open, to Peter's, and demanded: "But, oh Peter, I am so miserable I am almost dead. I have said you were a rock, and you are a rock. peter, can you get me out of this?"

"Sure," said Peter grimly. "Merely a case of living up to your blue china, even if it happens to be in the form of hieroglyphics instead of baked pottery. Give me the letters, Linda. Give me a few days to study them. Exchange typewriters with me so I can have the same machine. Give me some of the paper on which you have been writing and the address you have been using, and I'll guarantee to get you out of this in some way that will leave you Donald, and your friendship with Marian quite as good as new."

At that juncture Peter might have been kissed, but his neck was very stiff and his head was very high and his eyes were on a far-distant hilltop from which at that minute he could not seem to gather any particular help.

"Would it be your idea," he said, "that by reading these letters I could gain sufficient knowledge of what has passed to go on with this?"

"Of course you could," said Linda.

Peter reached in his side pocket and pulled out a clean handkerchief. He shook it from its folds and dried her eyes. Then he took her by her shoulders and set her up straight.

"Now stop this nerve strain and this foolishness," he said tersely. "You have done a very wonderful thing for me. It is barely possible that Marian Thorne is not my dream woman, but we can't always have our dreams in this world, and if I could not have mine, truly and candidly, Linda, so far as I have lived my life, I would rather have Marian Thorne than any other woman I have ever met."

Linda clapped her hands in delight.

"Oh, goody goody, Peter!" she cried. "How joyous! Can it be possible that my bungling is coming out right for Marian and right for you?"

"And right for you, Linda?" inquired Peter lightly.

"Sure, right for me," said Linda eagerly. "Of course it's right for me when it's right for you and Marian. And since it's not my secret alone I don't think it would be quite honorable to tell Donald about it. What hurts Marian's heart or heals it is none of his business. He doesn't even know her."

"All right then, Linda," said Peter, rising, "give me the letters and bring me the machine and the paper. Give me the joyous details and tell me when I am expected to send in my first letter in propria persona?"

"Oh, Peter," cried Linda, beaming on him, "oh, Peter, you are a rock! I do put my trust in you."

"Then God help me," said Peter, "for whatever happens, your trust in me shall not be betrayed, Linda."

CHAPTER XXIX. Katy Unburdens Her Mind

Possibly because she wished to eliminate herself from the offices of Nicholson and Snow for a few days, possibly because her finely attuned nature felt the call, Marian Thorne boarded a train that carried her to Los Angeles. She stepped from it at ten o'clock in the morning, and by the streetcar route made her way to Lilac Valley. When she arrived she realized that she could not see Linda before, possibly, three in the afternoon. She entered a restaurant, had a small lunch box packed, and leaving her dressing case, she set off down the valley toward the mountains. She had need of their strength, their quiet and their healing. To the one particular spot where she had found comfort in Lilac Valley her feet led her. By paths of her own, much overgrown for want of recent usage, she passed through the cultivated fields, left the roadway, and began to climb. When she reached the stream flowing down the rugged hillside, she stopped to rest for a while, and her mind was in a tumult. In one minute she was seeing the bitterly disappointed face of a lonely, sensitive man whose first wound had been reopened by the making of another possibly quite as deep; and at the next her heart was throbbing because Linda had succeeded in transferring the living Peter to paper.

The time had come when Marian felt that she would know the personality embodied in the letters she had been receiving; and in the past few days her mind had been fixing tenaciously upon Peter Morrison. And the feeling concerning which she had written Linda had taken possession of her. Wealth did not matter; position did not matter. Losing the love of a good man did not matter But the mind and the heart and the personality behind the letters she had been receiving did matter. She thought long and seriously When at last she arose she had arrived at the conclusion that she had done the right thing, no matter whether the wonderful letters she had received went on and offered her love or not, no matter about anything. She must merely live and do the best she could, until the writer of those letters chose to disclose himself and say what purpose he had in mind when he wrote them.

So Marian followed her own path beside the creek until she neared its head, which was a big, gushing icy spring at the foot of the mountain keeping watch over the small plateau that in her heart she had thought of as hers for years. As she neared the location strange sounds began to reach her, voices of men, clanging of hammers, the rip of saws. A look of deep consternation overspread her face. She listened an instant and then began to run. When she broke through the rank foliage flourishing from the waters of the spring and looked out on the plateau what she saw was Peter Morrison's house in the process of being floored and shingled. For a minute Marian was physically ill. Her heart hurt until her hand crept to her side in an effort to soothe it. Before she asked the question of a man coming to the spring with a pail in his hand, she knew the answer. It was Peter Morrison's house. Marian sprang across the brook, climbed to the temporary roadway, and walked down in front of the building. She stood looking at it intently. It was in a rough stage, but much disguise is needed to prevent a mother from knowing her own child. Marian's dark eyes began to widen and to blaze. She walked up to the front of the house and found that rough flooring had been laid so that she could go over the first floor. When she had done this she left the back door a deeply indignant woman.

"There is some connection," she told herself tersely, "between my lost sketch and this house, which is merely a left-to-right rehearsal of my plans; and it's the same plan with which Henry Anderson won the Nicholson and Snow prize money and the still more valuable honor of being the prize winner. What I want to know is how such a wrong may be righted, and what Peter Morrison has to do with it."

Stepping from the back door, Marian followed the well-worn pathway that led to the garage, looking right and left for Peter, and she was wondering what she would say to him if she met him. She was thinking that perhaps she had better return to San Francisco and talk the matter over with Mr. Snow before she said anything to anyone else; by this time she had reached the garage and stood in its wide-open door. She looked in at the cot, left just as someone had arisen from it, at the row of clothing hanging on a rough wooden rack at the back, at the piled boxes, at the big table, knocked together from rough lumber, in the center, scattered and piled with books and magazines; and then her eyes fixed intently on a packet lying on the table beside a typewriter and a stack of paper and envelopes. She walked over and picked up the packet. As she had known the instant she saw them, they were her letters. She stood an instant holding them in her hand, a dazed expression on her face. Mechanically she reached out and laid her hands on the closed typewriter to steady herself. Something about it appealed to her as familiar. She looked at it closely, then she lifted the cover and examined the machine. It was the same machine that had stood for years in Doctor Strong's library, a machine upon which she had typed business letters for her own father, and sometimes she had copied lectures and book manuscript on it for Doctor Strong. Until his house was completed and his belongings arrived, Peter undoubtedly had borrowed it. Suddenly a wild desire to escape swept over Marian. Her first thought was of her feelings. She was angry, and justly so. In her heart she had begun to feel that the letters she was receiving were from Peter Morrison. Here was the proof.

Could it be possible that in their one meeting Peter had decided that she was his dream woman, that in some way he had secured that rough sketch of her plans, and from them was preparing her dream house for her? The thought sped through her brain that he was something more than human to have secured those plans, to have found that secluded and choice location. For an instant she forgot the loss of the competition in trying to comprehend the wonder of finding her own particular house fitting her own particular location as naturally as one of its big boulders.

She tried to replace the package of letters exactly as she had found them. On tiptoe she slipped back to the door and looked searchingly down the road, around, and as far as possible through the house. Then she gathered her skirts, stepped from the garage, and began the process of effacing herself on the mountain side From clump to clump of the thickest bushes, crouching below the sage and greasewood, pausing to rest behind lilac and elder, without regard for her traveling suit or her beautifully shod feet, Marian fled from her location. When at last she felt that she was completely hidden and at least a mile from the spot, she dropped panting on a boulder, brushing the debris from her skirts, lifting trembling hands to straighten her hat, and ruefully contemplating her shoes. Then she tried to think in a calm, dispassionate, and reasonable manner, but she found it a most difficult process. Her mind was not well ordered, neither was it at her command. It whirled and shot off at unexpected tangents and danced as irresponsibly as a grasshopper from one place to another. The flying leaps it took ranged from San Francisco to Lilac Valley, from her location upon which Peter Morrison was building her house, to Linda. Even John Gilman obtruded himself once more. At one minute she was experiencing a raging indignation against Henry Anderson. How had he secured her plan? At another she was trying to figure dispassionately what connection Peter Morrison could have had with the building of his house upon her plan. Every time Peter came into the equation her heart arose in his defense. In some way his share in the proceeding was all right. He had cared for her and he had done what he thought would please her. Therefore she must be pleased, although forced to admit to herself that she would have been infinitely more pleased to have built her own house in her own way.

She was hungry to see Linda. She wanted Katherine O'Donovan to feed her and fuss over her and entertain her with her mellow Irish brogue; but if she went to them and disclosed her presence in the valley, Peter would know about it, and if he intended the building he was erecting as a wonderful surprise for her, then she must not spoil his joy. Plan in any way she could, Marian could see no course left to her other than to slip back to the station and return to San Francisco without meeting any of her friends. She hurriedly ate her lunch, again straightened her clothing, went to the restaurant for her traveling bag, and took the car for the station where she waited for a return train to San Francisco She bought a paper and tried to concentrate upon it in an effort to take her mind from her own problems so that, when she returned to them, she would be better able to think clearly, to reason justly, to act wisely. She was very glad when her train came and she was started on her way northward. At the first siding upon which it stopped to allow the passing of a south-bound limited, she was certain that as the cars flashed by, in one of them she saw Eugene Snow. She was so certain that when he reached the city she immediately called the office and asked for Mr. Snow only to be told that he had gone away for a day or two on business. After that Marian's thought was confused to the point of exasperation.

It would be difficult to explain precisely the state of mind in which Linda, upon arriving at her home that afternoon, received from Katy the information that a man named Snow had been waiting an hour for her in the living room. Linda's appearance was that of a person so astonished that Katy sidled up to her giving strong evidence of being ready to bristle.

"Ye know, lambie," she said with elaborate indifference, "ye aren't havin' to see anybody ye don't want to. If it's somebody intrudin' himself on ye, just say the word and I'll fire him; higher than Guilderoy's kite I'll be firin' him."

"No, I must see him, Katy," said Linda quietly. "And have something specially nice for dinner. Very likely I'll take him to see Peter Morrison's house and possibly I'll ask him and Peter to dinner. He is a San Francisco architect from the firm where Marian takes her lessons, and it's business about Peter's house. I was surprised, that's all."

Then Linda turned and laid a hand on each of Katy's hairy red arms.

"Katherine O'Donovan, old dear," she said, "if we do come back for dinner, concentrate on Mr. Snow and study him. Scrutinize, Katy! It's a bully word. Scrutinize closely. To add one more to our long lists of secrets, here's another. He's the man I told you about who has asked Marian to marry him, and Marian has refused him probably because she prefers somebody nearer home."

Then Linda felt the tensing of every muscle in Katy's body. She saw the lift of her head, the incredulous, resentful look in her eyes. There was frank hostility in her tone.

"Well, who is there nearer home that Marian knows?" she demanded belligerently.

"Well, now, who would there be?" retorted Linda.

"Ye ain't manin' John Gilman?" asked Katy.

"No," said Linda, "I am not meaning John Gilman. You should know Marian well enough to know that."

"Well, ye ought to know yourself well enough to know that they ain't anybody else around these diggin's that Marian Thorne's going to get," said Katy.

"I imagine Marian will get pretty much whom she wants," said Linda laughingly. "In your heart, Katy, you know that Marian need not have lost John Gilman if she had not deliberately let him go. If she had been willing to meet Eileen on her own ground and to play the game with her, it wouldn't have happened. Marian has more brains in a minute than Eileen has in a month."

When Linda drew back the portiere and stepped into the living room Eugene Snow rose to meet her. What either of them expected it might be difficult to explain. Knowing so little of each other, it is very possible that they had no visualizations. What Snow saw was what everyone saw who looked at Linda—a girl arrestingly unusual. With Linda lay the advantage by far, since she had Marian's letters for a background. What she saw was a tall man, slender, and about him there was to Linda a strong appeal. As she looked into his eyes, she could feel the double hurt that Fate had dealt him. She thought she could fathom the fineness in his nature that had led him to made home-building his chosen occupation. Instantly she liked him. With only one look deep into his eyes she was on his side. She stretched out both her hands and advanced.

"Now isn't this the finest thing of you?" she said. "I am so glad that you came. I'll tell you word for word what happened here."

"That will be fine," he said. "Which is your favorite chair?"

"You know," she said, "that is a joke. I am so unfamiliar with this room that I haven't any favorite chair. I'll have to take the nearest, like Thoreau selected his piece of chicken."

Then for a few minutes Linda talked frankly. She answered Eugene Snow's every question unhesitatingly and comprehensively. Together they ascended the stairs, and in the guest room she showed him the table at which she and Marian had studied the sketches of plans, and exactly where they had left them lying overnight.

"The one thing I can't be explicit about," said Linda, "is how many sheets were there in the morning. We had stayed awake so late talking, that we overslept. I packed Marian's bag while she dressed. I snatched up what there were without realizing whether there were two sheets or three, laid them in the flat bottom of the case, and folded her clothing on top of them."

"I see," said Mr. Snow comprehendingly. "Now let's experiment a little. Of course the window before that table was raised?"

"Yes, it was," said Linda, "but every window in the house is screened."

"And what about the door opening into the hall? Can you tell me whether it was closed or open?"

111

"It was open," said Linda. "We left it slightly ajar to create a draft; the night was warm."

"Is there anyone about the house," inquired Mr. Snow, "who could tell us certainly whether that window was screened that night?"

"Of course," said Linda. "Our housekeeper, Katherine O'Donovan, would know. When we go down we'll ask her."

On their return to the living room, for the first time in her life Linda rang for Katy. She hesitated an instant before she did it. It would be establishing a relationship that never before had existed between them. She always had gone to Katy as she would have, gone to her mother. She would have gone to her now, but she wanted Katy to make her appearance and give her information without the possibility of previous discussion. Katy answered the bell almost at once. Linda went to her side and reached her arm across her shoulders.

"Katy," she said, "this is Mr. Eugene Snow of San Francisco He is interested in finding out exactly what became of that lost plan of Marian's that we have looked for so carefully. Put on your thinking cap, old dear, and try to answer accurately any question that Mr. Snow may wish to ask you."

Katy looked expectantly at Eugene Snow.

"In the meantime," said Linda, "I'll be excused and go bring round the Bear Cat."

"I have only one question to ask you," said Mr. Snow. "Can you recall whether, for any reason, there was a screen out of the guest-room window directly in front of which the reading table was standing the night Miss Marian occupied the room before leaving for San Francisco?"

"Sure there was," answered Katy instantly in her richest, mellowest brogue.

She was taking the inventory she had been told to take. She was deciding, as instantly as Linda had done, that she liked this man. Years, appearance, everything about him appealed to Katy as being exactly right for Marian; and her cunning Irish mind was leaping and flying and tugging at the leash that thirty years of conventions had bound upon her.

"Sure," she repeated, "the wildest santana that ever roared over us just caught that screen and landed it slam against the side of the garage, and it set inside for three days till I could get a workman to go up the outside and put it back. It had been out two days before the night Marian was here."

"Did Miss Linda know about it?" asked Snow.

"Not that I know of," said Katy. "She is a schoolgirl, you know, off early in the morning, back and up to her room, the busiest youngster the valley knows; and coin' a dale of good she is, too. It was Miss Eileen that heard the screen ripped out and told me it was gone. She's the one who looked after the housekapin' and paid the bills. She knew all about it. If 'twould be helpin' Miss Marian any about findin' them plans we've ransacked the premises for, I couldn't see any reason why Miss Eileen wouldn't tell ye the same as I'm tellin' ye, and her housekapin' accounts and her cheque book would show she paid the carpenter, if it's legal business you're wantin'."

"Thank you, Katy," said Mr. Snow. "I hope nothing of that kind will occur. A great wrong has been perpetrated, but we must find some way to right it without involving such extremely nice young women in the annoyance of legal proceedings."

Katy folded her arms and raised her head. All her share of the blarney of Ireland began to roll from the mellow tip of her tongue.

"Now, the nice man ye are, to be seein' the beauty of them girls so quick," she said. "The good Lord airly in the mornin' of creation thought them out when He was jist fresh from rist, and the material was none shopworn. They ain't ladies like 'em anywhere else in the whole of California, and belave me, a many rale ladies have I seen in my time. Ye can jist make up your mind that Miss Linda is the broth of the earth. She is her father's own child and she is him as two pase in the pod. And Marian growed beside her, and much of a hand I've had in her raisin' meself, and well I'm knowin' how fine she is and what a juel she'd be, set on any man's hearthstone. I'm wonderin'," said Katy challengingly, "if you're the Mr. Snow at whose place she is takin' her lessons, and if ye are, I'm wonderin' if ye ain't goin' to use the good judgment to set her, like the juel she would be, in the stone of your own hearth."

Eugene Snow looked at Katy intently. He was not accustomed to discussing his affairs with household helpers, but he could not look at Katy without there remaining in his vision the forte of Linda standing beside her, a reassuring arm stretched across her shoulders, the manner in which she had presented her and then left her that she might be free to answer as she chose with out her young mistress even knowing exactly what was asked of her. Such faith and trust and love were unusual.

"I might try to do that very thing," he said, "but, you know, a wonderful woman is an animated jewel. You can't manufacture a setting and put her in and tighten the clasps without her consent."

"Then why don't you get it?" said Katy casually.

Eugene Snow laughed ruefully.

"But suppose," he said, "that the particular jewel you're discussing prefers to select her own setting, and mine does not please her."

"Well, they's jist one thing," said Katy. Her heels left the floor involuntarily; she arose on her tiptoes; her shoulders came up, and her head lifted to a height it never had known before. "They's jist one thing," she said. "Aside from Miss Linda, who is my very own child that I have washed and I have combed and I have done for since she was a toddlin' four-year-old, they ain't no woman in this world I would go as far for as I would for Miss Marian; but I'm tellin' ye now, ye Mr. Eujane Snow, that they's one thing I don't lend no countenance to. I am sorry she has had the cold, cruel luck that she has, but I ain't sorry enough that I'm goin' to stand for her droppin' herself into the place where she doesn't belong. If the good Lord ain't give her the sense to see that you're jist the image of the man that would be jist exactly right for her, somebody had better be tellin' her so. Anyway, if Miss Linda is takin' ye up to the house that Mr. Pater Morrison is buildin' and the Pater man is there, I would advise ye to cast your most discernin' eye on that gintleman. Ye watch him jist one minute when he looks at the young missus and he thinks nobody ain't observing him, and ye'll see what ye'll see. If ye want Marian, ye jist go on and take her. I'm not carin' whether ye use a club or white vi'lets, but don't ye be lettin' Marian Thorne get no idea into her head that she is goin' to take Mr. Pater Morrison, because concernin' Pater I know what I know, and I ain't goin' to stand by and see things goin' wrong for want of spakin' up. Now if you're a wise man, ye don't nade nothing further said on the subject."

Eugene Snow thought intently for a few moments. His vision centered on Katherine O'Donovan's face.

"You're absolutely sure of this?" he said at last.

"Jist as sure as the sun's sure, and the mountains, and the seasons come and go," said Katy with finality. "Watch him and you'll see it stickin' out all over him. I have picked him for me boss, and it's jist adorin' that man crature I am."

"What about Miss Linda?" inquired Snow. "Is she adoring him?"

"She ain't nothing but a ganglin' school kid, adorin' the spade with which she can shoot around that Bear Cat of hers, and race the canyons, and the rely lovely things she can strike on paper with her pencil and light up with her joyous colors. Her day and her hour ain't come, and the Pater man's that fine he won't lay a finger on her to wake her up when she has a year yet of her schoolin' before her. But in the manetime it's my job to stand guard as I'm standin' right now. I'm tellin' ye frank and fair. Ye go on and take Marian Thorne because ye ought to have her. If she's got any idea in her head that she's goin' to have Pater Morrison, she'll have to get it out."

Eugene Snow held out his hand and started to the front door in answer to the growl of the Bear Cat. As he came down the steps and advanced to the car, Linda, with the quick eye that had been one of her special gifts as a birthright, noted a change in him. He seemed to have been keyed up and toned up. There was a different expression on his face. There was buoyancy in his step. There was a visible determination in his eye. He took the seat beside her and Linda started the car. She looked at him interrogatively.

"Can you connect a heavy wind with the date of the lost plan?" he inquired.

"There was a crack-a-jack a few days before," said Linda. "It blew over some trees in the lot next to us."

"Exactly," said Snow; "and it plucked a screen from your guest-room window. Katy thinks that the cheque to the carpenter and the cost of the repairs will be in your sister's account books."

"Um hm," nodded Linda. "Well, that simplifies matters, because Peter Morrison is going to tell you about a trip Henry Anderson made around our house the morning Marian left."

"I think that is about all we need to know," said Mr. Snow conclusively.

"I think so," said Linda, "but I want you to see Peter's house for yourself, since I understand that according to your contract the rights to reproduce these particular plans remained with you after you had paid prize money for them."

"Most certainly," said Mr. Snow. "We should have that much to show for our share of the transaction."

"It's a queer thing," said Linda. "You would have to know me a long time, and perhaps know under what conditions I have been reared in order to understand a feeling that I frequently have concerning people. I tobogganed down a sheer side of Multiflores Canyon one day without my path having been previously prepared, and I very nearly landed in the automobile that carried Henry Anderson and Peter Morrison on their first trip to Lilac Valley. I was much interested in preserving the integrity of my neck. I fervently hoped not to break more than a dozen of my legs and arms, and was forced to bring down intact the finest Cotyledon pulverulenta that Daddy or I had found in fourteen years of collecting in California. I am telling you all this that you may see why I might have been excused for not having been minutely observant of my surroundings when I landed. But what I did observe was a chilly, caterpillary sensation chasing up my spine the instant I met the eyes of Henry Anderson. In that instant I said to myself that I would not trust him, that I did not like him."

"And what about his companion?" asked Eugene Snow lightly. "Oh, Peter?" said Linda. There was a caress in her pronunciation of the name. "Why, Peter is a rock. The instant I deposited my Cotyledon in a safe place I would have put my hand in Peter Morrison's and started around the world if he had asked me to go. There is only one Peter. You will recognize that the instant you meet him."

"I am altogether willing to take your word for it," said Mr. Snow.

"And there is one thing about this disagreeable business," said Linda. "It was not Peter's coat that had the plan in it. He knew nothing about it. He has had his full service of stiff war work, and he has been knocking around big cities in newspaper work, and now he has come home to Lilac Valley to 'set up his rest,' as in the hymn book, you know. He built his garage first and he is living in it because he so loves this house of his that he has to be present to watch it grow in minute detail. Once on a time I saw a great wizard walking along the sidewalk, and he looked exactly like any man. He might have been you so far as anything different from other men in his appearance w as concerned."

Linda cut down the Bear Cat to its slowest speed.

"What is on my mind is this," she said. "I don't think Peter could quite afford the amount of ground he has bought, and the house he is building. I think possibly he is tying himself up in obligations. It may take him two or three years to come even on it; but it is a prepossession with him. Now can't you see that if we go to him and tell him this sordid, underhand, unmanly tale, how his fine nature is going to be hurt, how his big heart is going to be wrung, how his home-house that he is building with such eager watchfulness will be a weighty Old Man of the Sea clinging to his back? Do you think, Mr. Eugene Snow, that you're enough of a wizard to examine this house and to satisfy yourself as to whether it's an infringement of your plans or not, without letting Peter know the things about it that would spoil it for him?"

Eugene Snow reached across and closed a hand over the one of Linda's nearest him on the steering wheel.

"You very decent kid, you," he said appreciatively. "I certainly am enough of a wizard to save your Peter man any disillusionment concerning his dream house."

"Oh, but he is not my Peter man," said Linda. "We are only the best friends in the world. Really and truly, if you can keep a secret, he's Marian's."

"Is he?" asked Mr. Snow interestedly. And then he added very casually, in the most offhand manner—he said it more to an orange orchard through which they were passing than he said it to Linda—"I have very grave doubts about that. I think there must be some slight complication that will have to be cleared up."

Linda's heart gave a great jump of consternation.

"Indeed no," she said emphatically. "I don't think he has just told Marian yet, but I am very sure that he cares for her more than for any other woman, and I am equally sure she cares for him; and nothing could be more suitable."

"All right then," agreed Mr. Snow.

Linda put the Bear Cat at the mountain, crept around the road, skirted the boulders, and stopped halfway to the garage. And there, in a low tone, she indicated to Mr. Snow where they had lunched, when she found the plans, how she had brought out the coat, where she had emptied the mouse nest. Then she stepped from the car and hallooed for Peter. Peter came hurrying from the garage, and Eugene Snow was swift in his mental inventory. It coincided exactly with Linda's. He would have been willing to join hands with Peter and start around the world, quite convinced of the fairness of the outcome, with no greater acquaintance than one intent look at Peter, one grip of his sure hand. After that he began to act on Katy's hint, and in a very short time he had convinced himself that she was right. Maybe Peter tried to absorb himself in the plans he was going over, in the house he was proud to show the great architect; but it seemed to the man he was entertaining that his glance scarcely left Linda, that he was so preoccupied with where she went and what she did that he was like a juggler keeping two mental balls in the air at the same time.

It seemed to Peter a natural thing that, the architect being in the city on business, he should run out to call on Miss Thorne's dearest friend It seemed to him equally natural that Linda should bring him to see a house in which she was so kindly interesting herself. And just when Peter was most dexterous in his juggling, just when he was trying to explain the very wonderful step-saving' time-saving, rational kitchen arrangements and at the same time watch Linda on her course down to the spring, the architect halted him with a jerk. Eugene Snow stood very straight, his hands in his coat pockets, looking, Peter supposed, with interest at the arrangements of kitchen conveniences. His next terse sentence fairly staggered Peter. He looked him straight in the eye and inquired casually: "Chosen your dream woman to fit your house, Morrison?"

Peter was too surprised to conceal his feelings. His jaws snapped together; a belligerent look sprang into his eyes.

"I have had a good deal to do with houses," continued Mr. Snow. "They are my life work. I find that invariably they are built for a woman. Almost always they are built from her plans, and for her pleasure. It's a new house, a unique house, a wonderful house you're evolving here. It must be truly a wonderful woman you're dreaming about while you build it."

That was a nasty little trap. With his years and worldly experience Peter should not have fallen into it; but all men are children when they are sick, heart sick or body sick, and Peter was a very sick man at that minute. He had been addressed in such a frank and casual manner. His own brain shot off at queer tangents and led him constantly into unexpected places. The narrow side lane that opened up came into view so suddenly that Peter, with the innocence of a four-year-old, turned with military precision at the suggestion and looked over the premises for the exact location of Linda. Eugene Snow had seen for himself the thing that Katy had told him he would see if he looked for it. Suddenly he held out his hand.

"As man to man, Morrison, in this instance," he said in rather a hoarse, breathless voice, "don't you think it would be a good idea for you and me to assert our manhood, to manage our own affairs, to select our own wives if need be? If we really set ourselves to the job don't you believe we can work out our lives more to our liking than anyone else can plan for us? You get the idea, don't you, Morrison?"

Peter was facing the kitchen sink but he did not see it. His brain was whirling. He did see Snow's point of view. He did realize his position. But what Mr. Snow knew of his affairs he could only guess. The one thing Mr. Snow could not know was that Linda frankly admitted her prepossession for her school chum, Donald Whiting, but in any event if Peter could not have Linda he would much prefer occupying his dream house alone. So he caught at the straw held out to him with both hands.

"I get you," he said tersely. "It is not quite up to the mark of the manhood we like to think we possess to let our lives be engineered by a high school kid. Suppose we do just quietly and masterfully assert ourselves concerning our own affairs."

"Suppose we do," said Snow with finality.

Whereupon they shook hands with a grip that whitened their knuckles.

Then they went back to Lilac Valley and had their dinner together, and Linda and Peter escorted Eugene Snow to his train and started him on his return trip to San Francisco feeling very much better. Peter would not allow Linda to drive him home at night, so he left her after the Bear Cat had been safely placed in the garage. As she stood on the walk beside him, strongly outlined in the moonlight, Peter studied Linda whimsically. He said it half laughingly, but there was something to think about in what he said:

"I'm just picturing, Linda, what a nice old lady you will be by the time that high school kid of yours spends four years in college, one on the continent, and the Lord knows how many at mastering a profession."

Linda looked at him with widened eyes.

KATY UNBURDENS HER MIND

"Why, what are you talking about, Peter? Are you moonstruck?" she inquired solicitously. "Donald's only a friend, you know. I love him because he is the nicest companion; but there is nothing for you to be silly about."

Then Peter began to realize the truth. There wasn't anything for him to be concerned about. She had not the slightest notion what love meant, even as she announced that she loved Donald.

CHAPTER XXX. Peter's Release

Eugene Snow returned to San Francisco enthusiastic about Linda, while he would scarcely have known how to express his appreciation of Katherine O'Donovan. He had been served a delicious dinner, deftly and quietly, such food as men particularly like; but there had been no subservience. If Katherine O'Donovan had been waiting on her own table, serving her own friends she could not have managed with more pride. It was very evident that she loved service, that she loved the girl to whom she gave constant attention. He understood exactly what there was in her heart and why she felt as she did when he saw Linda and Peter together and heard their manner of speaking to each other, and made mental note of the many points of interest which seemed to exist between them. He returned to San Francisco with a good deal of a "See-the-conquering-hero-comes" mental attitude. He went directly to his office, pausing on the way for a box of candy and a bunch of Parma violets. His first act on reaching the office was to send for Miss Thorne. Marian came almost immediately, a worried look in her eyes. She sat in the big, cushioned chair that was offered her, and smiled faintly when the box was laid on her lap, topped with the violets. She looked at Eugene Snow with an "I-wish-you-wouldn't" expression on her face; but he smiled at her reassuringly.

"Nothing," he said. "Picked them up on the way from the station. I made a hasty trip to that precious Lilac Valley of yours, and I must say it pales your representation. It is a wonderfully lovely spot."

Marian settled back in the chair. She picked up the violets and ran an experienced finger around the stems until she found the pin with which she fastened them at her waist. Then as they occupied themselves making selections from the candy box he looked smilingly at Marian. Her eyes noted the change in him. He was neither disappointed nor sad. Something had happened in Lilac Valley that had changed his perspective. Womanlike, she began probing.

"Glad you liked my valley," she said. "We are told that blue is a wonderful aura to surround a person, and it's equally wonderful when it surrounds a whole valley. With the blue sky and the blue walls and a few true-blue friends I have there, it's naturally a very dear spot to me."

"Yes," said Mr. Snow, "I can see that it is. I ran down on a business matter. I have been deeply puzzled and much perturbed over this prize contest. We have run these affairs once a year, sometimes oftener, for a long time, so I couldn't understand the peculiar thing about the similarity of the winning plans and your work this year. I have been holding up the prize money, because I did not feel that you were saying exactly what was in your heart, and I couldn't be altogether satisfied that everything was right. I went to Lilac Valley because I had a letter from your friend, Miss Linda Strong. There was an enclosure in it."

He drew from his pocket the folded sheet and handed it to Marian. Her eyes were surprised, incredulous, as she opened the missing sheet from her plans, saw the extraneous lines drawn upon it and the minute figuring with which the margin was covered.

"Linda found it at last!" she cried. "Where in this world did she get it, and whose work is this on it?"

"She got it," said Eugene Snow, "when she undertook to clean Peter Morrison's workroom on an evening when she and her cook were having supper with him. She turned a coat belonging to his architect that hung with some of his clothing in Peter Morrison's garage. She was shaking the nest of a field mouse from one of the side pockets. Naturally this emptied all the pockets, and in gathering up their contents she came across that plan, which she recognized. She thought it was right to take it and very wisely felt that it was man's business, so she sent it to me with her explanations. I went to Lilac Valley because I wanted to judge for myself exactly what kind of young person she was. I wanted to see her environment. I wanted to see the house that she felt sure was being built from these plans. I wanted to satisfy myself of the stability of what I had to work on before I mentioned the matter to you or Henry Anderson."

Marian sat holding the plan, listening absorbedly to what he was saying.

"It's an ugly business," he said, "so ugly that there is no question whatever but that it can be settled very quietly and without any annoyance to you. I shall have to take the matter up with the board, but I have the details so worked out that I shall have no difficulty in arranging matters as I think best. There is no question whatever, Marian, but that Anderson found that sketch on the west side of the Strong residence. When you left your plans lying on a table before a window in the Strong guestroom the night before you came to San Francisco you did not know that the santana which raged through the valley a day or two previously had stripped a screen from the window before which you left them. In opening your door to establish a draft before you went to bed you started one that carried your top drawing through the window. Waiting for Miss Strong the next morning, in making a circuit of the grounds Anderson found it and appropriated it to most excellent advantage. Miss Linda tells me that your study of architecture was discussed at the dinner table that night. He could not have helped realizing that any sheet of plans he found there must have been yours. If he could acquit his conscience of taking them and using them, he would still have to explain why he was ready to accept the first prize and the conditions imposed when he already had a house fairly well under construction from the plans he submitted in the contest. The rule is unbreakable that the plans must be original, must be unused, must be our sole property, if they take the prize."

Marian was leaning forward, her eyes wide with interest, her breast agitated. She nodded in acquiescence. Eugene Snow reached across and helped himself to another piece of candy from the box on her knee. He looked at her speculatively and spoke quietly as if the matter were of no great importance.

"Would it be agreeable, Marian, if the prize committee should announce that there were reasons as to why they were not satisfied, that they have decided to return all plans and call off the present contest, opening another in a few months in which interested parties may again submit their drawings? I will undertake swiftly and comprehensively to eliminate Henry Anderson from California. I would be willing to venture quite a sum that when I finish with the youngster he will see the beauty of going straight hereafter and the desirability of a change of atmosphere. He's a youngster. I hate to make the matter public, not only on account of involving you and your friends in such disagreeable business, but I am sorry for him. I would like to deal with him like the proverbial

'Dutch uncle,' then I would like to send him away to make a new start with the assurance that I am keeping close watch on him. Would you be satisfied if I handled the matter quietly and in my own way? Could you wait a few weeks for justice?"

Marian drew a deep breath.

"Of course," she said, "it would be wonderful if you could do that. But what about Peter Morrison? How much did he know concerning the plans, and what does he know about this?"

"Nothing," said Mr. Snow. "That most unusual young friend of yours made me see the light very clearly concerning Peter Morrison. There is no necessity for him ever to know that the 'dream house,' as Miss Linda calls it, that he is building for his dream woman has any disagreeable history attached to it. He so loves the spot that he is living on it to watch that house in minutest detail. Miss Linda was fairly eloquent in the plea she made on his behalf. He strikes me as a very unusual person, and she appealed to me in the same way. There must be some scientific explanation concerning her that I don't just get, but I can see that she is most unusual when I watched them together and heard them talk of their plans for the house and the grounds and discussing illustrations that she is making for articles that he is writing, I saw how deep and wholesome was the friendship existing between them. I even heard that wonderful serving woman, whom they so familiarly speak of as 'Katy,' chiding Peter Morrison for allowing Linda to take her typewriter to him and do her own work with a pen. And because Miss Linda seems so greathearted and loving with her friends, I was rather glad to hear his explanation that they were merely changing machines for the time being for a very particular reason of their own."

"Do you mean," asked Marian, "that you think there is anything more than casual friendship between Linda and Peter Morrison?"

"Not on her part," answered Eugene Snow. "Anybody can see that she is a child deeply engrossed in all sorts of affairs uncommon for a girl of her age and position. Her nice perceptions, her wonderful loyalty to her friends, her loving thought for them, are manifest in everything she says or does. If she ever makes any mistakes they will be from the head, not from the heart. But for the other end of the equation I could speak authoritatively. Katy pointed out to me the fact that if I would watch Peter Morrison in Miss Linda's presence, I should see that he adored her. I did watch, and I did see that very thing. When I taxed him about building a dream house for a dream woman, his eyes crossed a plateau, leaped a brook, and started up the side of a mountain. They did not rest until they had found Linda."

Marian sat so still that it seemed as if she were not even breathing. In view of what Katy had said, and his few words with Peter Morrison, Eugene Snow had felt justified in giving Marian a hint as to what was going on in Lilac Valley. Exactly what he had done he had no means of knowing. If he had known and had talked intentionally he could not have made clearer to Marian the thing which for months had puzzled her. She was aware that Eugene Snow was talking, that he was describing the dinner he had been served, the wonderful wild-flower garden that he had seen, how skillfully Linda drove the Bear Cat. She heard these things and dimly comprehended them but underneath, her brain was seizing upon one fact after another. They had exchanged typewriters. The poor, foolish little kid had known how her health was wracked, how she was suffering, how her pride would not let her stoop to Eileen's subterfuges and wage war with her implements for a man she did not want if her manner of living her everyday life did not appeal to him. Linda had known how lonely and heart hungry and disappointed she had gone away, and loyally she had tried to create an interest in life for her; and she had succeeded entirely too well. And then in a panic she must have gone to Peter Morrison and explained the situation; and Peter must have agreed to take over the correspondence. One by one things that had puzzled her about the letters and about the whole affair began to grow clear. She even saw how Linda, having friendly association with no man save Peter, would naturally use him for a model. The trouble was that, with her gift of penetration and insight and her facility with her pen, she had overdone the matter. She had not imitated Peter; she had BEEN Peter. Marian arose suddenly.

She went home, locked the door, and one after another she read the letters that had piqued, amused, comforted, and finally intrigued her. They were brilliant letters, charming, appealing letters, and yet, with knowledge concerning them, Marian wondered how she could have failed to appreciate in the beginning that they were from Linda.

"It goes to prove," she said at last, "how hungry the human heart is for love and sympathy. And that poor kid, what she must have suffered when she went to Peter for help! And if, as Mr. Snow thinks, he cares for her, how he must have suffered before he agreed to help her, as no doubt he did. What I have to do is to find some way out of the situation that will relieve Linda's anxiety and at least partially save my face. I shall have to take a few days to work it out. Luckily I haven't answered my last letter. When I find out what I really want to say then I will be very careful how I say it. I don't just exactly relish having my letters turned over to Peter Morrison, but possibly I can think of some

117

way—I must think of some way—to make them feel that I have not been any more credulous than they."

While she thought, both Linda and Peter were doing much thinking on the same subject. Linda's heart was full of gratitude to Peter for helping her out of her very disagreeable situation. Peter had not yet opened the packet of letters lying on his table He had a sickening distaste for the whole transaction. He had thought that he would wait until he received the first letter he was to answer. If it gave him sufficient foundation in itself for the answer, he would not be forced to search further. He had smoked many pipes on this decision. After the visit of Mr. Snow, Peter had seen a great light and had decided, from the mood and the attitude of that gentleman after his interview with Katy, that he very likely would be equal to any complication that might arise when he reached San Francisco. Mulling over the situation one day Peter said reflectively to the spring which was very busy talking to him: "I am morally certain that this matter has resolved itself into a situation that closely resembles the bootblack's apple: 'they ain't goin' to be any core.' I am reasonably certain that I never shall have a letter to answer. In a few days probably I shall be able to turn back that packet to Linda without having opened it."

To make up for the perturbation which had resulted in failure in class and two weeks of work that represented her worst appearances in high-school history, Linda, her mind freed from the worry over Marian's plans, and her heart calmer over the fiasco in trying to comfort her, devoted herself absorbingly to her lessons and to the next magazine article that she must finish. She had decided that it was time to write on the subject of Indian confections. Her first spare minute she and Katy must busy themselves working out the most delicious cactus candy possible. Then they could try the mesquite candy. No doubt she could evolve a delicious gum from the mesquite and the incense plant. She knew she could from the willow milkweed; and under the head of "sweets" an appetizing jelly from manzanita. There were delightful drinks too, from the manzanita and the chia. And better than either, the lemonade berry would serve this purpose. She had not experimented to an authoritative extent with the desert pickles. And among drinks she might use the tea made from blue-eyed grass, brewed by the Indians for feverish conditions; and there was a whole world of interest to open up in differing seeds and berries, parched or boiled for food. And there were the seeds that were ground for mush, like the thistle sage, and the mock orange which was food and soap also, and the wild sunflowers that were parched for meal, and above all, the acorns. She could see that her problem was not going to be one of difficulty in securing sufficient material for her book; it would be how to find time to gather all these things, and put them through the various processes and combinations necessary to make edible dishes from I them. It would mean a long summer of interesting and absorbing I work for her and for Katy. Much of it could not be done until the I summer was far advanced and the seeds and the berries were I ripe. She could rely on Donald to help her search for the material. With only herself and Katy in the family they could give much of their time to the work.

"Where Katy will rebel," said Linda to herself, "is when it comes to gathering sufficient seeds and parching them to make these meal and mush dishes. She will call it 'fiddlin' business.' She shall be propitiated with a new dress and a beautiful bonnet, and she shall go with me frequently to the fields. The old dear loves to ride. First thing I do I'll call at the bank again and have our affairs properly straightened and settled there in the light of the letter Daddy left me. Then I shall have money to get all the furniture and the rugs and things we truly need. I'll repaint the kitchen and get Katy some new cooking utensils to gladden her soul. And Saturday I must make my trip with Donald account for something worth while on the book."

All these plans were feasible. What Linda had to do was to accomplish them, and this she proceeded to do in a swift and businesslike manner. She soon reached the place where the whole house with the exception of Eileen's suite had been gone over, freshened and refurnished to her liking. The guest-room furniture had been moved to her rejuvenated room. On the strength of her I returns from the book she had disposed of her furniture and was finding much girlish delight in occupying a beautiful room, daintily decorated, comfortably furnished with pieces of her own selection. As she and Katy stood looking over their work when everything was ready for her first night of occupancy Katy had said to her:

"It's jist right and proper, lambie; it's jist the way it ought to be; and now say the word and let me clean out Eileen's suate and get it ready for Miss Marian, so if she would drop down unexpected she would find we was good as our word."

"All right," said Linda.

"And what am I to do with the stuff?" inquired Katy.

"Katy, my dear," said Linda with a dry laugh, "you'll think I am foolish, but I have the queerest feeling concerning those things. I can't feel that Eileen has done with them; I can't feel that she will never want them again; I can't feel that they should go to some second-hand basement. Pack all of her clothing that you can manage in her trunk and put it in the garret, and what the trunk won't hold pack in a tight box and put that in the garret also. She hasn't written me a line; she has sent me no address; I don't know what to do; but, as I have said before, I am going to save the things at least a year and see whether some day Eileen won't think of something she wants to do with them. Clean the rooms and I will order Marian's things sent."

According to these arrangements it was only a few days until Linda wrote Marian that her room was ready for her and that any time she desired to come and take possession she could test the lovingness of the welcome that awaited her by becoming intimately acquainted with it. Marian answered the letter immediately. She said that she was planning to come very soon to test that welcome. She longed for the quiet of the valley, for its cool, clean, wild air. She was very tired; she needed rest. She thought she would love the new home they were offering her. Then came two amazing paragraphs.

The other day Dana and I went into one of the big cafes in the city to treat ourselves to a taste of the entertainment with which the people of wealth regale themselves. We had wandered in laughingly jesting about what we should order, and ran into Eileen in the company of her aunt and uncle and a very flashy and loudly dressed young man, evidently a new suitor of Eileen's. I don't think Eileen wanted to introduce us, and yet she acted like a person ravenous for news of her home and friends. She did introduce us, and immediately her ponderous uncle took possession of us. It seems that the man is a brother of Eileen's mother. Linda, he is big and gross, he is everything that a man of nice perceptions would not be, but he does love Eileen. He is trying conscientiously to please her. His wife is the kind of person who would marry that kind of man and think everything he said and did was right. And the suitor, my dear, was the kind of man who could endure that kind of people. Eileen was almost, if not quite, the loveliest thing I ever have seen. She was plain; she was simple; but it was the costly simplicity of extravagance. Ye gods! but she had pearls of the size she had always wanted. She tried with all her might to be herself, but she knows me well enough to know what I would think and what I would write to you concerning the conditions under which I met her. We were simply forced to lunch with them. We could only nibble at the too rich, too highly seasoned food set before us. And I noticed that Eileen nibbled also. She is not going to grow fat and waddle and redden her nose, but, my dear, back deep in her eyes and in the curve of her lips and in the tone of her voice there were such disappointment and discontent as I never have seen in any woman. She could not suppress them; she could not conceal them. There was nothing on earth she could do but sit quietly and endure. They delivered us at our respective offices, leaving both of us dates on which to visit them, but neither of us intends to call on them. Eileen's face was a tragedy when her uncle insisted on making the arrangements. I can at least spare her that.

And now, my dear, life is growing so full and my time is so taken with my work at the office and with my widening friendships with Dana and her friends and with Mr. Snow, that I really feel I have not time to go farther with our anonymous correspondence. It is all I can do to find time to write you letters such as the one I am writing I have done my best to play up to what you expected of me and I think I have succeeded in fooling you quite as much as you felt that you were fooling me. But, Linda dear, I want you always to know that I appreciate the spirit in which you began this thing. I know why you did it and I shall always love you a trifle more for your thought of me and your effort to tide over the very dark days you knew I would be facing in San Francisco. I think, dear friend of mine, that I have had my share of dark days. I think there is very beautiful sunlight ahead for me. And by and by I hope to come into happiness that maybe is even more than my share. I am coming to see you soon and then I will tell you all about it.

There was more of the letter, but at that point Linda made one headlong rush for the Bear Cat. She took the curve on two wheels and almost ran into the mountain face behind the garage before she could slow down. Then she set the Cat screaming wildly for Peter. As he came up to the car she leaned toward him, shaking with excitement.

"Peter," she cried, "have you opened that packet of letters yet?"

"No," said Peter, "I have not."

"Then give them to me quickly, Peter," said Linda.

Peter rushed into the garage and brought out the packet. Linda caught it in both hands and dropped it in her lap.

"Well, thank God," she said devoutly. "And, Peter, the joke's on me. Marian knew I was writing those letters all the time and she just pretended that she cared for them to make the game interesting for me. And when she had so many friends and so much to do, she hadn't time for them any longer; then she pretended that she was getting awfully in earnest in order to stop me, and she did stop me all right."

Linda's face was a small panorama of conflicting emotions as she appealed to Peter.

"Peter," she said in a quivering voice, "you can testify that she stopped me properly, can't you, Peter?"

Peter tried to smile. He was older than Linda, and he was thinking swiftly, intently.

"Yes, kid," he said with utmost corroboration, "yes, kid, she stopped you, but I can't see that it was necessary literally to scare the life out of you till she had you at the point where you were thinking of taking off from a mountain or into the sea. Did you really mean that, Linda?"

Linda relaxed suddenly. She sank back into the deeply padded seat of the Bear Cat. A look of fright and entreaty swept into her dark eyes.

"Yes, Peter, I did mean it," she said with finality. "I couldn't have lived if I had hurt Marian irreparably. She has been hurt so much already. And, Peter, it was awfully nice of you to wait about reading these letters. Even if she only did it for a joke, I think Marian would rather that you had not read them. Now I'll go back home and begin to work in earnest on the head piece of 'How to Grow Good Citizens.' And I quite agree with you, Peter, that the oath of allegiance, citizenship, and the title to a piece of real estate are the prime requisites. People have no business comma to our country to earn money that they intend to carry away to invest in the development and the strengthening of some other country that may some day be our worst enemy. I have not found out yet how to say it in a four-by-twelve-inch strip, but by the time I have read the article aloud to my skylight along about ten tonight I'll get an inspiration; I am sure I shall."

"Of course you will," said Peter; "but don't worry about it, dear; don't lose sleep. Take things slower. Give time for a little more flesh to grow on your bones. And don't forget that while you're helping Donald to keep at the head of his classes it's your first job to keep at the head of your own."

"Thank you," said Linda. "How is the dream coming?"

"Beautifully," said Peter. "One of these days you're going to come rushing around the boulders and down the side of the building to find all this debris cleared away and the place for a lawn leveled. I am fighting down every possible avenue of expertise on the building in the effort to save money to make the brook run and the road wind where you have indicated that you want them to follow you."

Linda looked at Peter while a queer, reflective light gathered in her eyes. At last she said soberly: "Well, I don't know, Peter, that you should make them so very personal to me as all that."

"Why not?" asked Peter casually. "Since there is no one else, why not?"

Linda released the clutch and started the car. She backed in front of the garage and turned. She was still thinking deeply as she stopped. Once again she extended a hand to Peter.

"Thank you a thousand times for not reading these letters, Peter," she said. "I can't express how awfully fine I think it is of you. And if it's all right with you, perhaps there's not any real reason why you should not run that brook and drive that road the way I think they should go. Somebody is going to design them. Why shouldn't I, if it pleases you to have me?"

"It pleases me very greatly," said Peter—"more than anything else I can think of in all the world at this minute."

And then he did a thing that he had done once or twice before. He bent back Linda's fingers and left another kiss in the palm of her hand, and then he closed her fingers very tightly over it.

CHAPTER XXXI. The End of Donald's Contest

The middle of the week Linda had told Katy that she intended stocking up the Bear Cat for three and that she would take her along on the next Saturday's trip to her canyon kitchen. It was a day upon which she had planned to gather greens, vegetables, and roots, and prepare a dinner wholly from the wild. She was fairly sure exactly where in nature she would find the materials she wanted, but she knew that the search would be long and tiring. It would be jolly to have Katy to help her prepare the lunch. It would please Katy immensely to be taken; and the original things she said in her quaint Irish brogue greatly amused Donald. The arrangement had been understood among them for some time, so they all started on their journey filled with happy expectations. They closed the house and the garage carefully. Linda looked over the equipment of the Bear Cat minutely making sure that her field axe, saw, knives, and her field glasses were in place. Because more food than usual was to be prepared in the kitchen they took along a nest of cooking vessels and a broiler. They found Donald waiting before either of them were ready, and in great glee, with much laughing and many jests they rolled down the valley in the early morning. They drove to the kitchen, spread their blankets, set up their table, and arranged the small circular opening for their day's occupancy. While Katy and Linda were busy with these affairs Donald took the axe and collected a big heap of wood. Then they left Katy to burn the wood and have a deep bed of coals ready while they started out to collect from the canyon walls, the foot of the mountains, and the near-by desert the materials they would use for their dinner.

Just where the desert began to climb the mountain Linda had for a long time watched a big bed of amole. Donald used the shovel, she the hatchet, and soon they had brought to the surface such a quantity that Donald protested.

"But I have two uses for them today," explained Linda. "They must serve for potatoes and they have to furnish our meat."

"Oh, I get you," said Donald. "I have always been crazy to try that."

So he began to dig again enthusiastically.

"Now I'll tell you what I think we had better do," said Linda. "We will skirmish around this side of the mountain and find a very nice tender yucca shoot; and then we'll take these back to Katy and let her bury them in the ashes and keep up the fire while we forage for the remainder of our wild Indian feast."

Presently they found a yucca head that Linda said was exactly right, a delicate pink, thicker than her wrist and two feet in length. With this and the amole they ran back to Katy. She knew how to prepare the amole for roasting. Linda gave her a few words of instruction concerning the yucca. Then from the interior of the Bear Cat she drew a tightly rolled section of wire window screening. Just where a deep, wide pool narrowed at a rocky defile they sank the screening, jammed it well to the bottom, fastened it tight at the sides, and against the current side of it they threw leaves, grass, chunks of moss, any debris they could gather that would make a temporary dam. Then, standing on one side with her field knife, Linda began to slice the remainder of the amole very thin and to throw it over the surface of the pool. On the other, Donald pounded the big, juicy bulbs to pulp and scattered it broadcast over the water. Linda instructed Katy to sit on the bank with a long-handled landing net and whenever a trout arose, to snatch it out as speedily as possible, being careful not to take more than they would require.

Then the two youngsters, exhilarated with youth, with living, with the joy of friendship, with the lure of the valley, with the heady intoxication of the salt breeze and the gold of the sunshine, climbed into the Bear Cat and went rolling through the canyon and out to the valley on the far side. Here they gathered the tenderest heart shoots of the lupin until Linda said they had enough. Then to a particular spot that she knew on the desert they hurried for the enlarged stems of the desert trumpet which was to serve that day for an appetizer in the stead of pickles. Here, too, they filled a bucket from the heart of a big Bisnaga cactus as a basis for their drink. Among Katherine O'Donovan's cooking utensils there was a box of delicious cactus candy made from the preserved and sun-dried heart meat of this same fruit which was to serve as their confection. On the way back they stopped at the bridge and gathered cress for their salad. When they returned to Katy she had five fine trout lying in the shade, and with more experienced eyes and a more skillful hand Linda in a few minutes doubled this number. Then they tore out the dam, rinsed the screen and spread it over a rock to dry. While Donald scaled the fish Linda put the greens to cook, prepared the salad and set the table. Once, as he worked under her supervision, Linda said to Donald: "Now about bread, kid—there's not going to be any bread, because the Indians did not have it when they lived the way we are living today. When you reach the place where your left hand feels empty without a piece of bread in it, just butter up another amole and try it. It will serve the same purpose as bread, and be much better for the inner man."

"If you would let me skin these fish," said Donald, "I could do it much faster and make a better job of it."

"But you shouldn't skin them; you want the skin to hold the meat together when it begins to cook tender; and you should be able to peel it off and discard it if it burns or gets smoky in the cooking. It's a great concession to clean them as we do. The Indians cooked them in the altogether and ate the meat from the bones."

"Oh my tummy!" said Donald. "I always thought there was some dark secret about the Indians."

Linda sat on a rock opposite him and clasped her hands around her knees. She looked at him meditatively.

"Did you?" she asked. "Suppose you revise that opinion. Our North American Indians in their original state were as fine as any peoples that ever have been discovered the round of the globe. My grandfather came into intimate contact with them in the early days, and he said that their religion, embracing the idea of a great spirit to whom they were responsible for their deeds here, and a happy hunting ground to which they went as a reward for decent living, was as fine as any religion that ever has been practiced by people of any nation. Immorality was unknown among them. Family ties were formed and they were binding They loved their children and reared them carefully. They were hardy and healthful. Until the introduction of whiskey and what we are pleased to term civilized methods of living, very few of them died save from war or old age. They were free; they were happy. The moping, lazy, diseased creature that you find sleeping in the sun around the reservations is a product of our civilization. Nice commentary on civilization, isn't it?"

"For heaven's sake, Linda," said Donald, "don't start any big brainstorming trains of thought today! Grant me repose. I have overworked my brain for a few months past until I know only one thing for certain."

"All right then, me lad, this is the time for the big secret," said Linda. "I just happened to be in the assembly room on some business of my own last Thursday afternoon when my sessions were over, and I overheard your professor in trigonometry tell a marl I did not know, who seemed to be

121

a friend visiting him, that the son of Judge Whiting was doing the finest work that ever had been done in any of the Los Angeles high schools, and that undoubtedly you were going to graduate with higher honors than any other boy ever had from that school."

Donald sat thinking this over. He absently lifted an elbow and wiped the tiny scales from his face with his shirt sleeve.

"Young woman," he said solemnly, "them things what you're saying, are they 'cross your heart, honest to goodness, so help you,' truth, or are they the fruit of a perfervid imagination?"

Linda shook her head vigorously.

"De but', kid," she said, "de gospel but'. You have the Jap going properly. He can't stop you now. You have fought your good fight, and you have practically won it. All you have to do is to carry on till the middle of June, and you're It."

"I wish Dad knew," said Donald in a low voice.

"The Judge does know," said Linda heartily. "It wasn't fifteen minutes after I heard that till I had him on the telephone repeating it as fast as I could repeat. Come to think of it, haven't you noticed a particularly cocky set of his head and the corksome lightness about his heels during the past few days?"

"By Jove, he has been happy about something!" said Donald. "And I noticed that Louise and the Mater were sort of cheery and making a specialty of the only son and brother."

"Sure, brother, sure," said Linda. "Hurry up and scrape those fish and let's scamper down the canyon merely for the joy of flying with wings on our feet. You're It, young man, just It!"

Donald was sitting on a boulder. On another in front of him he was operating on the trout. His hands were soiled; his hair was tousled; he was fairly well decorated with fine scales. He looked at Linda appealingly.

"Am I 'It' with you, Linda?" he asked soberly.

"Sure you are," said Linda. "You're the best friend I have."

"Will you write to me when I go to college this fall?"

"Why, you couldn't keep me from it," said Linda. "I'll have so many things to tell you. And when your first vacation comes we'll make it a hummer."

"I know Dad won't let me come home for my holidays except for the midsummer ones," said Donald soberly. "It would take most of the time there would be of the short holidays to travel back and forth."

"You will have to go very carefully about getting a start," said Linda, "and you should be careful to find the right kind of friends at the very start. Christmas and Thanksgiving boxes can always be sent on time to reach you. It won't be so long for you as for us; and by the time you have Oka Sayye beaten to ravelings you will have such a 'perfect habit' that you will start right in with the beating idea. That should keep you fairly busy, because most of the men you come up against will be beaters themselves."

"Yes, I know," said Donald. "Are you going to start me to college with the idea that I have to keep up this beating habit? If I were to be one of fifty or a hundred, wouldn't that be good enough?"

"Why, sure," said Linda, "if you will be satisfied with having me like fifty or a hundred as well as I do you."

"Oh, damn!" said Donald angrily. "Do I have to keep up this top-crust business all my days?"

Linda looked at him with a queer smile on her lips.

"Not unless you want to, Donald," she said quietly; "not unless you think you would rather."

Donald scraped a fish vigorously. Linda sat watching him. Presently the tense lines around his eyes vanished. A faint red crept up his neck and settled on his left cheek bone. A confused grin slowly widened his naturally wide mouth.

"Then it's me for the top crust," he said conclusively.

"Then it's me for you," answered Linda in equally as matter-of-fact tones; and rising, she gathered up the fish and carried them to Katy while Donald knelt beside the chilly stream and scoured his face and hands, after which Linda whipped away the scales with an improvised brush of willow twigs.

It was such a wonderful day; it was such an unusual and delicious feast. Plump brook trout, fresh from icy water, delicately broiled over searing wood coals, are the finest of food. Through the meal to the point where Donald lay on his back at the far curve of the canyon wall, nibbling a piece of cactus candy, everything had been perfect. Nine months would be a long time to be gone, but Linda would wait for him, and she would write to him.

He raised his head on his elbow and called across to her: "Say, Linda, how often will you write to me?"

Linda answered promptly: "Every Saturday night. Saturday is our day. I'll tell you what has happened all the week. I'll tell you specially what a darned unprofitable day Saturday is when you're three thousand miles away."

Bending over the canyon fireplace, her face red with heat and exertion, Katherine O'Donovan caught up her poker and beat up the fire until the ashes flew.

"Easy, Katy, easy," cautioned Linda. "We may want to bury those coals and resurrect them to warm up what is left for supper."

"We'll do no such thing," said Katy promptly. "What remains goes to feed the fish. Next time it's hungry ye are, we're goin' to hit it straight to Lilac Valley and fill ourselves with God's own bread and beefsteak and paraties. Don't ye think we're goin' to be atin' these haythen messes twice in one day."

To herself she was saying: "The sooner I get you home to Pater Morrison, missy, the better I'll be satisfied."

Once she stood erect, her hands at her belt, her elbows widespread, and with narrowed eyes watched the youngsters. Her lips were closed so tightly they wrinkled curiously as she turned back to the fireplace.

"Nayther one of them fool kids has come to yet," she said to herself, "and a mighty good thing it is that they haven't."

Linda was looking speculatively at Donald as he lay stretched on the Indian blanket at the base of the cliff. And then, because she was for ever busy with Nature, her eyes strayed above him up the side of the cliff, noting the vegetation, the scarred rocks, the sheer beauty of the canyon wall until they reached the top. Then, for no reason at all, she sat looking steadily at a huge boulder overhanging the edge of the cliff, and she was wondering how many ages it had hung there and how many more it would hang, poised almost in air, when a tiny pebble at its base loosened and came rattling and bounding down the canyon face. Every nerve in Linda tensed. She opened her mouth, but not a sound came. For a breathless second she was paralyzed. Then she shrieked wildly: "Donald, Donald, roll under the ledge! Quick, quick!"

She turned to Katy.

"Back, Katy, back!" she screamed. "That boulder is loose; it's coming down!"

For months Donald Whiting had obeyed Linda implicitly and instantly. He had moved with almost invisible speed at her warning many times before. Sometimes it had been a venomous snake, sometimes a yucca bayonet, sometimes poison vines, again unsafe footing—in each case instant obedience had been the rule. He did hot "question why" at her warning; he instantly did as he was told. He, too, had noticed the falling pebble. With all the agility of which he was capable he rolled under the narrow projecting ledge above him. Katherine O'Donovan was a good soldier also. She whirled and ran to the roadway. She had barely reached it when, with a grinding crash, down came the huge boulder, carrying bushes, smaller rocks, sand, and debris with it. On account of its weight it fell straight, struck heavily, and buried itself in the earth exactly on the spot upon which Donald had been lying. Linda raised terrified eyes to the top of the wall. For one instant a dark object peered over it and then drew back. Without thought for herself Linda rushed to the boulder, and kneeling, tried to see back of it.

"Donald!" she cried, "Donald, are you all right?"

"Guess I am, unless it hit one foot pretty hard. Feels fast."

"Can you get out?" she cried, beginning to tear with her hands at the stone and the bushes where she thought his head would be.

"I'm fast; but I'm all right," he panted. "Why the devil did that thing hang there for ages, and then come down on me today?"

"Yes, why did it?" gasped Linda. "Donald, I must leave you a minute. I've got to know if I saw a head peer over just as that stone came down."

"Be careful what you do!" he cried after her.

Linda sprang to her feet and rushed to the car. She caught out the field classes and threw the strap over her head as she raced to the far side of the fireplace where the walls were not so sheer. Katherine O'Donovan promptly seized the axe, caught its carrying strap lying beside it, thrust the handle through, swung it over her own head, dropped it between her shoulders, and ripping off her dress skirt she started up the cliff after Linda. Linda was climbing so swiftly and so absorbedly that she reached the top before she heard a sound behind her. Then she turned with a white face, and her mouth dropped open as she saw Katy three fourths of the way up the cliff. For one second she was again stiff with terror, then, feeling she could do nothing, she stepped back out of sight and waited a second until Katy's red head and redder face appeared over the edge. Realizing that her authority was of no avail, that Katy would follow her no matter where she went or what she did, and with no time to argue, Linda simply called to her encouragingly: "Follow where I go; take your time; hang tight, old dear, it's dangerous!"

She started around the side of the mountain, heading almost straight upward, traveling as swiftly and as noiselessly as possible. Over big boulders, on precarious footing, clinging to bushes, they made their way until they reached a place that seemed to be sheer above them; certainly it was for

123

hundreds of feet below On a point of rock screened by overhanging bushes Linda paused until Katy overtook her.

"We are about stalled," she panted. "Find a good footing and stay where you are. I'm going to climb out on these bushes and see if I can get a view of the mountain side."

Advancing a few yards, Linda braced herself, drew around her glasses, and began searching the side of the mountain opposite her and below as far as she could range with the glasses. At last she gave up.

"Must have gone the other way," she said to Katy. "I'll crawl back to you. We'll go after help and get Donald out. There will be time enough to examine the cliff afterward; but I am just as sure now as I will be when it is examined that that stone was purposely loosened to a degree where a slight push would drop it. As Donald says, there's no reason why it should hang there for centuries and fall on him today. Shut your eyes, old dear, and back up. We must go to Donald. I rather think it's on one of his feet from what he said. Let me take one more good look."

At that minute from high on the mountain above them a shower of sand and pebbles came rattling down. Linda gave Katy one terrified look.

"My God!" she panted. "He's coming down right above us!"

Just how Linda recrossed the bushes and reached Katy she did not know. She motioned for her to make her way back as they had come. Katy planted her feet squarely upon the rock. Her lower jaw shot out; her eyes were aflame. She stood perfectly still with the exception of motioning Linda to crowd back under the bushes, and again Linda realized that she had no authority; as she had done from childhood when Katy was in earnest, Linda obeyed her. She had barely reached the overhanging bushes, crouched under them, and straightened herself, when a small avalanche came showering down, and a minute later a pair of feet were level with her head. Then screened by the bushes, she could have reached out and touched Oka Sayye. As his feet found a solid resting place on the ledge on which Linda and Katy stood, and while he was still clinging to the bushes, Katherine O'Donovan advanced upon him. He had felt that his feet were firm, let go his hold, and turned, when he faced the infuriated Irishwoman. She had pulled the strap from around her neck, slipped the axe from it, and with a strong thrust she planted the head of it against Oka Sayye's chest so hard that she almost fell forward. The Jap plunged backward among the bushes, the roots of which had supported Linda while she used the glasses. Then he fell, sliding among them, snatching wildly. Linda gripped the overhanging growth behind which she had been screened, and leaned forward.

"He has a hold; he is coming back up, Katy!" she cried.

Katy took another step forward. She looked over the cliff down an appalling depth of hundreds of feet. Deliberately she raised the axe, circled it round her head and brought it down upon that particular branch to which Oka Sayye was clinging. She cut it through, and the axe rang upon the stone wall behind it. As she swayed forward Linda reached out, gripped Katy and pulled her back.

"Get him?" she asked tersely, as if she were speaking of a rat or a rattlesnake.

Katy sank back limply against the wall. Linda slowly turned her around, and as she faced the rock, "Squeeze tight against it shut your eyes, and keep a stiff upper lip," she cautioned. "I'm going to work around you; I want to be ahead of you."

She squeezed past Katy, secured the axe and hung it round her own neck. She cautioned Katy to keep her eyes shut and follow where she led her, then they started on their way back. Linda did not attempt to descend the sheer wall by which they had climbed, but making a detour she went lower, and in a very short time they were back in the kitchen. Linda rushed to the boulder and knelt again, but she could get no response to her questions. Evidently Donald's foot was caught and he was unconscious from the pain. Squeezing as close as she could, she thrust her arm under the ledge until she could feel his head. Then she went to the other side, and there she could see that his right foot was pinned under the rock. She looked at Katy reassuringly, then she took off the axe and handed it to her.

"He's alive," she said. "Can't kill a healthy youngster to have a crushed foot. You stand guard until I take the Bear Cat and bring help. It's not far to where I can find people."

At full speed Linda put the Cat through the stream and out of the canyon until she reached cultivated land, where she found a man who would gather other men and start to the rescue. She ran on until she found a house with a telephone. There she called Judge Whiting, telling him to bring an ambulance and a surgeon, giving him explicit directions as to where to come, and assuring him that Donald could not possibly be seriously hurt. She found time to urge, also, that before starting he set in motion any precautions he had taken for Donald's protection. She told him where she thought what remained of Oka Sayye could be found. And then, as naturally and as methodically as she had done all the rest, she called Peter Morrison and told him that she was in trouble and where he could find her.

And because Peter had many miles less distance to travel than the others she had summoned, he arrived first. He found Linda and Katy had burrowed under the stone until they had made an opening into which the broken foot might sink so that the pain of the pressure would be relieved. Before the rock, with picks and shovels, half a dozen sympathetic farmers from ranches and cultivated land at the mouth of the canyon were digging furiously to make an opening undermining the boulder so that it could be easily tipped forward. Donald was conscious and they had been passing water to him and encouraging him with the report that his father and a good surgeon would be there very soon. Katherine O'Donovan had crouched at one side of the boulder, supporting the hurt foot. She was breathing heavily and her usually red face was a ghastly green. Linda had helped her to resume the skirt of her dress. At the other side of the rock the girl was reaching to where she could touch Donald's head or reassuringly grip the hand that he could extend to her. Peter seized Linda's axe and began hewing at the earth and rock in order to help in the speedy removal of the huge boulder. Soon Judge Whiting, accompanied by Doctor Fleming, the city's greatest surgeon, came caring into the canyon and stopped on the roadway when he saw the party. The Judge sprang from the car, leaped the stream, and started toward them. In an effort to free his son before his arrival, all the men braced themselves against the face of the cliff and pushed with their combined strength. The boulder dropped forward into the trench they had dug for it enough to allow Peter to crowd his body between it and the cliff and lift Donald's head and shoulders. Linda instantly ran around the boulder, pushed her way in, and carefully lifting Donald's feet, she managed to work the lithe slenderness of her body through the opening, so that they carried Donald out and laid him down in the open. He was considerably dazed and shaken, cruelly hurt, but proved himself a game youngster of the right mettle. He raised himself to a sitting posture, managing a rather stiff-lipped smile for his father and Linda. The surgeon instantly began cutting to reach the hurt foot, while Peter Morrison supported the boy's head and shoulders on one side, his father on the other.

An exclamation of dismay broke from the surgeon's lips. He looked at Judge Whiting and nodded slightly. The men immediately picked up Donald and carried him to the ambulance. Katherine O'Donovan sat down suddenly and buried her face in the skirt of her dress. Linda laid a reassuring hand on her shoulder.

"Don't, Katy," she said. "Keep up your nerve; you're all right, old dear. Donald's fine. That doesn't mean anything except that his foot is broken, so he won't be able, and it won't be necessary for him, to endure the pain of setting it in a cast without an anesthetic; and Doctor Fleming can work much better where he has every convenience. It's all right."

The surgeon climbed into the ambulance and they started on an emergency run to the hospital. As the car turned and swept down the canyon, for no reason that she could have explained, Linda began to shake until her teeth clicked. Peter Morrison sprang back across the brook, and running to her side, he put his arm around her and with one hand he pressed her head against his shoulder, covering her face.

"Steady, Linda," he said quietly, "steady. You know that he is all right. It will only be a question of a short confinement."

Linda made a brave effort to control herself. She leaned against Peter and held out both her hands.

"I'm all right," she chattered. "Give me a minute."

Judge Whiting came to them.

"I am getting away immediately," he said. "I must reach Louise and Mother before they get word of this. Doctor Fleming will take care of Donald all right. What happened, Linda? Can you tell me?"

Linda opened her lips and tried to speak, but she was too breathless, too full of excitement, to be coherent. To her amazement Katherine O'Donovan scrambled to her feet, lifted her head and faced the Judge. She pointed to the fireplace.

"I was right there, busy with me cookie' utensils," she said, "Miss Linda was a-sittin, on that exact spot, they jist havin finished atin' some of her haythen messes; and the lad was lyin, square where the boulder struck, on the Indian blanket, atin' a pace of cactus candy. And jist one pebble came rattlin' down, but Miss Linda happened to be lookin', and she scramed to the b'y to be rollin' under where ye found him; so he gave a flop or two, and it's well that he took his orders without waitin' to ask the raison for them, for if he had, at the prisint minute he would be about as thick as a shate of writing paper. The thing dropped clear and straight and drove itself into the earth and stone below it, as ye see."

Katherine O'Donovan paused.

"Yes," said the Judge. "Anything else?"

"Miss Linda got to him and she made sure he had brathin' space and he wasn't hurt bad, and then she told him he had got to stand it, because, sittin' where she did, she faced the cliff and she thought she had seen someone. She took the telescope and started climbin', and I took the axe and I started climbin' after her."

Katy broke down and emitted a weird Irish howl. Linda instantly braced herself, threw her arms around Katy, and drew her head to her shoulder. She looked at Judge Whiting and began to talk.

"I can show you where she followed me, straight up the face of the canyon, almost," she said. "And she never had tried to climb a canyon side for a yard, either, but she came up and over after me, like a cat. And up there on a small ledge Oka Sayye came down directly above us. I couldn't be mistaken. I saw him plainly. I know him by sight as well as I do any of you. We heard the stones coming down before him, and we knew someone was going to be on us who was desperate enough to kill. When he touched our level and turned to follow the ledge we were on, I pushed him over."

Katy shook off Linda's protecting arm and straightened suddenly.

"Why, ye domned little fool, ye!" she screamed. "Ye never told a lie before in all your days! Judge Whiting, I had the axe round me neck by the climbin' strap, and I got it in me fingers when we heard the crature comin', and against his chist I set it, and I gave him a shove that sint him over. Like a cat he was a-clingin' and climbin', and when I saw him comin' up on us with that awful face of his, I jist swung the axe like I do when I'm rejoocin' a pace of eucalyptus to fireplace size, and whack! I took the branch supportin' him, and a dome' good axe I spoiled din' it."

Katy folded her arms, lifted her chin higher than it ever had been before, and glared defiance at the Judge.

"Now go on," she said, "and decide what ye'll do to me for it."

The Judge reached over and took both Katherine O'Donovan's hands in a firm grip.

"You brave woman!" he said. "If it lay in my power, I would give you the Carnegie Medal. In any event I will see that you have a good bungalow with plenty of shamrock on each side of your front path, and a fair income to keep you comfortable when the rheumatic days are upon you."

"I am no over-feeder," said Katy proudly. "I'm daily exercisin' me muscles enough to kape them young. The rheumatism I'll not have. And nayther will I have the house nor the income. I've saved me money; I've an income of me own."

"And as for the bungalow," interrupted Linda, "Katherine, as I have mentioned frequently before is my father, and my mother, and my whole family, and her front door is mine."

"Sure," said Katy proudly. "When these two fine people before you set up their hearthstone, a-swapin' it I'll be, and carin' for their youngsters; but, Judge, I would like a bit of the shamrock. Ye might be sendin' me a start of that, if it would plase Your Honor."

Judge Whiting looked intently at Katherine O'Donovan. And then, as if they had been on the witness stand, he looked searchingly at Linda. But Linda was too perturbed, too accustomed to Katy's extravagant nonsense even to notice the purport of what she had said. Then the Judge turned his attention to Peter Morrison and realized that at least one of the parties to Katherine's proposed hearthstone had understood and heartily endorsed her proposal.

"I will have to be going. The boy and his mother will need me," he said. "I will see all of you later."

Then he sprang across the brook and sent his car roaring down the canyon after the ambulance.

Once more Katy sank to the ground. Linda looked at her as she buried her face and began to wail.

"Peter," she said quietly, "hunt our belongings and pack them in the Bear Cat the best you can. Excuse us for a few minutes. We must act this out of our systems."

Gravely she sat down beside Katy, laid her head on her shoulder, and began to cry very nearly as energetically as Katy herself. And that was the one thing which was most effective in restoring Katy's nerves. Tears were such an unaccustomed thing with Linda that Katy controlled herself speedily so that she might be better able to serve the girl. In a few minutes Katy had reduced her emotions to a dry sniffle. She lifted her head, groped for her pocket, and being unable to find it for the very good reason that she was sitting upon it, she used her gingham hem as a handkerchief. Once she had risen to the physical effort of wiping her eyes, she regained calmness rapidly. The last time she applied the hem she looked at Peter, but addressed the Almighty in resigned tones: "There, Lord, I guess that will do."

In a few minutes she was searching the kitchen, making sure that no knives, spoons, or cooking utensils were lost. Missing her support, Linda sat erect and endeavored to follow Katy's example. Her eyes met Peter's and when she saw that his shoulders were shaking, a dry, hysterical laugh possessed her.

"Yes, Katy," she panted, "that WILL do, and remember the tears we are shedding are over Donald's broken foot, and because this may interfere with his work, though I don't think it will for long."

"When I cry," said Katy tersely, "I cry because I feel like it. I wasn't wapin' over the snake that'd plan a death like that for anyone"—Katy waved toward the boulder—"and nayther was I wastin' me tears over the fut of a kid bein' jommed up a trifle."

"Well, then, Katy," asked Linda tremulously, "why were you crying?"

"Well, there's times," said Katy judicially, "when me spirits tell me I would be the better for lettin' off a wee bit of stame, and one of them times havin' arrived, I jist bowed me head to it, as is in accordance with the makings of me. Far be it from me to be flyin' in the face of Providence and sayin' I won't, when all me interior disposhion says to me: 'Ye will!'"

"And now, Linda," said Peter, "can you tell us why you were crying?"

"Why, I think," said Linda, "that Katy has explained sufficiently for both of us. It was merely time for us to howl after such fearful nerve strain, so we howled."

"Well, that's all right," said Peter. "Now I'll tell you something. If you had gone away in that ambulance to an anesthetic and an operation, no wildcat that ever indulged in a hunger hunt through this canyon could have put up a howl equal to the one that I would have sent up."

"Peter," said Linda, "there is nothing funny about this; it's no tame for jest. But do men have nerves? Would you really?"

"Of course I would," said Peter.

"No, you wouldn't," contradicted Linda. "You just say that because you want to comfort us for having broken down, instead of trying to tease us as most men would."

"He would, too!" said Katy, starting to the Bear Cat with a load of utensils. "Now come on; let's go home and be gettin' craned up and ready for what's goin' to happen to us. Will they be jailin' us, belike, Miss Linda?"

Linda looked at Peter questioningly.

"No," he said quietly. "It is very probable that the matter never will be mentioned to you again, unless Judge Whiting gets hold of some clue that he wishes to use as an argument against matured Japs being admitted in the same high-school classes with our clean, decent, young Americans. They stopped that in the grades several years ago, I am told."

Before they could start back to Lilac Valley a car stopped in the canyon and a couple of men introducing themselves as having come from Judge Whiting interviewed Katy and Linda exhaustively. Then Linda pointed out to them an easier but much longer route by which they might reach the top of the canyon to examine the spot from which the boulder had fallen. She showed them where she and Katy had ascended, and told them where they would be likely to find Oka Sayye.

When it came to a question of really starting, Linda looked with appealing eyes at Peter.

"Peter," she said, "could we fix it any way so you could drive Katy and me home? For the first time since I have begun driving this spring I don't feel equal to keeping the road."

"Of course," said Peter. "I'll take your car to the nearest farmhouse and leave it, then I'll take you and Katy in my car."

Late that evening Judge Whiting came to Lilac Valley with his wife and daughter to tell Linda that the top of the cliff gave every evidence of the stone having been loosened previously, so that a slight impetus would send it crashing down at the time when Donald lay in his accustomed place directly in the line of its fall. His detectives had found the location of the encounter and they had gone to the bottom of the cliff, a thousand feet below, but they had not been able to find any trace of Oka Sayye. Somewhere in waiting there had been confederates who had removed what remained of him. On the way home Mrs. Whiting said to her husband: "Judge, are you very sure that what the cook said to you this afternoon about Miss Strong and Mr. Morrison is true?"

"I am only sure of its truth so far as he is concerned," replied the Judge. "What he thought about Linda was evident. I am very sorry. She is a mighty fine girl and I think Donald is very much interested in her."

"Yes, I think so, too," said Donald's mother. "Interested; but he has not even a case of first love. He is interested for the same reason you would be or I would be, because she is intellectually so stimulating. And you have to take into consideration the fact that in two or three years more she will be ready for marriage and a home of her own, and Donald will still be in school with his worldly experience and his business education not yet begun. The best thing that can happen to Donald is just to let his infatuation for her die a natural death, with the quiet assistance of his family."

The Judge's face reddened slightly.

"Well, I would like mighty well to have her in the family," he said. "She's a corking fine girl. She would make a fine mother of fine men. I haven't a doubt but that with the power of his personality and the power of his pen and the lure of propinquity, Peter Morrison will win her, but I hate it. It's the best chance the boy ever will have."

And then Louise spoke up softly.

"Donald hasn't any chance, Dad," she said quietly, "and he never did have. I have met Peter Morrison myself and I would be only too glad if I thought he was devoted to me. I'll grant that Linda Strong is a fine girl, but when she wakes up to the worth of Peter Morrison and to a realization of what other women would be glad to be to him, she will merely reach out and lay possessive hands upon what already belongs to her."

It was a curious thing that such occurrences as the death of Oka Sayye and the injury to Donald could take place and no one know about them. Yet the papers were silent on the subject and so were the courts. Linda and Katy were fully protected. The confederates of Oka Sayye for reasons of their own preferred to keep very quiet.

By Monday Donald, with his foot in a plaster cast, was on a side veranda of his home with a table beside him strewn with books and papers. An agreement had been made that his professors should call and hear his recitations for a few days until by the aid of a crutch and a cane he could resume his place in school. Linda went to visit him exactly as she would have gone to see Marian in like circumstances. She succeeded in making all of the Whiting family her very devoted friends.

One evening, after he had been hobbling about for over a week, Linda and Peter called to spend the evening, and a very gay and enjoyable evening it was. And yet when it was over and they had gone away together Donald appeared worried and deeply thoughtful. When his mother came to his room to see if the foot was unduly painful or there was anything she could do to make him more comfortable, he looked at her belligerently.

"Mother," he said, "I don't like Peter Morrison being so much with my girl."

Mrs. Whiting stood very still. She thought very fast. Should she postpone it or should she let the boy take all of his hurts together? Her heart ached for him and yet she felt that she knew what life had in store for him concerning Linda. So she sat on the edge of the bed and began to talk quietly, plainly, reasonably. She tried to explain nature and human nature and what she thought the laws of probability were in the case. Donald lay silent. He said nothing until she had finished all she had to say, and then he announced triumphantly: "You're all wrong. That is what would happen if Linda were a girl like any of the other girls in her class, or like Louise. But she has promised that she would write to me every Saturday night and she has said that she thinks more of me than of any of the other boys."

"Donald dear," said Mrs. Whiting, "you're not 'in love' with Linda yourself, and neither is she with you. By the time you are ready to marry and settle down in life, Linda in all probability will be married and be the mother of two or three babies."

"Yes, like fun she will," said Donald roughly.

"Have you asked her whether she loves you?" inquired Mrs. Whiting.

"Oh, that 'love' business," said Donald, "it makes me tired! Linda and I never did any mushing around. We had things of some importance to talk about and to do."

A bit of pain in Mrs. Whiting's heart eased. It was difficult to keep her lips quiet and even.

"You haven't asked her to marry you, then?" she said soberly. "Oh good Lord," cried Donald, "'marry!' How could I marry anyone when I haven't even graduated from high school and with college and all that to come?"

"That is what I have been trying to tell you," said his mother evenly. "I don't believe you have been thinking about marriage and I am absolutely certain that Linda has not, but she is going to be made to think about it long before you will be in such financial position that you dare. That is the reason I am suggesting that you think about these things seriously and question yourself as to whether you would be doing the fair thing by Linda if you tried to tie her up in an arrangement that would ask her to wait six or eight years yet before you would be ready."

"Well, I can get around faster than that," said Donald belligerently.

"Of course you can," agreed his mother. "I made that estimate fully a year too long. But even in seven years Linda could do an awful lot of waiting; and there are some very wonderful girls that will be coming up six or seven years from now here at home. You know that hereafter all the girls in the world are going to be very much more Linda's kind of girls than they have been heretofore. The girls who have lived through the war and who have been intimate with its sorrow and its suffering and its terrible results to humanity, are not going to be such heedless, thoughtless, not nearly such selfish, girls as the world has known in the decade just past. And there is going to be more outdoor life, more nature study. There are going to be stronger bodies, better food, better-cared-for young people; and every year educational advantages are going to be greater. If you can bring yourself to think about giving up the idea of there ever existing any extremely personal thing between you and Linda, I am very sure I could guarantee to introduce you to a girl who would be quite her counterpart, and undoubtedly we could meet one who would be handsomer."

Donald punched his pillow viciously.

"That's nice talk," he said, "and it may be true talk. But in the first place I wish that Peter Morrison would let my girl alone, and in the second place I don't care if there are a thousand just as nice girls or even better-looking girls than Linda, though any girl would be going some if she were nicer and better looking than Linda. But I am telling you that when my foot gets better I am going to Lilac Valley and tell him where to head in, and I'll punch his head if he doesn't do it promptly."

"Of course you will," said his mother reassuringly; "and I'll go with you and we'll see to it that he attends strictly to his own affairs."

Donald burst out laughing, exactly as his mother in her heart had hoped that he would.

"Yes, I've got a hand-painted picture of myself starting to Lilac Valley to fight a man who is butting in with my girl, and taking my mother along to help me beat him up," he said.

Mrs. Whiting put her arms around her boy, kissed him tenderly, and smoothed his hair, and then turned out the lights and slipped from the room. But in the clear moonlight as she closed the door she could see that a boyish grin was twisting his lips, and she went down to tell the Judge that he need not worry. If his boy were irreparably hurt anywhere, it was in his foot.

CHAPTER XXXII. How the Wasp Built Her Nest

The following weeks were very happy for Linda. When the cast was removed from Donald's foot and it was found that a year or two of care would put him even on the athletic fields and the dancing floor again, she was greatly relieved.

She lacked words in which to express her joy that Marian was rapidly coming into happiness. She was so very busy with her school work, with doing all she could to help Donald with his, with her "Jane Meredith" articles, with hunting and working out material for her book, that she never had many minutes at a time for introspection. When she did have a few she sometimes pondered deeply as to whether Marian had been altogether sincere in the last letter she had written her in their correspondence, but she was so delighted in the outcome that if she did at times have the same doubt in a fleeting form that had not been in the least fleeting with Peter Morrison, she dismissed it as rapidly as possible. When things were so very good as they were at that time, why try to improve them?

One evening as she came from school, thinking that she would take Katy for a short run in the Bear Cat before dinner, she noticed a red head prominent in the front yard as she neared home. When she turned in at the front walk and crossed the lawn she would have been willing to wager quite a sum that Katy had been crying.

"Why, old dear," said Linda, putting her arms around her, "if anything has gone wrong with you I will certainly take to the warpath, instanter. I can't even imagine what could be troubling you." Linda lowered her voice. "Nothing has come up about Oka Sayye?"

Katy shook her head.

"I thought not," said Linda. "Judge Whiting promised me that what use he made of that should be man's business and exploited wholly for the sake of California and her people. He said we shouldn't be involved. I haven't been worried about it even, although I am willing to go upon the stand and tell the whole story if it will be any help toward putting right what is at present a great wrong to California."

"Yes, so would I," said Katy. "I'm not worryin' meself about the little baste any more than I would if it had been a mad dog foaming up that cliff at ye."

"Then what is it?" asked Linda. "Tell me this minute."

"I dunno what in the world you're going to think," said Katy "I dunno what in the world you're going to do."

Her face was so distressed that Linda's nimble brain flew to a conclusion. She tightened her arm across Katy's shoulder.

"By Jove, Katy!" she said breathlessly. "Is Eileen in the house?"

Katy nodded.

"Has she been to see John and made things right with him?"

Katy nodded again.

"He's in there with her waitin' for ye," she said.

It was a stunned Linda who slowly dropped her arm, stood erect, and lifted her head very high. She thought intently.

"You don't mean to tell me," she said, "that you have been CRYING over her?"

Katy held out both hands.

"Linda," she said, "she always was such a pretty thing, and her ma didn't raise her to have the sense of a peewee. If your pa had been let take her outdoors and grow her in the sun and the air, she would have been bigger and broader, an' there would have been the truth of God's sunshine an' the glory of His rain about her. Ye know, Linda, that she didn't ever have a common decent chance. It was curls that couldn't be shook out an' a nose that dassen't be sunburned and shoes that mustn't be scuffed and a dress that shouldn't be mussed, from the day she was born. Ye couldn't jist honest say she had ever had a FAIR chance, now could ye?"

"No," said Linda conclusively, "no, Katherine O'Donovan, you could not. But what are we up against? Does she want to come back? Does she want to stay here again?"

"I think she would like to," said Katy. "You go in and see her for yourself, lambie, before ye come to any decision."

"You don't mean," said Linda in a marveling tone, "that she has been homesick, that she has come back to us because she would like to be with us again?"

"You go and see her for yourself; and if you don't say she is the worst beat out and the tiredest mortal that ye have ever seen you'll be surprisin' me. My God, Linda, they ain't nothin' in bein' rich if it can do to a girl what has been done to Eileen!"

"Oh, well," said Linda impatiently, "don't condemn all money because Eileen has not found happiness with it. The trouble has been that Eileen's only chance to be rich came to her through the wrong kind of people."

"Well, will ye jist tell me, then," said Katy, "how it happened that Eileen's ma was a sister to that great beef of a man, which same is hard on self-rayspectin' beef; pork would come nearer."

"Yes," said Linda, "I'll tell you. Eileen's mother had a big streak of the same coarseness and the same vulgarity in HER nature, or she could not have reared Eileen as she did. She probably had been sent to school and had better advantages than the boy through a designing mother of her own. Her first husband must have been a man who greatly refined and educated her. We can't ever get away from the fact that Daddy believed in her and loved her."

"Yes," said Katy, "but he was a fooled man. She wasn't what we thought she was. Many's the time I've stood injustice about the accounts and household management because I wouldn't be wakin' him up to what he was bound to for life."

"That doesn't help us," said Linda. "I must go in and face them."

She handed her books to Katy, and went into the living room She concentrated on John Gilman first, and a wee qualm of disgust crept through her soul when she saw that after weeks of suffering he was once more ready to devote himself to Eileen. Linda marveled at the power a woman could hold over a man that would force him to compromise with his intellect, his education and environment. Then she turned her attention to Eileen, and the shock she received was informing. She studied her an instant incredulously, then she went to her and held out her hand.

"How do you do?" she said as cordially as was possible to her. "This is unexpected."

Her mind was working rapidly, yet she could not recall ever having seen a woman quite so beautiful as Eileen. She was very certain that the color on her cheeks was ebbing and rising with excitement; it was no longer so deep as to be stationary. She was very certain that her eyes had not been darkened as to lids or waxed as to lashes. Her hair was beautifully dressed in sweeping waves with scarcely any artificial work upon it. Her dress was extremely tasteful and very expensive. There was no simper on her lips, nothing superficial. She was only a tired, homesick girl. As Linda looked at her she understood why Katy had cried over her. She felt tears beginning to rise in her own heart. She put both arms protectingly around Eileen.

"Why, you poor little thing," she said wonderingly, "was it so damn' bad as all that?"

Eileen stood straight. She held herself rigidly. She merely nodded. Then after a second she said: "Worse than anything you could imagine, Linda. Being rich with people who have grown rich by accident is a dreadful experience."

"So I have always imagined," said Linda. And then in her usual downright way she asked: "Why did you come, Eileen? Is there anything you wanted of me?"

Eileen hesitated. It was not in Linda's heart to be mean.

"Homesick, little sister?" she asked lightly "Do you want to come here while you're getting ready to make a home for John? Is that it?"

Then Eileen swayed forward suddenly, buried her face in Linda's breast, and for the first time in her life Linda saw and heard her cry, not from selfishness, not from anger, not from greed, but as an ordinary human being cries when the heart is so full that nature relieves itself with tears. Linda closed her arms around her and smiled over her head at John Gilman.

"Finish all of it before you stop," she advised. "It's all right. You come straight home. You didn't leave me any word, and I didn't know what to do with your things, but I couldn't feel that you would want to give up such beautiful things that you had so enjoyed. We had planned for Marian to spend her summer vacation here so I put her things in your suite and I had moved mine into the guest room, but I have had my room done over and the guest room things are in there, and every scrap of yours is carefully put away. If that will do, you are perfectly welcome to it."

Eileen wiped her eyes.

"Anything," she sobbed. "I'd rather have Katy's room than be shamed and humiliated and hurt any further. Linda, I would almost like you to know my Aunt Callie, because you will never understand about her if you don't. Her favorite pastime was to tell everyone we met how much the things I wore cost her."

Linda released Eileen with a slight shake.

"Cheer up!" she said. "We'll all have a gorgeous time together. I haven't the slightest ambition to know more than that about your Aunt Callie. If my brain really had been acting properly I would never have dismantled your room. I would have known that you could not endure her, and that you would come home just as you should. It's all right, John, make yourself comfortable. I don't know what Katy has for dinner but she can always find enough for an extra couple. Come Eileen, I'll help you to settle. Where is your luggage?"

"I brought back, Linda, just what I have on," said Eileen. "I will begin again where I left off. I realize that I am not entitled to anything further from the Strong estate, but Uncle was so unhappy and John says it's all right—really I am the only blood heir to all they have; I might as well take a comfortable allowance from it. I am to go to see them a few days of every month. I can endure that when I know I have John and you to come back to."

When Eileen had been installed in Linda's old room Linda went down to the kitchen, shut the door behind her, and leaning against it, laid her hand over her mouth to suppress a low laugh.

"Katy," she said, "I've been and gone and done it; I have put the perfect lady in my old room. That will be a test of her sincerity—even dainty and pretty as it is since it's been done over. If she is sincere enough to spend the summer getting ready to marry John Gilman—why that is all right, old girl. We can stand it, can't we?"

"Yes," said Katy, "it's one of them infernal nuisances but we can stand it. I'm thinkin', from the looks of John Gilman and his manner of spakin', that it ain't goin' to be but a very short time that he'll be waitin'."

"Katy," said Linda, "isn't this the most entertaining world? Doesn't it produce the most lightning-like changes, and don't the most unexpected things happen? Sort of dazes me. I had planned to take a little run with you and the Cat. Since we are having—no, I mustn't say guests—since John and Eileen have come home, I'll have to give up that plan until after dinner, and then we'll go and take counsel with our souls and see if we can figure out how we are going to solve this equation; and if you don t know what an equation is, old dear heart, it's me with a war-club and you with a shillalah and Eileen between us, and it's 'damned' to us if we can't make an average, ordinary, decent human being out of her. Pin an apron on her in the morning, Katy, and hand her a dust cloth and tell her to industrialize. We will help her with her trousseau, but she SHALL help us with the work."

"Ye know, lambie," whispered Katy suddenly, "this is a burnin' shame. The one thing I DIDN'T think about is that book of yours. What about it?"

"I scarcely know," said Linda; "it's difficult to say. Of course we can't carry out the plans we had made to work here, exactly as we had intended, with Eileen in the house preparing to be married. But she tells me that her uncle has made her a generous allowance, so probably it's environment and love she is needing much more than help. It is barely possible, Katy, that after I have watched her a few days, if I decide she is in genuine, sincere, heart-whole earnest, I might introduce her and John to my friend, 'Jane.' It is probable that if I did, Eileen would not expect me to help her, and at the same time she wouldn't feel that I was acting indifferently because I did not. We'll wait awhile, Katy, and see whether we skid before we put on the chains."

"What about Marian?" inquired Katy.

"I don't know," said Linda thoughtfully. "If Marian is big enough to come here and spend the summer under the same roof with Eileen and John Gilman, and have a really restful, enjoyable time out of it, she is bigger than I am. Come up to the garret; I think Eileen has brought no more with her than she took away. We'll bring her trunk down, put it in her room and lay the keys on top. Don't begin by treating her as a visitor; treat her as if she were truly my sister. Tell her what you want and how you want it, exactly as you tell me and as I tell you. If you see even a suspicion of any of the former objectionable tendencies popping up, let's check them quick and hard, Katy."

For a week Linda watched Eileen closely. At the end of that time she was sincere in her conviction that Eileen had been severely chastened. When she came in contact with Peter Morrison or any other man they met she was not immediately artificial. She had learned to be as natural with men as with other women. There were no pretty postures, no softened vocal modulations, no childish nonsense on subjects upon which the average child of these days displays the knowledge of the past-generation grandmother. When they visited Peter Morrison's house it was easy to see that Eileen was interested, more interested than any of them ever before had seen her in any subject outside of clothing and jewels. Her conduct in the Strong home had been irreproachable. She had cared for her own room, quietly undertaken the duties of dusting and arranging the rooms and cutting and bringing in flowers. She had gone to the kitchen and wiped dishes and asked to be taught how to cook things of which John was particularly fond. She had been reasonable in the amount of time she had spent on her shopping, and had repeatedly gone to Linda and shown interest in her concerns. The result was that Linda at once displayed the same interest in anything pertaining to Eileen.

One afternoon Linda came home unusually early. She called for Eileen, told her to tie on her sunshade and be ready for a short ride. Almost immediately she brought around the Bear Cat and when they were seated side by side headed it toward the canyon. She stopped at the usual resting place, and together she and Eileen walked down the light-dappled road bed. She pointed out things to Eileen, telling her what they were, to what uses they could be put, while at the same time narrowly watching her. To her amazement she found that Eileen was interested, that she was noticing things for herself, asking what they were. She wanted to know the names of the singing birds. When a big bird trailed a waving shadow in front of her Linda explained how she might distinguish an eagle from a hawk, a hawk from a vulture, a sea bird from those of the land. When they reached the bridge Linda climbed down the embankment to gather cress. She was moved to protest when Eileen followed and without saying a word began to assist her, but she restrained herself, for it suddenly occurred to her that it would be an excellent thing for Eileen to think more of what she was doing and why she was doing it than about whether she would wet her feet or muddy her fingers. So the protest became an explanation that it was rather late for cress: the leaves toughened when it bloomed and were too peppery. The only way it could be used agreeably was to work along the edges and select the small tender shoots that had not yet matured to the flowering point. When they had an armload they went back to the car, and without any explanation Linda drove into Los Angeles and stopped at the residence of Judge Whiting, not telling Eileen where she was.

"Friends of mine," said Linda lightly as she stepped from the car. "Fond of cress salad with their dinner. They prepare it after the Jane Meredith recipe to which you called my attention, in Everybody's Home last winter. Come along with me."

Eileen stepped from the car and followed. Linda led the way round the sidewalk to where her quick ear had located voices on the side lawn. She stopped at the kitchen door, handed in the cress, exchanged a few laughing words with the cook, and then presented herself at the door of the summerhouse. Inside, his books and papers spread over a worktable, sat Donald Whiting. One side of him his mother was busy darning his socks; on the other his sister Louise was working with embroidery silk and small squares of gaily colored linen. Linda entered with exactly the same self-possession that characterized her at home. She shook hands with Mrs. Whiting, Mary Louise, and Donald, and then she said quietly: "Eileen and I were gathering cress and we stopped to leave you some for your dinner." With this explanation she introduced Eileen to Mrs. Whiting. Mary Louise immediately sprang up and recalled their meeting at Riverside. Donald remembered a meeting he did not mention. It was only a few minutes until Linda was seated beside Donald, interesting herself in his lessons. Eileen begged to be shown the pretty handkerchiefs that Mary Louise was making. An hour later Linda refused an invitation to dinner because Katy would be expecting them. When she arose to go, Eileen was carrying a small square of blue-green linen. Carefully pinned to it was a patch of white with a spray of delicate flowers outlined upon it, and a skein of pink silk thread. She had been initiated into the thrillingly absorbing feminine accomplishment of making sport handkerchiefs. When they left Eileen was included naturally, casually, spontaneously, in their invitation to Linda to run in any time she would. Mary Louise had said she would ride out with Donald in few days and see how the handkerchiefs were coming on, and more instruction and different stitches and patterns were necessary, she would love to teach them. So Linda realized that Mary Louise had been told about the trousseau. She knew, even lacking as she was in feminine sophistication, that there were two open roads to the heart of a woman. One is a wedding and the other is a baby. The lure of either is irresistible.

As the Bear Cat glided back to Lilac Valley, Eileen sat silent. For ten years she had coveted the entree to the Whiting home perhaps more than any other in the city. Merely by being simple and natural, by living her life as life presented itself each day, Linda with no effort whatever had made possible to Eileen the thing she so deeply craved. Eileen was learning a new lesson each day—some days many of them—but none was more amazing more simple, or struck deeper into her awakened consciousness. As she gazed with far-seeing eye on the blue walls of the valley Eileen was taking a mental inventory of her former self. One by one she was arraigning all the old tricks she had used in her trade of getting on in the world. One by one she was discarding them in favor of honesty, unaffectedness, and wholesome enjoyment.

Because of these things Linda came home the next afternoon and left a bundle on Eileen's bed before she made her way to her own room to busy herself with a head piece for Peter's latest article. She had taken down the wasp picture and while she had not destroyed it she had turned the key of a very substantial lock upon it. She was hard at work when she heard steps on the stairs. When Eileen entered, Linda smiled quizzically and then broke into an unaffected ejaculation.

"Ripping!" she cried. "Why, Eileen, you're perfectly topping."

Eileen's face flamed with delight. She was a challenging little figure. None of them was accustomed to her when she represented anything more substantial than curls and ruffles.

Linda reached for the telephone, called Gilman, and asked him if he could go to the beach for supper that evening. He immediately replied that he would. Then she called Peter Morrison and asked him the same question and when Peter answered affirmatively she told him to bring his car. Then she hastily put on her own field clothes and ran to the kitchen to fill the lunch box. To Katy's delight Linda told her there would be room for her and that she needed her.

It was evening and the sun was moving slowly toward the horizon when they stopped the cars and went down on the white sands of Santa Monica Bay. Eileen had been complimented until she was in a glow of delight. She did not notice that in piling things out of the car for their beach supper Linda had handed her a shovel and the blackened iron legs of a broiler. Everyone was loaded promiscuously as they took up their march down to as near the water's edge as the sands were dry. Peter and John gathered driftwood. Linda improvised two cooking places, one behind a rock for herself, the other under the little outdoor stove for Katy. Eileen was instructed as to how to set up the beach table, spread the blankets beside it, and place the food upon it. While Katy made coffee and toasted biscuit Linda was busy introducing her party to brigand beefsteak upon four long steel skewers. The day had been warm. The light salt breeze from the sea was like a benediction. Friendly gulls gathered on the white sands around them. Cunning little sea chickens worked in accord with the tide: when the waves advanced they rose above them on wing; when they retreated they scampered over the wet sand, hunting any small particles of food that might have been carried in. Out over the water big brown pelicans went slowly fanning homeward; and white sea swallows drew wonderful pictures on the blue night sky with the tips of their wings. For a few minutes at the reddest point of its setting the sun painted a marvelous picture in a bank of white clouds. These piled up like a great rosy castle, and down the sky roadway before it came a long procession of armored knights, red in the sun glow and riding huge red horses. Then the colors mixed and faded and a long red bridge for a short time spanned the water, ending at their feet. The gulls hunted the last scrap thrown them and went home. The swallows sought their high cliffs. The insidiously alluring perfume of sand verbena rose like altar incense around them. Gilman spread a blanket, piled the beach fire higher, and sitting beside Eileen, he drew her head to his shoulder and put his arm around her. Possibly he could have been happier in a careless way if he had never suffered. It is very probable that the poignant depth of exquisite happiness he felt in that hour never would have come to him had he not lost Eileen and found her again so much more worth loving. Linda wandered down the beach until she reached the lighthouse rocks. She climbed on a high one and sat watching the sea as it sprayed just below. Peter Morrison followed her.

"May I come up?" he asked.

"Surely," said Linda, "this belongs to the Lord; it isn't mine."

So Peter climbed up and sat beside her.

"How did the landscape appeal to you when you left the campfire?" inquired Linda.

"I should think the night cry might very well be Eight o'clock and all's well," answered Peter.

"'God's in his heaven, all's right with the world?'" Linda put it in the form of a question.

"It seems to be for John and Eileen," said Peter.

"It is for a number of people," said Linda. "I had a letter from Marian today. I had written her to ask if she would come to us for the summer, in spite of the change in our plans; but Mr. Snow has made some plans of his own. He is a very astute individual. He wanted Marian to marry him at once and she would not, so he took her for a short visit to see his daughter at her grandmother's home in the northern part of the state. Marian fell deeply in love with his little girl, and of course those people found Marian charming, just as right-minded people would find her. When she saw how the little girl missed her father and how difficult it was for him to leave her, and when she saw how she would be loved and appreciated in that fine family, she changed her mind. Peter, we are going to be invited to San Francisco to see them married very shortly. Are you glad or sorry?"

"I am very glad," said Peter heartily. "I make no concealment of my admiration for Miss Thorne but I am very glad indeed that it is not her head that is to complete the decoration when you start the iris marching down my creek banks."

"Well, that's all right," said Linda. "Of course you should have something to say about whose head finished that picture. I can't contract to do more than set the iris. The thing about this I dread is that Marian and Eugene are going to live in San Francisco, and I did so want her to make her home in Lilac Valley."

"That's too bad," said Peter sympathetically. "I know how you appreciate her, how deeply you love her. Do you think the valley will ever be right for you without her, Linda?"

"It will have to be," said Linda. "I've had to go on without Father, you know. If greater happiness seems to be in store for Marian in San Francisco, all I can do is to efface myself and say 'Amen.' When the world is all right for Marian, it is about as near all right as it can be for me. And did you ever see much more sincerely and clearly contented people than John and Eileen are at the present minute?"

Peter looked at Linda whimsically. He lowered his voice as if a sea urchin might hear and tattle.

"What did you do about the wasp, Linda?" he whispered.

"I delicately erased the stinger, fluffed up a ruffle, and put the sketch under lock and key. I should have started a fire with it, but couldn't quite bring myself to let it go, yet."

"Is she going to hold out?" asked Peter.

133

"She'll hold out or get her neck wrung," said Linda. "I truly think she has been redeemed. She has been born again. She has a new heart and a new soul and a new impulse and a right conception of life. Why, Peter, she has even got a new body. Her face is not the same."

"She is much handsomer," said Peter.

"Isn't she?" cried Linda enthusiastically. "And doesn't having a soul and doesn't thinking about essential things make the most remarkable difference in her? It is worth going through a fiery furnace to come out new like that. I called her Abednego the other day, but she didn't know what I meant."

Then they sat silent and watched the sea for a long time. By and by the night air grew chill. Peter slipped from the rock and went up the beach and came back with an Indian blanket. He put it very carefully around Linda's shoulders, and when he went to resume his seat beside her he found one of her arms stretching it with a blanket corner for him. So he sat down beside her and drew the corner over his shoulder; and because his right arm was very much in his way, and it would have been very disagreeable if Linda had slipped from the rock and fallen into the cold, salt, unsympathetic Pacific at nine o'clock at night—merely to dispose of the arm comfortably and to ensure her security, Peter put it around Linda and drew her up beside him very close. Linda did not seem to notice. She sat quietly looking at the Pacific and thinking her own thoughts. When the fog became damp and chill, she said they must be going, and so they went back to their cars and drove home through the sheer wonder of the moonlight, through the perfume of the orange orchards, hearing the night song of the mockingbirds.

CHAPTER XXXIII. The Lady of the Iris

A few days later Linda and Peter went to San Francisco and helped celebrate the marriage of Marian and Eugene Snow. They left Marian in a home carefully designed to insure every comfort and convenience she ever had planned, furnished in accordance with her desires. Both Linda and Peter were charmed with little Deborah Snow; she was a beautiful and an appealing child.

"It seems to me," said Linda, on the train going home, "that Marian will get more out of life, she will love deeper, she will work harder, she will climb higher in her profession than she would have done if she had married John. It is difficult sometimes, when things are happening, to realize that they are for the best, but I really believe this thing has been for the level best. I think Marian is going to be a bigger woman in San Francisco than she ever would have been in Lilac Valley. With that thought I must reconcile myself."

"And what about John?" asked Peter. "Is he going to be a bigger man with Eileen than he would have been with Marian?"

"No," said Linda, "he is not. He didn't do right and he'll have penalty to pay. Eileen is developing into a lovable and truly beautiful woman, but she has not the intellect, nor the education, nor the impulse to stimulate a man's mental processes and make him outdo himself the way Marian will. John will probably never know it, but he will have to do his own stimulating; he will have to vision life for himself. He will have to find his high hill and climb it with Eileen riding securely on his shoulders. It isn't really the pleasantest thing in the world, it isn't truly the thing I wanted to do this summer—helping them out—but it has seemed to be the work at hand, the thing Daddy probably would have wanted me to do, so it's up to me to do all I can for them, just as I did all I could for Donald. One thing I shall always be delighted about. With my own ears I heard the pronouncement: Donald had the Jap beaten; he was at the head of his class before Oka Sayye was eliminated. The Jap knew it. His only chance lay in getting rid of his rival. Donald can take the excellent record he has made in this race to start on this fall when he commences another battle against some other man's brain for top honors in his college."

"Will he start with the idea that he wants to be an honor man?"

Linda laughed outright.

"I think," she said, "his idea was that if he were one of fifty or one hundred leading men it would be sufficient, but I insisted that if he wanted to be first with me, he would have to be first in his school work."

"I see," said Peter. "Linda, have you definitely decided that when you come to your home-making hour, Donald is the man with whom you want to spend the remainder of your life?"

"Oh, good gracious!" said Linda. "Who's talking about 'homes' and 'spending the remainder of lives'? Donald and I are school friends, and we are good companions. You're as bad as Eileen. She's always trying to suggest things that nobody else ever thought of, and now Katy's beginning it too."

"Sapheads, all!" said Peter. "Well, allow me to congratulate you on having given Donald his spurs. I think it's a very fine thing for him to start to college with the honor idea in his head. What about your Saturday excursions?"

"They have died an unnatural death," said Linda. "Don and I fought for them, but the Judge and Mrs. Whiting and Mary Louise were terrified for fear a bone might slip in Don's foot, or some revengeful friend or relative of Oka Sayye lie in wait for us. They won't hear of our going any more. I go every Saturday and take Donald for a very careful drive over a smooth road with the Bear Cat cursing our rate of speed all the way. All the fun's spoiled for all three of us."

"Think I would be any good as a substitute when it comes to field work?" inquired Peter casually. "I have looked at your desert garden so much I would know a Cotyledon if I saw it. I believe I could learn."

"You wouldn't have time to bother," objected Linda. "You're a man, with a man's business to transact in the world. You have to hustle and earn money to pay for the bridge and changing the brook."

"But I had money to pay for the brook and the bridge before I agreed to them," said Peter.

"Well, then," said Linda, "you should begin to hunt old mahogany and rugs."

"I hadn't intended to," said Peter; "if they are to be old, I won't have to do more than to ship them. In storage in Virginia there are some very wonderful old mahogany and rosewood and rugs and bric-a-brac enough to furnish the house I am building. The stuff belonged to a little old aunt of mine who left it to me in her will, and it was with those things in mind that I began my house. The plans and finishing will fit that furniture beautifully."

"Why, you lucky individual!" said Linda. "Nowhere in the world is there more beautiful furniture than in some of those old homes in Virginia. There are old Flemish and Dutch and British and Italian pieces that came into this country on early sailing vessels for the aristocrats. You don't mean that kind of stuff, do you, Peter?"

"That is precisely the kind of stuff I do mean," answered Peter.

"Why Peter, if you have furniture like that," cried Linda, "then all you need is Mary Louise."

"Linda," said Peter soberly, "you are trespassing on delicate ground again. You selected one wife for me and your plan didn't work. When that furniture arrives and is installed I'll set about inducing the lady of my dreams to come and occupy my dream house, in my own way. I never did give you that job. It was merely assumed on your part."

"So it was," said Linda. "But you know I could set that iris and run that brook with more enthusiasm if I knew the lady who was to walk beside it."

"You do," said Peter. "You know her better than anyone else, even better than I. Put that in your mental pipe and smoke it!"

"Saints preserve us!" cried Linda. "I believe the man is planning to take Katy away from me."

"Not FROM you," said Peter, "WITH you."

"Let me know about it before you do it," said Linda with a careless laugh.

"That's what I'm doing right now," said Peter.

"And I'm going to school," said Linda.

"Of course," said Peter, "but that won't last forever."

Linda entered enthusiastically upon the triple task of getting Donald in a proper frame of mind to start to college with the ambition to do good work, of marrying off Eileen and John Gilman, and of giving her best brain and heart to Jane Meredith. When the time came, Donald was ready to enter college comfortable and happy, willing to wait and see what life had in store for him as he lived it.

When she was sure of Eileen past any reasonable doubt Linda took her and John to her workroom one evening and showed them her book contract and the material she had ready, and gave them the best idea she could of what yet remained to be done. She was not prepared for their wholehearted praise, for their delight and appreciation.

Alone, they took counsel as to how they could best help her, and decided that to be married at once and take a long trip abroad would be the best way. That would leave Linda to work in quiet and with no interruption to distract her attention. They could make their home arrangements when they returned.

When they had gone Linda worked persistently, but her book was not completed and the publishers were hurrying her when the fall term of school opened. By the time the final chapter with its exquisite illustration had been sent in, the first ones were coming back in proof, and with the proof came the materialized form of Linda's design for her cover, and there was no Marian to consult about it. Linda worked until she was confused. Then she piled the material in the Bear Cat and headed up Lilac Valley. As she came around the curve and turned from the public road she saw that for the first time she might cross her bridge; it was waiting for her. She heard the rejoicing of the water as it fell from stone to stone where it dipped under the road, and as she swung across the bridge she saw that she might drive over the completed road which had been finished in her weeks of absence. The windows told another story. Peter's furniture had come and he had been placing it without telling her. She found the front door standing wide open, so she walked in. With her bundle on her arm she made her way to Peter's workroom. When he looked up and saw her standing in his door he sprang to his feet and came to meet her.

"Peter," she said, "I've taken on more work than I can possibly finish on time, and I'm the lonesomest person in California today."

"I doubt that," said Peter gravely. "If you are any lonesomer than I am you must prove it."

"I have proved it," said Linda quietly. "If you had been as lonesome as I am you would have come to me. As it is, I have come to you."

"I see," said Peter rather breathlessly. "What have you there, Linda? Why did you come?"

"I came for two reasons," said Linda. "I want to ask you about this stuff. Several times this summer you have heard talk about Jane Meredith and the Everybody's Home articles. Ever read any of them, Peter?"

"Yes," said Peter, "I read all of them. Interested in home stuff these days myself."

"Well," said Linda, dumping her armload before Peter, "there's the proof and there's the illustration and there's the cover design for a book to be made from that stuff. Peter, make your best boy and say 'pleased to meet you' to Jane Meredith."

Peter secured both of Linda's hands and held them. First he looked at her, then he looked at the material she had piled down in front of him.

"Never again," said Peter in a small voice, "will I credit myself with any deep discernment, any keen penetration. How I could have read that matter and looked at those pictures and not seen you in and through and over them is a thing I can't imagine. It's great, Linda, absolutely great! Of course I will help you any way in the world I can. And what else was it you wanted? You said two things."

"Oh, the other doesn't amount to much," said Linda. "I only wanted the comfort of knowing whether, as soon as I graduate, I may take Katy and come home, Peter."

From previous experience with Linda, Peter had learned that a girl reared by men is not as other women. He had supposed the other thing concerning which she had wanted to appeal to him was on par with her desire for sympathy and help concerning her book. At her question, with her eyes frankly meeting his, Peter for an instant felt lightheaded. He almost dodged, he was so sweepingly taken unawares. Linda was waiting and his brain was not working. He tried to smile, but he knew she would not recognize as natural the expression of that whirling moment. She saw his hesitation.

"Of course, if you don't want us, Peter—"

Peter found his voice promptly. Only his God knew how much he wanted Linda, but there were conditions that a man of Peter's soul-fiber could not endure. More than life he wanted her, but he did not want her asleep. He did not want to risk her awakening to a spoiled life and disappointed hopes.

"But you remember that I told you coming home from San Francisco that you knew the Lady of my Iris better than anyone else, and that I was planning to take Katy, not from you, but with you."

"Of course I remember," said Linda. "That is why when Marian and Eileen and Donald and all my world went past and left me standing desolate, and my work piled up until I couldn't see my way, I just started right out to ask you if you would help me with the proof. Of course I knew you would be glad to do that and I thought if you really meant in your heart that I was the one to complete your iris procession, it would be a comfort to me during the hard work and the lonesome days to have it put in two-syllable English. Marian said that was the only real way—"

"And Marian is eminently correct. You will have to give me an ordinary lifetime, Linda, in which to try to make you understand exactly what this means to me. Perhaps I'll even have to invent new words in which to express myself."

"Oh, that's all right," said Linda. "It means a lot to me too. I can't tell you how much I think of you. That first day, as soon as I put down the Cotyledon safely and tucked in my blouse, I would have put my hand in yours and started around the world, if you had asked me to. I have the very highest esteem for you, Peter."

"Esteem, yes," said Peter slowly. "But Linda-girl, isn't the sort of alliance I am asking you to enter with me usually based on something a good bit stronger than 'esteem'?"

"Yes, I think it is," said Linda. "But you needn't worry. I only wanted the comfort of knowing that I was not utterly alone again, save for Katy. I'll stick to my book and to my fight for Senior honors all right."

Peter was blinking his eyes and fighting to breathe evenly. When he could speak he said as smoothly as possible: "Of course, Linda. I'll do your proof for you and you may put all your time on class honors. It merely occurred to me to wonder whether you realized the full and ultimate significance of what we are saying; exactly what it means to me and to you."

"Possibly not, Peter," said Linda, smiling on him with utter confidence. "Everyone says I am my father's daughter, and Father didn't live to coach me on being your iris decoration, as a woman would; but, Peter, when the time comes, I have every confidence in your ability to teach me what you would like me to know yourself. Don't you agree with me, Peter?"

Making an effort to control himself Peter gathered up the material Linda had brought and taking her arm he said casually: "I thoroughly agree with you, dear. You are sanely and health fully and

136

beautifully right. Now let's go and take Katy into our confidence, and then you shall show me your ideas before I begin work on your proof. And after this, instead of you coming to me I shall always come to you whenever you can spare a minute for me."

Linda nodded acquiescence.

"Of course! That would be best," she said. "Peter, you are so satisfyingly satisfactory."

Made in the USA
Monee, IL
08 October 2023

44201016R00083